The Book of Thornhold

Judith Arnopp

for all my children

Copyright©JudithArnopp2023
First Edition

The author has asserted their moral right under the Copyright, Designs and Patents Act, 1988, to be identified as the author of this work.

All Rights reserved. No part of this publication may be reproduced, copied, stored in a retrieval system, or transmitted, in any form or by any means, without the prior written consent of the copyright holder, nor be otherwise circulated in any form of binding or cover other than that in which it is published and without a similar condition being imposed on the subsequent purchaser.
NO AI TRAINING: Without in any way limiting the author's [and publisher's] exclusive rights under copyright, any use of this publication to "train" generative artificial intelligence (AI) technologies to generate text is expressly prohibited. The author reserves all rights to license uses of this work for generative AI training and development of machine learning language models.

Previously published under the author name: Julie May Ruddock

A CIP catalogue record for this title is available from the British Library.

Introduction by the Author

The Book of Thornhold was first written way back in 2004. It is the second full length piece I ever completed so is not perhaps as polished as my later work. It was previously published under the pseudonym, J. M Ruddock, but it was read by few. After I began writing seriously, I published under my own name, Judith Arnopp, becoming well-known for medieval and Tudor novels. On the advice of peers and colleagues, I have now given *The Book of Thornhold* a wash and brush up and brought it under my own banner.

I was inspired to write this story while on a university trip to the National museum of Wales where I was privileged to handle my first ever historic manuscripts. Some of them were very famous, like the Ellesmere manuscript of Chaucer's Canterbury Tales, highly illuminated and exquisitely made. Other artifacts were humbler, and a good deal older. One, a nondescript book of grammar, had an inscription near the front, clearly written by a child. It read, "This book was gifted to me by my mother," and I was struck by the incredible chance of that boy's book from the 10th century (as I recall) to the present day - and for me to hold it. I felt that child had reached across time to place it my hands.

It was a fabulous moment.

On the way home, I began to think of all the things that book would have witnessed and I was struck by the idea of a novel, featuring one artefact on its journey through history. The more I thought about it, the more the idea appealed, and I began to include a manor house and generations of the same family. By the time I had made all the notes and added characters and adventures it became clear the book was going to be extremely long.

In the end, I compromised but skipping through time, stopping at key moments in English history. Unfortunately, I couldn't include all eras, or I would still be writing it, so the book is comprised of several short stories beginning with the book's creation circa 793 in Northumberland where it is bothered by Vikings. Then, it journeys south, pausing at the time of the Norman conquest at a Saxon settlement named Thornholding. The next stop is during the plague years when the holding has evolved into Thornhold Manor. Part four takes place during the war of the roses where we briefly encounter Edward IV and his brothers. Then the narrative moves to the Monmouth Rebellion when the inhabitants of Thornhold flirt with treason. We also pause during the Victorian era when Jamie Thornbury is preparing to leave for the Crimean War. In 2005 the narrative all comes together when young historian, Laura Gardener, begins to research the history of the manor where she works. She quickly discovers that all is not as it seems!

As a novice author, unaware of the many rules of crafting a novel, I had great fun writing this book; nearly twenty years later as an experienced author, I had rather less fun chopping it up, rewriting chunks, and salvaging other parts to turn it into a passable book. It is not my best work but still worth a read, I think. I apologise for any flaws the drastic surgery may have caused.

Part One
The Beginning

*Before he leaves on his fated journey
No man will be so wise that he need not
Reflect while time still remains
Whether his soul will win delight
Or darkness after his death-day.*
(Attributed to Bede)

Northumberland – 729AD

At nightfall they extinguished their candles, took off their clothes and crept into the woods to celebrate the pivoting season in the old way. Beneath the golden canopy of the woods of Alricsleah, the night throbbed and something primeval shifted in the dark. Back at the settlement, in his half-erected church, Alric heard the drums and lifted his head from prayer.

"Ungrateful whoresons," he swore but, swiftly repenting his anger, he rose from his knees and followed them into the night.

The wood was dank and dark. Swirling mist obscured his vision, and brambles in league with the devil, snarled his robes and snapped like fiends at his heels. Alric gritted his teeth and quickened his pace, trying to ignore the beating drums that throbbed in his head, and pulsed within his blood.

"I should let them rot in their filth for this. Let them trust to Nerthus to save their miserable souls."

He stumbled into a clearing where an abandoned fire sulked forth smoke. It writhed about the forest floor before dissipating into the darkness. His quarry were not far ahead. Alric hitched up his robe and padded on but, each time he drew near, the drumming ceased, only to start up again farther off as his prey fled deeper into the wood.

Changing direction and ascending a sharp hill, Alric hurried on, the unaccustomed exercise making him pant. Other men would have given up, but Alric was not that sort. At the summit, he paused, and with a hand to his aching ribs, he looked down to where his flock writhed in a demonic dance. They were so far gone in devilry that they did not hear their priest give vent to ungodly rage.

When his anger was spent, Alric fell to his knees in the loamy soil. "Lord? Why did you give me a flock who refuse to be reached? Why will they not listen?"

But God made no reply. Alric's thin body was still shaking with sobs when he heard something rustling in the undergrowth and lifted his head. Drawing a hand across his wet eyes, he noticed a figure crouching at the base of a tree. Instinctively, Alric's arm snaked out and his hand clamped down upon a fragile wrist. With a snarl, he dragged his victim into the moonlight.

A pair of green eyes stared back at him, eyes that were full of fear. She was the last person he had expected to find here. He swallowed, licked his lips. His heart marking time with the devil's drums.

Alric knew her well. She was a quiet, hard-working girl from the village, and a credit to her kin. He would have laid down his soul that she was chaste but, this night, with her workaday tunic put aside and her hair falling free, the moonlight transformed her into something exotic.

"Rheda?" he whispered. "What are you doing? Here … like this?"

He did not want to look at her nakedness, but Alric couldn't help it. He held her at a distance and let his eyes sweep over her body. Dry leaves and moss were trapped in Rheda's russet hair, and to mark the onset of her fertility, her breasts and the bowl of her belly were encircled with a ring of blue paint. She was different from the girl he knew. This was a woman, wild and fragrant with damp earth and wood smoke.

Of the conflicting powers of Heaven and Earth, Rheda's was momentarily the greater; the sorcery of her green eyes cast out the priest, leaving only the defenceless man.

In the swirling darkness, Alric clung to her.

* * *

In the morning, the village people returned to their everyday lives as if the wild woodland ceremony had never happened. Praying that it would be the last time, the priest too went about his daily life as usual. He was working in his garden, prying weeds from between rows of vegetables. The work made him ache from head to toe, but a man had to eat. He stood up and pressed a hand to his back. The sun was high and sweat dripped from his brow. Taking a swig of ale, he looked around the enclosure and admired the results of his labour. The lines of neat vegetables, the beans that entwined the makeshift trellis were satisfying, filled him with pride but also calmed his fear of a hungry winter. But pride being one of the deadly sins, he sent up a swift repentant prayer.

When Alric first arrived in the tiny hamlet they now called Alricsleah the people had not learned the word of God but now a small wooden church stood at one end of the settlement, testament to three long years of labour. In the beginning Alric had worked alone, felling the trees, trimming branches and hewing logs into planks but over time, as the people responded to his stories, and the first converts lent their aid. Now, although the walls were unfinished and the windows were still unshuttered, a thatched roof protected the altar from the elements and the rough building had come to resemble a proper church. Each day the village children gathered boulders and laid them out to form a boundary wall, and Alric sanctified the interior as holy land. When the time came, the people of Alricsleah would be laid to rest beneath the sod.

Today, Alric was glad when the sun reached its zenith, and he could take a break from the toil. Wiping the worst of the soil from his hands, he sought out the shade and rested his back against a tree as he ate his meal. Soon the first of his afternoon pupils began to struggle up the hill.

"Hello, Brother Alric," called the largest of the twelve children. "I've bought you an egg from my hen. It is the first she has ever laid and it's brown and speckled. Mother says we should have eggs a plenty this year."

The boy held out the prize and Alric accepted the gift gratefully.

"I thank you, child. I shall have the egg for my supper. Now, will you join me in the shade for today's story, or shall we continue work on the boundary wall?"

"Oh, a story, a story please, Brother Alric," they cried in unison. "We have worked all morning, clearing stones in the fields."

The priest smiled and settled himself more comfortably against the tree. Not realising they were Alric's pupils, the children quietened so his tale could begin.

"I have heard that far away in the east lies the noblest of lands, famous among men. The face of the land is not to be found across the world by many of the Earth's dwellers, but by God's might it is set afar off from evildoers…"

Alric always embroidered his tales with just enough of the familiar heroic tradition to please them. He hoped that the message they ingested with the colourful stories he wove would ultimately prove to be a Christian one.

The village elders never came to listen, they thought the priest a harmless mad man. They accepted his singing and strange beliefs because they knew he was fundamentally good. The women welcomed him because he minded the children and did what he could for the sick or injured. While their infants attended his lessons, the women were spared the onus of caring for their offspring for a few hours each day. They trusted him and knew they'd be safe.

Today was no different. The children were quiet. The older ones spellbound by his words and the smaller infants, lulled to sleep by his hypnotic voice, slumbered in the shade. These children were the future of the settlement and Alric knew that, should he succeed, Christianity would blossom in them. He spoke softly, answered their questions patiently, and often he was as absorbed with his audience as they were with him. As the afternoon wore on Alric grew restive, glancing every so often toward the gate. His mouth was dry, his voice hoarse from speaking and when the sun began to sink toward the west, he was glad of it.

"It is time you returned to your others now," he said. "I will see you tomorrow. God give you good rest."

"Goodbye, Brother Alric. Thank you for the tale. Next time, can we have some riddles?"

"Yes, yes, of course, remind me tomorrow and we will have riddles all the afternoon."

He waved them off, watched as they dwindled down the hill toward the village. Then, with dread and delight merging in his heart, he looked toward the gate again.

She was there.

She was always there. The position of the sun in the skies could be predicted by her arrival. Never once had he acknowledged her presence. He hoped she would grow tired of waiting and go away. He glanced back again. She had not moved, and he knew she waited for him to acknowledge her but, he would not speak. How could he?

He did not know what to say.

She was no longer the sensual woman of the woods. Her glorious hair was hidden beneath a coif, her glorious breasts disguised beneath a shapeless tunic.

But he knew now how she looked without her clothes.

Week after week, while Alric went about his business, Rheda waited, eyes downcast, hands clasped, the picture of innocent sorrow. Alric was as ignorant of women as Rheda was of priests and the stalemate between them could not be overcome. The jewel that Alric had taken from her could not be given back, and Rheda could not forget the gift that she had given.

After dark, when he should be sleeping, he burned with the memory of the glorious passion that had raged between them. He sweated as he remembered every warm curve, the fragrance of her breath, and taste of her skin. And when he'd finished remembering, he rose from his cot and cast himself upon the dirt floor to pray for forgiveness and a release from the terrible knowledge.

Yet still, Rheda waited.

The afternoon sun gilded the halo of her hair and cast her long shadow across the grass. Alric forced himself not to look but just before it grew dark, his resolve broke and he looked in her direction, just in time to see her walk away. The dying sun silhouetted her body against the sky, and for the first time he noticed her swollen stomach that screamed in silent accusation of the sin they had committed.

* * *

Alric prayed and worked as never before, unable to sleep or to find peace. God remained silent. The walls of his church rose as swiftly as Rheda's belly expanded and as day by day she grew more dejected, the priest became more fearful.

"Help me, Lord," he prayed. "Send me strength to resist her. Put her far from my reach, Lord, and help me to be a good servant, I pray you."

And then, one day Rheda did not come.

Alric's spade jarred upon a large stone, sending pain shooting to his elbow. He threw the tool into the mud. *Where is she?* The evening was drawing in. He looked to where she usually waited and ran a hand through his hair. *I must find out where she is.* Taking up his wide brimmed hat he decided to walk to the village.

It was a fine afternoon, the trees just beginning to change colour, and the earth was dusty after a long summer. A group of men were gathered by the well, when they saw him they beckoned him to join them in a jug of ale. It took all Alric's self-control not to immediately enquire as to Rheda's whereabouts. He asked about their expectation of a fat harvest, if the pigs were fattening in the byre but then, as he opened his mouth to ask another question, a cry issuing from one of the huts made his blood run cold. His mouth fell open, his unasked question answered by Rheda's father.

"The girl's been screeching all day, Brother, she's having a bad time, I reckon. My woman birthed all six of ours with barely a whimper. Is there anything ye can do for her, Brother?"

"Oh no, n-n-n-not, not unless I am summoned. A birthing is no place for a man, but once she is safely delivered I – I will call. In the meantime, I will offer up prayers."

He hurried away, stumbling his way toward the church, pausing now and then to look over his shoulder. The men turned back to their business, allowing the women to get on with theirs.

***

Rheda stopped going to the church, but Alric heard the gossip of how she refused to name her child's father. In their eyes bringing up her child without the protection of a man risked both the wrath of the old gods, and the displeasure of the new.

But, despite their prophecies of misfortune, the boy she bore grew strong. Alric watched him from afar, noting that the boy's eyes were the colour of the sky, and his hair the same red-brown hue as the dampened soil upon which he was conceived.

Alric avoided Rheda and, if she found herself in his company she mumbled an excuse and slipped away.

The next time the seasons turned, and the villagers slipped into the woods, Alric locked himself in his cell. As he lay on his narrow cot and watched the torchlight flicker on the walls, he couldn't help but wonder if Rheda ran naked through the forest with dry leaves snarled in her russet hair.

Alric opened his bible. It was an ancient thing, penned and illuminated by some ancient monk to glorify God's word. It showed signs of much devotion and Alric knew it would not last many more years. He would miss it when it finally became too ragged to be of use. As he turned the pages he was suddenly struck with an idea to make recompense to God for his continuing wrongs.

The sin of bodily lust could be atoned by prayer, but cowardice and denial required greater penance. He resolved to make a copy of the book and in doing so perpetuate God's word. From that day, when he was not praying or preaching to his congregation, he turned his attention to his pen.

Forgetting that pride was as deadly a sin as lust, Alric sharpened his feather into a quill, seeing in his mind's eye the completed manuscript. His book would be bigger, brighter, more beautiful and more perfect than the original. It would enrich the humble church he had built and help to swell his congregation and spread God's word.

***

A few months later while Alric was praying, a drip of water fell on the back of his neck, a short time later, it was followed by another. In the end, he was forced to fetch a vessel in which to contain the water. On the next fine day, he took a ladder and climbed up to attempt to repair the church roof. He whistled through his teeth, happy to be in the fresh air, doing the Lord's work. It was shortly after noon when, from his vantage point, he saw a group of women and children walking toward the nearby woodland.

Alric put down his hammer.

The women were carrying baskets, and skins of ale, and the atmosphere was one of holiday. As their chatter dwindled, he climbed from his ladder, wiped the back of his hand across his mouth, and decided that he too would seek the silence of the broad-leafed glade. Carefully he descended from the roof and put his tools away.

Inside the wood, the drop in temperature was considerable, the world was green and hushed beneath the spreading canopy. At first he walked briskly but when he spied the women someway ahead, he slowed his pace. Keeping them in sight, he followed in the wake of their soft laughter, his attention mainly on Rheda and her infant.

They did not linger in the woodland but headed for the cliffs on the far side. The women and children often made excursions to the seashore to collect shellfish from the rock pools. Small fish, shrimps and crab were always a welcome supplement to their meagre diet.

Alric followed and, as the shade gave way to rough meadow he paused beneath a tree. He smiled to see how the excited children ran ahead to the sand dunes. Alric filled his lungs with sea air but didn't follow further. Instead, he sat on the grass and watched them cross the rippled sands toward the water's edge.

The afternoon was hot, and he envied the women wading through rock pools with their skirts hitched high as they searched out shellfish. He smiled at the boys digging their bare feet deep into the wet sand, and the girls splashing in the sun-warmed shallows. Their happy laughter mingled with the cry of the gulls, and soon his idleness made him sleepy. He yawned and turned back to watch the women. It took a moment for his to realise that Rheda was not among them.

As the other women stripped off their tunics to freshen their dusty bodies in the cold sea, he sought out Rheda, finally spotting her higher up the sands where the land merged with the beach.

The child was at her breast, she rocked him to and fro, and Alric guessed she was singing. He watched as the child fell asleep, and she lay him down and covered him with her cloak. She stood high on a rock looking south across the bay, then she closed her eyes, swaying on her toes as she enjoyed the kiss of the sun and the caress of the salty air. Her hair blew from her face, like a pennant in the stiff breeze, her tunic moulded to her body.

Alric swallowed and tried to moisten his lips, but his tongue was parched.

When she put up a hand to unfasten her shoulder clasps he fought the impulse to stand, but sat up a little straighter, his eyes fastened greedily upon her. He was so lost in the pleasure of her unveiling that he did not at first acknowledge the silent mummery of her awakening fear.

She peered out to sea, then backed away, her hand clamped to her mouth. Alric frowned, puzzled until a cry from the lower beach drew his attention back to the other women. He opened his mouth and dived face first into the springy turf, pressing his body close to the ground and scrambling to the edge of the low cliff to watch the unfolding horror.

The small ship had drawn quietly onto the beach. Twenty or more armed men clambered over the side and waded to shore. The women grabbed for their children, and leapt long-legged through the waves, their movements hampered by the frisky surf.

"No God, no, no, no!"

Alric stayed where he was, unable to move as he witnessed the northmen take hold of the hysterical women. They carried them like screaming animals to their ship. A bearded Dane silenced the noisiest of them with his fist.

Paralysed, Alric prayed that Rheda would have the sense to stay where she was. He could see her, safely hidden in the rocks and knew that God intended her to be spared but, as the ship was almost full of wailing women and making ready to pull away, he heard a sound, like the far-off call of a lonely gull. It grew louder and floated out across the beach.

A splash of russet tunic as Rheda abandoned her hiding place and ran toward her child. Alric leapt up, screaming soundlessly into the wind as she sped across the sand.

"Stay there, Rheda. Lie down!"

But one of the men had heard. He turned, and let fly his weapon, the axe somersaulting across the beach and lodging with sickening finality in the back of Rheda's skull.

She dropped like a stone onto the sand.

By the time Alric reached her, the raiding party was already offshore. High above the beach, gulls keened a mourning cry but only the disturbance of the sand betrayed the tragedy that had occurred. Soon the tide would cover the marks of desperate feet, and nothing would remain to tell the tale.

Except for Rheda.

He ran stumbling across the beach to where she lay face down in the sand. Flies already swarmed in the congealed globules of blood in her hair. Alric fell to his knees and turned her body over. The eyes that stared back did not see his grief. The bloodied, sandy lips that he remembered kissing did not curve in welcome. With grief tearing at his soul, he took her in his arms, stroked back her hair and placed his lips upon her high clear brow. The body that had for so long robbed him of sleep was stilled, all sensuality diminished. As he covered her with her tunic, he heard a sound, and remembered the child.

The boy was still pink from sleep. He drew a wet, red thumb from his mouth before clambering to his feet and holding out his arms, demanding to be picked up. For a long moment Alric stared back at the boy.

He could not carry them both. The child would have to walk. It would be a long, slow journey but there was no other way. He led him to his mother and taking a deep breath, hoisted her into his arms, and indicated to the child that he should hold onto his robe.

It was no easy task ascending the shifting dunes with a dead woman in his arms, and a two-year-old child in tow. The boy grizzled to be carried but Alric coaxed him onward with promises of milk and a chicken bone to suck when they arrived back at the settlement.

Rheda was bad company upon the journey. The tunic with which he'd covered her continually slipped, revealing her ruined face. Her body jolted against his, mocking the memory of their brief love, and exacerbating the horror of the long journey through dappled glade.

Alric wept.

***

The next morning Rheda's mother brought the boy to the church.

"My man says you must take the child. "He says, it's your duty for we don't want him. Make him into a priest like yourself. It is what his mother would have wanted."

Looking at neither the child nor the priest, she walked away. Alric stared at the boy in bemusement. He knew nothing of children. As she neared the gate, he moved forward and called for her to wait, and she halted, her body silhouetted in the gateway, the sun picking out the grey in her faded red hair.

He raised both arms before letting them drop again.

"The boy?" he said. "What am I to do with him? I do not even know his name!"

She stared at him for a long emotionless moment.

"Rheda named him Alricson," she said.

***

They knew! They'd known all along!

It took many months for Alric's shame to fade. At first, before the lessening of grief, he blamed the child. He prayed to God to relieve him of the burden but as time went on, Alric found comfort in him. The trials of infancy were testing, and Alric knew nothing of teething or changing and cleaning linen but with God's help, he managed.

As the boy grew older and assumed some independence, Alric discovered not just a companion, but an assistant. Alric's stories found fertile ground and the boy's winning ways found friends among the villagers. He worked happily and willingly at Alric's side and helped draw Alric closer to the people, who loved the boy for the sake of Rheda's memory.

"You are four summers now, Alricson, and so I think you can look after the hens. You will feed them grain and collect their eggs each day."

The boy nodded. "Alric, will you help me build a small hut to protect them from the fox."

Usually, the birds took refuge at night in the lean-to shed where Alric kept his tools and grain, but the boy was insistent; to him the fox embodied the fearfulness of the devil. Together they worked every evening after prayers until the roof was watertight, the floor dry and the door secure.

One day when the boy failed to appear for his midday meal, Alric discovered him at the chicken coop, with a hen on his knee while the others scratched diligently in the dust. As he drew near, he heard the boy reciting the scriptures and was surprised at how accurately the child told his tale.

"Come Child, your food is waiting."

As they walked hand in hand back to the church, he suggested that poultry were undeserving of the scriptures.

"Why?" asked Alricson. "Are they not God's creatures too?"

"They are but chickens, my child, and do not understand your tales. Even though they were created by God, he does not expect them to worship him for he knows they have no learning. Men are set apart from animals by their capacity for reason and judgement; it is only the intelligent who are required to follow the teachings of the church."

Alricson thought for a while,

"But what about Anton, the boy in the villages who drools and cannot speak at all? He has a small brain, I think; does that mean he is not one of God's creatures? Because he cannot think, does that mean God has ceased to love him?"

Inadequate in the face of the child's perception, Alric muttered something about the food growing cold. As he helped Alricson onto his stool and watched him make his prayer of thanks, he wondered how he would cope as the boy grew older and his questions grew more complex. It was clear, even now, that the boy's intellect would eventually outstrip his own.

"What shall you be when you are grown, Alricson?"

The child swallowed a spoonful of broth.

"Why, I shall be a priest, Alric, what else should I be? I will be just like you."

Alricson was not his father's equal, however. In both intellect and godliness, he far surpassed the tormented priest. Once he learned his letters, he began to assist Alric with his book of gospels, copying the Latin script in a large round hand. Alricson possessed an inner peace that quite eluded Alric and, untroubled by Earthly concerns, he remained unblemished by sin, and effortlessly followed God's path. He watched with envy as his son grew to be the man Alric had always longed to be.

Alric was working on a carpet page, a central double cross with concentric circles and swirls of yellow, interlaced with zoomorphic patterning. It was an intricate artistic masterpiece and Alric's heart leapt with joy each time he contemplated its perfection. He had just one small section to complete but since the light was fading, he decided to continue work in the morning. Before he tidied it away he called Alricson to admire it.

The boy held up the folio to the light and smiled his angelic smile.

"It is a fine piece of work, Alric, and fit to grace the grandest of cathedrals, but I think you should leave it as it is."

"What, unfinished?" thundered Alric. "Whatever for? It would be a sin not to complete such a perfect piece. It is to be my gift to God, to glorify his name!"

The boy's sandals barely made a sound upon the dirt floor as he paced back and forth.

"I don't think it would be a sin not to complete it," he frowned. "Alric, you are a Christian priest and as such should seek humility. This work is not a simple glorification of God's name; it is a considerable work of art that is approaching perfection. You should leave the work incomplete as a testament of your humility. Men may never understand your motive, but God will, and I believe he will bless you for it, Alric."

Alric stared into the child's unblinking eyes, slammed down his pen and stalked from the room. Damn the boy! He was unnatural. Inhuman!

Through the window he watched as Alricson carefully replaced the parchment on the worktable, the boy's glowing serenity was a harsh contrast to the dark pride that lodged in his own heart. But, remembering his sins, he became penitent again. The boy was right about so many things. As an adult and a priest, Alric should have realised the work lacked humility. The page that a short time ago had filled him with pleasure was spoiled now; he could only feel guilt at the joy he had taken in his own skill; a talent that he owed to God.

Alric left the page incomplete.

He moved on to a portrait of St Matthew, a piece of work that also took many months but, as it neared completion, he was careful to include a few errors in the interlaced design so as to keep his earthly humility intact.

This time when he showed the work to Alricson, the boy patted him approvingly as if he were the teacher, and Alric the pupil.

***

The village took many years to recover from the loss of their young women; a whole generation of mothers was not easily replaced. Once the initial grief lifted, some of the younger men journeyed inland in search of new wives. Gradually new children were born to compensate those lost to the Northmen. None, however, were close to Alricson's age and his childhood was a solitary one. By the time he reached his thirteenth year he was far better read than Alric and the priest knew the day would come when the boy would require more than he or the village could ever offer.

He was a well-built youth who worked tirelessly, taking joy in the church they'd built. It had become a centre of village life, standing prominently in the clearing, the solid walls a spiritual haven from the harshness of life. After services they held meetings there, exchanged stories, and received bodily as well as spiritual guidance. But, despite this Alricson learned nothing of the wider world.

He knew the woods and the shoreline well, but since that far off day when he lost his mother, he had never experienced danger. He was ignorant of his beginnings and Alric put off telling him of it for as long as he could. But one day, as they looked out across the ocean the priest somehow found the strength to relate the tale of the wild men who had sailed over the horizon to murder his mother.

"I think I remember," the boy said. "I think there were gulls and my feet hurt. I was walking through the wood with no sandals. I always thought it was a dream."

Alric stared at the boy, unable to voice the questions that teemed his mind. Instead, he described Rheda, and thankfully the boy missed the note of longing in Alric's voice. He spoke of her russet hair and green eyes while Alricson nodded wisely, as if he recalled her. To Alric's great relief, the boy never asked about his father and since his grandparents were long dead, there was no-one to tell him the full truth.

One evening as they discussed theology over a cup of ale, Alricson leaned forward, his eyes bright in the candle's flame.

"I want to be a priest like you, Alric, or perhaps a monk at one of the great monasteries you told me of: Lindisfarne or Jarrow perhaps. I wish for a life of solitude."

"Perhaps you will one day, Alricson," replied Alric, suppressing a squirm of misgiving. "I could write a letter for you to take to Lindisfarne by way of introduction. I knew a scribe who entered there. I do not know if he is still living but they would welcome you, I am sure."

Alricson's next question was interrupted by the sound of the tolling village bell.

Alric froze in his seat.

"What is it?" Alricson whispered.

Alric padded to the door and peered blindly into the night, alert to the sharp smell of burning that hung heavily in the air. Knowing instinctively that danger was coming, he turned to the boy and gripped him by the shoulders,

"There is trouble in the village, Alricson, I must go and help. Stay here. No, do not stay here. Collect the book and my wooden cross. There are a few coins beneath my bed, take them and hide with them in the deepest part of the woods until I return. Do *not* come out whatever happens. Promise me, Alricson! Protect our book and protect yourself. God will be with you, my son!"

After kissing the boy quickly, Alric plunged into the night. As he dissolved into the dark, the boy sped to the workroom and thrust the book into a large skin bag. The wooden cross had no value, save that of age but it had witnessed many a desperate and lonely prayer. The boy shoved it into the sack and tucked the moneybag into his belt before running into the woods.

Outside, a damp chill lay heavy on the air and, underfoot, the leaves were soggy, clinging to his feet and legs as he scrambled through the undergrowth. On the rise of the hill, he halted and peered back through the trees toward the village, and what he saw chilled his soul. Huts were burning, screaming women and children scattering from the raiders. He dropped to his knees. Too stunned to pray, he closed his eyes and covered his ears with his hands. The village men were not fighting men but, although they had no chance against the Northmen, they stood their ground. One by one they fell, and soon the smell of blood mingled with that of burning.

Alricson watched as a burly trio of northmen herded the villagers with their short swords. He held his breath when he heard Alric's familiar voice. He looked up in time to see him run forward, arms outstretched, and throw himself before the wailing women. They clutched their babies to their breasts, and over their cries rose the imploring voice of the priest.

"Have mercy on these women. You have slaughtered their men and burned their homes, at least spare their lives!"

The muddied and be-draggled women crawled close to Alric and clung to his robes. He represented the only safety they knew. They remembered his stories of God protecting the righteous, and believed he could save them.

A thickset Dane laughed and pushed the priest aside before roping the women one to the other, pulling the bonds tight. The women's wails rose, their cries drowning Alric's pleas.

"In the name of God, do not harm these people! Think of your own women and show pity! God will have mercy on those who harken to his word!"

The raider turned.

"Peace Priest!" he snarled and with a vicious upward swipe, struck out with his axe. Alric's eyes rolled; he clutched at his intestines as they slid, sinuous as snakes, to the ground. Alric fell at his murderer's feet.

Roaring at the women, the Dane continued to bind them but, having no time for infants, he snatched a newborn from its mother and tossed it away, it lay unmoving on the ground.

With sickness in his throat, Alricson watched as the captives were marched away. Each time the women dared to turn the heads for a last look at home, their captors forced them on. Alricson knew they would never return to the village. If they survived the journey, they would live and die in a foreign land, slaves to an uncivil master. How long before the village of Alricsleah was forgotten. Alricsleah: built by a priest whose blood and entrails were even now drying in the early morning sun.

Alricson did not move for hours but he finally summoned the courage to leave his hiding place and creep back to what remained of the village. The abandoned infant was crying weakly. He stooped over it and, taking pity on the helpless misery of hunger, he tucked the child's wrap tightly around it before moving off to check the other bodies for signs of life.

The raiders had done their work well. None were left living. Wiping his tears on his sleeve, the boy braced his shoulders and began to drag the bodies to the churchyard. Without pausing for rest, he found Alric's spade and began to dig, stopping only to chase off dogs when they crept too close to sniff at the corpses. Steadily, though his body protested, and his hands blistered, the line of graves extended until he was faced with the most difficult task of all.

Alric lay where he had fallen; his eyes turned heavenward, his hands clasped to his belly, blood congealed upon his torso and the earth upon which he lay.

Alricson prayed.

And then he began to dig again. He was exhausted now, his belly churning for want of food. Flies plagued him, hindering his progress, but he beat them away, hating the thought that they had so recently feasted upon his friends. He wiped his eyes and blew his nose before wrapping Alric's body in a winding sheet and rolling it into the grave.

Into the dark.

Only yesterday, the village had thronged with life. How long, he wondered, until the graves he'd dug became indistinguishable from the surroundings. God would send the wind and rain, wild animals would disturb the piled soil and slowly, from want of someone to tend it, the undergrowth would grow up to cover the site.

The wooden houses in the village would crumble, the vegetable patches would be overgrown and the church on the hill would gradually retreat back into the woods. Alricson hesitated; perhaps he should stay. It's what Alric would have wanted … but then the thin wail of the child reminded him of what he must do.

743 AD

Alricson walked for days. The babe yelled and kicked, it slept and then yelled again before, far in the distance, he spied a thin column of smoke. The thought of a fire and people quickened his pace. The inhabitants of the hamlet watched warily as he entered the clearing. With a word to nobody, he walked straight to the well and drank deeply before collapsing in the dirt. Only then did the people of the hamlet come forward, plucking at his clothes, and lifting the child from his arms.

It was dark when he awoke. His fingers felt fur and he knew he was lying upon warm skins in a hut lit only by a central fire. Sensing he was not alone, he stirred, and a figure moved closer and laid a hand upon his forehead. It was Alricson's first remembered touch of a woman. Looking into her eyes, he saw kindness and thanking God, he relaxed and gave himself up to her care.

When he was sufficiently recovered and his strength restored by food and rest, he looked around the hut, his eyes falling upon the woman. She sat at the hearth with a child at her breast. He turned his head away, his movement drawing the woman's attention.

"It is fortunate that I recently birthed a daughter," she said softly. "What is the child called?"

"I don't know," he replied, his voice hoarse. "But my name is Alricson."

"You are welcome, Alricson. This is the hut of my man, Beocca."

A figure loomed huge in the darkness and Alricson noticed another swaddled child was cradled in the crook of his arm.

"I am Beocca, and this is my woman, Edith, and our first born, Eta. We are curious to know your story."

When Alricson told them of the attack on Alricsleah, and the slaughter and abduction that followed, Beocca and Edith grew alarmed. All of Northumbria, they said, knew of the raiders, and those nearest to the coast lived in constant fear of further attacks. As he related the story, sparing no detail, the woman grew agitated, and the infant in her arms whimpered.

Alricson gestured to the child.

"That child and I are the only survivors from a village of perhaps thirty people. The priest who raised me died trying to save the women, but they were taken anyway. What do you think will happen to them?" he demanded of Beocca. "The Danes killed my mother when I was a child. Why will they not live peaceably? Why do they steal our women?"

Beocca rubbed a rough finger across his nose. "Because they can, son," he replied. "Because they are heathen. Those they do not keep for themselves will be sold as slaves, and the infants likewise, if they survive. God rot them!"

And at his words, a tiny light returned to Alricson's world because he knew that, mercifully, he had fallen among Christians.

He stayed for several weeks before leaving the infant in the care of Edith and Beocca. They gave their promise to raise the boy as a brother to Eta. They were good people and Alricson knew they would keep their word. As reward for their goodness, he pressed the few coins from Alric's hoard into their hands before he said goodbye.

"It is some thirty leagues to the Holy Island," Beocca told him. "But be sure you cross to the island when the tide is low. Many have perished attempting to cross on the incoming tide."

Alricson walked, he slept and walked again but when at last he stood upon the windy shore and looked across at the island, surrounded by sea, bombarded by seabirds, he knew in his heart, he had been called to this place.

The community shook their sorrowful heads when they heard Alricson's tale. They welcomed him into their hearts, added him to their prayers, and took him into the bosom of their brotherhood. The profound peace of the island aided his spiritual recovery and, despite the roaring, spume spattering seas and the crying gulls, Alricson felt closer to God than ever before. As he worked in the scriptorium, the chanting of the brothers soothed his raging sorrow, and created reason out of the chaos in his mind.

As he healed, Alricson found miracles in the smallest sparrow that pecked crumbs from the sill outside his window and smiled to watch the tiniest daisy trail the sun across the heavens. When not at prayer, or working in the scriptorium, Alricson found solace in menial tasks, milking the sheep, tilling the land or labouring in the kitchens, and on the day he was finally ordained as a holy man, he began to embellish the book that Alric had begun.

Making full use of Lindisfarne's materials, he dedicated himself to garnishing the gospel pages, spending painstaking hours adding ten thousand red dots around each folio capital. He highlighted the robes of the apostles with gold and lapis lazuli, beautifying every page but never forgetting to leave a flaw, a small imperfection to mark his inferiority to God.

For only God was perfect.

Alric's book, with a tooled leather cover, adorned with gold and studded with precious stones, was added to Lindisfarne's treasure store. And at the back of the book Alricson added an inscription in faultless Latin:

"Alric of Alricsleah in Northumbria began this book in God's glory, assisted by his pupil, Alricson, who carried it with him to Lindisfarne where it was made complete in Alric's memory. By grace of God."

And so, Alric's book joined the vast library at Lindisfarne while Alricson, abandoning his dreams of physically spreading the word of God, experienced a contentment so profound that he often sought penance for his comfort. Sometimes, when life grew too easy, he emulated Saint Cuthbert, and stood with his feet in the freezing midnight sea so that he should suffer a little, as Christ had.

Lindisfarne - 793 AD

Fifty years later, on just such a evening, when Alricson was an old man, he ventured once more to the beach. The island had lately been battered by a spate of unprecedented winds and forked lightening that lit up the Northumbrian skies with fiery dragons, but this night was calmer. His ankles and knees protested as he immersed himself in the foamy surf, but he did not withdraw. He stayed all night, embracing the pain as he chanted and praised God.

When dawn broke and the sun began to climb above the rim of the world, the old man eased his rheumatic feet from the waves and prepared to journey back. As he turned away, his eye was caught by a splash of colour far offshore among the waves. He squinted, dazzled by the rising sun on the sea and, sailing wraithlike through swirling mist he beheld a fleet of ships. Hoisting his robes to his knees, Alricson fled across the shingle to raise the alarm.

The monks were already busy about their daily tasks but even so, the tide was high and escape to the mainland was impossible. There was nothing to be done but stand and make ready to face their fate. Their conjoined prayer grew louder as the long ships grated onto the shore and the Northmen surged up the beach in an angry tide.

Alric's last moments loomed large in his son's mind.

Harsh accents shattered the silence, the chambers ringing with murderous rage. The Dane leader loomed from the haze, his arms and torso dwarfing those of the holy men. The monks cowered before Christ's altar and, at first, sensing no resistance, the invaders ignored them and concentrated on the plunder. When the first relics were scattered across the floor, Alricson stood firm, a comforting hand placed upon the shoulders of two novices who huddled at his feet. But his quiet prayers ceased when two brawny raiders emerged from the scriptorium laden with Christian tomes.

Alricson forced himself to continue praying, wrestling to keep faith and place his trust in God but when he saw Alric's treasured book flung carelessly into a casket, Alricson's faith floundered.

He wet his lips and turned toward the altar.

One of the raiders straddled the chancel railing and roared encouragement in his mother tongue. Then he turned abruptly, blond braids flying, as an accomplice entered the church with the abbot bound and tied. He flung him at the leader's feet where the priest begged incoherently for his life. The Northman screamed something incomprehensible and brought his axe down across the tonsured head.

Alricson saw the abbot fall but still he did not move. He'd seen for himself that the Vikings lacked mercy. The abbot's death made Alricson the senior monk, but he took no evasive action. Outside, screams split the morning air, and acrid smoke rolled into the nave but still Alricson remained calm.

"God will not forsake us," he whispered to the novices that clung to him.

A noviciate ran into the nave and tripped, skidding across the floor. The Danes roared as they grabbed his arms and legs, stretched him across the altar and proceeded to burn the soles of his feet. Why? Why? Why?

Hate surged through Alricson's body, the sensation unfamiliar, but willing himself to be calm, he prayed on. His old heart lurched, his breath became short, but something kept him going, something helped him overcome panic. At last, maddened by the pain, the tortured novice lapsed into unconsciousness and the Danes lost interest, leaving him spread-eagled, his body bleeding and his head broken.

When the burning church grew too hot even for the Vikings, they herded the surviving monks outside, where they wept at fresh atrocities.

Bodies were strewn in the daisy-studded grass and a steady stream of raiders trampled them as they bore away church treasures, and herded livestock toward the waiting ships. A few Danes systematically dispatched any survivor who moved until only Alricson and the two novices were left. The boys clung determinedly to Alricson's knees until they were ripped away, their throats sliced, and their bodies left to bleed into the holy soil. Alricson, wondering if he should have fought them after all, wept.

Alricson alone was left alive. He cried out when the huge raider grasped his robes and hurled him to the ground. Pain reverberated through his body. His hip was broken. It must be. He could not move but seeking God's presence, he closed his eyes and prayed aloud, bearing witness to the pain, the brutality, the sin. Strong hands grabbed his ancient body, the Dane straddled him and hauled him by the neck of his robe, so he was nose to nose with the raider. The brutish stench of the northman engulfed him. Cold blue steel pressed into his throat, and a trickle of blood ran down his neck. Alricson fought for breath, a warm stream of piss ran across his thigh. As his heart failed, he realised it was the last thing he would ever smell.

He would rather it were roses.

The knife was sharp against his windpipe, sticky, wet blood collecting in the hollow of his throat. The Dane's face was close to Alricson's, so close the priest could see coarse black stubble on his chin.

"We spare your life, Priest," the Viking snarled, as he wrenched Alricson's head back. "You must go forth and tell this tale. Tell them all. Tell your farmers in their mean huts, and your Ealdormen in their high halls, tell them we will return!"

He dropped Alricson to the ground. Silence fell. The northmen sailed away leaving the grieving gulls to vent their displeasure. Alone on the island, Alricson crawled to the enclosure wall, propped himself against it, and wept for his lost brethren, his father's lost book, and for the lost souls of all mankind.

He wept until gentle hands roused him and urged him to seek shelter from the returning storm. Safe on the mainland, Alricson did not witness the oceans rise in a storm of vengeance. He did not see the Viking ships cast, broken and battered, upon the rocky shore. And he did not see Alric's book in its wooden casket washed miraculously back to land.

Part Two
Weaver of Peace

When the bold warrior wrapped his arms about me,
I seethed with desire and yet with such hatred.
Wulf, my wulf, my yearning for you ...
(from Wulf)

Gloucestershire - September 1066

The hall was warm, Byrtha's cheeks burned from the heat of the flames that roared in the central hearth. As she wove a path through her father's retainers, topping up their mead, laughing at their quips, she accepted their compliments as her due. The men had known Byrtha for most of her life and she was perfectly at home among them, secure in her status as daughter of the Ealdorman, Oslac.

Her father's voice rang across the hall, his confidence in the ensuing battle infecting those around him. "We will send the Norwegians straight back across the northern sea where they belong!"

Cheers erupted. Although Ealdorman Oslac's days of war were over, as a veteran of the shield wall and an intrepid leader of men, Oslac was unsurpassed. He was proud to hold the king's trust and prouder still of his family. His sons were strong and already showing prowess on the battlefield, even the youngest. The elder two were already fathers while, Leofwine, still on the brink of manhood, would see his first battle tomorrow.

Byrtha's laugh drew Oslac's attention to where she whispered with her betrothed, Scef, the eldest son of their neighbour. He was a fine, well-made boy whose beard was still soft upon his chin. As she refilled his cup, Scef twirled the ends of Byrtha's flaxen braids, whispered in her ear making her blush. Oslac recognised desire for one another and was not displeased; passion was good in a marriage. Scef was a similar age to Byrtha, another aspect of the match that Oslac approved of. He was many years older than his own wife and knew the problems that disparity in age could bring.

Oslac searched for his wife and found her sitting some distance away, among the women. He scratched his belly and wondered again how, in his thirtieth year he'd been unwise enough to have his head turned by a pretty face. Sometimes he wondered if his wisdom was solely confined to the battleground.

"Oh, Gyða," he thought, letting his gaze flick over her. "Whatever happened to us? Where is that girl I joined with?"

As if sensing his eyes upon her, Gyða glanced up, their eyes momentarily clashing before she looked away again. Oslac sighed, realising that outside the concerns of the household, they would never have anything in common. When he turned back to his daughter, his sombre mood lifted.

The match she had made with young Scef promised only good things. The joining ceremony was set for next month and would cement his alliance with the neighbouring Ealdormen and strengthen their united fighting force. He dwelled happily upon the idea of a prosperous and comfortable old age, safe in the settlement while his sons undertook most of his duties, leaving him to peace and …relaxation. Something he had never had time for. His spirits rekindled, he balanced his cup of mead on his belly, and beamed across the hall.

Oslac's eldest son stood up, his drinking horn raised. He thumped the table to silence the hall. "To King Harold!" he cried, "and a swift victory!"

"And a safe return!" called out his young wife. Aethel raised her horn to that of her husband. She had come to them as a very young girl and Gyða had brought her up to be a good wife for her son. She knew better than to voice aloud her dread of the coming battle.

It would be a long march north to Jorvik where Harald Hardrada and Tostig, the renegade brother of the king, had invaded the land. God knew what hazards they would meet. The women were right to fear but if similar qualms beset the fighting men, they hid it well. The high hall rang loud with certain victory to come but, as the cries died down, just one dissenting voice spoke out.

It was a voice often heard in the household but seldom heeded.

The grandmother sat close to the hearth clutching her robes with a rheumatic hand. She groped in the ashes of the hearth, her nails blackened and broken, reading ill-omens and portents written in the cinders.

The grandmother was tolerated because she was Gyða's mother, although even their relationship was fraught. Byrtha was the only household member to show the grandmother any affection. Since infancy, indifferent to the old woman's noxious odours, she was often found snuggled in her grandmother's robes. The Grandmother told stories that few others could be bothered to listen to, and as she grew, even Byrtha thought them untrue.

The old woman claimed her mother had been a paramour of Thorkell the Viking who had dragged her daughter all over the land in pursuit of him. Even Gyða dismissed the claim as the ramblings of a crazed old woman. While she was a young woman people had listened, harkened to her warnings but now she was in her dotage, she was ridiculed. But now it was imperative to make them listen. She tugged Oslac's sleeve.

"Tell them to stay at home, Oslac, the signs are not good."

But Oslac shrugged her away, raised his horn and drank to the coming victory.

***

Byrtha dressed hurriedly the next morning and hastened into the sunshine while still fastening the ties on her apron. After the carousal of the night before, she had overslept, and the enclosure was already milling with horsemen. As she scanned the throng for her brothers, her dog pawed at her skirts, but spying Pallig and Aethel, she pushed him away, hurrying to join them. But when she noticed Aethel's face was crumpled with tears, she paused.

Aethel clung to Pallig's arm, a squalling babe on her hip while their two young sons huddled at her feet. The younger of the two, upset at his mother's distress, sucked hard on his thumb. As she hurried past, Byrtha stroked his head and gave him her cheeriest smile and, immediately transferring his faith to her, he took hold of her skirts and followed.

"Father…" But Oslac was busy bellowing instructions to Leofwine and paid no heed.

"Remember to stay close to your brothers. They will look after you. It's no shame; in battle every warrior depends upon the men next to and behind him. Keep your shield up and your head down, and stab and slash at the enemy's legs, as you have been taught. Where's Pallig? Pallig! Come over here boy!"

With one hand fastened to Leo's shoulder he waited for his other son's approach.

"Aethel is afraid for me, Father." Pallig pulled his wife into the crook of his arm, and she gave a wan smile, struggling to conceal her fear. Resettling her baby son on her hip but, not trusting her voice, she remained silent while Oslac bellowed instructions.

"I was advising Leo about the battle. You must try to stay together, all of you, if you can. You are to protect your brother and bring him safely back to us. If he so much as scratches a finger his mother's wrath will be fearsome! You young men may be brave but never forget your mother's tongue is sharper than a Viking axe! Why, Beowulf himself would tremble, Grendell's wrath being nothing in comparison. Humph, shush now, shush! See where she comes …"

Unrelenting childbirth had coarsened Gytha's figure and marred her once clear brow, but, in a good light, she was still comely. She was a woman of few words, but her ire could cower the most hardened of warriors. Today her ruddy cheeks were pale, but her face was stretched into a smile, her hands clasped tightly, her fear contained.

She stood next to Byrtha as the men prepared to mount. One by one they kissed their mother's reddened cheek and stroked the smooth pink one of their sister. Oslac the younger and Pallig gave their wives one last embrace and ruffled the hair of their children. As they rode away, the women stood calmly but the moment they were out of sight, Aethel abandoned all pretence of bravery.

At seventeen she was already mother to three children and had not seen her own family since the day she was betrothed to Pallig. Never managing to bond with her new family, she felt his loss keenly when he was absent. As the cavalcade of horse dwindled into the distance, Byrtha took Aethel's hand and squeezed it.

They waited until the men were out of sight before turning toward the hall again. As they neared the door, the Grandmother emerged, dishevelled still from sleep. She tottered on unsteady feet toward them and spat on the ground.

"Ye let them go then, Oslac, ye fool ye! I warned ye yester night 'tis an ill-starred fight but ye never listen to me, do ye, Boy? Ye never listen!"

Oslac, curling his lip at the travesty of femininity before him, pushed his way past, and the grandmother transferred her venom to Aethel. Her bony finger wagged beneath the girl's nose.

"Ye do well to grieve, my girl. Your man won't be back, we'll not see none of they again. The sky will shine with the hairy star come winter's end, and wolves will reign over Angleland for a long, long time to come."

She shuffled off, shaking her grey head but none heeded her. Only Byrtha felt a swathe of pimples run across her skin at the prophecy.

With a cry of despair, Aethel covered her face with her hands, drawing Gyða's ire.

"Show some dignity, Girl. Come, we have food to prepare, and cloth to weave. Our husbands wish to return to a thriving, prosperous community and snivelling won't solve anything."

Sweeping the youngest child into her arms, she settled it comfortably onto her hip and shepherded everyone back to the hall. The enclosure fell silent.

As she worked, the Grandmother's prophecy echoed in Byrtha's mind. She helped Aethel clear the remains of yesterday' feast from the tables, while the other women warmed pots of cawl on the fire. Byrtha kept glancing to the corner where the Grandmother rocked on a three-legged stool.

The old woman pushed a piece of bread into her mouth and mangled in between her gums, her jaws working frantically to force the nourishment on its downward journey. Her cloudy eyes roamed around the hall before falling on her granddaughter. Then, her expression softened, and a solitary tear began a convoluted journey across the furrows of her face.

Byrtha's broom raised a cloud of fine ash into the air. As she worked she sang a lament, popular among the women. The children, soldiered along a trestle bench, munched their bread and listened, enjoying but not understanding her words.

> *"I draw these words from my deep sadness,*
> *my sorrowful lot. I can say that,*
> *since I grew up, I have not suffered*
> *such hardships as now, old or new.*
> *I am tortured by the anguish of exile.*
>
> *First my lord forsook his family*
> *For the tossing waves; I fretted at dawn*
> *As to where in the world my lord might be.*
> *In my sorrow I set out then,*
> *A friendless wanderer, to search for my man.*
> *But that man's kinsman laid secret plans*
> *To part us, so that we should live*
> *Most wretchedly, far from each other*
> *In this wide world; I was seized with longings….."*

"Byrtha," the Grandmother murmured. "You're the very image of me father. Since the minute ye was birthed I've known the blood of Thorkell pumps strongly in ye veins."

Grandmother knew, first hand, the pain women suffered for the sake of men. For years, her own mother had trailed her man across the sea, from one battle to another, carrying her only surviving child with her and burying others at the roadside along the way. The male preoccupation with blood feud, revenge and war left little time for tenderness and, once the initial bedding was over, there were no more gentle words, yet still her mother had remained, and endured.

"I've lost all my hopes but you, Byrtha, you are all I've left."

Byrtha who was destined for a fine match with young Scef. She was sure to raise a fine brood of sons; a sudden chill swept across the old woman's skin. She took a second look at her granddaughter and thought again. Was she really destined to be a mother to fine sons? There was something strange, dark and unseeable surrounding her. Suddenly afraid, she beckoned to Byrtha, and the girl put down the broom.

"What's the matter, Grandmother?"

She knelt at her knee, allowed the Grandmother to stroke her face and, as the old woman began to sing, she closed her eyes and drifted back to her childhood. When the words of the song faltered, Byrtha sat up.

"What is it?"

The old woman shook her head, croaked painfully.

"Come with me, Child, come. I must talk with ye, come, help me up."

Byrtha took the proffered arm and matched her steps to the old woman's as they shuffled to the corner where the Grandmother slept. Behind a stiff hide curtain was a stuffed mattress piled with noxious sleeping furs. A sheep's skull, small stones, rusted arrowheads and other treasures were lined along a wooden ledge. Easing onto a stool, the grandmother placed both hands on her knees and looked at Byrtha.

"Bad times are coming, and we must prepare for trouble. I've seen things written and they be bad things. I will not live to see the worst of it but, you child, will suffer what no woman should have to …but listen to me, ye be strong and ye will conquer the enemy in the end. It will be up to you to bend them to your will and make them serve ye. Do ye hear me, child?"

Byrtha made what she knew was the expected reply.

"Yes, I hear you, Grandmother, although I don't understand. I will try to do as you say. But what is going to happen?"

"I see things, child, I always have; waking, sleeping, who knows? And, often times, the things I see happen true. We must be prepared for the worst; being ready be half the battle."

Impatient at her grandmother's obscurity, Byrtha frowned.

"Prepared for what? What bad things? And when?"

"I know no more than I say, child, but I see death coming. I see dishonour. And I see wolves, hundreds of black wolves prowling around the walls of the enclosure. They will devour us if we let them."

Grandmother nodded knowingly and when Byrtha opened her mouth to speak again, the old woman forestalled her.

"Me days are short now, Granddaughter, and I have some things for you to keep in remembrance of me. You must care for them and pass them on, in time, to your own daughter."

Byrtha looked at the cobwebbed collection of treasures.

"Yes, Grandmother. I will be proud to look after your things."

The old woman cackled as she rocked to and fro on her stool.

"There's a good gel. 'twas always a good gel you were. Now, reach beneath my sleeping fur and you'll find a package, bring it out to me but mind, it is heavy, far too heavy for an old body like mine."

Groping beneath the rank bedcovers Byrtha's hand came to rest upon a large package. She drew it out, sat on the bed and the old woman took it from her, her gnarled hands trembling as she struggled to untie the strips of knotted hide that bound it.

"The knots have grown too tight, 'tis an age since I last loosened them. See if your fingers are nimbler, child."

Byrtha picked at the ties until they were loose, and then the old woman nudged her out of the way.

"Here let me do it, it's been so long …" Her hands shook as they drew off the covering and held out a tunic. "I want ye to keep this, 'tis a fine outfit given me by Thorkell. It's one of the few things he gave me, and I treasure it. I was wearing it on the feast day when I caught the eye of your grandfather but, nonetheless, I still treasure it." She held it up, her eyes misting. "Eh but I were a fine-looking thing, tall and straight like me father, I turned many a head in my time, but I fell for none of their pretty words until your grandfather happened along. May he rot!"

Byrtha took the garment and murmured thanks as she held it against herself, it was an ancient, faded thing, the once green cloth dulled to a sulkier shade, but the shoulder clasps still gleamed and, on closer examination, Byrtha found that they were silver and of the finest workmanship. She looked at the old woman with new eyes, trying to picture her young and handsome enough to catch the eye of a passing minstrel.

"What was grandfather like?"

"Pshwa, rubbish, a pile of stinking cat spew dressed to look like best mutton. Worst piece of muck that ever stuck to me shoe, I can tell ye! Now here's the real treasure…"

The laughter died on Byrtha's lips. Her eyes opened wide as a heavy book was placed in her hands.

"Where did you get this? What is it?"

"Thorkell had it. He stole it from somewhere, I expect but 'tis old I think and crafted by the gods by the looks of it. I've never showed it to a soul in case it were taken from me, and my father never let any set eyes on it but me. You must keep it safe, child … away from the wolves."

Byrtha laid the book on the bed and began to turn the pages. The cover was missing but the pages shone brightly, richly adorned with gold leaf. She ran a finger across the page, longing for the knowledge to read the words although the pictures were explicit enough. There were images of men and beasts, intertwined with glossy leaves and bright flowers. The colours that had been applied so many years ago looked as if they were painted yesterday. Here and there, a thumbprint showed in the margin where the craftsman had gripped the parchment tightly in concentration, a blob of candle wax, a ring left by a cup.

The book smelled musty and was stained about the edges. The first three or four pages were slashed as though scored with a dagger but, despite the damage, the book still radiated wealth and Byrtha felt somehow humbled by it. She traced the decoration of swirls and dots of gold with her finger and struggled to speak through her gathering tears.

"Grandmother, this is a great treasure, and I will guard it with my life. It shall pass to my sons, and they will pass it to theirs. I will ensure it is preserved forever."

Putting a hand on her granddaughter's knee, the old woman spoke quietly.

"Twill maybe prove some comfort in the black times that are coming, child. When the days are dark, you can look at it and think of me."

As Byrtha wrapped the nettle green gown around the book she felt a surge of kinship with her grandmother and, for the first time, gave real credence to her stories. With his book in her hands, Thorkell suddenly seemed very real.

That evening while Oslac pondered the outcome of the ensuing battle, the Grandmother kept a rare peace as she rocked on her stool. She offered no comment when Oslac spoke of the thegns' plan to combine forces with the Earls, Edwin and Morcar just outside York.

"I don't know when a king has faced such foe as now face King Harold. William the Bastard is threatening from Normandy, and now Harold's renegade brother, Tostig, has joined with Hardrada and threatens from the north. We'd decided that the thegns should fight the Norwegians so that Harold could stay in the south to deal with the Normans ... if they come ... but the sacking of Scarborough means there is more to contend with than we bargained for, and we will need Harold's assistance. It will be a devilish thing to defend both ends of the realm at once. I'd not want to be in Harold's shoes, that's for certain but I'd be at his side were I a few years younger. Pass the flagon, Byrtha, child."

Byrtha filled her father's cup before replenishing those of the women with short beer from a separate jug.

"But we will win, won't we, Father, and the men will come home safely?"

She sat down, flicked a braid behind her back, and waited for his reply.

"Why surely! Surely, child! Have no doubt, our shield walls are invincible, and our army will force the invader back across the seas. Then the King will slit his brother's traitorous lying gizzard. Have faith, the boys will be home before lent, and everything will be as it was before."

Oslac buried his nose in his mead cup and failed to meet the women's gaze. Then he spluttered and coughed, clapped his hand, dispelling the darkness. "But this is a gloomy meeting, Let us have some entertainment. Where is the storyteller, fetch him at once. Fetch him forth!"

October 1066

The pedlar turned from the broad paved roadway built by the old people and travelled by way of the lesser tracks. The old Roman road was overgrown with brambles, and broken in places but, in contrast to the rutted mud path he now followed, it had been an easier passage. His mouth was dusty, and his donkey, laden with fine goods, hung its head as they began the slow pull up the slope that led to the outer limits of Oslac's domain. Usually, the pedlar's pace quickened when he approached this settlement, there was always a glad welcome waiting for him. Today, although he craved wine and a warm fireside, he was loath to arrive.

When he reached the outer ditch, the gatekeeper blew a long note on his horn to alert the settlement of an arrival. In a place where news from the outside world was sporadic, any visitor was a welcome distraction, and the pedlar was always a favourite of the women who hankered not just for the goods but for the news he carried. Today, with most of the men away, the women were more than usually eager for tidings.

As the warm summer weather extended into October the settlement was making the annual preparations for winter. Strips of mutton were strung out to dry in the sun, and a second harvest of late grain was in being stored away, ready for the long cold months. To make the most of the fine weather, the younger women had brought their work outside and were spinning and weaving in the sunshine. When they saw the pedlar coming, they dropped their work and clustered around him, chattering and pushing, the same questions on every lip.

Gyða forced a way through the throng.

"Peace, peace! Let the man breathe. Aethel, fetch him bread and ale."

While refreshment was bought Gyða ushered the man to a seat and sent one of her grandsons to fetch Oslac. The pedlar always relieved the monotony of the settlement and the inhabitants had come to know and like him. He was an honest man, whose news was reliable, and his goods were of the best quality but today his lack of cheer was notable.

While Gyða waited patiently for her husband to join them, she leant forward, clutched the pitcher tightly. "Well? What news?"

The pedlar snatched off his cap and rubbed it across his face.

"I have heard that a great battle at Stamford was won and our army victorious. Hardrada is slain, and Earl Tostig too. The fight was bloody, and the losses were many, and they say that the enemy, who'd arrived in three hundred ships were sent home in just four and twenty…"

"But this is good news surely!" interrupted Oslac, 'so why so despondent? Our cause is won, and our men will soon be home; it's a time of cheer, is it not?"

A buzz of excitement ran through the company, but the pedlar held up a hand and cut the celebration short.

"No Sir, it's not. I have few details as yet, but it seems another battle was fought at Fulford … before the King's arrival, and all was lost. There was great slaughter, and it's said the river ran red with blood. In their victory the invaders used the bodies of our dead as a bridge across the marsh. Many of our bravest are slaughtered…I am sorry … Oslac … your son … Pallig was among them."

Aethel's pent-up grief burst. Gyða put her hands over her face as Asa pushed to the front of the group, her breath coming in gasps.

"What of Oslac the younger? What of him? Does he live?"

"Aye, I believe so, Lady. They say he was wounded but not badly. He will live, and he and the young one have ridden south with the fyrd to fight the Bastard Duke who has set sail from Normandy. Harold disbanded the army after Stamford, and planned to call for arms in the south but the fyrd chose to follow him. Many fighting men refused to abandon their liege lord. It was a brave thing…"

Oslac fumbled for his wife's hand and pulled Byrtha close. Through the din of Aethel's weeping, he bewilderedly repeated what he'd just been told.

"Leo has ridden forth with the King. And Oslac too?"

The empathic sun slipped behind clouds, and sensing rain in the air, Byrtha led her parents inside. As she helped her mother to her bed, her attention was drawn by a rustling movement from the far corner.

The grandmother scratched her forearm, leaving wheals.

"I was right then, was I? Which of they be gone? Pallig or Oslac?"

There was no triumph on her grandmother's face, only sorrow. Byrtha put her arms about her, absorbing the tremors of her old body, sharing her grief. Today, despite her own pain, Byrtha had to be strong for everyone. She patted the old woman's hand and stared to where her mother and father were lying, side by side yet some distance apart.

Gyða's great body shook with grief, but Oslac was so motionless he could be dead. Huddled with the grandmother, despite the furs she piled on the bed, Byrtha could not warm herself. She shivered as she rocked back and forth, her face washed with tears.

After a time, from the Grandmother's regular breathing Byrtha knew the old woman slept. She drew her furs higher about her shoulders before creeping from the hall, surprised to see that the sunshine shone brightly again, and the hens were still scratching in the dirt as if nothing had happened.

She blinked against the brightness and as her vision cleared she saw the pedlar watering his donkey and sorting through his pack. She approached him, her movements so quiet that she had to cough to gain his attention.

"Lady," he exclaimed. "Your soft tread escaped my ears."

With a sad smile, she motioned for him to walk with her to the palisade where she sat and looked down at her hands that were twisted in her lap.

"I was wondering if you had news of Scef?"

'Scef? Nay Lady, I don't, but if he were among the dead, I should have learned of it. No one reported him fallen, either at Fulford or Stamford. I imagine he has ridden south with the others."

Byrtha clutched at this possible truth.

"I hope you are right. It is the sort of thing he would do. I thank you. In which direction do you travel now?"

The pedlar looked into the distance.

"South, Lady. As soon as I have further news, I will send you word of it. Please do not worry, mistress, all will be well. The King will prevail."

In the weeks that followed, survivors began to trickle home, bringing stories of both defeat and glory. Byrtha's time was divided between caring for the men, and nursing Gyða who had fallen sick with a fever. Lost in a nightmare, Byrtha's mother tossed and turned, and each time she woke and remembered, she fell to weeping again. "My son, my lovely child …"

Oslac remained in a bemused state, leaving the onus of leadership in Byrtha's hands. There was no option but to put aside her private grief and wade through the mire of problems. And if her days became waking nightmares, her sleeping hours were not much better, her rest was continually shattered by dreams. She dreamt the horn at the gate sounded, welcoming her brothers home. When they rode proudly through the gates, she ran out with a cry of welcome. It was so real yet each time she woke to the realities of a cold, comfortless dawn, she grieved afresh.

As the seasons turned, the sunshine was defeated, and strong winds blew. Day and night, the moan filled her ears and confused her mind, and, by the hearth, the Grandmother rocked back and forth …back and forth.

"D' ye hear them howling, Child?" she asked in her sing-song voice. "It's the wolves, ye know. They be coming closer. Slow but steady, slow but steady; devouring all in their path."

When she could bear no more, Byrtha snatched up her basket and escaped the confines of the hall and made for the silence of the woods. Plucking a cluster of hazelnuts, she dropped them into her basket. The wind was lighter in the wood, dry leaves fell like copper raindrops, and eddied about the woodland floor. They crackled beneath her feet, betraying her approach, sending squirrels darting into the canopy.

Her basket was not even half full when she heard the blast of the settlement horn. At first, she mistook it for the soughing wind, but the second blast was unmistakable. For a moment she froze while she determined what to do, then lifting her skirts she ran as fast as she could back to the holding.

The pedlar was just finishing a flagon of ale when she arrived. When he saw her duck beneath the lintel, he wiped his mouth on the back of his hand and stood up. One look at his face told her his news was not good. Forgetting her manners, she sank to her knees and grasped his arm.

"Tell me." she demanded.

The pedlar shook his head, swallowed.

"All is lost, Lady, all is lost. They slayed him. Shot him clean through the eye. They say we have a new king now. There's a Norman bastard on England's throne." He spat in the dirt. "He's been given a poor welcome so far, and his retaliation has been bloody. I've heard talk of burnings and routings. The common folk resist them where they can but there are few Ealdorman left to instruct or defend us. All are either slain or fled. I am sorry, lady. I wish I could offer you comfort, but I fear, all is lost."

He drained his already empty flagon.

Byrtha frowned. "And what of my brothers, and Scef? What of them?"

"I know nothing of that, Lady. I only know there was carnage and many of our men fell but we have been given no names. Those who escaped the field speak of butchery; afterwards, even the king's body parts were scattered so far abroad that only his lady could identify them. The death toll will be high, for they fought on long after Harold had fallen. They fought, but to no avail. All we can do is wait for the survivors to come home … if they can. I advise you to double your guard, look out for the approach of Norman troops for, if the enemy come, they will show you no mercy."

"What shall I do? How can we defend ourselves? My parents are ailing, and the women are grieving. The only men remaining are either old or wounded or too young. I have not been trained for leadership. I am weak and I will fail."

With a wry smile, the pedlar placed his weather roughened hand on hers.

"Not you, Lady, you are strong. Haven't I heard it said that the blood of Thorkell floods through your veins? Why, Lady, you are invincible."

***

A funeral procession began the slow climb uphill, a buffeting wind snatching at their robes and hair. Gyða lay serenely on her funeral bier; her comfortable body was clad in festive robes, and a golden torque was fastened about her throat. A complex person in life, her funeral reflected her mix of beliefs. She was laid in the grave, facing east to west in the Christian manner, but ignoring the frowns of the priest, small personal treasures were laid beside her, the custom of an older, pagan world. A finely crafted bowl of grain, a small ivory handled knife, and a drinking beaker were arranged around her body.

Lost in his uncertain world, Oslac held tight to Byrtha's hand as his wife was lowered into her grave, while the grandmother droned a lengthy narrative of daughter's conception and childhood: a narrative that nobody heeded.

As they returned to the hall a sudden squall of scudding rain hastened their return to Thorn Holding. They hurried heads down, to the comfortless hall where a sulky fire refused to warm them. Byrtha, rubbed moisture from her hair and ordered a slave to bring hot broth for the Grandmother. Perhaps the distraction of food and drink would stem her continuing warnings of imminent tragedy.

November 1066

It was another cold day and the first hint of the frigid winter to come crept through the crevices in the walls, and between the layers of their clothing. The community had taken refuge in the hall and Byrtha was enjoying an afternoon of leisure. She sat beside the fire, the children clustered at her feet as she told them a story. If she closed her eyes and tried to think back to the time before, it seemed like a dream. Byrtha had to remind herself she hadn't always lived like this, with her nerves on edge, forever waiting for an onslaught. Different scenarios ran through her head, tactics to defeat or deceive the enemy but when the first notes of the horn sounded, she was unprepared, her careful plans thrust into disarray.

"Normans!"

She ran aimlessly from the hearth to the door, and back to the hearth again before finally gathering her senses and forcing her feet to be still.

"Stay where you are," she told the women. "Look after the little ones, look after Grandmother."

Then Byrtha left the hall alone.

Running toward the palisade she clambered a ladder and saw in the distance, a troop of horse. It was clear they were not Saxons.

Their clothes were like nothing she'd ever seen, an artificial splash of colour on a neutral landscape, and as they drew closer, she saw the men wore no moustaches. Used to the full beards of her father and brothers, the naked faces of the Normans appeared both obscene and juvenile. But, soft cheeked or not, they were armed to the teeth. Dangerous! Her life, and the lives of all at the settlement depended entirely upon her.

The Normans rode in single file, the merry jingling harness belying their joyless faces, but it was not a war party. Some of the men carried hawks and, judging from the game that hung from their saddles, they'd taken the opportunity to hunt along the way. With quaking knees, she descended the ladder and took a deep breath, swallowing the bile that suddenly surged into her throat. She positioned herself defensively in the centre of the enclosure, and slowly, almost unnoticed, members of the community crept out to stand behind her.

The Norman horses surged through the gate, Byrtha knew they must seem a bedraggled group of old or injured men and half-fledged boys. Most of the women were indoors, keeping the infants quiet, but Byrtha suddenly realised the Grandmother was there; standing tall at Byrtha's side, all signs of pain vanquished by defiance.

Four men and a few foot soldiers rode through the inner gate. They did not dismount but surveyed the group from their saddles, the great iron shod hooves churning the damp ground to mud. Two of the Normans obviously outranked the others, their strange haircuts, shaved faces and elegant clothing setting them apart. The elder of the two sported a leaping stag upon his chest. His horse pranced but he kept it in check and looked down his nose before addressing the gathering. His tones were harsh and authoritative, his words incomprehensible.

Byrtha stepped forward, nodded her head as she had seen her father do, and greeted them in English.

"Welcome to Thorn holding. My name is Byrtha. I am the daughter of Oslac the Elder who is the ealdorman here."

The horse came close to her, the rider looking down disdainfully. Byrtha stood her ground, her heart hammered like a drum. Turning to his companions, he said something in a quick foreign accent. Something disdainful.

Byrtha looked one from the other, trying to determine some sense of what was happening. Then, the horseman shouted to the men who waited in the outer enclosure, and a scuffle broke out amid much shouting. A moment later, two Norman foot soldiers entered dragging a figure between them. They threw him in the dust at Byrtha's feet and she saw it was a cleric. Dashing forward to assist him, she saw the priest's habit was filthy, and his chin had lacked the benefit of a blade for some time.

The horseman spoke harshly, and the priest fell sweating to his knees before answering breathlessly in French.

"Yes, my Lord, yes of course. I am only too happy to be of service." Then, turning to Byrtha, he spoke in the Saxon tongue.

"This man is now your Lord. As a reward for his loyal service in the recent battle at Hastings, King William has awarded him ownership of this and other nearby settlements. You must do as he commands, or you will be punished. I must warn you that their punishments are severe."

A great howl of despair rose from the crowd as the priest stepped back, his chin in his chest but, as if her limbs were worked by someone else, Byrtha stepped forward.

"No," she cried. "There is some mistake. My *father* is the Ealdorman here, as was his father before him. It has always been so. He took no part in the battle so why should he suffer penalty?"

The priest cringed before relating her words to the Norman who, turned toward her and snarled a few clipped sentences. The priest interpreted.

"My child, they know that your father provided arms and men to Harold at Hastings. His son Oslac was captured and slaughtered. These lands are sequestered by the crown, and the King chooses to endow them upon this Norman Lord. The land, the settlement and all in it are at his disposal."

Byrtha tried to think quickly, the painful confirmation of her brother's death swamped by the immediacy of the present tragedy. She had to protect the people in her care. She groped wildly for a solution.

What would father do?

He was so sick and frail, surely they wouldn't punish a sick old man. Trying not to glare, she entreated the cleric instead.

"I beg you, Sir, do not repeat my words to these men. There must be something I can do. My father still lives but he is sick, he is… not himself. The shock of losing his sons, and the death of his wife has temporarily turned his mind. I took no part in Hastings or any battle and, as I have legal possession of these lands, see no reason why I should be punished? I am defenceless, Sir, but I question the legality of this Norman action. Can you help us?"

The cleric's eyes flicked from her to the Norman and back to Byrtha.

"No, Child, I cannot help you, nor can anyone. There is no help for any of us. I would advise acquiescence or … you could pray if you are of a mind to." Then, turning back to the Norman, he repeated, word for word, everything Byrtha had said.

The Norman Lord stared at her, long and hard. Byrtha, as if bewitched by his stare, unable to move. Slowly, he dismounted from his horse, his leather harness creaking as he moved toward her. He circled her, assessing her, the disdain on his face suggesting he did not like what he saw. Throughout the long moment, Byrtha stood unmoving with her chin lifted. He was so close that she could see the sprouting stubble on his chin, and smell the horse sweat and garlic engrained in his clothes. Placing one gauntleted finger beneath her chin, he turned her face up to his and inspected it. She stared back, her scorn as marked as his. Then, suddenly releasing her, he turned and shouted a curt order to his men. As he remounted, his soldiers sprang into action, and a cry went up as two men lay hold of Byrtha and the priest and began to drag them away.

She kicked and twisted in their grip, her mouth wide in an outraged scream. Her people surged forward and as the settlement fell into skirmish, she twisted in the soldier's grip and brought her knee up, hard, into his groin.

He released her so quickly that she fell and began to crawl away toward the hall. The mounted Normans unsheathed their swords and rode their mounts into the crowd, driving them back toward the hall. Byrtha was exposed again. This time, as strong hands grabbed her beneath the arms and began to haul her off, she saw her grandmother run out, her old arms flailing as she cursed them.

"Misbegotten Shitedogs!" she cried, "May the gods rot ye all!" The Norman horses surged forward again, the hooves thrashing. There was a cry and a clash of steel, followed by a long-drawn-out scream. The grandmother's protests were severed forever.

"Grandmotherrrrrrrrrrrr!"

***

It was so dark in the hut that they could not see each other's faces. The cleric's breath came in gasps as he heaved himself to his feet. Byrtha heard him slapping the dirt from his robe. He grunted as he groped his way toward where she lay, stunned on the floor.

"Are you hurt, Child?"

The sound of his voice was all she had.

"My grandmother. My grandmother. I saw her fall beneath his horse. Oh God, let me out. I must help her. Grandmother! Grandmother!"

She dragged herself up again to bang on the wooden door until her hands ached, and her voice failed. The cleric gently touched her shoulder.

"You waste your energies, Child. They will not let you out; your sorrows are unimportant to them. Any resistance will be treated harshly. They have brought me with them, against my will, all the way from Essex because I can speak their tongue. I should not like to describe the atrocities I have seen but you must believe me when I tell you that resistance is useless. I have learned the hard way it is better to humour them and live … than to resist them and die."

He began to pace the dirt floor, rasping his hand across his stubbly chin. He had not shaved in days, and even his tonsure was almost indistinct. "Surrender the settlement and they will let you leave. Have you no kin you can go to? It is better that you leave here, you are not safe among them."

The voice, disembodied in the dark, did not soothe, it did the opposite. Byrtha made a sudden movement and the priest sensed that she stood close before him.

"Oh no," she hissed, "I will not give up this settlement. I should rather die than let that Norman shite take possession of my father's lands. My brothers may yet return and, when they do, they will learn that I defended this settlement and our people with *all* of my weapons, and to my last breath!"

The priest backed away from the face of her venom, and fell to praying aloud, as much for his own comfort as that of the girl. On his travels he has seen Norman atrocities such as he'd never imagined but, although he listed them throughout the remainder of the night, Byrtha would not heed him. She huddled in the opposite corner while the priest's voice droned on … and on.

***

The cock, which had been crowing since dawn, eventually fell silent and gradually sounds of activity began to filter through the walls of their prison. The first chinks of light crept through the wattle walls and Byrtha rose stiff backed from the corner. She pressed an eye to a knot hole.

Everything appeared normal; a slave crossed the yard to milk the sheep, chickens scratched in the dirt, dogs scavenged at the rubbish tip, and smoke spiralled from the cooking fires. The only difference was the silence, the absence of laughter or music, or children. Byrtha guessed their mothers kept them close.

The priest stirred, farted and slept again. Byrtha was thirsty and hungry, and felt a pressing need to pee. Drawing comfort from the dark interior and the less than heavenly snores issuing from her fellow prisoner, she lifted her tunic and urinated upon the floor.

The morning dragged by, and the sun was high in the sky when the door was finally opened, and a young Norman guard allowed a red-nosed Aethel to place a dish of cawl just inside the entrance. Byrtha had ever been more pleased to see anyone in her life. She stuffed a piece of rye bread in her mouth, speaking with her mouth full.

"What is happening, Aethel? What are they doing? Is everyone all right?"

"Oh Byrtha, no! When you were taken, the horses charged at us and several of us fell and were wounded. The... the Grandmother refused to be pushed back and stood firm, shaking her fists and calling them piss pot scum."

The two girls half smiled at the memory and then sobered, looked at each other.

"She's dead, isn't she?"

Byrtha's tone was dull and Aethel's expression confirmed her fears. Her throat closed, and tears pricked at her eyes, but this was not the time to give way. Grandmother would not give way, and neither would Byrtha.

Resolutely she pushed the sorrow away and turned her mind to practicalities but when she spoke, her voice was cracked with grief.

"Does it look as though they might leave soon?"

"Nay, not at all, Byrtha. That big fellow, the lord on the black horse has commandeered the best chamber and ordered the able-bodied to start work on a ditch. He orders that one should be dug all about the outer defences. A huge ditch with sides as steep as a gorge. They're working us like devils – all of us. I was sent back with some of the women to prepare food for this evening and I managed to get the heathen guarding the door to understand that you needed food too. I can't stay long, Byrtha, or worse will befall me." She clung suddenly to Byrtha's arm. "Oh, what is going to happen to us? Do you think my father knows of this? I am certain he will come with a force of arms to help me when he hears of it."

Byrtha doubted if Aethel's father, if he were alive, was in any better position than they to fight against the edicts of the new King but she said nothing. Instead, she chewed her food and wracked her brains for a solution.

In the far corner the old cleric, still sticky with sleep, sucked and slurped at his gruel. When Byrtha spoke to him, he jumped and spilt a spoonful of gravy down his robes.

"Father, what do you think will happen next? You know better than we the workings of their minds. What do you think they want?"

The priest paused in his feeding.

"On my journey here with them," he began, and then paused to swallow a mouthful of bread. "I saw men struck dead for lesser crimes than you and your people committed yesterday. I saw homesteads burned, women violated, livestock stolen, and innocent people murdered. However, it seems that even a Norman hesitates before slaying women in cold blood ... although, if you were ugly I imagine you may have fared worse. I should think your behaviour, unusual as it is, has made him uncertain what to do with you. He has probably sent to the King for orders as to how to proceed. You can be sure of only one thing. He will not relinquish this property, and a mere woman will not stand in his way."

"But it is so unjust. I did not fight for the king and neither did my father. Why should Thornholding be forfeit if we have committed no offence? Even my brothers were only fighting for their anointed King. Where is the crime in that?"

The priest scratched his scalp and examined a grimy fingernail.

"Madam, I know not. Be thankful that you live and take some comfort from that. Remember those that have suffered worse torment than you suffer now. "All you can do is pray for peace."

"Where was God when the Normans stole the throne? Where was He when my brothers were taken? Where was He when my grandmother was butchered? Do not seek to comfort me with your religion, Sir."

The priest scrabbled for words.

"Everything is part of God's pl......" he began, but Byrtha cut him short, turning to Aethel who still hesitated in the doorway as if she expected the power of heaven to strike her sister-in-law dead. Everyone paid lip service to the church and none openly defied God, certainly not in the presence of a priest. Byrtha snapped her fingers, regaining her sister-in-law's attention.

"Aethel, go back to the hall and deliver a message to this Norman fellow. Tell him that, as the Ealdorman's daughter, I demand to be released."

For the rest of the day, the priest avoided eye contact with Byrtha. While she restlessly paced back and forth, he pretended to sleep but kept one eye open and, fearing she was beset by devils, sent up prayers for deliverance.

Night was falling before they were summoned into the Norman's presence. Byrtha noted the pink tinged evening sky and rued the loss of an entire day. When she entered the hall and found him sprawled in her father's chair, she wanted to kill him. She imagined his severed head, his blood running thick and cold, lapped up by the dogs. The time is not yet right, she told herself, I cannot kill him yet. Instead, she acknowledged him coldly, while the priest bowed and fawned at the Norman's feet. Ignoring the grovelling priest, the Lord turned his attention upon Byrtha.

He smiled a slow smile and, for the first time, spoke her name in a thick foreign accent. "Byrrrrtha, n'est pa?" he drawled.

Barely recognising her name, Byrtha nodded in affirmation. While she moistened her dry lips, he gestured the priest to translate his words into English.

"He says he has a letter from the King." The priest indicated the parchment that the Norman was waving in the air. Then a stream of unintelligible language issued from the Lord, followed by silence as the priest processed the information.

"The letter confirms that the settlement known as Thorn holding is indeed forfeit to the crown, and it is the King's pleasure that it be given into the possession of this man, Rainald de Caen."

Byrtha stepped forward but her words were immobilised when the priest continued. "It is also the King's pleasure that the Ealdorman Oslac be brought before him in person, and that the hand of Oslac's daughter, Byrtha of Thorn holding, be given in marriage to Lord Rainald. A union designed to bring peace between Saxon and Norman."

Byrtha's jaw dropped, her determination to remain calm extinguished by the idea of marriage to this man.

"By God! I will not be hand-fasted with him. You can tell your king that I am already betrothed to another, our vows were sworn before God, in the presence of our fathers. Not even a Norman can gainsay a pledge taken before witnesses."

The vehemence of her refusal amused the Norman. He settled himself more comfortably in his chair and stroked his upper lip with two forefingers. He raised his brows at the priest, silently requesting clarification of her ire.

Fortunately, the priest valued his skin and described the predicament of her prior alliance with more diplomacy. The Norman leaned forward in his chair, a stream of French words, and a gesture of dismissal erased her protest, and the priest once more coughed before interpreting.

"Baron Rainald regrets to inform you that your betrothed, Scef of Thorndyke, was slain at Hastings and no longer constitutes a bar to your union. He says that the King wishes the marriage to take place without delay, and ... and so tomorrow forenoon you will both be joined... with or without your consent."

Byrtha's hopes crashed, the whole weight of the last few months falling heavily upon her. Grief for her brothers, her mother, the Grandmother and the sickness of her father, had been held at bay by the one slim hope that Scef and Leo had survived and would soon ride home to liberate her.

Rainald rose from his seat and approached her. She did not move, even when he stood too close, even when he whispered his strange words close beside her ear. The priest continued to translate. "My Lady, I am not a cruel man..." Rainald turned swiftly and batted him about the ear, his endearments clearly not meant for sharing.

She listened, unwillingly and during supper let him ply her with food and drink, eating sparingly although she was ravenously hungry. His dark eyes smouldered and his voice was gentle as she listened with murder flourishing in her heart. At length, growing tired of her lack of response, he straightened in his chair and called for a servant. When Aethel appeared, he sent the pair of them away with a Norman guard.

In the outer chamber the priest was informing the settlement of the wedding that was to take place between Byrtha and their new lord. As the guard led her through the hall, their eyes followed her. There were no calls of friendship or good wishes, her presence was met with a hostile silence. As the curtain fell behind her she heard one word.

"Traitor!"

***

Aethel came at first light to help her wash, braid her hair and put on a fresh gown. As the garment was drawn over her head, she remembered painstakingly stitching it, ready for her hand fasting with Scef.

"What am I to do, Aethel? How can I exchange vows with that- that *monster*?"

Her grief for Scef was still raw, it always would be. Her feelings of helplessness made worse by her own predicament. If she refused to join with the Norman he might force her from the holding, or worse. And what would befall her people then?

The feel of the fine fabric on her skin and the smell of the herbs brought back memories of the day she had began to sew it, the day she'd first tried it on. Days of optimism. Tears sprung to her eyes. If someone had told her then, that a few months later Scef and her brothers would be dead and herself forced to marry a stranger, she'd have scoffed at the idea. In the course of two battles, everything had been changed, and just as Harold had lost his life and kingdom, so was she in danger of losing hers. She had no option but to comply. Like a lamb to the slaughter, she must sacrifice herself for the well-being of her people. Her chin began to tremble, her chest tight with tears but as she teetered on the edge of despair, she remembered the words of the Grandmother. Byrtha was no lamb. She was a lioness.

In a joyless ceremony in a frigid chapel, Rainald and Byrtha were joined. He was dressed in rich, blue garments and gold rings glinted on his fingers. When their hands were joined, his fingers were warm and dry. Byrtha's were cold.

"I now declare you are man …and wife."

Before the words had left the priest's mouth, Rainald bent over and pressed his lips against her clammy wrist. Then, as if blind to her hostility, he guided her to the hall where a feast had been prepared in their honour.

Byrtha, seated in her mother's chair, took no part in the celebration. The surviving elders of Thornholding sat far from the Normans but some of the young women moved up and down the table, serving drinks. Byrtha saw some of them exchanging pleasantries with the soldiers. It seemed much had changed in her two days of incarceration, and her people were already beginning to accept and adapt to the change in Lordship.

She noted the names of the girls who flirted with the soldiers and those who shunned them; she would reward them accordingly. But how long, she wondered, would it be before the first Norman bastard was conceived? How long before the blood of her people was diluted, tainted!

If her marriage to Rainald was seen as a form of acceptance, she would soon prove them wrong.. Byrtha would never give up the fight. Throughout the meal Rainald spoke quietly to her but she did not acknowledge him. Instead, she sought courage in the depths of her mead cup. The unaccustomed strong drink made her weak, maudlin tears she had held back for so long pricked at her eyes. She blinked them away and drank deeper. She wanted to be drunk, disgustingly drunk, and blot out the horror that was to come.

It was not long before her head grew light, and the heat in the hall oppressive. She leaned her head back and watched the smoke eddy about the roof space, seeking escape into the night air. *I wish I could escape so easily*, she thought. *If only I could just disappear.*

Rainald's leaned forward, covered her hand with his and said something. She longed to snatch her hand from his and leave the hall but feared he might mistake her departure as eagerness for the joining that was to follow. She had no choice but to listen and, after a while she came to recognise the rhythm of his words and distinguish where one word ended and another began. His meaning was lost but his sentiment was not, and as the evening turned to night his voice deepened and softened.

He picked up the end of her rope like braid, she remembered Scef doing the same. *Pray God he does not tickle my nose with it.* Her throat tightened and her eyes burned. Fighting tears, she breathed slowly while Rainald feasted his eyes on her bare white throat.

"très bien, ma petite, très bien."

When Rainald rose suddenly to his feet, the music petered out and Byrtha opened her eyes. A mischievous cheer went up from the soldiery, but Rainald raised a hand and silenced them. Usually at a wedding, there was ribaldry and fun; the marriage bed would be adorned with flora, the odd prank of a sprig of holly or family of mice hidden in the covers. But as the new lord took Byrtha's hand and led her across the stifling hall, nobody uttered a word.

***

Outside, the night was still and cold. Rainald paused, looked up at the sky and gestured for her to do the same. Byrtha filled her lungs with air and regarded the blue mantle that was drawn across the sky, pinned with bright stars. The moon hung low, like a jewel, its benign face seeming to mock her. Behind them in the hall the sounds of revelry resumed and Rainald murmured something and laughed gently before placing his arm about her shoulder. She did her best not to shrink away.

They stood for a long while, drinking in the beauty of the mist-streaked valley, inhaling the earthy, green fragrance of the wood and Byrtha tried not to recall other nights, with another suitor.

No wonder the Normans coveted this rich, fertile land. She turned slightly watching him unobserved. His eyes were closed, his nose slightly hooked, and his chin was sharp. He was foreign and he looked it but, monster though he was, he was handsomely made. His face and body well-formed and strong. If circumstances were different he would be a desirable husband.

At length, he opened his eyes and turned toward her, smiling. She looked quickly away, stiffening when he reached out to stroke her cheek. The night was perfect, and she was very drunk, and she wished with her whole being he was Scef. But while Scef lay cold in an unmarked grave, she must bed a Norman.

In Rainald's chamber a fire burned brightly, and rich furs were piled in his sleeping place. A leather curtain kept out the worst of the chill, and a plate of cold meat and a flagon of wine were laid before the fire. When Rainald poured a cup and handed it to her, she downed the liquor quickly, wiping the back of her hand across her mouth. She knew what was going to happen and if she was to bear it, she needed to be as drunk as possible. As the wine took hold it was as if her head detached from her body. She seemed to be observing from a great height as her enemy seduced her.

Rainald sat down and drew her onto his knee. She sat stiffly, keeping her eyes fixed on the flames. While he ran his hands across her body, his warm fingers stroking her back and buttocks she did not respond and was determined not to give him the satisfaction of fighting.

She had expected roughness. She had imagined he would throw her onto the furs and tear off her clothes, do what was to be done straight away. Instead, as he stroked her skin, he murmured in her ear, matching his tone to the gentleness of his touch. By the time he turned her face toward him and kissed her, she was relaxed, ready but still unwelcoming.

She had only been kissed by a boy before. Rainald was a man and as he grew more insistent, his face harsh against hers, she tried to pull away. But Rainald held her head firm, his tongue hot in her mouth, his hands roaming her body.

"No!" she wailed, but he did not stop.

"*Oh, oui, oui Madame. Oui, oui.*"

Rainald stood up suddenly, sending her tumbling from his lap. Scrambling to her feet, she lunged for the door, but he caught her by the wrist and, leading her firmly to the sleeping place, indicated that she was to lie upon the furs. She searched frantically for a way out, a way to make him stop. If he would just give her time to …She considered fighting but at the back of her mind, she knew the thing was going to happen anyway. Being taken by force would be far worse than compliance.

She climbed onto the bed and lay stiffly, her face craned toward the wall. As he began to loosen her braids, his murmuring words were almost a song. He nuzzled at her neck like a kitten, sending goose bumps across her flesh but rejecting the pleasure of it, Byrtha bit her lip. He freed her hair, as if he'd done so many times before and arranged it prettily on the pillow. His lips found her earlobe and he nibbled gently, making her gasp involuntarily. She opened her eyes wide, breathing in short, distressed gasps.

Imperceptibly his left hand began drawing up her skirts, his fingers working a way up her thigh. With panic rising, and her head swimming, Byrtha foundered beneath his touch. Her breast, somehow freed from her gown, was in his palm and he massaged, sending strange sensations through her body. Then he fastened his lips around her nipple, at first flicking with his tongue and then pulling, drawing on it deeply … rhythmically.

With her head reeling, Byrtha lay still. Compliant.

"Byrtha," he murmured, her name exotic on his tongue. She tried to think, tried to hate him, tried to fight it but he pressed his body against hers, his mouth coming down hard, his exploring hands sending fire surging through her. She groaned aloud. She tried to struggle but something, perhaps it was the wine, made her weak. Scef's pale face melted sadly away, leaving only Rainald.

He reared before her, ignoring the restraining hand she placed upon his chest, he prised her knees apart as he pushed gently against her yielding body.

"I hate you," she murmured, making one last attempt to withstand the attack. But she had used all her weapons, and his assault was too strong; her determination wavered, her protests a limp, white flag in the night.

Thin fingers of daylight crept through the shutter, revealing their discarded clothing, an overturned flagon and rumpled bed covers. As the memory of the previous night returned, Byrtha looked at the stranger sleeping beside her. His dark beard grew strong on his chin, and his mouth was open, his regular breathing lifting her hair that lay tangled on the pillow.

Guilt bit savagely when she recalled how weakly she had fought him; shame when she recalled the delight toward the end. She had betrayed everything she believed in; her family, her country and herself. Shifting her position, she began to move gingerly away from his warmth. Carefully, she lifted the sheet, the revelation of his unconscious form giving her pause. His arms and chest were covered in dark hair, his penis curled, pink and innocuous in its nest. Rainald snored on.

Reaching for her tunic, Byrtha noticed the hilt of his heavy sword, discarded among their clothing. It taunted her in the half-light. She should have resisted him last night; she was dishonourable, weak! She felt a resurgence of hate, now mixed with shame. Yesterday, she would have snatched up the sword and plunged it deep into his heart. Like Judith, she would have hacked off his head, run outside to display the trophy to her people and lead them all to freedom.

Her fingers crept toward the scabbard, but the sheet slipped aside and revealed the red marks his mouth had left upon her skin. A sudden vivid memory of her body entwined with his drew her up short; she had never imagined such feelings existed.

She left the sword where it lay.

By the time Rainald stirred, Byrtha was fully dressed. He rolled onto his side; his greeting smile sensuous. He threw back the covers, exposing his early morning pride and Byrtha looked quickly away, her cheeks flushing scarlet. He laughed softly, held out his arms, and judging from his earnest words, apparently wished her to return to bed. She drew back her shoulders and spoke clearly although she knew he could not understand.

"As your wife, my Lord, I have other duties to attend to. This settlement will not run itself. I will no doubt see you at table later in the day."

Somehow understanding and mercifully accepting her denial, Rainald uttered a profanity and flung himself back upon the pillows. By the time Rainald emerged from his hut no sign of the lover remained, he was once more the formidable Norman soldier. With his priestly interpreter at his heels, he issued orders and organised the men of the settlement into working parties.

The men, ailing and ageing as they were organised into groups and set to work on a defensive ditch that was to encircle the enclosure.

"We will be separated from the rest of the world," Byrtha thought when she saw it. "They are imprisoning us, cutting off our chances of escape."

Even some of the stronger women were set to work. After many weeks, the ditch was complete the people were told to begin felling timber for further construction. Byrtha, of course, was spared this labour and tried to persuade Rainald to let her take her turn. The Norman refused, taking her arm and propelling her back to the hall. He thrust her into a chair.

"I can't just sit here!" she cried. "I must be of some use."

Rainald smiled, pointed to a jug and told her to pour.

"Women work." He said, in halting English. With the jug in her hand, Byrtha turned and placed a cup before him.

"Well," she said. "I'd imagined you would expect me to learn your tongue, not the other way about."

He smiled again, uncomprehendingly and raised his cup.

Outside, incessant rain hampered the progress of the defensive structure, and the mud, and relentless work increased the people's resentment for this new Lord. Hatred simmered on all sides, and it fell to Byrtha to try to keep the peace. She tried to explain the futility of resistance and encourage the labourers to do as they were bid. Even now, with her hatred for Rainald tempered, she still clung to the fragile hope that a Saxon army would come to drive the invaders away.

The war may be over, but the conflict continued. Byrtha's time was spent pacifying the small skirmishes that broke out daily. When a Norman took one of the girls to his bed, she had to speak to Rainald and persuade him they should marry. One of the soldiers killed and ate a milking goat, Byrtha had to explain they were not for eating but for providing the settlement with milk. Small atrocities carried out by Normans were inflated in the eyes of the Saxons and it took all her diplomacy to prevent rebellion. During the day she hated the invaders as much as any other at the settlement but when she was summoned to his bed at nightfall, the pleasure she took there made her forget he was the enemy.

Her feelings fluctuated from frigid indifference to burning delight. She was confused, appalled by her own behaviour but the benefits of being his wife were considerable. She had never slept apart from the rest of the community, but she soon came to prefer it. The central hall noisy, even in the night; sounds of insomnia, sickness, or coupling often disturbed her but, in the quiet of their own sleeping hut, only Rainald's attentions kept her from sleep. And it was increasingly difficult to resent it.

Before too many weeks had passed Rainald began to seek her out during the day. Sometimes it was to ask her opinion on something, or for assistance with the villagers. In public, she continued to treat him coldly but they both knew their relationship was transitioning. She began to understand some of his words and phrases and came to realise that in his eyes what she construed as harshness, was actually justice.

He was performing his duty to his Norman king as he saw it, and as part of the invasion force, he was constrained to follow orders. She knew from the priest's stories that Rainald could have been very much worse.

Across England other settlements were suffering much more than Thornholding, they heard tales of rape and murder. Byrtha began to count her blessings. Rainald may not be the husband she had looked for, but he was not old, he was handsome and strong, with a head full of teeth and he was prosperous too. As long as she behaved, he treated her well enough. In fact, there were far worse husbands among her own people.

As the months passed it became easier to accept her old life was over. Her mother and grandmother were dead, her brothers killed or exiled, and her father imprisoned. She must make the best of a bad situation; her family would expect her to do no different. She still grieved every day for her lost kin and wondered how her father was faring in the Norman gaol. She hoped that his loss of memory protected him from the reality of what was happening. It tortured her to think of Oslac imprisoned and alone. She prayed for him, begging God to keep him well.

In many ways, once the defences were in place, life at the holding went on as it always had; the women made cloth and prepared food and raised infants, while the men and half-grown boys farmed and hunted.

The only change was that the orders now came from Rainald.

She would never admit that she was excited by the new wooden castle Rainald was having built on the central mound. The first time he led her around the half-constructed building, pointing out the various rooms and demonstrating how his improvements would greatly improve the defences, she couldn't quite believe what she was seeing. The structure was sturdy, promising to be less damp than the old hall and since the cooking would be performed on the lower floors, the upper chambers would be warm and free of vermin.

***

Rainald was away and taking advantage of it Byrtha was being lazy. She sat beside the well, watching the activities around her. In his absence the atmosphere at the settlement was more relaxed and, apart from the usual sounds of hammering issuing from the keep, she could almost pretend the invasion had never happened. She listened to the children playing nearby, their voices mingling with those of the women who were spinning in the sun. Already, their language was peppered with French expressions and curses, and the boys' games heavily influenced by the conflict.

They had formed themselves into two groups and, armed with stout sticks, advanced toward each other and began to fight. Byrtha watched, so absorbed she didn't at first hear the clear notes of the horn sounding.

"The horn, Byrtha, the horn. Someone is here." She leapt up when Aethel's voice penetrated her reverie. Putting a hand to her brow she squinted into the distance.

"It is Rainald," she said, and the other women, disappointed it wasn't someone bringing salvation, returned to their tasks.

Byrtha went to meet her husband. His black horse was gleaming with sweat, the long mane streaming in the wind, the nostrils distended and red. She drew back as the cavalcade thundered into the enclosure and milled about in the half-frozen mud. Grooms came running to take charge of the horses but when Rainald slid from his saddle he didn't greet her at once. Instead, he turned to help someone else dismount, someone whose steps were unsteady when he found himself on firm ground. Shielding her eyes with one hand, Byrtha blinked into the blaze of sunlight as Rainald led the guest toward her.

The old man halted, looked about the enclosure with a vague smile. Byrtha's heart leapt, she ran toward him, flung her arms about his neck, her lips peppering his flaccid cheek with kisses.

Imprisonment had stripped Oslac the Elder of his girth and his clothes hung loosely on his frame. He patted her shoulder absently, as if he had just returned from a fishing trip.

"Byrtha, my dear!" he said. "Where is your mother? Is she within?"

Byrtha hesitated, glanced at Rainald, who shrugged his shoulders in apology. She gave him her best smile.

"I thank you, my Lord," she said before turning to follow her father into the old hall.

Rainald watched them go.

"Today was the first time you have smiled at me during daylight, before others." Rainald spoke in French, Byrtha understanding the gist of his statement.

"That is because you gave me something to smile about."

He laughed, showing his strong teeth, a glint in his eye.

"I'll make you smile more later."

The guard standing nearby nudged one another and chuckled, making eyes at her and with her cheeks burning, Byrtha fled into the hall.

***

"Look, Byrtha," said Rainald. 'See what I bring from court."

Byrtha turned from her task to see him pulling a rich tapestry from his pack.

"Oh, hangings for the keep! They are very fine." She shook them, spread them out so they could appreciate the design. "I want to hang them now. I want to see how they will look."

The sun was climbing towards its zenith as they hurried toward the half-built castle. Rainald gesticulated with his arms as he spoke of his plans, pointing out how each room would be used. His excitement triggered a reaction in his wife.

"I'm most excited about the sleeping chamber," she said. "I've never had such a thing before."

"It is barbaric the way you English all sleep together in one place. A lord needs his privacy."

Catching hold of her hand, he pulled her into a large chamber and, speaking too rapidly for her to follow, he spun around the floor indicating where their bed was to be placed and where the new Flemish tapestry should hang.

"And I bring this for you, also" he cried, shaking out a tunic of sea green wool. Holding it against himself, he postured like a woman.

Byrtha laughed out loud, her hand to her mouth. Rainald dropped the gown and took both her hands in his and kissed her. As if pushed from behind, she moved easily toward him, and his arms slipped around her shoulders. Then, suddenly self-conscious, they pulled apart again, unsure of how to deal with the feelings flaring between them in the light of day. Byrtha was aware that their relationship was shifting toward something else, and she closed her eyes, anticipating Rainald's kiss before he lowered his head.

The hangings that were still strewn about the floor became a couch for their lovemaking. He took her tenderly, softly, as if she might break. When it was over, tears ran down Byrtha's cheeks, her heart full of joy. Seeing her wet cheeks, Rainald wiped the tears away.

"What? Why you weep? Did I hurt you?"

"Do not worry, Rainald, they are good tears. Happy."

How can I be joyful? How have I forgotten Scef so quickly?

Rainald's brow furrowed.

"You need more words…" He shrugged his shoulders, indicating he did not understand. And then, shy at their newfound intimacy, he played the part of a maid and helped her to dress.

The afternoon was almost over when they left the keep and walked hand in hand across the enclosure. The people paused in their work to watch them pass and the cook's boy, who was in the act of pulling a cockerel's neck, relaxed his grip letting the bird escape. He set off in pursuit, but the bird fluttered to a rooftop to crow his victory.

Rainald, sharing his triumph, joined in.

March 1068

Steady rain turned the hard packed earth of the settlement to sticky mud. It clung to the feet of the children and the skirts of the women. March winds howled like wolves around the keep where Byrtha huddled at a table with the priest who was teaching her her letters. Her grasp of the French tongue had been so rapid she was now able to converse in simple terms. Rainald, quick to recognise his wife's agile brain, now wanted to improve her literacy and Byrtha was determined to excel.

She dipped her quill into the inkwell and, with the tip of her tongue showing at the corner of her mouth, began to copy the script provided by the priest. When she'd finished the set piece, she sat up and pushed the work across the table for his inspection. It was neatly but plainly done, and she knew it in no way compared with the artistry of the writing in the book bequeathed her by the Grandmother.

A whole year had passed since her marriage to Rainald, and their friendship had blossomed so much that she could scarce remember a time when he was not part of her life.

One afternoon, Byrtha decided it was time to show her husband the book. When she drew it from the hiding place and unfolded the wrapping, he took it from her and laid it reverently upon their bed. He turned one page and turned to her, his eyes gleaming.

"This is a wonder …a treasure," he marvelled. "I have seen such things in churches and great houses in Normandy but … where did you come by it? Its value is great, I am sure."

Byrtha told him of the Grandmother, and her Viking father, detailing her grandmother's life, her great strength of character.

"The Grandmother knew her own value and saw little need to behave other than she saw fit. She refused to conform, and my own mother despaired of her. They had little to do with each other toward the end of her life, but I was always very close to her. I treasure this book, Rainald, not because of its value but because she gave it to me, as her father entrusted it to her. If I am lucky enough to have a child one day, I will pass it into his keeping when the time comes."

Rainald continued to examine the book, turning further pages.

"It seems to have had an outer cover at some time but that is long gone now, and here see, there are some water marks on the edge of the pages. I wonder; where was it made?"

"There are some words in the back, that are plainer, unembellished and I have often wondered at their meaning."

She turned to the relevant page and indicated the place in the text and Rainald leaned over to see if he could decipher the handwriting. He cleared his throat and then read in halting Latin.

"Alric of Alricsleah in Northumbria began this book and was helped by his pupil, Alricson who carried it with him after Alric's death to Lindisfarne where it was made complete in his memory." Why this is amazing, Byrtha! The book has travelled all the way from the North of the Humber to here. I wonder who these people were. Obviously they must have been clerics of some sort. How strange it is to hold in our hands the work of people so long dead."

Byrtha pondered on that thought for a while and then began to rewrap the book in its soft covering.

"We will never know that, Rainald; my great grandfather gave it to my grandmother but did not say how it came into his possession. He was a Viking so maybe he stole it, or it was part of his reward. We will never know."

Fascinated, Rainald sat down and pulled her onto his knee, inhaling the scent of her hair. "Your grand-mère; chérie. When did she die?"

Byrtha's ears began to ring, her face burned as she fumbled with the book's wrapping, sudden tears stinging the back of her eyes. Suddenly sickened, she shook her head before replying huskily.

"It was when you came, Rainald. Don't you remember? She tried to prevent me from being mishandled …She was mown down beneath the hooves of your horse."

Rainald stood up, spilling his wife from his lap. He moved to the window, his face white, watching her from the corner of his eye as, embracing the book in her arms, she moved slowly away.

Rainald cursed quietly as she closed the door.

***

The atmosphere between them was strained for a few days but Byrtha was determined not to let the issue come between them. She had to remain practical. One night, as they lay upon their bed, she asked him if he would teach her how to write her name.

"Oh, I would were I not so busy but perhaps the priest is better equipped than I."

She proved a willing pupil and quickly learned the rudiments of committing her thoughts and wishes to parchment. This particular morning, however, she was feeling queasy and, as soon as she could, excused herself from the room, leaving the comforts of the keep and crossing the holding in the scudding rain.

When she arrived at the old hall her hair was jewelled with drops of rain and the hem of her skirts muddied. Shaking herself free of the worst of the wet, she joined a small group at the central fire. Although the building of the castle was now complete and proved a much more comfortable shelter than anything they had known before, the older members of the community preferred to conglomerate in the ancestral hall – as they always had. Rainald had intended to tear the old building down, but Byrtha pleaded with him to let it stand because it was where her father seemed happiest.

Oslac was sitting close to the hearth wrapped in a fur cloak while Aethel spooned broth into his mouth. The girl straightened up at Byrtha's approach and handed her the bowl. Byrtha took her place at her father's side.

Poor Aethel, she thought, *she has lost her husband and her status. Now she is little better than a slave.*

Unless she joined with a Norman underling, Aethel now had no prospect of remarriage, and her children were obliged to grow up fatherless and without privileges. Byrtha, on the other hand, had retained her status, had a grand new keep to live in and fine clothes to wear. While her prosperity increased, Aethel and Asa became work-worn, and their futures unpromising.

Byrtha enjoyed her afternoons with Oslac, and loved to sing to him as she teased the knots from his thin hair. He gazed about the hall, listening in vain for the footfall of the wife he had always imagined he didn't love.

The rain had stopped at last, and puddles reflected the tall keep and the clearing skies above. As she tiptoed gingerly through them, a disturbance caught her attention and she saw three Norman soldiers dragging a young boy across the settlement toward the stocks. In her father's time the stocks had seen little use, being a deterrent rather than a punishment, and she watched in dismay as the boy was forced to the ground and secured by the wrists and feet. His mouth gaped and tears spouted from his eyes. As she hurried forward, his sobbing mother rushed toward her.

"Oh, Lady, it must be a mistake. He's a good boy is Eadred and wouldn't do no wrong. Please stop them, he has not yet seen seven summers and yet they say he is to have a flogging."

The woman continued to weep, intermittently wiping her nose on her hood and beseeching God to intercede. Byrtha didn't know what to do. A crowd was gathering, all of them looking to her for support, and the Norman soldiers were growing belligerent.

Why was Rainald not here? He never seemed to be here when she needed him, and today he was supervising a shipment of wool and wouldn't be back before nightfall. She must act before the situation got out of hand.

Brushing the fawning villagers away, she forced a way through the crowd.

Two soldiers guarded the boy; they looked at her stonily. She tried to address them in halting French until she realised they were smirking at her accent. She switched to English.

"I forbid you to punish this boy further. He is too young for such treatment. What has he done to deserve such roughness?"

The taller of the soldiers hesitated, her status unclear. She was the wife of his lord, but she was also English and despised by his king.

"The law is the law, and this boy took a bow and a quiver of arrows, an offence by anyone's standards and, in the absence of Lord Rainald, I must act according to Norman law."

"My *husband*," she said, trying not to clip her words, "will return shortly and he will be displeased if you do not do as I ask. I demand that you free this child!"

"I'll free him when my Lord commands me and not before. To go against the law is more than my life is worth. Rules must be followed."

The villagers clustered around her; their silence ominous, their hatred humming like a swarm of bees. Byrtha stood at their head, keenly aware of the capabilities of these men. What would Rainald do? She licked her lips, her voice belying her lack of confidence,

"Very well then, we will all wait for my husband to return. He will be little more than an hour now, and it will do no harm if the punishment is delayed."

The villagers shuffled their feet, their disapproval rumbling. The boy's mother tugged at her sleeve again.

"But Lady, tis coming on to dark, and rain is threatening. Eadred takes the fever so easily, what if your Lord don't return, my boy could be dead before morning."

Byrtha spoke into the woman's ear.

"If we provoke them, everyone will suffer. Lord Rainald is not here to control them, so please be calm. We must wait. I'm sure he will come soon!"

But the mother's patience had run out, desperation to protect her son overcoming judgement.

"It's a shame, that's what," she cried, addressing the soldiers through gritted teeth. "Your betters would never have treated a child thus, God-forsaken Norman curs."

The soldier took one look at her hate-twisted face and struck her hard across the mouth. She sprawled into the mud. With a scream, Byrtha crouched to assist the woman who clung to her, and spat bloody drool onto the soldier's boots.

The soldier kicked her again and, this time, the woman lay still.

Silence fell, for a brief moment the only sound was birdsong, but hatred screamed around them. One villager moved, an old man, his arm raised, inciting violence, a surge of anger rising in response. Byrtha was pushed aside, the force of the crowd spinning her around. Hearing the fray, other Normans came running, their weapons raised. Without thought for her own safety, Byrtha clambered onto the stocks and screamed at the crowd.

'Stop!" she cried. 'Stop now. This will do no good; look, more soldiers are coming. You cannot win. Stop now before it is too late. Listen to me, listen, I say!"

Those closest heard her, saw the men at arms bearing down upon them and understood what was about to happen. They urged those close by to desist and, before the Normans reached them, the villagers were quieter although fermenting with anger.

Breathless and dishevelled, Byrtha tucked a stray strand of hair beneath her cap and addressed the fray again.

"I know you think I am weak because I do not fight. I know you think me a traitor because I interact with the invaders but … suppose I did not? Where would we be today? Would you be here? Would you be still living? Would your children be fed and your bellies full? Who would nurse you in your sickness and protect your livelihood? Do you think any of us would be left alive? What would you have me do? Fight and be killed and let Thornholding pass completely into Norman hands? This conflict is *not* about King Harold or King William, or any other potential King. It is about us, and the continuity of our settlement.

If we fight your way then we all perish, and England along with it, but my way, we get to remain here. The blood of my father runs in my veins and, God willing, one day I will have a son, who will not be just half Norman but half Saxon too! I urge you to comply with these men, because, in the end, we will triumph. The good blood that flows in our veins will water down that of the Normans. Lord Rainald will be back soon, and he will free the child. That I promise you."

Quieter now, the villagers began to slowly disperse. The boy's mother was helped to her feet, her face bathed, and a salve applied. Byrtha, sending up a thankful prayer, climbed down from the stocks but, as she did so, she caught sight of a figure standing in the shadow of the gate.

As he moved into the light, she realised her husband had returned in time to witness her impassioned speech. She smiled uncertainly and waited for him to draw near.

He gave her no welcoming smile as he took her arm and gruffly ordered them to release the child. As the men fumbled with the ties that bound him, and the boy's mother led him home, Rainald hurried Byrtha away.

'So, Madame?" he spat as they went. "You guarantee my leniency in my absence as though I am some lapdog? You feign affection for me merely to keep hold of your father's settlement, and you breed with me only to get sons to win back your father's land?"

Byrtha opened her mouth to reply but he cut her short, forcing her against a rough wall, and thrusting his face close to hers.

"I had thought better of you, Byrtha," he snarled. "Do you think I am the fool, Madame, to be gulled by a woman? Oh! You made a good show of pretending love for me; I admit it. I was deceived. You are no simpleton and that makes you a very dangerous enemy, an overly intelligent, deceitful enemy. What do you think I should do, Madame? Should I beat you perhaps, or renounce my vows and cast you off? Oh Byrtha! I thought I had a friend in this God-forsaken country, yet you are a serpent."

While she fumbled for the right words, he ran his hand through his hair, and her heart turned over at the thought of losing him.

"No Rainald! That is not so. All I did was try to keep the peace in your absence. It was my duty to do so. Your men are unreasonable and hostile and provoke my villagers who are understandably resentful. You came among us and killed our kin. When you took me in unwelcome wedlock I complied with everything you said, uncomplainingly. Admittedly, at first, I hated you, but I have since come to respect and admire you my lord. I am proud to be your wife and I am proud to bear your child but there must be trust between us if we are to succeed."

Rainald held up a hand to silence her. He stood unmoving, but she could see he was thinking; his eyes narrowed as he scrutinised her face, searching for truth in her words. With her hands wrapped tightly in her skirts she tried to still her thumping heart. Slowly Rainald's expression altered, his voice grew calmer.

"Forgive me, my English is not good. Did you say, "I *am* proud to bear your child:" or, "I *would* be proud to bear your child?"

Byrtha raised her head. "I said I *am* proud to bear your child, my Lord."

***

Swords of sunlight lanced the high windows. Byrtha and Rainald stirred simultaneously and turned toward each other. The covering had slid from the bed and Byrtha tugged at it as she sat up, shielding her body. Rainald made a face, pulling at the sheet until her breasts were exposed, and then he lay his head on her shoulder and began to play with them. They were larger than usual and traced with faint blue veins, but only the slight curve of her stomach betrayed her secret. Rainald slid his hand from her breast to cup and gently stroke her belly. Byrtha watched the caress.

"A boy, do you think, My Lord, or a girl?"

"I care not," he replied, 'so long as his mother is safe."

"Ha!" she exclaimed triumphantly, "you said 'his mother' so you do want a son!"

Rainald continued to stroke her silky skin, pondering the question before replying.

"No, honestly, I have no preference. A son would be nice, every man wishes for an heir, but a girl will be fine too, just so long as she has the thick flaxen hair and blue, blue eyes and the heart of a dragon."

Byrtha snorted. 'Sounds like a monster, my love."

She dived playfully beneath the covers, evading his clutching hands before emerging once more, laughing and tempting him to lunge for her again.

The news of their coming child had changed everything for they were now both invested in a united future. Rainald, growing serious again, stroked the hair from her brow and began to kiss her. She pulled away.

"Aethel will be here any moment to help me dre…" His kiss staunched her words, and her body melted beneath his touch.

The day ahead was full of duties, but Aethel would have to wait.

Bracing himself for the shock, Rainald poured cold water over his head, rubbing it dry before quickly dressing, and blowing a kiss to his wife. After he quit the chamber, Byrtha slid down into the sheets again and waited for Aethel to arrive.

Today she would work on her Latin, instruct the women in the kitchens and then spend time with her father. She had told him about the child, done all she cold to try to make him understand but he didn't comprehend the enormity of what she was saying.

This child would be the first Anglo-Norman child born at Thornholding. He would unite enemies, blur the boundaries between them. Choosing his name was a delicate matter and they had not yet come to an agreement. While Rainald favoured Norman names like Oddo or Roger, she preferred Eadwald or Brithnoth. A compromise was required and, as Aethel brushed the tangles from her hair and confined it in tight braids, they considered the alternatives.

The villagers clustered in the bailey as a lathered horse skidded to a halt and a young, mailed archer leapt from his mount.

"Quick," he called. "Give me a drink."

He doused his head with water from the well before tipping back his head and pouring ale into his throat, spilling most of it down his front. Wiping his mouth on his sleeve, he scanned the yard, searching for someone in authority. Noticing Rainald's approach, he bowed perfunctorily and between breaths explained his errand from the king.

As Rainald led the messenger out of ear shot, Byrtha strained to hear their words. Her husband didn't look happy. *Not more bad news*, she thought fearfully.

"I must ride with the king. There is trouble at Exeter."

"What trouble, Rainald?"

"From what I can gather, the mother of your late King Harold has sought refuge there but, instead of keeping out of trouble, she has roused the citizens to revolt. Now the residents refuse to either pay their taxes or swear fealty to the King. The stupid woman has brought disaster upon the town for William now turns his army upon them. He will show little mercy."

The action was to be a swift and effective swipe at the resistance and the king required an immediate response. Rainald swore darkly.

"It is a bad time to leave you, Byrtha. I am reluctant to expose you to the danger of rebellion when you are with child. And there is so much to do here. I've had enough of war. I've given King William enough of my life. I want time to enjoy my reward for helping him to victory."

He placed a heavy hand on her shoulder while he hollered curt orders to his sergeant to ready his men for a long march south.

She resisted the instinct to cling to his sleeve and beg him to stay for she knew she'd be ignored. The King had the prior claim. The hustle of preparation reminded her uncomfortably of the days before her brothers had ridden off. She had never seen them again. Sieges could last months, years even, and he expected her to be strong and entrusted her to keep charge of the settlement in his absence.

He itemised his orders, striking them off on his fingers.

"I will leave enough men to protect you; men who will be under orders to obey your every command."

She gulped and, summoning her stores of courage, followed in Rainald's wake as he listed the many instructions she was to follow. She hadn't expected to be trusted with the sole responsibility for the safety and peace within the settlement. His faith was touching, and she was determined to do it justice.

***

It was time for Rainald to leave. The weapons had been cleaned and the baggage packed upon wagons. When she watched him make ready, he seemed changed, distanced and distracted, his mind already on battle. Seeing him in full armour again, the leaping stag emblazoned on his chest, memories were triggered of his capacity for violence, and a flutter of uncertainty stirred in the pit of her stomach.

Perhaps she didn't really know him at all.

His horse, a beast bred and trained for combat, arched its head and stamped its huge hooves. The same hooves that had cut down her grandmother. Byrtha shied away, hanging back until Rainald urged the horse closer. She looked up at him, the sunlight on his helmet girding him with a flashing halo. Sliding from the saddle again, he kissed her goodbye.

"Take care," he whispered as his lips brushed her cheek. Then, turning abruptly, he remounted and settled himself in the saddle. With a last gentle smile, he raised a hand and cantered off at the head of the cavalcade.

Byrtha's tears diluted the spectacle but ignoring the ache in her throat, she waited until they were gone. Then she wiped her face dry and returned into the darkness of the keep. As she passed, one of the Norman guards saluted her, and Byrtha straightened her shoulders and lifted her chin.

The mantle of responsibility proved a heavy one and Byrtha wearied beneath the combined strains of administration and early pregnancy. She missed Rainald and worried that, although most of the men under her command were ostensibly obedient, they secretly resented her authority. She had heard mutters that some of them resented being left behind, playing nursemaid when they could have been enjoying a siege. Although no outright conflict had broken out, she sensed their resentment; the resulting tension tainting her days and making them long. By the time night fell her head ached and concentration was difficult; she could barely stay awake. As her pregnancy advanced, she retired to her chamber earlier and earlier each night.

As darkness fell the settlement was still at work, chopping wood, milking and feeding livestock and making ready for the night. Her chamber was welcoming, the fires stoked and the torches lit. She stared longingly at her bed, piled high with furs, but her duties were not yet over. A pile of parchment, secured by a heavy silver inkwell, awaited her attention. She sat down, and pulled the candle closer, the only sound the whispering flames in the hearth.

Byrtha sighed. The documents needed signing, there were goods to be paid for, deliveries to check but she just couldn't face them, not tonight. She dropped her pen and summoned Aethel to bring a soothing balm.

"I'm so tired. I'll see to the papers first thing in the morning" she promised.

As Byrtha drifted off to sleep she was aware of Aethel tidying her comb and the jar of salve away. She heard the door open, and close again as her servant crept from the room. "Just a few moments, that's all I need," she murmured to the empty chamber.

An hour or so later, the fire had burned low, and the embers slumped in the grate, rousing Byrtha from her dreams. She sat up, a little refreshed and extremely hungry and was glad that somebody had placed a tray of victuals close beside the bed. She had slept through supper and missed evening prayers again.

It wasn't good enough.

She hurried to the garderobe before dining. She sank her teeth into a cold cut of pork and tore off a hunk of bread, gulped a goblet of wine before leaving the chamber.

There was such a great hubbub in the hall, that few noticed her arrive. The remnants of the evening meal were still on the tables and children and dogs were chasing one another around the rush-strewn floor. A musician stroked his lyre, and some of the younger men and women were dancing at the far end of the hall. Byrtha, looking forward to the entertainments, reached the bottom of the stairwell and as she crossed the hall to join them, Aethel approached and whispered in her ear.

"There be a messenger, he will speak to none but you. He arrived just after you fell asleep; he says he has news that will gladden your heart!"

"A messenger from Rainald? So soon!"

She looked about the hall.

"Nay Byrtha, It's not from Rainald. It's the pedlar, he has some happy news but will impart it to none but you. He is with your father in the old hall. Come, I will go with you, let me fetch a light."

Aethel grabbed a flaming torch, and the two women made their way outside, cutting through the darkness and making straight for the old hall. Inside, it was dim and smoky and Oslac sat at his usual place beside the central hearth. Beside him, still wrapped in cloak, sat the familiar figure of the pedlar. Noticing Byrtha's approached, he rose from his seat, and bowed over her hand.

"Greetings, Lady, it is good to see you so well."

"And I you, friend." She cupped his hand between her palms. "It does my heart good to see old faces in these troubled times. Tell me, what news have you? Do you come from Exeter?"

The pedlar looked startled.

"Nay, Lady. Exeter is not a good place to be. I have other news. I have seen your brother."

Byrtha frowned, fumbling to locate a stool. She sat on it, her head swimming.

"My Brother? Oslac still lives? I had thought him long dead. Where is he? Is he imprisoned? If so, we must ransom him. Rainald will help me."

The pedlar sighed, shook his head.

"Nay, Lady, I'm told that Oslac was slain as they fled from Hastings. It's Leofwine who sent me."

"Leo?" Byrtha breathed incredulously. "Leo lives! Oh, the good Lord be praised. Where is he? Is he safe? I thought, of all my brothers, he would be the first to die."

She clapped her hands but as she realised her companions did not share her joy, her smile froze. She sat up straighter, trapping her hands between her knees.

"There is more, isn't there? He is not safe is he? I can tell by your expression. Oh, I will be quiet while you tell all."

The pedlar cleared his throat.

"I was travelling north, Lady, from the coast near to Ipswich. All England is hostile; the people put their trust in no one, not even pedlars, so to avoid trouble, I travel by the old roads and keep my head low until I come to a place of friendship, which are sadly few.

Many homesteads and holdings have been taken by the enemy. Anyway, I came upon a wood and thought it a good place to pass the night but … as I was unloading my pack, I was set upon by desperate men. They were rough with me but, once they realised I was only an honest pedlar, they spared my life and began to question me. They were a desperate lot, unwashed and half-starved, and they told me how after fighting for the true king at Hastings they'd managed to escape the aftermath. As I began to relate my own tale, a young fellow thrust through the group and clapped me on the shoulder. He said he knew me well and told his companions I am an honest fellow. I knew his name, although it was hard to recognise your brother, even beneath the dirt that begrimed his face it was evident he is changed."

"And he is unharmed?" Byrtha leaned forward in her chair.

The pedlar frowned and swirled the mead in his cup.

"Well, he lives, Lady. He suffered a wound at Hastings, and although it has healed, his looks are spoiled. He is half starved and sickly but as yet, undefeated. He needs your help, I think."

"Where is he? Is he close by? Can he meet me at the wood on the morrow? I shall be there at noon."

May 1068

Summer sunshine dappled the woodland floor, casting shadowy caverns at the base of the ancient beeches. The earth was soft beneath the girls' feet as they hurried toward the central clearing where Byrtha's brother would be waiting. Many a childhood afternoon had been spent there, lounging and playing, cushioned on bracken as they feasted on berries and nuts.

It was fast approaching noon. Aethel carried a basket of victuals and a stone flagon of mead. On reaching the clearing they found it empty but made themselves comfortable on a mossy log. The birds were silent today and the wind had dropped, and after a while a stealthy noise jolted the girls to their feet. They peered through the trees, pregnant with hope.

Before long, a man limped into view and stood waiting, his arms hanging at his sides. At first Byrtha did not recognise him as her brother, for he was the picture of defeat. His handsome features were marred by a scar which ran from crown to chin, the wound passing through his left eye and neatly parting his eyebrow. It was evident from the clouded iris that his vision was impaired. The rags he wore had once been fine, and a tattered sword swung from his narrow hip, yet somehow Byrtha recognised the stranger as her brother.

"Byrtha. How nice."

He took her basket and began rummaging through it, drawing out a roasted fowl.

"Leo!"

She stepped closer, reached up to kiss him but he pulled away, more interested in the contents of the basket than in reunion. She gestured toward the log. "Please, sit and eat, we can talk after."

As he tore the flesh from the bone, Byrtha watched him. The last time she'd seen him, on the day the men all rode off to war, Leo had been a fresh-faced boy. Now he was a bearded, desperate man. Once his appetite was appeased, he wiped the grease from his lips and reached for the flagon. Then he turned to her.

"Well, Sister," he nodded, probing food scraps from his teeth with his tongue. "You look well enough; are they are treating you fairly?"

"Yes, Leo, yes they are. But what about you? Where have you been, and where are you heading?"

"I'm travelling with a war band. They are awaiting my return in the forest. Rebellion is brewing in the north, and we mean to be part of it. The Normans must and will be vanquished, and when they are, I shall come home and retake my property."

Byrtha swallowed, doubting that victory would be so easy.

"The Norman's are strong, Leo, and there is every chance you will only make things worse for yourself. Would it not be better to take refuge overseas, as others have done? Save yourselves and begin life again in exile?"

Leo looked at her; his one good eye menacing, the other blank and empty.

"Is that what you've done, Byrtha? Forgotten our heritage and rolled over like a dog beneath your Norman master? I cannot so easily forget my dead father and brothers, the loss of my lands and privileges OR my murdered king!"

"But Father is not murdered. He is here. He is sick and sad, but he's alive, Leo. *Alive.*" She nodded as she spoke, trying to convince him. Leo looked at the ground, lost in thought.

"That is good news in a sorry time, but it makes no difference. We must scourge the enemy from the land, and I will not rest until they've gone, and neither will our countrymen. I must go to York and join the rebellion; Edgar the Atheling is coming, and we will crown him King. In the meantime, you must see Father is looked after, and mother too, but first I need your help. I need horses, food and coin and I know you can supply them; they are rightfully mine anyway. You must bring or send them here before nightfall so that I can be on my way."

A lengthy silence. His eyes bored into hers until Byrtha was forced to look away. She was aware of the warm sun on her neck and the roughness of the tree bark through her tunic. The memory of the time before stirred, the laughter, the security they had once enjoyed. But then another memory, of a warm hand upon her skin, husky laughter in her ear. The exquisite joy of loving and being loved.

"I cannot help you, Leo. What you ask is impossible."

"Byrtha, what are you saying?" Aethel tugged at her elbow. "You have to help him."

Leo stepped closer; his face thrust close to hers.

"Yes, Byrtha, what are you saying?"

"What you ask is too dangerous. I must think of the people in my charge, and I must think of myself. I have been left in a position of trust, and should I break it, *everyone* at Thornholding will suffer. I will not risk the lives of the community. Whatever the outcome of your battle, my life will continue here. If I help you and you fail, Leo, what then? Prison, when I could be here. Death, when I could live. For what purpose? The Normans will not be easily vanquished, they are here to stay, and I think we must make the best of it. Take my advice and go overseas Leo; make a new life for yourself."

She turned to walk away but Leo grabbed her arm and spun her round to face him. Aethel dropped the basket and rushed after them, her gaze darting from brother to sister.

"Make a new life for myself?" Leo sneered. 'So that my sister can continue whoring for a Norman? Oh, I think not, Madam."

He shifted his vicious grip to her chin and backed her against a tree. Clenching his fingers hard, he squeezed her face, making a pout of her lips. Shaken to the root of her soul, Byrtha stared into his crazed eyes and knew that not a vestige of her brother remained in the body of this man.

"You will give me the horses and the coin, Byrtha, and you will give them to me tonight. If I have to kill you and fire the holding to get them, I will have those horses!"

Byrtha peered up hill. Through the trees she could just make out the outer palisade of the settlement. Leo grabbed her braids and pressed a rusty dagger to her throat, his marred face too close to hers. Acutely aware of the unborn child curled vulnerably between her and her assailant, she swallowed bile and thanked God that her brother was ignorant of her condition.

From the corner of her eye, she saw Aethel backing slowly away, her eyes wide and her mouth open with horror. As she was swallowed into the wood, Byrtha searched for a persuasive argument, something to stave off his anger and perhaps trick him into believing she would help him after all.

Byrtha's mind worked quickly, dismissing new ideas as soon as they were born. She briefly toyed with the idea of giving him the horses and coin and then casting herself on Rainald's mercy when he returned … *if* he returned.

If Leo's rebellion was successful and the Normans scourged from the land, what would become of her and her child? She would never see Rainald again. Her mind whirled with conflict. It was her brother and country versus the man she loved and her unborn child. Suddenly, it all became clear.

She loved her Norman husband and passionately coveted Thornholding, not for herself but for her sons. She wanted to see *her* son become ealdorman, not Leo's. It was essential that the stories the Grandmother had told her of Thorkell the Tall were passed down the generations. She was not prepared to give that up, not for the sake of her brother, and not for the sake of Edgar the Atheling, either.

It made little difference to Byrtha who was King of England; what mattered was that Rainald kept control of Thornholding for their family. She made her decision and, with the cold steel pressing into her softness, she let a tear slide down her cold cheek.

"I'm sorry, Leo. I will help you. I see now that it is what Father would want. It is my duty to help you. I am just a silly weak woman, and I was afraid."

The pressure of the knife relaxed slightly so that she was able to turn her head. She managed to smile.

"Come, Leo, come with me. I will give you horses now. It is quite safe."

As dusk washed in around them, Byrtha and her brother approached the outer gate of the settlement. The guard, recognising his mistress, lowered his bow and let them enter, curiously regarding the ragged stranger. Byrtha led Leo toward the stables where Aethel and the pedlar were whispering in the shadow of the wall. They turned, wide eyed when Byrtha and Leo walked across the yard and halted before the captain.

The soldier rose to his feet, saluted his mistress.

"Good afternoon, Otto," she said in perfect French. "I want you to arrest this man and hold him secure until such time as my husband returns. He does not speak your tongue and he is an enemy to King William."

Leo waited, his wiry frame alert, his head turning from side to side, watching until a heavy footfall made him lunge for his dagger. He ran a few paces forward, but a line of Norman archers cut off his escape. Their arrows trained directly at this heart.

Dropping his knife and dragging his sword from its scabbard, he grabbed Byrtha's hair and pulled her close against him, his arm about her throat. A Norman shouted across the bailey, another replied but unable to interpret the foreign tongue, Leo panicked, his gaze darting this way and that.

"What are they saying?" he snarled. "Tell me."

He yanked Byrtha's head, but she remained mute. Another shouted command and an archer let fly an arrow that glided swiftly across the bailey and lodged deeply in Leo's thigh. With a scream of pain, he half collapsed, just managing to maintain his hold on his sister's throat.

Dragging her toward the well, he sprawled in the dirt, pulling her down with him.

"Give it up, Leo, they have you. Give it up!"

"Never," he gasped through the pain. "I refuse to submit to dogs such as these."

His blood trickled down, seeping into Byrtha's tunic. Another arrow flew, bit deeply into his shoulder and his grip on Byrtha slackened a fraction. Sensing her moment, she jabbed an elbow into his ribs and twisted away, scrambling on all fours, like a dog, to safety. As a further arrow struck his knee Leo screamed and rolled, defeated in the dust.

Byrtha huddled against a wall, tears of terror and grief soaking her cheeks. Even now, after such cruelty, if Leo surrendered she would forgive him but, before he lost consciousness, his voice ripped across the enclosure.

"May God curse you for your treachery, Byrtha. May your womb shrivel, and all your children be twisted."

Byrtha allowed herself one last look at her brother. *That it should have come to this* -she thought as she was assailed by a thousand memories. Leo toddling across the enclosure to greet his father. Leo teasing her, pulling her braids, stealing her food. Leo and her other brothers learning the art of war, training to be men, soldiers, to protect the holding and the realm. It was all over now – blown away like chaff in the wind. The past is gone and can never be reclaimed. She must grasp the future, make new memories, discover new ambition, new hopes. Her sadness transformed into pride. She had defended and held her property – as she had promised to.

She was irrevocably Norman now. She nodded to Aethel, silently dismissing her and, as she passed the priest who cowered in the shadow of the wall she said, "Pray attend to my brother, Father, and make sure he is shriven."

***

Rainald returned to Thornholding at the head of a band of weary men. His left leg was bound where a stray arrow had struck his knee. It was only a flesh wound but the location of the strike, just above the joint, made healing slow and movement awkward. The physicians were confident that no infection had entered the joint but warned it would take months to fully heal.

Byrtha, feeling strangely shy after so many months apart, waited beneath the arch while Rainald limped through the chaos of his arrival. He stopped a few feet away and looked at her for a long time, noting her changed shape, her flushed cheeks before moving closer and taking her hand. The glinting approval in his eye informed her that news of her action had reached him.

"You are well, my wife, I trust? And the child too?"

"Oh yes," she replied as she walked informally into his arms. "I am very well, my lord."

January 1069

Byrtha awoke and lay staring into the absolute darkness, wondering what had woken her. An unspecific sense of unease assailed her. She strained her ears but all she could hear was the regular tic of Rainald's breathing, and the crackle of the fire.

Somewhere a dog was barking, a curt voice cut across the night calling for silence, and far off a door slammed. The frigid black silence resumed, and the sense of disquiet grew stronger. Something was wrong. Sliding from Rainald's embrace she swung her legs over the side of the bed and taking a cup from the nightstand, rinsed her mouth with wine. As she shifted to a more comfortable position she felt a gentle pop and warm fluid washed down her inner thighs. Looking down at the spreading stain upon the sheet, she realised that her child was coming.

She shook Rainald by the shoulder. He stirred, snorted and raised his head.

"What's the matter?" he asked huskily, turning over and pulling himself up. "Are you ill?"

Byrtha pressed a hand either side of her distended stomach and blew hard through her mouth, Rainald wiped a hand across his face forcing the sleep away.

"Not ill, My Lord, but I feel a small matter queasy, and the birth waters have broken. I think you should send for the midwife."

Rainald leapt up, struggling into his jerkin, and brought the night candle closer to the bed.

"Is it time? Stay where you are!" he cried as Byrtha started to rise. "I will fetch Aethel and send for the midwife."

Byrtha smiled as Rainald hopped around with one foot in his leggings, but a renewed tightening of her uterus chased the humour away. The sensation tightened into real pain, located at the base of her spine. She gasped, stirred her lower limbs, trying to shift the discomfort.

When the feeling abated, she rose and taking a taper, ignited the candles. Her mouth was dry, so she took more wine, swilling it around her mouth before swallowing. Below stairs Rainald was hollering, and she was comforted by the sound of scurrying feet hastening to their lord's command.

It was not long before the braziers had been stirred back to life and the torches lit in her chamber. The women brought piles of linen and the midwife was busy setting out her tools along with potions, salves and a birthing bowl and swaddling bands for the infant. Byrtha's fears increased as she perched on the edge of the bed and tried to ignore the increasing intensity of pain.

The midwife clucked into the room like an old hen and without ceremony, lifted Byrtha's nightgown. "That's it, duck, lie back and let me feel your belly so I can tell how long we have to wait."

She pursed her lips as she probed Byrtha's stomach. Then she stood up and squeezed each nipple making a bead of watery milk drip onto her gown. Demurely, she covered her charge's knees again.

"It's early days yet, me duck. I'll keep close by, so you just call if you need me."

Aethel sat by the bed and took Byrtha's hand.

"Oh Aethel," murmured Byrtha in disbelief. 'She says it will be a long time yet, but I am in sore pain already. Do you think she may be mistaken and maybe the birth is imminent?"

"Fryda knows her business; remember she's been birthing the settlement for twenty years. Why, she knew that my Æthelwine was a girl even before her head had crowned. She is preparing a mother's brew to ease you in the later stages. Come, do not fret, Byrtha; you are strong and will easily bear the pain."

Byrtha was not so sure. She gasped as the band tightened about her loins again, and gripped the bedpost, gritting her teeth and puffing hard. The women in the chamber seemingly unmoved by her plight, diligently sewed, and passed the time by sharing tales of their own traumatic births.

Fryda insisted that the night air was fatal for mother and child, ordering the fire to be built up and the draughty windows muffled. The heat in the chamber was soon stifling.

When the pain grew too much, Byrtha was dosed with a potion which made her relax and grow drowsy. She dreamed of her grandmother and Thorkell and at times she felt again the cold heat of Leo's dagger at her throat. She cried out against it until Aethel soothed her fears with more wine. Sweating and twisting on the bed she felt detached from reality, unreachable through the belladonic haze.

She wept, and when it seemed she could bear no more, Fryda heaved herself from her stool by the fire and urged Byrtha onto her hands and knees. Her body was leaden and solid, but she heaved herself onto all fours. Her braided hair dangled from her ears and her nightgown was pulled up, exposing her nether regions for Fryda's examination.

"Not long now, me duck," the old woman encouraged, patting her bottom. "When the next pain hits you can push the little tinker out."

With the weight of the child removed from her spine, the pain was more bearable and Byrtha regained some control. She risked a quick look about the chamber and wished she was sewing with the women, so smug in their pain-free serenity.

The agony expanded in waves, and she tried to breath with it; as her body laboured Byrtha strained, hanging onto the twisted length of cloth that Fryda had tied to the bedstead, her face distorting as she pushed. Then the pain receded again, and she collapsed, face down onto the mattress, panting and gasping.

Aethel brought more malmsey but before Byrtha could drink the pain returned. She was sure it was stronger, and reared up, her knees parted and her head back, shrieking. She prayed for respite, begged for it, but her body was governed by some unknown force, and urged her on.

Barely noticing the cool touch of the flannel, she panted for breath, knowing the next assault was imminent. But then, a new sensation. Something hard, pressing and burning. She put down her hand and felt her child's head hot, sticky and pulsing with life, wedged fast between her legs. Without waiting to be told, she put her chin to her chest, gritted her teeth and pushed her son into the world.

Sponged and clean, her hair brushed and her face shining, Byrtha cradled her tightly swaddled new-born son. He gripped tightly to her forefinger with a strong, encouraging grasp and surveyed his mother through slit eyes. Byrtha examined his battered and bruised face and declared him the handsomest thing she had ever seen.

"Don't be afeared, me duck, it will heal in a week." Freyda leant over the bed. "Now, let me show you how to get him to latch on to your dug."

A few moments later, Aethel popped her head around the chamber door and, seeing that Byrtha was awake, slipped in and came to the side of the bed.

"Your Lord is desperate to see you, Byrtha. Can he come up? He has been pacing about like a crazy man all day, haunting the lower keep and accosting us all with questions. He fell into such a rage when I didn't understand his heathen tongue."

Byrtha laughed. "Oh, his bark is worse than his bite, you know that. Has he been told of our new son?"

"Yes, of course, straight away but Old Fryda forbid him to come up until you were rested. It's odd how the toughest of men grow meek beneath the tongue of an old wife. Shall I fetch him for you?"

Byrtha turned her attention back to her son who was sucking fractiously on his own fist. She adjusted her gown and attached him to her nipple as she had been shown. The sensation of his pulling mouth, and the exquisite touch of his tiny hand were new pleasures to Byrtha. She was smiling so tenderly at her child that she did not at first notice the opening door.

Byrtha left a soft kiss upon her son's brow and closed her eyes. Slowly, she came aware of the figure standing silently beside her and turned to find her husband. He bent over to look closely at his son who had fallen into a slumber.

"I have been in purgatory, My Byrtha, waiting and waiting; I thought it would never end. They tell me you are both well, is that so?"

"Oh yes, My Lord, although for a while I feared death was near. Old Fryda assures me it was the potion she fed me, and that there was never any real danger, but from my end it seemed very different. I thought I was going to die! I wish it were possible for you to bear our next child, Rainald, it would do you good to experience true peril for once."

They laughed and, after a while, Byrtha laid their son in his father's arms and watched as he counted the pink new-born toes.

"Très adorable, très adorable…"

The fire burned low, the shifting logs and cinders disturbing the three from their slumbers. Rainald placed the child in his basket then, turning to his wife, he picked up a thick flaxen braid.

"Is there anything you need, Chérie?"

"Not really, Rainald, although you could fetch The Book from the coffer."

Rainald opened the lid of Byrtha's chest and, beneath an old, nettle-green gown he found The Book securely wrapped in its coverings. Marvelling again at the weight of the volume, he placed it on Byrtha's knee and brought forth a quill and ink, and a candle from the nightstand.

Byrtha slowly turned the pages, remarking anew at the workmanship and the brightness of hue until she reached the last few pages of the book where Alricson had written, chronicling the book's beginnings and immortalising its maker. Byrtha took up her quill and dipped it into the inkwell, thinking for a while before she put the nib to the page; then she leaned forward and wrote in her unformed hand,

"Today on the nineteenth day of January, in the year of our lord, 1069 was born to Rainald of Caen and Byrtha of Thornholding, a son, Robert, an emblem of future peace."

Part Three
Pestilence

'Such as I was you are, and such as I am you will be.
Wealth, honour and power are of no value at the hour of your death."
(from the 14th century psalter of Robert de L isle)

Thornhold Manor – July 1348

The great dog curled its lip, displaying yellowed teeth. A globule of blood dripped from one fang, and his eyes glowed orange in the half-light. A dead kitten lay across his front paws, the blue ribbon that had been so lovingly tied about its tiny neck, unravelled and soiled. Molly swallowed and backed slowly away on hands and knees, retracing the path she had taken through the undergrowth. The dog watched her go, his blood smeared muzzle twitching. As soon as she reached the gap in the hedge through which her kitten had disappeared, Molly hastened her retreat and scrambled backside first into the churchyard.

"Molly!" Mary grabbed Molly's arm and began ferociously brushing the mud from the child's skirts.

"Where on earth have you been, child? I take my eyes from you for a second and you disappear! Lucky for you your parents are busy with the priest and didn't notice your absence. Just look at your gown, you bad girl."

Molly knuckled a tear from her eye, the horror of what she had just seen depriving her of speech. As the nursery maid left her to attend another of her charges, Molly whimpered.

In the shadow of the church wall, Thomas was scuffling with some of the village boys. When his nurse's palm caught the back of his ear, he put a hand to his head. Molly felt no emotion as she watched her brother begin to wail, all she could think of was her kitten. If she hadn't squeezed him so tightly he'd have not sought escape and fallen into the path of the dog.

Cats were welcome at Thornhold manor; their hunting skills kept the rats at bay in the midden. There were cats in the house kitchen, cats in the mill, and cats in every barn. It was only a few days since she had stumbled across the litter of kittens in the malt house and old George, who tended the farm stock, had said she could take one and good riddance to it.

There were four balls of fluff to choose from, each with pink tongues, stiff tails and bright eyes. There were two tabbies, a black and white one, and a fluffy black one with a white smudge on its nose. At first she warmed toward the one with the smudge but when she pulled it rudely from the nest by its scruff, a tiny paw shot out and scratched her. She dropped it abruptly and rubbed her wound while the rest of the litter spilled from the nest, running off in all directions in search of mischief.

But one of the tabbies stayed behind and mewed silently at Molly, showing the inside of its pink mouth. The girl picked up the kitten and it pushed its face against hers, establishing and marking its territory. Needing no further encouragement, Molly got to her feet and carried it to the dairy to find it a bowl of milk. The kitten, whom she named Mouser, became her constant companion. She smuggled him beneath her apron into dinner, tucked him beside her into her narrow bed, and even carried him in her basket to church. It was there, during the interminably long sermon, that her head lolled onto her big sister's arm, and she fell asleep.

Molly had known the moment she woke that something was wrong. As the congregation trooped into the sunshine, she discovered that Mouser was missing from his basket. She ran back into the nave, vainly searching every corner, calling his name, and making the kissing noise with her lips that usually brought him to her side.

When she emerged into gleaming wet daylight, the sky was a dangerous deep blue, but the sun shone, illuminating the white church tower against the dark skies. Shielding her eyes from the glare, she glimpsed Mouser in his Sunday best blue ribbon, disappearing into the undergrowth that flanked the vestry wall.

***

Now he was dead. She stood in the churchyard, isolated from the rest of her family, the sun slipped behind a cloud and a chill sprung suddenly from the stillness. The rain hissed quickly across the already sodden ground and Bella, seizing Molly by the wrist, forced her to run all the way from the church yard to the manor house.

Bella held her head down, but Molly turned her face up to feel the cool drops on her overheated cheeks. Sometimes, when it rained she liked to stand with her mouth open, trying to catch the drops on her tongue but today there was no time for that, her short legs found it difficult to keep up. Mud splattered their skirts as the girls dashed through the downpour, and behind them the rest of the family followed, laughing and skidding in the puddles. They tumbled into the great hall, exclaiming at the suddenness of the deluge.

"Damned weather," exclaimed Henry Thornbury, throwing off his soaking cloak. "Is there no end to it? The wheat is lying ruined in the top field and if the barley fails again this year they'll be no ale and no barley bread for the villagers again. This rain is like a curse, and a failed crop, together with the pestilence the sheep are suffering will mean another hard winter for rich and poor alike."

His voice trailed away as he quit the room with his wife, Isabel, still shaking droplets of water from her hair. As the door closed on their parents, the children could hear their mother's soothing tones as she endeavoured to calm her husband down.

Harry, the eldest of the Thornbury children, went to the window, threw back the shutter and looked out.

"Father's right, it has been raining forever. My horse stands idle in the stable while I grow soft away from the butts, and there is so little amusement indoors. Bella, take up your lute and play for us, the little ones can dance."

He flopped into a low chair and watched his sister pick up her instrument. She ran her fingers across the strings and adjusted the tuning keys. She smiled across at her younger sister who was shivering before the fire.

"Come, Molly, take Tom's hand and dance for us."

Thomas, who was playing beneath the table, scowled.

"I'm not dancing," he challenged from his stronghold. "Dancing is for girls, and I'm to be a soldier when I'm grown up. Soldiers don't dance; they fight."

The band of horror that had been constricting Molly's tears snapped suddenly. She opened her mouth wide, her face drenched with tears as she wrung her hands and wept as though her heart would break. Bella put down the lute and rushed to comfort her sister. She put her arm around Molly's shoulder.

"What is it? You've been odd since the sermon."

Harry watched, noticing how inefficient the tiny kerchief was for mopping up such copious tears. After a while, unable to bear her painful sobs any longer, crawled out from beneath the table.

"Oh, all right then, Molly; stop weeping and I will dance with you, if I must."

October 1348

For the remainder of the summer the rain continued, lasting throughout the summer into early autumn. There was little to alleviate the ennui of enforced inactivity, and while the villagers slopped about in the mud trying to attend to their seasonal tasks, the children were cooped up in Thornhold Manor, growing ever more disgruntled.

An endless round of routine; day followed day, meal followed meal, and night followed night. To leaven the boredom, mother brought The Book of Thornhold from its place of honour in father's study. The Latin text did little to lighten their boredom but when Mother showed them the colourful illustrations, even Tom couldn't fail to be impressed. Nobody could be bored by the book's radiance.

Since Grandfather had it recovered, it had stood on a lectern in the study. Although they'd heard the story many times, it was always thrilling, always some new discovery to be made. The book had been crafted by monks hundreds of years ago and had fallen into disrepair until it came into the possession of the Thornbury family. Mother claimed it had magical qualities and that, as long as the Thornbury family cared for The Book, so it would protect and look after them. Warm and dry in the solar, listening to Mother read from it, a spell was cast, making them forget the drear realities of the world.

There was no escaping the hardship that would quickly follow the failed harvest, and already crimes were being committed in the village. Jem Bailey had been called before the manor court for illegal fishing, and there had been reports of eggs and apples mysteriously missing from the kitchens at Thornhold Manor. Food theft was a sure sign of hunger for the villagers were usually God-fearing people, not given to sin. Because of this, Henry Thornbury dealt leniently with the thefts and did his best to find a way to alleviate the suffering.

In such hard times it was difficult enough to keep his own family fed and watered, and Henry wondered how bad things would become if the next harvest also failed. What with the rain and the sheep sickness it was almost like a curse. Perhaps it was as the priests claimed, and mankind's increasing sinfulness had incurred God's wrath.

Hunger rapidly decreased the workforce of Thornhold Manor and deprived of nutrition the young and old fell sick, leaving only a handful of able-bodied men and half-grown boys to tend the stock and till the fields. In his private study, Henry made his mark at the bottom of the page and closed his account book. The figures were worrying. Rising from his chair, he placed the book in a coffer with his small hoard of coin, turned the key and went down to breakfast.

"Mother, can I get down from the table, please?"

Gaining her mother's permission, Molly went to the window, as she did each day, and opened the shutter to leave some breadcrumbs for the birds.

"A rat!" Molly cried. "A great big one, eating the crusts I put out for the birds."

Mother dropped her knife at her daughter's shriek and joined Molly at the window in time to see the sleek grey body whisk from sight. She leaned out to look at the sky. Each morning she and Molly delighted in the wild birds that came down to feed, the child loved their bright colours and pretty habits, but today the crumbs from the previous day had scarcely been touched.

Molly frowned as she brushed away the stale crumbs and replaced them with fresh ones. "That's funny, they haven't eaten the food from yesterday yet."

She whistled to the birds in hope that they'd come down, but she received no response and, after a while she grew bored. "Oh well," she murmured to Mother who had returned to her breakfast. "Perhaps they aren't hungry this morning."

Bella was helping the women sort wool for the new tapestry cushions they planned for the great hall.

"There you are," Molly said, when she joined them. "I searched everywhere."

"Not everywhere," Bella replied, "Or you'd have found me sooner."

Molly stuck out her tongue, and taking her place at the table, began to sort out all the green shades and wind them onto cards to make the task easier for the stitchers. She would only be allowed to add a few stitches to the work; it was the elder skilled women who would contribute the most. Her mother's voice drifted in and out as Molly wound the thread about the wooden holders, she heard but paid no attention to the conversation for her mind was far away.

Isabella Thornbury and the household women gathered every morning to work on their needlework. The continual rain had little effect on their routine and the rich hues of the embroidery silk, and the proposed tapestry design took their minds from the troubling times. The threat of failed harvests and sick livestock became less prominent, and they were all so involved in their work that none of them so much as raised their heads when Harry opened the door.

"Mother, there is a very wet pedlar in the kitchen. Shall I show him into the lower hall, or would you like me to send him on his way?"

The women, abandoning their work, leapt up and jostled to be first out of the door after their mistress. Just as curious as their elders, Molly and Bella followed.

Being far off the beaten track, visitors to Thornhold Manor were few and the pedlar always welcome. It wasn't only the luxurious goods he brought from town; it was the news he carried from the outside world.

In exchange for a few pennies, the pedlar offered unguents and potions for the face and hands, silks and velvets fresh from the trade ports, and spices from the Far East. He carried buttons and ribbons, needles and trinkets that could not be easily made. To the women, the pedlar's visits were red-letter days.

The pedlar was tired, wet and dirty yet he greeted them gladly. He pulled off his cap and mopped his forehead with a large kerchief. When a tankard of ale was placed before him, he thanked them gladly and took a large draught. His donkey was led to the stables where he enjoyed a sample of the Manor's precious store of hay.

The women stared at the pedlar's pack imagining the glories it concealed. Impatiently, they waited until he put down his tankard, wiped the froth from his lips, and began to loosen the ties that kept his treasures safe.

He pulled out some samples of fine yellow cloth.

"I got this straight off a ship at Bristol, and they assured me it is fresh from Flanders. Ah, now ladies, this shade would make the perfect gown and look here, I have slippers to go with it; bejewelled and studded just like the Queen's."

As the women clustered about the table, the pedlar freed himself from the crush and let them search through the treasures themselves. He joined Harry at the fireside.

"How be things with you, Young Sir?"

"Damned dull with all this rain. I swear I have not been off the manor all summer. My father says the tenants are struggling to keep afloat because of sheep sickness and crop failure. What harvest we have taken was wet, and is rotting in the barns, and Father says another famine cannot be avoided. Our tenants suffered last season from hunger and many a new-born was lost. It's unheard of for the weather to be so unseasonable. It's as if God has abandoned us."

The pedlar held out his hands to the flames, as he began to speak his words were halted by a coughing fit but, recovering himself, he begged pardon and wiped spittle from his lips with the back of his hand.

"Ah, Sir, worse things happen at sea, as they say. There be sickness in Bristol port. I'm hoping it's not the same thing that's been plaguing them across the channel, for when I left the port, folks was sweating and swealing away, in a matter of days, it seemed. I thought it wise to make myself scarce, having no wish to go the same road."

"That sounds wise. Ah, here is my father now, he will also wish to hear your news."

The next day dawned as heavy as the last, the oppressive air unseasonal for October. Against all medical advice, the shutters in the family chambers stood open, letting the cool of the night aid restful slumber. Unable to sleep, Molly slid from her bed and stood at the window but the stagnant air did little to refresh her, and she went in search of Mary. As she trailed along the corridor to the nursery, she untied the strings of her linen night cap and pulled it from her head. While her nurse untangled her hair, she listened to the stream of chatter.

"It is only a few weeks now until my wedding," said Mary. "Will has been busy odd jobbing, thatching and shearing and the like; working all the hours so as to afford to rent a cottage. Now that old Seth has passed, the Master says we can have his place for our own."

Molly was not at all interested in Mary's forthcoming marriage, but she murmured her congratulations; she knew Mary was fortunate indeed to be going straight into her own cottage, for most newly-weds lived with their parents, often until their children were grown.

"I'll ask Mother if we can look out some bits of furniture from the attics, some of them are full of things that we never use."

"Ooh, Miss, do you think so? We have next to nothing and what we do have has been scrounged from here and there. My Will has mended the leaky thatch, killed off most of the vermin, and we're all set to move in after our joining, a month hence."

"I'm sure she will have something," assured Bella, who had been listening at the chamber door. "I will ask for you, she is more likely to listen to me than Molly."

"Oh, thank you, Miss Bella, that'd be grand. The wedding won't be much, just the joining at the church door and a small celebration afterward in the barn; but it would mean a lot to me if you children were to share my special day."

Mary wasn't a bad sort and Molly tried to summon some enthusiasm for the wedding, but her head felt heavy, her limbs leaden. When they joined the family for breakfast, she held tightly to her nurse's hand. At one end of the chamber, Molly climbed onto a bench beside her sister and waited for the blessing to be read.

Isabella Thornbury sat at the head of the table and her husband usually sat opposite but today he was busy with his bailiff. Mother gave the children permission to start their food without waiting for him. Presently, the door opened, and he hurried forward, and whispered into his wife's ear.

"Keep the children indoors, Isabella, there is trouble in the village. I will be back when I know more."

Allowed no time to reply, Isabella rose from her seat as he hurried away.

"Henry" she called after him. "What sort of trouble? Can it not wait until after you have eaten? This is scarcely the time to scrimp on your morning victuals."

Her words gave Henry pause, and he came back, took her elbow and drew her away from the children.

"The bailiff says there is some sort of sickness. That pedlar who called here two days since was found dead, and the fellow he took lodging with is sick of the same fever. It may be that sickness that we heard tell of. So, I want you all to stay indoors, all of you, until we have ascertained what manner of illness this is. And send for the priest, would you."

Isabella called a servant boy and sent him to summon the priest; she then resumed her place at the table, pretending nothing was amiss.

Oblivious to the ensuing drama, the children chattered, their minds on sundry things. One of the hunting dogs was in pup and there was much excitement about the imminent birth. They viewed her distended belly with awe, certain that she would birth twelve or thirteen pups at least. Father had promised Harry one to raise as his own, and Tom and Molly thought this most unfair. Tom was perfectly old enough to handle a dog of his own, and Molly could see no reason why she shouldn't have one too, especially since she'd lost her kitten.

"Mother," she said sweetly between mouthfuls. 'Suppose Diana has a little tiny pup that nobody else wants; could I have it if she does, do you think?"

Isabella's thoughts were with her husband who was putting himself at the risk of some unspecific contagion, and she answered inattentively.

"Perhaps Dear. We will see, you must ask your father."

Molly's eyes lit up. "Oh, thank you, Mother."

Tom scooped up his food while Bella poked fingers of bread into her mouth.

"Mother said I can have a pup, Bella!" Molly cried. "Won't it be lovely? What should I call him, do you think?"

"No, she didn't," replied Tom. "She said, 'she'd see' and that's different from saying 'yes'. Grown-ups always say 'we'll see' when they really mean 'no.'"

Molly pushed away her half-eaten breakfast and went to the open window. Outside, she saw her father hurrying across the bailey toward the house. If she asked him about the pup now, he'd be bound to agree. She rushed from the room and down the stairs and caught up with her father who had paused on his way to the hall to speak to the priest.

She flung her arms unceremoniously around his knees.

"Father, Oh Father! Please may I have one of Diana's pups? I will take such good care of it, as good care of it as any boy would."

Henry thrust her away.

"Get away from me, child!" he cried. "Away, for the love of God! Go back to your nurse and stay with her!"

Unaccustomed to his anger, Molly backed away and slunk up the stairs. Father never shouted. He always greeted her with a kiss and called her his "little sweetheart". Sometimes, he lifted her and threw her into the air and caught her again, and the thrill of flying before jolting back into the safety of his arms never waned. Sometimes, he made her laugh so much she got hiccups, but today his face was hard and white and cross. She ran from him, but when she reached the turn in the stair, she paused and dared to take another look.

He was speaking rapidly, gesticulating, the white-faced priest nodding as he turned to do Father's bidding. They did not even notice she was still there. Sadly, she returned to the great hall and climbed onto the window seat again, pulling the curtain closed and shutting herself away from the rest of the house. She scowled as she laid her head against the cold glass, and hugging a cushion tightly to her stomach, put her thumb into her mouth.

After being kept indoors because of the weather, the Thornbury children were now forced to stay in because of the sickness. The pedlar and the villager that had offered him lodging were now buried in Thornhold churchyard, and a white cross was painted on the front door of the lodging house to warn everyone that the pestilence had arrived.

The future had already looked dreary, but now things were much bleaker. Mary made posies of herbs and flowers for the family to inhale to help defray any lingering infection, and the children were forbidden to leave the confines of the house. Even when, for the first time in months, the late summer sun showed itself, the children were told the gardens were out of bounds. They were instructed to stay away from the kitchens and restricted to the nursery or the parlour. As if to spite them, the rain ceased, and the sun emerged, and the children looked longingly from the windows while the outdoors called to them.

Harry dreamed of galloping his horse across the meadow and complained it would grow flabby and unfit in the paddock. So far, there was no sickness in the house, but news filtered through that two of the village children had fallen sick and died. Henry Thornbury sent to the Cistercian monks at Hayles Abbey, asking for assistance, for the white monks were famed for their medicinal skills. A few days after the summons, a white clad figure arrived on an old donkey.

***

"But I'm not a bit tired," said Molly crossly. "Why do I have to go to bed? I've done nothing all day, and it is too hot to sleep, Mary. Will you ask Harry to come and tell me a story?"

"Master Harry is busy, Miss. He is helping move the stock to the top fields for all the forage in the lower pasture has gone. Now, give over and try to sleep."

The monk, Brother John, advised the family to keep fires burning in the night chambers, and to seal the windows to prevent the harmful night air from entering the house. This was done, making their rooms so hot it impossible to sleep. It was after mid-night when Molly sat up and fumbled for the cup at her bedside. But even with her thirst quenched, she couldn't rest and, after several hours of trying, she threw back the coverlet and slid from the bed.

As she crept along the passage, shadows leapt on the walls and a rat, disturbed from his nocturnal prowling, glared at her from the wainscot. Close to her parent's chamber, she was pushed suddenly and roughly aside by Brother John as he swept into the room. Molly peeped around the door.

A candle burned at the bedside, a fire blazed in the grate and her mother, clad in only her shift, was bending over the bed. Brother John handed Mother a bowl and she began to dab a wet cloth over Father's body. Recognising the tangy aroma of vinegar, Molly realised he must be ill.

Molly slid quietly down the wall and sat on the floor, hugging her knees and resting her chin upon them. Swamped in misery, she knew Father was very sick, that much was clear, and from the urgency of her mother's movements, Molly knew he could be sick unto death.

Every so often he groaned aloud, called out in a hoarse voice that was quite unlike Father's. Mother reacted by applying the cloth more frantically, murmuring comfort. The priest knelt, fingering his rosary and beseeching God to help them. Mother pushed her hair impatiently from her face and turned to him.

"What else can be done, Brother John? There must be something!"

The monk's calm voice did nothing to soothe.

"There is nothing to be done until the swelling appears, My Lady, then we can lance it, but even so, it will be no guarantee that he will live."

He lifted Henry's right arm and probed for a sign of swelling and then did the same to the other. He stood up and shook his head. "There is no sign of it yet, my lady…unless…"

He drew back the sheet and began to examine his lower torso. Then he stood up again, alert and surprised.

"It is as I suspected, the buboes have erupted in his groin, but they are small yet. When they are large enough we can lance them to release the contagion, and then we must apply a poultice. Order your women to make up a mixture of tree resin, roots of white lilies, and some dried excrement, preferably that of the Lord himself. Then we can smear it into the incisions we will make. It will help to draw away the fever."

Isabella looked at the monk in disbelief.

"Tree resin?" she cried. "White lily root? Where am I supposed to get those from at this time of night? There is plenty of shite in yonder chamber pot for the drying, but as to the other things, where am I to find them?"

Throwing the cloth into the slopping bowl, she slumped into a chair and put a hand to her head, letting go of her carefully controlled panic. Molly had never seen her mother cry before. Her woman, Martha, emerged from the shadows and placed a hand on her shoulder.

"Madam," she said quietly. "The old widow, Ma Jenkins in the village makes potions to help girls rid themselves of freckles and unwanted babes and such." The monk rolled his eyes and crossed himself as Martha continued defiantly. "She may have such things in her stores, lily root is a common enough thing…"

The monk coughed.

"If I could interrupt, Madam. I have some lily root myself, all I require is someone to supply the resin and the excrement, and perhaps some bandages…" Martha was gone before he finished speaking, her skirts brushing Molly's face as she hurried briskly past.

As Henry began to thrash and call out, Mother wept helplessly. Each time he threw off the coverings, she replaced them, tucking them about his neck, trying to restrain his tearing hands. His curses were loud and profane, and once or twice he caught her with his fist. Molly heard her gasp, saw her wipe a tear from her cheek, but she worked on, continuing to bathe his burning skin, and crooning to him as if he was a child.

There was no sign that he was aware of her ministrations. In the guttering candlelight while Mother laboured on, the priest continued to pray. Only Molly noticed when the sky began to lighten imperceptibly in the east.

Morning was coming. They said he'd be dead by morning. Molly prayed harder.

At length, as the first fingers of daylight crept over the horizon, the monk drew back the covers and examined Thornbury's groin again. He straightened up.

"I think it's time Madam, where is your woman?"

"Here we are mistress!" reassured Martha as, followed closely by a kitchen boy, she waddled into the room bearing a laden tray. "Widow Jenkins had most of the stuff we need. She suggested we place a live hen next the swelling; she said it's a sure to draw away the pestilence, so I bought this as well. She was roosting in the kitchen – providential, I call it."

The kitchen boy crept forward and held out a startled looking white hen, until the enraged expression of the white monk forced him to tuck it beneath his arm again.

Ignoring the boy, the monk brought a candle closer to the bed and drew back the coverlet again. With unexpected strength, he held Henry's arching body still while his wrists were bound to the bed posts. Molly strained to see, unable to tear her eyes away when the knife swiped down and her father's blood spurted across the counterpane. She could not look away, but when the women applied the hot poultice and tied the bandages in place, she covered her ears to shut out his screams of agony.

Gradually, his screams turned to whimpers, and then to heavy breathing and, at last, satisfied that he slept, Mother collapsed into a chair.

After tidying the room, Martha and Mary prepared to leave but pulled up short when they discovered Molly standing forlornly in the doorway.

"I didn't feel well," Molly explained. "And I wanted another drink. Is Father going to get better now?"

With a cry, Martha scooped Molly into her arms. By the light of the candle, she looked into the child's flushed face and placed a hand to her forehead.

"Oh, dear God in heaven," she wailed. "She is burning hot!"

* * *

Molly woke suddenly and tried to sit up. Her throat was on fire, her chest hurt, her breath rasped. A fire raged in the grate, casting demons upon the chamber walls. At the foot of her bed, a figure knelt, its head lowered in shadow, and a voice murmured in a monotonous chant. It grew in volume until her head was filled with the sonorous sound.

Credo in Deum Patrem Omnipotentem

Heaving onto her side, she tried to reach for the flagon but as she did so she realised that the bed was towering above the floor. She was high, high up by the wooden vaulted ceiling and the table with its thirst-quenching flagon lay far below, out of reach, close to the droning figure and the satanic fire.

Menacing black rats scampered in corners. She coughed and whimpered, calling for her mother and suddenly she was there, her sweet face replete with love. She stroked Molly's brow, but her touch seemed to brand blisters into Molly's skin. Isabella drew back her hand and instead held a cup of cool drink to her daughter's blackened lips. The child struggled to sit up and grabbed the huge goblet to staunch her terrible thirst, but the contents burned, and she spat the foul liquid across the counterpane, and threw the cup aside.

The voice continued.

Passus sub Pontio Pilato,
Crucifixus
Mortuus, et sepultus

Voices were all around her, speaking at once. Molly strained to see but the figures were shadowy and distorted, the voices indistinguishable. The strap around her throat tightened. The pain intensified and skeletons were hiding in the curtains about her bed. She knew them from the wall paintings in the church; the three skeletons who warned the three kings that they too must perish. The priest had said this could happen. He said the devil would get her if she were naughty.

"As we are, so shall you be," they warned, shaking their cadaverous heads and rattling their bones.

Molly writhed beneath the covers and tried to free her limbs from the constraints of the blankets, but Isabella drew them up tight and tucked them in, determined to keep the harmful night air at bay.

A new pain had begun beneath her arm and Molly writhed on the bed, until her wrist was caught in a firm grasp. Brother John's face loomed close to hers and she recognised a friend.

"Brother John," she whispered. "The devils are here; they are in the room. You must help me, Brother John, or they will take me for sure. They are hiding, there, look in the bed hanging."

Brother John didn't seem to hear, he drew away again, leaving her alone. Alone with the dead. Her eyes streamed tears and her hair was stuck to her skull. Her mouth gaped wide, her tongue was dry and cracked. She knew she would die here un-shriven. She remembered the warnings of the priest against sin and levity, and knew she must be a terrible sinner to suffer so. Time and time again they had told her that only the wicked died un-shriven, bound for hell to suffer pain everlasting.

Molly did not want to die.

Vivos et mortuos

Credo in Spiritum Sanctum.

Her father's hunting dog, Diana, leapt heavily on to the bed and began to lick her face, her saliva tasting peculiarly of vinegar and marigolds. Fretfully, Molly tried to push her away and, as her arm fell to the bed again, there arose a terrible squawking and she realised that there was a hen in the chamber.

White feathers rained softly down, settling like snow upon her face and upon her aching limbs. Then Brother John was back, and he had a knife, a big one!

Molly hugged Diana, crying out as the knife slashed down toward them and the monk plunged the dagger into the distended abdomen of the dog. Molly's despair overflowed as the puppies spilled wetly onto the bed.

There were hundreds and hundreds of puppies leaping and jumping to lick Molly's face; she tried to push them away, but her arms were weak, and there were too many. Soon, they turned into miniature hounds of hell. They jumped up, their teeth ripping at her throat and at the tender skin beneath her arms. She knew, no matter how hard she struggled, in the end they would draw her down to hell.

Remissionem peccatorus

Carnis ressurectionem

Et vitam aeternam.

Too exhausted to care, Molly gave herself up to everlasting torture and let them take her. Their loud yelping hurt her head but somehow, although the pain remained, the pressure beneath her arms was relieved.

It could be no worse in hell than it was right here on earth.

The droning voice returned, or perhaps it had never stopped, perhaps the horror of her last moments had merely obscured the sound. Everything but the monotonous rhythm of the voice drifted away, and Molly slept.

Descendit ad inferna
Tertia die resurrexit a mortuis.

The puppies stirred again, rousing Molly from brief slumber. Someone placed a wet cloth on her forehead and squeezed liquid into her mouth. Molly pulled away, whimpered. A cool hand grazed her forehead, her mother's voice, pale and tired.

"God be praised but I think the crisis is passed, Harry. Oh, thank God."

* * *

The scarred oak table had stood at the centre of the great hall for generations, it had seen celebrations, births, deaths, and now Harry sat at it alone, cradling his head in his hands. Less than a month ago the bad harvest and the unseasonable weather had seemed insurmountable problems but now fate had brought the world down about his ears. At fifteen years old Harry, who had not learned the rudiments of manhood, found himself head of the family, or what was left of it. His father, mother and his sister Isabella were sewn into winding sheets, waiting to be taken for burial. The priest was quite insistent that their bodies should go into the lime pits with the rest of the villagers to stop the contagion from spreading but Harry refused to countenance it.

Thornburys had been buried in the family vault since the church was erected and he was not going to change that now. Even though life at Thornhold had changed forever, some traditions must remain.

There had been a break after Mother's death. A whole thirty-six hours during which time Harry had nurtured hope it was all over. But the nightmare returned, and now seven-year-old Tom was showing the first signs of fever.

Harry sent Martha to summon Brother John back and hurried to the deserted kitchens to snatch some stale bread and slightly rancid milk to subdue his hunger. He had to supplement his strength somehow. As he made his weary way back to the bedchamber he shared with his brother, Harry was aware of what awaited him. He knew what he had to do but still he was afraid, his only certainty was failure.

He was unable to pray. Certain that God had forsaken them, he pushed away the horror of tomorrow and concentrated instead on the task in hand. The monk insisted that the buboes should be lanced as soon as they appeared, this method had seemed to offer some relief to his mother and Harry was strongly persuaded the method had snatched Molly back from the brink.

Molly was still abed, mercifully growing stronger and their baby brother, Richard, was as yet, untouched by the pestilence. Harry dreaded the ensuing battle. When he reached the chamber door, he paused, loitered in the corridor waiting for Martha to return. He was not afraid of the disease himself, in fact, with his parents gone, survival seemed a far more frightening prospect than death. He had no-one to lean on, no-one to help him, and nothing to expect but sickness and suffering.

The whole village was in the grip of the epidemic, the strongest members taken first, leaving the old or the very young to fend for themselves. Everyone, it seemed, from the lowliest cotter to the bailiff, were looking to him for answers that he did not have. He was tired and feverish, but although he examined his own body regularly for signs of the sickness, so far, he had found nothing. The monk regarded it as some sort of a miracle for Harry had been exposed to it daily, from the beginning.

At first, he'd been unaware of the crisis. He hated himself for sleeping through his father's death but there would be time to pay that penance later. He did all he could to assist at Molly's bedside and afterwards had nursed his mother when she herself succumbed. Closing his eyes against the grief of her passing, he swallowed, unable to contemplate a future without her guidance. *What would happen to the family and the holding without father?* He cuffed the thought away, brushed his tears from his eyes and climbed the stairs, two at a time. He had to face this, he was the only one left.

When he at last opened the door, Mary looked up from her sewing. She put a finger to her lips. "He is sleeping, for now," she whispered, and Harry passed on to Molly's room. She was propped up upon pillows, her face pasty against the white linen. She managed a weak smile. "Oh, Harry," she said.

He sat down on the bed and took her hand.

"How are you feeling? And why are you all alone?" He put a hand to her forehead, glad it no longer burned.

"Oh, I'll be well enough," she replied, listlessly. "I sent Mary to sit with Tom, I could hear him whimpering…he has it too, doesn't he?"

Harry's throat closed again, robbing him of words. He nodded helplessly and Molly held out her arms, he felt them creep about his neck.

"Oh, God, Harry. What will happen if you all die, and I am left alone? Who will look after me? Oh, I wish I had died first! I want Mother."

Three days had passed since it became apparent Molly was going to survive and until now she had been too weak to grieve, but now, as her body grew stronger, so did her mind. Harry felt her sorrow heaving in her chest, sparking his own misery. At length she lay back again and tried to smile, her chin wobbling as she tried to speak.

"Harry, you should go and see to Tom. He will need you and it is selfish of me to keep you from him. I need to sleep again now."

She was right. She usually was. Reluctantly, he rose from the bed, hanging to his sister's hand until the last. When he entered Tom's chamber, Harry saw with relief that Martha had returned but she proved little comfort. She clutched his sleeve.

"Oh, Master Harry, Brother John will not come back. He says the priest is stricken with the fever now and cannot be left! He says we shall have to make do until he can get here."

She turned weeping onto Mary's shoulder.

Harry thrust a hand through his hair. "Then we must manage as best we can."

"But who is going to pray? The child grows weaker and there is no-one left in the village. The bodies are piled in the church yard although there are none left alive to bury them! The stench out there is revolting, and the dogs are beginning to scavenge…"

"Martha! Hush …I cannot think."

Harry shook his head against the images evoked by her words. Pushing his inner panic away, he bent over his brother's bed. There would be time for that later. He stood up, summoning a façade of confidence.

"We will have to manage," he said. "We have no choice… Martha fetch the unguents and salves from my mother's chamber and some cordial, if you can find any."

While she was gone, Mary stoked the fire and prepared to boil up the ingredients for the poultices. Harry, trying to remember the method the Cistercian had used, examined Tom's armpits for swellings and tried to get him to drink. The boy stared at Tom as if he were a stranger, come to kill him. Delirium was the hardest part of the illness, it drove the patient mad, and Harry himself was already not too far from insanity.

Not only did Tom not recognise his brother, he also didn't realise he was trying to help. He viewed Harry as an enemy, his thrashing limbs turning every aspect of care into a struggle, from the simple offering of liquids to the lancing of the buboes. The boy was trapped in some nightmare from which only death would release him.

The women continued to heap fuel on the fire and, as the flames leapt up the chimney, the heat within the room intensified but, remembering the warnings of Brother John, they kept the windows firmly closed. Even outside, it was unseasonably warm with no hint of a breeze. The bedside candle flame burned tall and yellow, and sweat dripped into Harry's eyes as he bathed the infant's body in vinegar.

It took a long while for the swellings to appear, hours in which the boy grew weaker, hotter, and more violent. When they finally erupted, Harry was nonplussed. There were not one or two swellings as he had seen upon his mother and sister, but many hard, black nodules scattered across Tom's upper torso and limbs.

Harry had no idea where to make the incision.

The boy sweated and strained against the restraints around his wrists. The combined smell of vinegar and excrement permeated the room, the stench of death, the venom of contagion. Harry hesitated, the knife wavering in his grip.

Mary licked her parched lips, her eyes darting from the face of her young master to the stricken child.

"I'll run ask Brother John," she cried, and without waiting for his consent she fled from the room. Her footsteps skittered down the stairs, shortly followed by a distant bang as the door slammed behind her. Harry was alone.

***

Outside it was dark and Mary had forgotten to bring a lamp. She edged her way along the walls of the manor house until her eyes became used to the dark and she was able to discern the shadowy outline of buildings. A dog barked and another, closer by, answered. It wasn't far to the church lodging; she should know the way blindfold, but she was loath to leave the safety of the house. She closed her eyes and prayed hard, gathering all her strength, before plunging into the night.

The church tower loomed dark against the darker sky, and she kept her eyes fastened upon it. Before she had gone far, the churchyard gate loomed out of the darkness. The gate where she had waited in better days, for Will to take her a-courting in the greenwood. It was also the place where, God willing, in a few weeks' time, they would meet on their wedding morning.

She groped for the latch and as she began to creep along the path that wove through the gravestones, she was assailed by an ungodly stench. She clamped her apron over her nose, retching as she passed the bodies piled outside the chantry door. Turning her face away, she hurried on.

Something moved in the grass, she peered through the darkness, her scalp prickling in horror when she identified a colony of rats, revelling in human despair. A cry of horror escaped her but squaring her shoulders, she hurried on toward the open church door. The candles were burned out and there was nobody praying. Somebody should be praying for if ever prayers were needed, it was now. But she headed on, toward the priest's lodgings and thumped loudly on the door.

"Brother John, Brother John, you must come." She called again and again, until at last, a window opened on the upper floor. A single candle appeared, followed by a face.

"What is it child? The priest is dying. I cannot come just now."

Out of breath, her heart banging as if she had been running, Mary took her courage in her hands and answered him back.

"You must listen, Brother John, I've come from the manor. You must come! The child, Master Tom, his sickness is different from the others, and we are at a loss as to what to do. His symptoms are different. There are hard black lumps all over his limbs, but we don't know which swelling to lance. We are at our wit's end. You must come! Master Harry sent me to fetch you."

"I have said I will come when this priest is released from suffering; it should not be long now, but I must guide him on his way to Heaven."

"But what about the child. Is he of less worth to God than a priest? We don't know how to treat him! Are we to let him die? There is no one to pray for his tiny soul should we lose him …"

There was a long silence and the light at the window extinguished, plunging Mary into darkness. She lingered, not knowing if she should knock again or return, empty handed to the house. But, after a moment, the heavy door opened and Brother John stood before her, the light from his candle revealing a face ravaged with exhaustion. He was a good man but one who often found himself impatient with the disingenuous. He touched Mary's arm, attempting to soften the blow of the words he must speak.

"If the child has many small hard lumps and no individual large swelling then there is no hope of recovery. There is nothing you can do except to make him comfortable. As for prayers, come with me and I will ordain you. If I do not get there in time, then you must perform his last rites and pray for him until the end."

Mary was aghast.

"Me! But I'm not a priest. I'm not even a man! How can a woman, and a serving woman at that, perform the services of a priest? I don't even know the proper words…"

Mary's indignation was nearing hysteria as Brother John calmly recited the priestly ordinance over her.

"My child, this is a time of such extreme crisis, and we can only hope that God will recognise our predicament and forgive our liberty in allowing a woman to perform such a role."

Then, leaving Mary sobbing on the doorstep, he went inside and closed the door.

With no hope to spur her on, Mary found the way back to the manor far worse than the outward journey. She had no faith in her status as confessor and knew if the boy did not survive he would go to his grave un-shriven. She was running through a nightmare, a dream of horror which seemingly had no end.

As she drew close to the churchyard gate, she heard the click of the latch and froze to a stand-still. Straining to see through the darkness, she heard a labouring breath, and the sound of something heavy being dragged along the path toward her. She had often heard the phrase 'my blood ran cold,' but until now had not understood it. If some demon approached to drag her off to hell, the last few days had prepared her for it.

"Who's there?" she cried out with false bravado. "I am Mary from the manor. Now, tell me why you are skulking about. What are you up to?"

She heard a dull thud and then footsteps before a tiny figure loomed out of the darkness. When the figure clutched her arm, Mary almost leapt from her skin.

"Oh, Mary love, 'tis Good Wife Cotter! I'm glad you're still living, lass. How are they faring up at the house? 'Tis weeks since we saw you. We feared the pestilence had taken you too."

Mary crossed herself.

"Not yet, it hasn't, Goodwife," she replied, fear rising like bile in her throat as she returned the old woman's embrace. "How is it with you? And what are you doing here alone?"

"I'm bringing my lad, Nick," the old woman replied. "He passed on earlier today and I'm taking his body to the churchyard for burial.

There's no-one else hail enough to do it. Those that haven't fled are either sick or dead. I don't believe there be many of us left now at all."

Mary thrust her own problems aside.

"Let me help you, Goodwife," she said, lifting the feet of the shrouded body as his mother took the head. It was heavy work. She wondered that the old woman had been able to bring the body so far on her own. Just a few days ago, the corpse had been a lively thirty-year-old with a young family. Her thoughts darted to the man she was to wed in a few days."

"What about Will, Mother Cotter? Why couldn't he help you?"

The old woman made a noise in the back of her throat before her voice came shakily through the dark.

"Young William be sick unto death himself, Mary. He knows nothing of his brother's passing, or of his two nephews dying yester night. Oh, Mary child! Why didn't God take me instead? I'm old, I am, and when William is gone, my life will be over anyway. That's the truth of it. I don't know what we ever did to deserve such a terrible judgement, but judgement it must be! I just hope the end comes swift. Life for a widow woman with no sons is no life at all."

Will's face swam into Mary's mind. She couldn't breathe. She remembered him laughing and twirling a piece of grass in his fingers, trying to tickle her neck with the seed head while she shrieked and tried to escape his embraces. Was that happy afternoon really just a few weeks ago? It seemed a lifetime.

Dropping the feet of the corpse, Mary crashed to the ground and collapsed, vomiting into the grass.

***

Molly knew without being told that Tom's sickness was critical. For a long time, she hid beneath the bedcovers, praying for his survival, praying for guidance, begging for help. Then, after what seemed hours, she stopped and raised her head, listening. She strained her ears in the darkness trying to filter the new sound from the anguish of Tom's cries.

When it came again she realised it was the baby, Richard, crying in the nursery, and from the sound of it he had been crying for a while. The thin wail of neglect echoed along the corridor. When she could bear it no more, she threw back the bedclothes, fought her way through the heavy hangings.

Her legs were weak, and her head swam as she bent over and lifted him into her arms. He was wet, so she laid him on his back and lifted his gown. His tears stopped and, pleased to be free of his sodden napkin, he grabbed at her nose. To her surprise, Molly found she was smiling. She carried him back to her chamber, tucked him into bed with her and tried to block out the sounds from the sickroom.

Presently they both fell asleep.

She dreamed that she was in Mother's solar. The sun streamed through the huge windows, and everything was calm, tranquil. There was no famine, no rain and no sickness; everything was as it had been before. In the dream, Molly felt again the solid presence of her mother as Isabella put down her needlework and began to show her The Book of Thornhold.

It was a beautiful, the family's treasure kept secure in her father's private chambers. In the dream, her mother pointed to the illustrations, and turned the pages reverently, explaining that it had been made by monks long, long ago, and that it had come to the family by chance and had been in their possession ever since.

"Our family must always look after the book," Mother smiled, "or harm might befall us. As long as we protect the book, so the book will protect us in return."

The decorated pages gleamed, illuminating Isabella's face as she turned them. She looked like an angel, and blinded by her brilliance, Molly reached for her.

When she awoke the sun was shining onto her face. She blinked, rubbed her eyes and turned to find Richard, fidgety and hot, beside her. Reality rushed back in, obliterating the happy dream.

Molly looked more closely at her brother.

His face was flushed, and his lips slightly tinged with blue. Fear bit into her empty stomach. She struggled from the bed and as fast as she could, she hurried into Tom's chamber and dumped Richard on Martha's lap.

Mary was kneeling by Tom's bed, intoning a mixture of prayer and grief, the words of which were indiscernible.

Molly rudely interrupted.

"Mother spoke to me in a dream, Martha, and you should know, Richard is sick too. In the dream, Mother told me how to help them. I won't be long. You must comfort him while I am gone."

Molly hurried from the room again as Martha struggled to her feet to embark upon yet another futile attempt to save a life.

The stairs to Father's private apartment seemed to go on forever. Molly had never realised how steep and tiring they were. When she finally reached his chamber and crossed the floor toward the lectern where the book was kept, her legs were shaking so badly, she wondered if she'd have the strength to do what she must do.

She lifted the book down carefully and clasped it tight, struggling to walk because it was so heavy, and the jewelled covering jabbed through her nightgown.

As she passed the solar she noticed her mother's needlework discarded on a chair, the needle as she had left it, half in and half out of the fabric, awaiting her return. A sharp stab of pain disrupted the rhythm of Molly's breathing.

But somehow she struggled on.

Richard was lying across the bed, the early signs of the sickness already apparent upon his baby skin while Martha dabbed his limbs with vinegar. In one corner, Mary was kneeling at the prie-dieu praying so hard and so quickly, her words made little sense. She kept forgetting the words and beginning again, her hands were trembling, and hysteria not far away. Harry was weeping weakly by the bed, and with a wrench of grief, Molly saw he had drawn the sheet across Tom's face.

Her throat closed, but she quenched it. There would be time for sorrow later. She was too late to save Tom, but Richard's life was the important thing now.

She refused to think about the heroic future Tom had planned. Aware that the fortune of second-born sons was in their own hands, he had intended to ride to the crusades. He'd spent every spare moment practising and only a few weeks ago he'd been in disgrace for leaping on the table and breaking a jug with his wooden sword.

Don't think of it now, she scolded herself and opened the book to a random page and laid it on the bed, hastily covering it with a cloth.

"Lay him on it, Martha," she instructed.

"Whatever for, child?" asked Martha, automatically doing as she was bid. Harry lifted his head from his hands as he heard Molly reply.

'It will make Richard get better, Martha. The book has the power to heal, Mother told me so. If only we had thought of it before we might have saved them all. We must try, since all else seems to be failing. We can't let any more of us die."

Martha screwed up her face and breathed sharply through her nostrils but Harry, coming up and quietly placing his hand on Molly's shoulder, nodded for her to do as she was asked.

"Make up more poultice, Martha. Molly, you should go back to bed."

"If I am well enough to lay awake fretting all night long, I may as well be here with you. I am just very tired. Mother came to me in a dream and told me to fetch the book, Harry. It may have only been a dream, or even part of my sickness, but she seemed so very real, and … and well, we have to try."

It seemed hours before the buboes emerged on Richard's body but, in fact, it was just coming on to midday. He wailed and sweated and fought like a baby demon all morning but as the sun reached its zenith, Martha stood with a bowl of poultice, ready to apply it immediately the incision had been made.

It was a horrible moment. Richard lay limp and lifeless, his tiny chest heaving with the trauma of breathing. Molly held his limbs fast while Harry wielded the knife. The purple swelling was obscene against the baby's pure, blue-white skin. Harry's hand shook as he brought the knife to its target. Just as he was about to make the incision, Richard jerked, almost oversetting the poultice bowl. The careful planning of the moment spoiled Harry tried again. With Richard's screams rising, Harry sliced into the buboe, sending puss and blood arcing across the bedclothes.

The child's body went rigid, his black lips stretched and the veins upon his forehead distended. As he fought for freedom, the sheet beneath him shifted, exposing the bright pages of the book. Richard's hand flew from Molly's grasp and came down into the bowl of hot poultice just before Martha slapped the mixture firmly into his wound. He jerked his hand away and it came to rest on Alric's book, leaving an indelible red handprint upon the beautifully illuminated script.

The three of them worked tirelessly, binding the poultice in place, bathing his body in more vinegar, while Mary continued her frantic prayers. She only knew the Latin responses to the prayers that they heard in church every day, and had no notion of their meaning, but she hoped they would be sufficient. Just to be sure, she improvised by supplementing them with private entreaties of her own.

"Dear God, if you've any mercy in your soul then save this child from death." She repeated it over and over until it sounded more like a threat than a plea.

The day had passed into evening before the fever began to fall and Richard slipped into a heavy sleep. Harry drooped at his bedside, both physically and emotionally spent, and Molly, soiled and sweaty, immediately dropped asleep on his lap.

Mary ceased to pray, looked at her sleeping companions, and lay herself down before the hearth. Martha surveyed the chaos, the upended bowls and discarded rags. The dying embers of the fire slumped suddenly, and she turned toward Tom's body, grotesque beneath his sheet, and the sleeping babe beside him.

Wrung out with sorrow, she sat down beside the bed, and with the words of Mary's prayers still playing in her head, took up her needle and began to sew Tom into his winding sheet.

January 1349

Harry closed the manor house door and locked it, placing the keys safely in his pocket. Molly, thin and pale, shifted Richard to a more comfortable position on her hip and wiped his nose. She smiled encouragement at her elder brother as they descended the steps of the great hall for what might be the last time.

Wrapped against the January chill, they set off to the stable where Martha was waiting. Molly handed her the baby and picked up a pack which she threw upon her back. Harry's horse, grown thin during the weeks of neglect, was laden with saddlebags. The boy took the reins and led him under the gate and through the deserted village. Martha and Molly followed, their emotions in turmoil.

There was little else to be done now, except seek help from the Cistercian Abbey which lay twenty or so miles to the north. Brother John had not survived the pestilence. He had nursed the old priest, and then died quietly, alone and unshriven, in the priest's lodging. He had left a scribbled note detailing a last request that someone inform the Abbot of Hayles of his passing. Just when they thought it all over, Mary had fallen ill and followed them all to the grave. Now, only Martha remained to care for them.

With little food left in the storerooms, no rents coming in and nobody to bring in even a meagre harvest, the children had scoured the local hedgerows for fruit and nuts to supplement the thin pottage that served as their only source of nourishment. The house was empty without their parents, and it was cold, and they were without guidance.

The road that led through the village was deserted. The pestilence had spread quickly through the cottages, and many had fled the contagion to perish on the road. There were few villagers left alive to bid them farewell.

Some were slowly recovering but they were too few in number to enable the manorial way of life to resume. But, at the far end of the village, an elderly couple waited to bid farewell to the young master. The Thornbury family had always been regarded as fair landlords, better by far than some. They bore no ill will toward Harry for deserting them.

Harry raised his cap to the old woman before pressing some of his precious coin into the old man's hand. He felt bad leaving them to their fate but didn't know what else he could do; his prior duty was to his sister and still sickly infant brother.

The old couple, Abel and Alyce Gardner, were unwilling to leave the cottage they had shared since their youth. They assured Harry their son would return from overseas and care for them in their dotage, as he had promised. But Harry thought it more likely that they wanted to die in their home. They would survive for a while on scrawny vegetables salvaged from the winter gardens, and a few hens still scratched about the place. Their harshest foe would be the winter cold, and Harry was sure they'd not see another spring.

With their passing, village life would be over. The ramshackle cottages would dwindle into decay, the shutters would blow in, and the nettles would grow rank against the doors. Up at the manor, the plough would rot in the barn, the mill wheel not turn again, and the roof of the great hall would fall in, and trees take root in the floor.

As the children rode away, Harry prayed he could one day return to rebuild his inheritance, he would make it his life's work. On the brow of the hill, he drew the horse to a halt, and they all turned for a last look.

"We didn't know how lucky we were, did we?" Molly asked.

Harry rubbed a fist across his nose.

"I don't think we ever know happiness, until it has passed."

Silence fell. From this distance there was no sign of the tragedy that had befallen the manor. The house stood, as it had always done, in the shadow of the church; the defensive ditch dug by the Normans still distinguishable in the lush landscape, and the village buildings straggled up the hill and clustered against the manor walls. As the Thornbury children turned and walked away from their ancestral home, a dog barked repeatedly in the distance.

Part Four
Rose petals red; Rose petals white

> *England hath long been mad, and scarred herself:*
> *The brother blindly shed the brother's blood;*
> *The father rashly slaughtered his own son.*
> *The son, compelled, been butcher to the Sire.*
> *All this divided York and Lancaster..."*
> *(William Shakespeare, Richard III)*

Tewkesbury - May 1471

Dodging swords and flying arrows, the unarmed Welshman dived into the undergrowth, a few stray missiles whistling overhead as he scrambled a mile or so along the ditch in the direction of the abbey. His body was not built for agility but for strength, and his breath came in gasps, his barrel chest heaving. As he hauled his wet and bloody body onto a wooden bridge, the crash of battle raged on. He straightened up, deciding whether to run right or left when, out of nowhere, an equine scream ripped through the air, and iron shod hooves flailed around his head. As the horse came down again, Huw cowered in the mud, making rapid peace with God.

"God's teeth man, you near unseated me. Here quick, take my wrist!"

The knight reached out and hauled the Welshman up behind him before urging his steed hell for leather across the marsh. They rapidly overtook the fleeing remnants of Margaret's army and headed for St Mary's abbey that promised sanctuary to the fugitives. Abandoning the horse on the church steps, the two men fell into a nave and found it littered with wounded and dying men. The stench of fear and blood mingled with the aroma of incense. The knight took off his helmet and shook his hair, spraying blood and sweat over his companion. Huw the Bowman, his face marred by a gash on his temple, nodded gratitude and attempted to examine a sword-cut on his shoulder.

"My thanks, Lord, I am in your debt. It was a close-run thing. I am not built for speed."

The knight, his hands shaking with agitation, tore a strip from his mired surcoat and used it to staunch the bowman's wound.

"I thought we'd never outrun them," he gasped. "I swear I could feel Clarence's breath on my neck as we rode past the abbey mill. My men were scattered by Gloucester's flank attack. I see none of them here. My name is Thornbury, Sir Richard Thornbury. I'm glad to be of assistance."

Finding a space next to Huw against the font, Sir Richard exhaled a long breath and scanned the faces of the assembly. They appeared to be mostly commoners, foot soldiers and a few archers but there were some of nobler blood among them. He recognised Somerset, Clifton and Tresham in a huddle close to the rood screen where Lord St John was bleeding copiously onto the tiled floor. Subdued panic buzzed in the air while priests moved among them, offering water to staunch both thirst and blood, and prayed over those who needed it. Every soldier and priest were aware that York's army were not far behind.

Thornbury got up and took a flagon from a monk and handed it to Huw before crossing the nave to speak to Somerset.

"Where is Prince Edward, did you see which way he went?"

Grimly, Somerset shook his head.

"We were just determining who was the last of us to see him. I saw him before the battle, but Tresham here says …"

Tresham took up the tale.

"The last I saw of him he was mounted, in company and well-guarded. They were heading for the town. I'm certain he will have escaped. It can only be a good thing that he is not here with us."

Aware that the man spoke more from hope than conviction, Thornbury nodded.

"I trust that is so, Sir, our cause is lost else. York is fast on our heels, and we can expect no mercy."

A commotion at the entrance and Abbot Stensham bustled forward as the heavy oak door flew back on its hinges. Drawing all eyes toward him, a mounted knight clattered still mounted into the nave. In a blaze of defiant anger, the giant reined in his horse and looked down upon them.

"Somerset!" he bellowed and, spying his prey almost at once, urged his horse forward until a diminutive abbot bravely barred his way. The horse snorted, its huge, distended nostrils glowing red, his hooves sparking on the patterned floor. Trusting in God to provide him with the adequate courage the Abbot held out both arms protectively.

"What are you doing, Sir? You cannot enter God's house to do the devil's work. Turn around and leave this place. Have you not shed blood enough this day?"

As the Yorkist Knight threw back his visor, his soldiers arrived and clustered at his side. The mounted man looked down his nose.

"Out of my way, Stensham," he bellowed, "before I take my devil's sword to your miserable godly throat."

Recognising too late the authority of his king, the abbot fell to his knees.

"Oh, forgive me, Your Grace. I did not recognise you. Pray, come into my private chamber and let us discuss this amicably. I can offer you refreshment and rest. I do not need to remind you that God's house is not the place for violence."

King Edward of York reached for his sword and glared at the abbot; after a moment's hesitation, the old man faltered and took a step backward. The fugitives braced themselves, those that could scrambling to meet their bloody end on foot. The air in the nave simmered until a young monk bearing a tray of bread and wine, moved into the fray.

"Before God, Your Grace, you cannot enter here with drawn sword. Look how mired it is with blood, and how befouled your armour. These men came here for succour, and succour they shall receive. Go forth and cleanse yourself from the filth of battle, and let these men remain here until such time as you offer them their liberty."

Edward IV stared down at him as though he were something foul on his shoe. One swipe of his sword would finish him.

"God's teeth! Get out of my way, you wretch, or I shall have your guts. I have not come here to listen to you preach."

Leaping from the saddle, he raised his sword above the cowering form. As the monk prepared to die, a knight reached out and stayed the king's hand. Edward turned in fury, but seeing who it was, lowered his weapon and listened to his brother's reason.

Edward deflated and sheathed his sword, but his jaw remained clenched. The monk unfolded himself and watched his monarch remount. With one hand he steered the horse forward, its great hooves striking sparks from the stone floor as he addressed the company.

"Lucky for you, *monk*," the king said, making an insult of the word. "My brother of Gloucester suggests peaceful council. I shall consort with him. You are to guard them, Norfolk, and let no man venture forth."

***

When the news came they were to be pardoned, a half-hearted cheer issued around the nave as the battle-weary men prepared to return home. Several of their number had died of their wounds during the night, and more were as yet too sick to travel. Sir Richard Thornbury, refreshed after a night curled like a cat upon the tiled floor, splashed some water onto his face and knelt before the altar to give his thanks to God.

Huw the Bowman knelt beside him, his shoulder sore yet mercifully free of infection. He wondered what he would do, where he would go. His wound spelled an end to his career as a first-class bowman. Trained at the longbow, he had fought in the wars since he was little more than a boy, developing such strength in his upper body that his left arm was now far more muscular than his right. He loved the thrill of battle, the killing joy as he let go up to twenty arrows a minute, felling as many as he hit. He knew no other life. Huw had fought under Lord Wenlock's command; sometimes against York, sometimes against Lancaster, as the fickle heart of his Lord dictated.

"What does it matter who sits on England's throne," thought Huw, "as long as I'm engaged in battle."

Huw frowned as he considered his uncertain future. His lord was dead, and the Lancastrian army routed. Huw had watched helplessly as Somerset lost his temper and lashed out at Wenlock, splattering his brains at some perceived betrayal. Wenlock's failure to support Somerset's flank may have been intentional, it may have just been chance, but the outcome left Huw leaderless, and for the first time since leaving Wales more than twenty years ago he was directionless.

Thornbury produced a loaf of bread. It was stale but Huw tore into it and listened as his companion spoke warmly of his home in Gloucestershire.

"It's not so far from here, Huw. A modest manor set on the side of a valley. My family have been there since the Conquest, farming and prospering, in between wars. You should visit sometime when you are recovered. We can relive our adventures over a hearty meal. My wife Eleanor will welcome you, and my daughters always appreciate a visitor."

Huw nodded absently. "I'm from Powys, I am, Lord. A little place named Cwmdu. 'Tis years since I was there. I doubt you've heard of it, Lord."

"Nor any of those heathenish Welsh places, Huw. Where on earth does a name like that come from anyway?"

"It means, "dark valley," so they say. It's a tiny place, I doubt I'll ever see it again."

Huw helped Thornbury into his armour, fastening the straps and scrubbing off the dried blood as best he could. Many of the fugitives had already left but Huw, envious of their sense of purpose, still had not made up his mind which road to take.

Once in the saddle, Thornbury leant down and the two men clasped hands.

"God-speed," Thornbury smiled, his eyes warm, "and thank you, Huw. Remember my offer. Visit whenever you are passing."

Huw watched the nobles ride off together, leaving the common soldiers to swallow their dust as they followed on foot. He winced as he eased his wounded body into his leather jerkin and picked up his water skin. Instinct told him to quit Tewkesbury and its surroundings as soon as possible. He'd had a lucky escape and wanted many miles between himself and the battleground as possible.

The May sunshine was just beginning to warm the morning air and as the men emerged from the mist, the sheep in the meadow raised their heads. Although the future was uncertain Huw was cheerful to be free. Once out of the abbey precinct the travelling men parted and Huw, finding himself alone, hitched his pack higher and increased his pace. A mile or so along the track Huw stopped, cocked his head, listening, alert to the sounds of affray. Warily, he broke into a jog; ducking behind a hedge and using it as cover until he could determine the source of the trouble.

Through the rising dust Huw recognised a company of horse, intent on murder. He knew from the badges on their coats that Lancaster and York were at it again.

So much for reprieve, he thought, longing for his bow. It was clear there had been an ambush. From the cover of the thicket, he saw Somerset, Thornbury and others putting up a brave resistance but taken by surprise as they were, the Lancastrians were swiftly overpowered. From his hiding place Huw saw them disarmed, mishandled and taken into custody.

Huw remained in the shelter of the hedge until the dust had settled and the road empty before making a furtive way along the road, back toward the town.

A couple of soldiers were taking ale outside an inn. Huw sat down nearby, keeping his eye on the ground, his ears intent on their conversation.

"It's what they deserve," one of the men spat into the dust. "They fought against the king, 'tis only right they should stand trial for treason. It's the scaffold for them and once it's done, England will rest easy. It will teach the bitch of Anjou a lesson. Without Somerset at her side, she and her like will be silenced for good."

Huw swore roundly beneath his breath. Edward, the fiend of York, using false promises of pardon had tricked the men of Lancaster from sanctuary.

***

The makeshift courtroom was packed with Yorkists come to watch their enemies condemned to death. Stripped of their armour and weapons, the captives were herded into the hall; everyone knew the trial was a formality and their common fate already sealed. Huw wondered that York bothered going through the motions at all. The dishonour of trickery left a foul taste in his mouth. This was not justice, it was revenge; the young King Edward seeking retribution for the indignities heaped upon his father and brother, whose heads had been lopped, mocked with a paper crown, and displayed on York's Micklegate bar.

Thornbury waited in the dock. The penalty for treason was execution and disembowelment and the knowledge had bled him of colour, turned his eyes to dark hollows. It was an undignified end for a good knight, a gallant man. Huw hoped Thornbury had the balls to die well.

Spotting Huw almost at once in the crowded chamber, gave Thornbury some comfort. He prayed he would not die squawking like a woman. He could taste the acrid tang of defeat and knew the Lancastrian cause was over. There would be few left to fight on after this. The Duke of Warwick had been slain at Barnet, Wenlock was killed in this last battle, as were Courtenay and John Beaufort. And just this morning he'd heard it rumoured that Prince Edward, the hope of Lancaster, had also been hacked down.

Queen Margaret would be inconsolable. Thornbury was glad he'd not be the one to tell her of it. She was alone now; without Somerset's guidance the simple-minded King Henry could provide no leadership. Loyal as Thornbury was, England might as well have a stuffed dummy at its head than he. The country needed strong leadership, better the devil spawn of York than a puppet king. There was no getting away from it, Lancaster was finished now and York in the ascendancy. Thornbury's thoughts wandered to his son, and the effect the defeat would have on Thornhold.

A door opened at the other end of the room, drawing his attention to the present. A troop of dignitaries filed in to take their places at the long table. A boy, or a young man took the high chair, immediately engaging John Mowbray in conversation.

"It must be young Gloucester," thought Thornbury, although there was no familial resemblance to the king. Rumour said the boy was a great soldier and loyal subject. He wondered if the unshakable loyalty of this brother compensated King Edward for the treachery of the other.

As Constable of England, the boy bore a heavy responsibility; the power over life and death being a burden few would welcome, let alone a boy of nineteen. As the list of penalties were read out, Thornbury continued to watch the boy, and against his will, found himself impressed. Gloucester did not stutter over his words; his eye was firm, and his voice clear and business like. He was the sort of boy any man would be proud to sire.

Once more Thornbury's thoughts drifted back to his son, Edward. He was young to be master of the estate, his education was incomplete, and his experience limited. *What would he do without guidance? Who could he turn to?* Thornbury regretted not paying more attention to his training, and wished he'd taught him personally rather than leaving it to a tutor. *And Eleanor, what would it all mean to her?*

"Oh, Eleanor, what have I done?"

She had been a good wife; initially it was not a love match, but affection had blossomed, and she had given him two sons; one whom they had raised, the other who had lain since infancy in the family vault. His daughters, Katherine and Elizabeth, almost of an age to be wed. Even now, he smiled at the memory. They had lightened his troubles. He had imagined his senior years would be spent with grandchildren at his knee, and as he prepared for death, regret hung heavy on him. War, he realised belatedly, was for fools.

***

One by one, his comrades ascended the scaffold before him. He would have preferred to go first, to get it over with but being older, they left him until last. Each man died bravely. One boy, not yet twenty, sobbed as he stumbled up the blood-soaked steps, still looking over his shoulder in hope of reprieve. Thornbury wept for the child having fought for his anointed king, now died a traitor's death. It was too much.

Thornbury was the last to die. He watched as Edmund Beaufort, the last of the noble line of Somerset, bowed his neck to receive the axe. When his own time came, he almost gave way to panic. His feet taking him against his will, up the slippery steps to face his end.

He looked numbly across the heads of the crowd, nodded dumbly as he was absolved of sin and prepared him to greet his God. Never more alone in that last moment on the makeshift scaffold, panic threatened to overwhelm him. On the verge of dying like a jade, he suddenly saw a raised hand in the crowd and the rugged, familiar face of Huw the Bowman …smiling.

His last thoughts winged across the baying crowd to Huw and before he died he knew it had made their mark. Huw gave a nod of assurance and Richard Thornbury after a swift, final prayer, knelt to his destiny. The sun was warm on the back of his neck and then the axe came down, turning his world dark.

***

The door was wrenched open by a sulky squire who cast a disapproving eye over Huw's unkempt clothes, his scuffed shoes.

"What do you want?"

Huw kept his eyes low. "I would speak with the Lord Constable if 'tis convenient, Sir."

The squire looked down his long nose. "The Lord Constable? My Lord of Gloucester? What is your business with him, man?"

The boy leaned on the lintel and chewed the skin around his nails while Huw, having no intention of divulging the nature of his business, took a deep breath and tried not to sound impertinent.

"It's a private matter, Sir, begging your pardon. If the Lord Constable is not available then the Earl Marshall will do as well, the Duke of Norfolk, that is."

"I know who the Earl Marshall is, man. I need no instruction from you. Wait here, I shall enquire."

He backed out of the room, regarding the Welshman suspiciously before letting the door slam behind him and Huw was left kicking his heels in the antechamber. He sat on a rough bench and waited. Then he got up and began to pace the floor, then sat down again. Eventually, the squire returned.

"The Duke of Gloucester is with the King, and my Lord of Norfolk likewise. However, the Duke of Clarence has graciously consented to know the nature of your business. You will wait here until summoned and do try to tidy yourself before you are admitted."

Huw tugged at his jerkin and, spitting on his hands, slicked down his hair. Shortly afterwards he was shown into the hall. The Duke of Clarence was lounging with some companions by the fireside, a half empty flagon of wine on the table before them.

The fair head turned; his speech arrested.

"You wish to speak with me?"

"Well, Sir," replied Huw, moistening his lips. "I did wish to speak with the Lord of Gloucester, or Norfolk, but the young fellow at the door told me they was busy, Sir."

"Yes, yes well, won't I do? Come, what is it? Some boon, no doubt."

Huw found himself disliking the flushed face of the man before him, he didn't seem the type to dispense justice. He cleared his throat.

"Sir Richard Thornbury was executed this morning, and I crave permission to take his body home to his wife and family. He was a good man and deserves to be laid to rest among his kin, Sir."

"Then he should have had the good sense to stay home by his fireside, or at least to fight on the winning side. If I had my way, the remains of all his ilk would be tossed on the midden. No, you shall not have him. Don't bother me again."

Waving Huw away, Clarence turned back to his friends who, enjoying the Welshman's discomfort, joined him in laughter. Huw had never seen Clarence before, but he knew all about him. The whole country knew it was not long since he'd allied himself with the Duke of Warwick against his own brother, the king. Only the good nature of King Edward, which some saw as foolishness, had ensured his welcome into the bosom of the York faction. Greatly daring, Huw stepped forward.

"Forgiveness is a great thing, Lord, and sometimes men make mistakes. In these wicked times a man must follow his conscience but, 'tis easy to be led astray; you should know that My Lord. Thornbury's wife and family ..."

"You impudent dog! How dare you speak so to me?"

Clarence crossed the room in three strides. "You will suffer for this. I will see you strung up in the market square with the other traitors."

Taking an involuntary step backward, Huw forced himself to continue.

"King Edward said that commoners should be spared, My Lord. I have done nothing wrong, all I did was follow the orders of my betters. It's all I've ever done. I am here today because I want to do what's right and take my Lord's body home so he can lay at rest among his kin."

Clarence's eyes glinted, clenching his lips he unsheathed his sword. Huw knew he was lost. He should have minded his business and gone back to Wales. The duke was obviously unhinged. Aware that all eyes were upon him, Huw backed away until he found himself against a dresser. He groped behind him, searching for a weapon, anything until his fingers closed upon a candle stick. It was thick and heavy in his hand. He stood ready to swing it at Clarence's head.

The door was thrust open, and Gloucester entered, laughing at some joke of Norfolk's. The smiles faded as Richard of Gloucester moved quietly forward, his voice guarded.

"What now, George? What is the trouble here? Is this the fellow that wished to speak to me?"

"An impudent fellow, Brother, and one that will pay for his insolence."

Clarence's sword wavered a few inches from Huw's nose as Gloucester moved closer. Placing a hand upon his brother's shoulder, he spoke quietly.

"Has there not been enough killing for one day, George? He looks an honest fellow. Come put up your sword and tell me the trouble."

Clarence kept his sword levelled at Huw, intent on vengeance. Gloucester tried again.

"George, think, will you? What will Edward say if you commit murder in his hall. Has there not been enough strife? Come, put up your sword."

Clarence stepped away with a curse, and Huw relaxed his shoulders. Gloucester jerked his head and, relinquishing the candlestick, Huw followed him from the chamber.

"Take a seat," Gloucester slopped some wine into a goblet and offered it to Huw, who declined, eager to get the ordeal over. He began to tell his tale while the duke listened without comment. After a pause, he leaned back in his chair.

"So, you followed Thornbury in life, and now wish to fulfil your obligation to him in death. That is noble indeed, my friend. Tell me, were you at Barnet?"

Surprised at the change in direction the conversation was taking, Huw raised his brows before replying.

"I was, Lord, but I was not with Thornbury then. I have served under Lord Wenlock since childhood. He was slain on the field two days since by the Duke of Somerset, a sorry deed, My Lord, but I had lost my bow and taken a blow to the shoulder. I could neither save nor avenge him, so I fled with the others. Thornbury saved me from the fray, Sir, and brought me to Tewkesbury. The debt I owe him is for my life."

Gloucester took a sip of wine, nodding slowly, appreciative of an honest man.

"Many brave men died today, and I have seen blood enough in my short lifetime. For sixteen years we have fought and died for the English crown. Now it is with York, where it should be, I pray the wars shall cease. I always have need of a competent bowman though, Huw, should you wish to transfer your allegiance."

Huw flushed, both touched and embarrassed by the offer.

"To tell truth, My Lord, I little care who is on the throne. It makes no difference to a fellow like me. I'm a bowman and I just do my job, but I fear the injury I took on the field will end my days as an archer."

He drew aside his stained jerkin to reveal blood-soaked bandages. Gloucester started up in his chair.

"Good God. You must have it tended before you bleed to death in my chamber. You may have Thornbury's body and his horse and trappings. When you are patched up, go to Thornhold, where they can nurse you back to full health. I will prepare a letter of mark, to ease your passage."

Huw flashed Gloucester a look of gratitude as the duke continued, "You seem to be a good soul, Huw Bowman, and any man would be proud to have your loyalty. I wish you well. God speed and good luck."

Mid-May 1471

Eleanor laid aside her embroidery and moved to the window to watch the rain scudding across the gardens. "How many more weeks must we be incarcerated by this weather? May is the month of love and romance, a time of Maypoles and dancing but here we are, miserable and damp."

"I do believe it's rained since Easter day, M'lady. April it was when the master left, and it was raining then and has hardly stopped for a minute since."

Margery was right. The rain had begun to fall on the day when Richard left to muster with the Duke of Somerset. Eleanor felt she would soon go mad from inactivity. Despite the grand new solar windows that allowed daylight to flood in, her failing eyesight prevented her from stitching for too long. Turning from the window to the feminine domesticity of her women gathered beside the hearth with their needles, she sighed again. In the corner, Anne strummed upon her lute and sang a dirge of unrequited love.

"For heaven's sake, Anne, as if the day is not dismal enough. Can you not play something more uplifting?"

The tune ended discordantly, and Anne began to sing a ditty about a duck and a dairy maid.

"Has anyone seen the children today?" Eleanor asked.

"Master Edward has taken his hawk out, and Miss Libby is in the dairy helping Bessie try to get the butter to turn, but I've not seen Miss Katherine."

The women exchanged glances, but nobody had seen Katherine since breakfast. Eleanor sighed again and began to wind some thread onto spools, a task which was less strain upon her eyes than close stitching. It was bad enough to be cooped up like this in the winter, but in May, when they should be in the gardens, it was unbearable.

"Oh, how I wish my Lord would return, I am sure the sun will come out in celebration when he does. I feel so restless. Come Margery, walk with me, we will go in search of my daughters."

Margery had served Eleanor since her teens, offering much and demanding nothing. Her familiar chatter washed over her mistress as they passed through the long corridors to the gallery. When they reached the gallery above the great hall, they caught sight of Katherine in the room below. She was engaged in setting two of the castle dogs against each other.

She held them apart, the hounds snapping and snarling as they awaited the girl's signal to go to again.

"Katherine!" Eleanor's voice rang across the hall, but it was a little too late, and the dogs hurled themselves into the fray. Her eyes innocently wide, Katherine spun on her heel, to face her mother.

"Did you want me?" Her voice was sunny, belying her thrall with the dog's battle for domination.

"What do you think you are doing? Attend me in my private chamber immediately."

Katherine looked shamefaced as her mother signalled to a groom to return the hounds to the kennels. As she quit the gallery, Katherine looked down at her gown and found it was stained with blood and dog hair. Often in trouble but seldom contrite, Kate cursed her foolishness. She should have taken the dogs out to one of the barns; now she would probably be confined to her chamber for a week. Instead of attending her Mother straight away, she hurried to her chamber to change her gown and clean her face and hands.

Eleanor bit at her thumbnail. When the knock came upon the chamber door she jumped and wiped her fingers on her skirt. Rising from her chair, she turned to face her daughter, noting her fresh gown and tidied hair. There was no outward flaw in her daughter. Kate was fair and straight with an open, sunny expression. She was clever, competent and a stranger would never guess there was a ruthless streak marring the good, kind girl she had been trained to be.

"I really don't know what to say to you, Katherine. I cannot imagine what you were thinking. I know you love those dogs. I have seen you pet and fawn over them, and feed them titbits from the table, and yet you take pleasure in watching them fight. What would father say were you to incite his favourite dogs to kill each other?"

Kate shuffled her feet, her fine features contrite.

"I don't know, Mother. I am very, very sorry. I don't know what came over me. It has been so dull with all this rain; I long to get outside, yet the weather forbids it. While Ned has the liberty to ride out, I must stay indoors. It doesn't seem fair."

"Pray don't change the subject. Ned is almost a man, and you a gentlewoman… although sometimes I wonder. You will soon be seeking a husband and, above all, when looking for a wife a man looks for gentleness. How are we to ever settle you satisfactorily if you behave like a barbarian? Oh, I wish you were more like your sister."

Katherine's jaw clenched. She looked down at her clasped hands. A smear of blood was streaked across her wrist, and she pulled at her sleeve to hide it. Eleanor was waiting for an answer. Her eyes looked tired, and, with a twinge of remorse, Kate realised she had been weeping. She sighed crossly.

"I don't mean to be bad, Mother. I will be good from now on but when I am forced to stay indoors, I fill up with excess energy. I try to contain it but in the end it comes pouring out … although, I don't mean it to. I promise to be good from now on so, pray, don't be angry."

The women looked at each other. Eleanor was well aware that Katherine was attempting to gain permission to venture outside in the inclement weather, but Eleanor was not prepared to be so easily duped.

"Very well, Kate, I accept your explanation. You will be confined to your chamber every morning for a week, and every afternoon you will take some exercise, suitably accompanied, in the manor garden but that is to be the limit of your liberty. If I hear anything to your detriment, the entire matter will be reported to your father on his return. Do I make myself clear?"

"You do, Mother, and pray believe me when I say that you will hear nothing whatsoever bad about me, ever again!"

Unconvinced, Eleanor accepted her daughter's contrition. Rising from her chair, she smoothed her gown.

"Summon the ladies from the solar; the rain seems to have ceased for a while. Let us all take a turn in the garden before it begins again."

The shady walkways, designed to shield complexions from the harsh rays of the sun, showered them with raindrops as they passed beneath. The garden was in a sorry state. They looked with dismay at the fallen petals and slug-laced leaves. Most years the garden provided a delightful oasis from the bustling household but this year, it was muddy, the blooms struggled from little sun, and the camomile seats were too damp to rest upon.

Where the paths intersected at the centre of the garden, water leapt in a fountain before overflowing the cistern and cascading onto the flowery mead. The women paused to watch a robin take an energetic bath in a puddle and, as they lingered, large drops began to fall again.

"Oh no, not again!"

Lifting their skirts, the women hurried quickly across the grass to seek the shelter of the arbour. They twittered like canaries as they shook drips from their hoods and peered up at the clouds to ascertain how long the shower might last. They were still laughing when a footstep on the gravel betokened another arrival, and the women turned to see Libby, hunched against the rain.

"Libby" they cried, as she limped toward them, her fat white dog at her heels. "Hurry up, child, or you will be soaked through."

Damp and pink, the little girl hurried to join them beneath the shelter and threw herself onto her mother's lap. Eleanor laughed,

"Libby, you are as wet as a spaniel that fell in a pond!"

"Are you all mad walking in the gardens on such a day? I saw you from the dairy as you passed by, and thought to join you, but you walk so swiftly. I couldn't catch up."

The women dried her face with their kerchiefs; and Libby, enjoying the attention, snuggled into her mother's lap. Katherine watched without pleasure as her mother's recent words stung her again. "I wish you were more like your sister."

Everyone, without exception, loved Libby, and she was the darling of her mother's eye. Katherine had to confess that she too adored her. The moment she saw her newborn sister she had loved her but sometimes resentment was stronger, tarnished that love.

Katherine knew she was fairer than Libby. She was straight and slim, her body just beginning to bud into that of a woman; and her legs were perfectly formed. But Libby was darker, her skin sallow and from birth she'd been afflicted with a twisted foot. Libby was often naughty and was smacked far more often than her sister had ever been. Katherine's misdemeanours were sly, so she was seldom caught but Libby's mischief was open, and her apologies heartfelt. Nobody ever stayed cross with her for long. Now, in the damp arbour, Katherine watched miserably as once again, her little sister became the centre of attention.

Libby and the women began to play a counting game and, every so often, she would lose count and, put a hand across her mouth, releasing a gurgle of laughter. She was irrepressible, that was the thing; mischievous and lovable whereas Katherine was just beautiful, her goodness penetrating no deeper than her perfect complexion. She knew she was bad inside, and no matter how hard she tried she could never fight it. She could never be nice like Libby; no wonder they all loved Libby best.

"The rain has stopped, Mother. Should we not get back to the house before it starts again?"

Eleanor looked up from the game and held a hand outside the shelter.

"Yes, I suppose we should. Come along, ladies, let us not tarry. Come, Libby, let me carry you, Sweetheart." She scooped her daughter into her arms and the child scrambled joyfully onto her mother's back. As they hurried along the path, Hero the dog barked joyfully, heedless of the weather.

"Let me carry you," mimicked Katherine silently, pulling a face as she trailed along behind, carrying Libby's discarded cloak. The thought of watching her young sister revel in the attentions of the women held little attraction so, as they began to ascend the stone stairway that led to the solar, she ducked away and headed for the stables.

She patted her mare's nose and ran a hand down her neck, beneath her mane. Lacey exhaled, shook herself and blew down her nose. Katherine leaned across her back inhaling the wonderful scent that reminded her of galloping across meadows, leaping small streams, ducking under branches. *Would those days ever return?* Lacey was growing fat and lazy, cooped up every day in the stable.

Her father had picked Lacey up at market four years ago. She was a cream-coloured filly and they had learned the rudiments of good horsemanship together, and a bond had grown up between them. When Katherine missed her daily ride, her energy built up and her propensity for mischief sharpened, and Lacey also restive, gave the grooms a hard time. It was not fair that Edward, could ride out alone any time he wished. She too would like to strap a falcon to her wrist and escape for a day's hunting, but it wasn't allowed, because she was a girl.

Katherine pouted and began to comb her palfrey's mane. It was silken and blonde, not unlike her own hair. As the tension began to leave Katherine's body, Lacey, appreciative of the fuss snorted into the manger, scattering a cloud of oats and chaff. She rested a hind leg, leaning lazily against her mistress until the girl slapped her on the rump and told her to give over.

"It is too wet to ride out today," Katherine explained, "but soon, it will brighten, and we will go out every day as we used to. You will like that, won't you?"

Katherine confided in Lacey, as she did nobody else. The pony never argued back.

There was a commotion in the yard and Katherine recognised the voice of her brother's attendant, calling for a groom. She hurried outside and grasped the fellow's bridle, steadying his mount as he leapt from the saddle.

"What is it, Ben, has Ned taken a tumble?"

"Fetch the mistress, we spied Lord Thornbury's horse approaching along the town road, and Master Ned has ridden forth to meet him. Lord Thornbury is alone and looks to be injured, and the horse is drawing a litter too. Someone fetch Lady Thornbury."

As the grooms scattered, Katherine kicked off her pattens and flew along the road, her slippers quickly become mired, and her feet soaked. In the distance she could see her brother's horse leading another, she squinted to make them out better, but Father seemed to be slumped forward in the saddle. He must be dead tired.

Ignoring the sharp pain in her side, she hurried on. As she grew nearer she saw Ned was leading his father's horse. As he became aware of Katherine's presence, he dismounted, holding out his arms to halt her approach.

"No! Stay there, come no closer!"

He was crying; his face, that had begun of late to develop manly contours had dissolved again into that of a boy.

"Ned?" she questioned, feeling suddenly sick. "What is it? What is wrong with Father?"

The boy shook his head, his voice sounding husky and strange.

"It isn't father, it is some other fellow."

"It is Father's horse," Katherine pointed out. But, suspecting something of the truth; her face began to crumple. "He's dead isn't he? Father is dead?"

Ned nodded, his tears mingling with the rain. "Father's body is in the litter, and this fellow, I don't know who he is, is barely breathing."

The household gathered in the yard, began cheering when they saw the approaching cavalcade but when they saw the faces of the Thornbury children, their joy dwindled into silence. Eleanor covered her face with her hands.

When the horses came to a halt, the rain-sodden stranger slipped from the saddle and lay, like a corpse, in the mud. A squire rushed forward, loosening his clothing.

"A stranger; barely alive," he said but Eleanor did not move. As her servants busied themselves conveying the dying man into the house she stood, her back pressed against the barton wall, her eyes riveted on the shrouded body on the litter.

"Father is dead," Ned hung his head, bracing himself for the barrage of his mother's grief but her knees gave out so suddenly, none were ready to catch her. She fell senseless into the mire. The foundation upon which her life was built washed away by war.

Left alone in the barton, Katherine placed a hand on the horses' flank and stared at the bloody sheet beneath which her father's body lay. Something urged her to reach out and, with trembling fingers, she grasped the edge of the shroud. Drawing it back slowly she expected to see her father's familiar mop of black hair, his woolly black brows and ruddy cheeks – a face she loved. Instead, she was confronted with a tangled mess of sinew and flesh, his head separated from his body, his eyes, bereft of spirit, staring blindly back at her, his mouth gaping.

The daughter Richard Thornbury had loved best whirled into madness.

June 1471

A stream of unintelligible babble left the strangers lips as they battled to clean and bind the gash upon his chest.

"I swear he's possessed by devils," Margery exclaimed, stepping away from the bed. "Where's the priest, its ages since we sent for him?"

"He is still with the mistress, trying to calm her, poor lady."

They turned back to the man on the bed.

Whoever he was, he was in a bad way. Black stubble sprouted on his chin and his hair was damp with sweat but, as fast as the women bathed him he become drenched again. All the while the hole in his shoulder was cleansed and sutured, he raved and shouted, seemingly unaware of his surroundings. When at last he was clean and tidied to the best of their ability, Margery trickled wine into the patient's mouth; seconds later, he spat it back.

Margery dabbed at the splashes on her bodice.

"Definitely has a devil in him," she sniffed. "I will go and see if the priest will be much longer."

When she returned with her quarry in tow, the man on the bed was calmer but still restless, the odd shout interrupting his muttering as he twisted in his nightmare.

"Dewch yn ôl neu byddwch yn cael eich lladd…"

"You see?" Margery gasped, crossing herself. "Strange devilish words, Father."

"Those aren't the words of the devil, Margery. It is Welsh, although there are some who'd say that amounts to the same thing. We have a Welshman among us."

The priest blessed the patient and said prayers over his unconscious body and soon Huw calmed and slept more soundly. But the worst of his raving was far from over.

Bethan held the candle high as Margery leaned over Huw's body and carefully unwound the bandage; the wound was still inflamed and dangerously so. She probed with her finger, making Huw jump, and the women drew back, their hands to their noses.

"I don't know what to do for the best. Oh, how I wish Lady Thornbury was well enough to tend him. She'd know what to do."

"Maybe we should send for her" suggested Bethan. "Maybe it would draw her from her sorrow."

Margery shook her head. "I fear their grief is yet too raw. Lady Eleanor, I feel, will recover; but I'm not sure about Katherine. The mistress' heart is broken but young Katherine is raving. A girl's mind is a delicate thing. If only there was some herb that could take away the memory of what she saw."

"My Lord," bellowed the man on the bed. "Look to yourself, My Lord!" Huw twisted in the sheets while Beth murmured comfort and stroked his head.

"At least he is speaking English now," she said. "That gobbledegook he was speaking before was unnerving. He has no clue any of us are here. I wish we could reach him."

Hearing a sound, she looked past Margery to the door.

"Mistress Katherine!" she cried. "This is no place for you. You should be resting. Go back to your chamber, you can do no good here.!"

But, ignoring her, Katherine came closer to the bed. She looked at the blood daubed bandages, the soiled linen, the foul bowl in which they'd just washed him and did not turn away. Katherine's stomach was strong. She poked the bandage and did not flinch when Huw writhed at her touch. He was going to die; anyone could see that. Katherine thought it a shame. She watched him suffering for some time and then straightened up.

"It is The Book he needs, Margery. The Book of Thornhold. Father told me of its magical power. It is the only thing that can save him."

"The Book? But that is just a fairy tale, made up to amuse children. A book can't heal anyone."

"We can at least try."

***

Since there was no adult to gainsay her order, the Book of Thornbury was brought from its place in the library and placed upon a table before the roaring fire. Katherine, all traces of lunacy now passed, began to turn the thick leaves and, as she did so, a hush fell in the chamber.

Turning to a random page, Katherine and Bethan balanced the book between them while Margery poured rosemary water across the page, letting it trickle slowly across the text and into an earthenware bowl.

"How do you know what to do?" Bethan pulled a face at Margery that was intercepted by Katherine.

"Father told me that The Book has saved our family in the past. The story is that it saved a Thornbury child from the first plague, and when that child grew up he brought Thornhold back from ruin and reinstalled the book in the library. The Book has been held sacred by my family ever since. I don't really know if it will save this fellow, since he isn't family, but we can at least try."

Huw whimpered, and tossed his head from side to side, his lips drawn back over chattering teeth. Showing no sign of emotion, Katherine gently sponged the blessed water into his wound. Ignoring his cries of pain, she whispered a charm and then, while Bethan vomited nearby, she scooped out the evil humours, squeezing the wound until no more pus came. Then, using bowl after bowl of sanctified water, she cleansed it thoroughly. Unnerved by the strangeness of her behaviour, the women retreated to the outer edges of the room.

"She shouldn't be doing that, Margery," complained Bethan. "What on earth would her mother say? It's unseemly for a young miss to be looking on a man's nakedness! Can you imagine the trouble we are going to be in?"

But Margery raised a finger, silencing Bethan. She pointed to the bed, where Huw had stopped shivering and his breathing regulated.

***

"Hector Protector was dressed all in green;
Hector Protector was sent to the Queen.
The Queen did not like him,
Nor more did the King;
So Hector Protector was sent back again."

The voice warbled like a wren's. Huw turned his head toward it, surprised to find a young girl perched on the bed. As she sang she was making her rag doll dance to her tune. He let his eyes wander around the room. A middle-aged woman dozed before a small fire, a dog at her feet. He was thirsty and his head ached. When he stirred his limbs a dart of pain stabbed at his shoulder making him gasp. The girl looked up and smiled.

"At last! Do you know how long you've been asleep? I thought you'd never stir. Would you like a drink? I will fetch you one."

She brought a cup of water, and somehow, despite the pain, Huw pulled himself into a semi sitting position and drank. He grunted thanks.

"I'd better go tell the others you are awake, there's no point trying to wake Bethan, she is so deaf it would take all day. Stay there, I won't be long."

Huw lay back, wondering where she thought he might go. He didn't know where he was, or how he'd got there. He didn't even know how long he had been sick, but it seemed they had tended him well, and that was something to which an archer was unaccustomed.

The girl hurtled back into the room, a small white dog at her heel, and took up her doll again.

"They are coming," she announced as she climbed back onto the bed. "I forgot to ask your name, Sir, what are you called?"

"Huw" he said, his voice husky from little use. "They call me Huw the Bowman, and what do they call you?"

Straight backed and self-important, she said carefully, "My name is Elizabeth Eleanor Mary Thornbury, but everyone calls me Libby. On Sunday next I shall be twelve, Sir Huw the Bowman."

"No, you mistake me, Mistress, my name is simply, Huw the Bowman, there is no 'sir.' I am from simple stock. I was at Tewkesbury with Sir Richard Thornbury, last I recall."

Libby sobered suddenly; it was as if a cloud had passed over the sun.

"Father is dead, did you know that? Were you his friend? How did he die? They won't tell me. Were you with him?"

At the sudden recollection of Sir Richard's death Huw had the wit to give the child an edited version of events.

"He died bravely, Miss Elizabeth, as a man should. I was with him at the end, and he spoke of you and sent his love. He told me to tell you to be a good, brave girl."

Huw was heartened to see his words had given comfort.

"Really? He sent love to me? Oh, Huw the Bowman, thank you for being his friend. Look, here is my mother, Sir."

As a bevy of women sailed into the room, the girl scrambled from the bed and curtseyed. At a signal from her mother, she flashed a conspiratorial glance at Huw, and left the room.

"Well, Sir, how good it is to see you conscious. you've been a deal of worry to us over the last month or so. How do you feel? Is there anything you require?"

"Oh no, My Lady. I only fear I shall never be able to repay your goodness. It's far more than I deserve, and I thank you truly. I'm in your service, I am, Lady, for all time."

"Nay, Sir, it is we who are in yours, for you brought my husband home."

Her voice was soft with emotion. Huw shifted upon the mattress to see her better. She continued to speak as she tidied his blankets, plumped his pillow. "My youngest daughter knows nothing of the manner of her father's death, and I should be grateful if you would ensure that remains the case."

"Of course, My Lady. She did ask me of it almost the first moment I opened my eyes, but I suspicioned she had not been told all. Your man died bravely, My Lady, and extracted a promise from me to convey to you his love, and his regret."

Lady Thornbury's eyes grew moist. She peered at his bandage to check the wound.

"I think it best if we leave it alone now, too much interference could well cause further damage. I can take little credit for your recovery, Sir, save for being the mother of Katherine. It was my eldest daughter who tended you. She is out at present, but you shall see her on her return."

Libby reappeared in the doorway and came skipping to the bed. "Can I stay to talk with him, Mother. He can't be sleepy; he's been asleep for weeks and weeks."

The women laughed but her mother shook her head. "No, Libby. Huw needs all the rest he can get, and you must change that apron; just look at it!"

"If you please, My Lady, I should like the child to stay. Her chatter eases me. I will not let her overtire me, and I'm sure she will promise to go when I feel the need to sleep."

"Please, Mother…" Libby put on her most irresistible smile. Eleanor knew herself beaten.

"Very well, but don't stay for too long or he will relapse.

All smiles again, the child clambered on to the bed and, as the women quietly quit the chamber, began to tell Huw about the family of mice that had been found that morning living in her workbox.

When Katherine returned from her walk and learned Huw was awake, she hurried to the sickroom, regardless of her mired gown and windswept hair. At her sudden entrance Huw and Libby looked up from the game of cat's cradle they were playing. Libby was kneeling up over him in an attempt to retrieve the thread that was wound tightly about his stubby fingers.

"Oh, hello, Katherine!" called Libby. "Huw has woken up. He says he feels as though he has never even been ill."

"Well, he won't say that if you fall on him, you little fool, get down at once; whatever would Mother say?"

Libby scowled but obeyed. Huw watched as Katherine carried a stool to his bedside. "Mistress," he murmured.

"Sir," replied Katherine. "I hope you are quite recovered. Do you feel any pain, or light headedness?"

"Nay, mistress, I am tired, that's all. A few days rest and I shall be myself again. I understand it is you I have to thank for my recovery."

Katherine shrugged, blushing as she kept her blue eyes lowered, remembering her intimate probing of the man's body. Trying not to stare at his broad chest and thick muscled arms, she concentrated on his face. He was regarding her as though she was something to eat. She smiled shyly; her golden head poised delicately upon fine sloping shoulders.

By God, she's lovely, thought Huw. *Like a sad angel. Almost too lovely to look upon.*

"I wanted to welcome you to Thornhold," she said. "But we should leave you now, Sir, you need to sleep. Perhaps, after supper, you will be able to make the acquaintance of my brother, Edward. I know he longs to thank you for the great service you have done us. After supper, Sir."

Her sorrow did not mar her beauty. By the light of the window, he admired the clarity of her eyes, and the unblemished skin of her neck and breasts. But there was a shadow in her eyes, and Huw longed suddenly to see her laugh, to watch her ruby lips stretch into a proper smile. He was so taken with her beauty that he failed to notice the clods of mud that fell from her feet as she crossed the chamber floor.

***

Ill-equipped to cope with the running of the manor, Ned was totally reliant on his solicitor and estate manager. The king had demanded an extortionate fine, which although better than forfeiting the property to the crown, made things even more difficult. When he increased the rents, the tenants grew sullen. They didn't care that his taxes were sky high and the costs of keeping the women clothed was giving him headaches. Katherine demanded the latest fashions, the newest carriage, the fastest horse and Ned lacked the authority to deny her. More and more he turned to Huw for advice, but the bowman was no better suited to running a manor than Ned.

Huw intended to return to Wales but, each time he tried the family begged him to stay a little longer. They treated him, more or less, as an equal. Seeing him only as their father's friend, they enjoyed his strange tales and deep singing-voice. Huw's rough edges were softened by his natural gentleness, and one way or another, he began to fill some part of the void left by Sir Richard.

Eventually, everyone refused to countenance him ever leaving.

"I don't know what to do, Huw. A fellow has to make a living, but the holding can barely feed itself, and the taxes are such that I will never accumulate riches. How am I ever to take a wife if I cannot provide for one? And my sisters. How can they be wed if I cannot provide a dowry? Our coffers were emptied by the king's fine, and I cannot seem to refill them, no matter how hard I try. Thornhold soaks up any money I amass. We will not weather even the smallest storm, should one come. What do you think I should do?"

Huw rubbed his face. "I don't know, Ned. I suspect your father earned more wealth from battle than from rents, but there is scarce a noble left to fight for these days. Many who fought on the wrong side lost their lands completely so you're doing better than some."

"I have no skills, Huw. I cannot spend my life as a farmer and Father's attainder means I am not invited to court. I want to test my battle skills; ride in the lists if nothing else."

Offering Edward a cup of burgundy wine, Huw took a deep breath.

"I do have a sort of idea, Ned, although you make not like it. If I offer a suggestion, do you swear not to take offence?"

"Of course, Huw. Good God, what do you take me for?"

Huw emptied his goblet and placed it carefully on the table.

"After your father's ex … brave death, I sought an interview with Gloucester, the younger brother of the king."

"Yes, the Lord Constable, I know of him."

"I'd swear he's a good man, Edward, for all he wears the wrong livery and I'd as soon trust him as anyone. He seemed to be a fair man, and I think he prefers peace to war. When he heard I was without a lord to follow, he offered me a place with his bowyers, even though I'd fought for Lancaster. He even saw to it that my wounds were bound and found me your father's horse and set me on my way with a letter of mark. He promised if ever I needed anything, I'd only to ask. Now, it may just have been a form of politeness, but he seemed genuine; it's maybe worth a try."

Ned put down his wine. "What is worth a try, Huw? I think I am missing something. Please be more precise."

"Well, Lad, I'm thinking that we should write to Gloucester and seek a place for you among his household knights."

"What." exclaimed Ned. "Fight for York? After they killed my father? Christ man. It was Gloucester who sentenced him to death. How can I serve my father's murderer"

Huw shrugged, sheepishly.

"I thought you'd not like it, but it was only a suggestion. Sometimes, if he is to move on, a man has to let bygones be bygones. Think of your family penniless; your sisters spinsters; your mother ruined; your home lost, and then consider how a little humble pie could change all that. As a favourite of Gloucester you'd find good matches for your sisters; with money in your coffers you could buy fine furnishings and enjoy a household of contented women. There is no Lancaster left to fight for, and York, well, when all is said and done, Ned, York is very much the same. It is the man you'll be fighting under you should think of. I've never heard a breath of scandal about him, which when you consider the muck that clings to his brothers, is surprising."

"I don't like it, Huw but I've never known you offer bad advice yet. I will think on it. Maybe we will write your letter and see where it gets us; although I doubt my father will rest quiet in his grave."

Christmas 1474

It was Christmas Eve and Ned was due home from Middleham. A portrait of Sir Richard looked down from the wall above the fireplace to where Libby knelt at the window with Hero at her side. She pressed her nose against the thick glass, trying to see out while Katherine waited with the women close to the fire. Her head was down, as if concentrating upon her stitching but, in reality, she was hankering for Huw. He had ridden early into town on business, and Katherine knew that he would soon be home bearing New Year's gifts. It was the third Christmas since Father's death and this year, Katherine was determined, would be better. It was time to put off sorrow. Father had loved the festivities and had always contrived to spend it with them if he could.

"Libby, do you remember how father used to hide little trinkets about the place for us to hunt out?"

"Oh, yes I do," sighed Libby from the window. "And how he'd come home with surprises in his pockets for us. Oh, I wonder if we will ever stop missing him; sometimes it seems like yesterday he was here, and at others it seems a lifetime ago."

Katherine glanced at her mother, who was smiling up at the portrait, listening to the carol her woman was strumming on her lute. Although outwardly recovered, Eleanor showed no inclination to remarry and had refused several suitors in the last year alone. It seemed she was content to be a widow, and Edward had assured her that she could always rely upon a home with him at Thornhold.

"Huw is a bit like a father though, isn't he?" said Libby suddenly. "Maybe you should wed him, Mother, so we should be a proper family again."

Katherine's needle stabbed into her thumb, she put it in her mouth. Libby's words also startled Eleanor from her reverie.

"Marry Huw? Good Lord, Libby, what a suggestion. Pray never repeat it in Huw's hearing; the poor man would die of embarrassment."

Libby pouted. It seemed a fine idea to her. He was so funny and good-tempered; he would make a delicious father. She hugged Hero to her chest, closed her eyes until the dog began wriggling to escape.

***

Huw urged his flagging mount onward, eager to reach home before dusk. As he grew closer to Thornhold, he pondered his predicament. The problem had been brewing for some time and had now reached such proportions that it hovered on disaster. He should have nipped the thing in the bud before it grew out of hand.

Katherine was enamoured of him. She had not said so and he was sure nobody else had noticed but she sought him out at every opportunity, begging for a tale, and hanging on his every word. Sometimes she bumped into him as though by accident and suggested a turn around the castle garden and, not knowing how to refuse, he sometimes went with her.

He was uncomfortable in her company. She said little, but her silence spoke volumes. She was a beautiful girl, of course, but for the likes of Huw, her behaviour spelt danger. And he had no idea how to explain it to her, she wasn't easy like Libby. Katherine was deep, murky, and her determination to have him, lethal. Huw had only ever known camp followers, and there'd been no need of courtship there. He was out of his depth.

As he rode through the deepening dusk he reflected on a night last week when she had come across him in the corridor when he was on his way to bed.

"Huw, you are just the man. I know I can rely upon your wisdom." She immobilised him with her luminous eyes and foolishly, he allowed her to lure him into a small side chamber. Fumbling for his tinder, he lit a candle and prepared to listen to her woe.

"Mother is cross with me again, Huw, and I don't know how to appease her. I thought maybe a small gift or something to cheer her and convince her of my regret. Have you any ideas?"

His exasperation threatened to overflow.

"Katherine," he exclaimed. "What do I know of women's gifts, or how to placate a mother? I suggest you speak to Margery who will be far better able to help you, knowing your mother as well as she does."

He tried to leave but, before he could do so, she began to weep. There was nothing that troubled Huw more than women's tears. She sat at the table, her head drooped on her hands, her shoulders gently shaking. As if he were touching a hot coal, Huw placed a comforting hand upon her shoulder, patting awkwardly, trying not to notice the way her hair curled in wisps on the nape of her neck. Quite suddenly, taking him by surprise she was up and sobbing into his chest, so that he was holding her in his arms.

Her body pressed tight against him. and Huw found himself rocking and crooning, his lips in her hair, her perfume like nothing he had ever smelled before. His senses swimming, she turned her face up to his and parted her lips. Lips that were red and moist; she closed her eyes, waiting, just waiting...

Huw thrust her away and fled.

Since then, he had tried to avoid her, but she was constantly coming upon him, tormenting him with her wiles. She was like an itch that he longed to scratch. He did not love her and was under no illusion that he did. He was well aware that very little lurked beneath Katherine's beauty. Over the years he had witnessed many small cruelties and knew her to be an unpleasant woman. Her conversation bored him, her passionate nature discomforted him, and her desire to bed him was more frightening than an army of hostiles.

He could have her if he wished, but he knew it wouldn't end with a quick tumble. If he bedded Katherine, it would represent a betrothal.

And that could never happen. His only option was to leave Thornhold for good.

***

Libby watched the dancing from the table, her dog secreted in her lap. She clapped her hands as they twirled and leapt to the piping of the minstrels. So far Christmas had been wonderful. The great hall was festooned with holly and ivy, the tableware sparkled in the torchlight. It was good to have Ned home from Yorkshire. He was seated at the head table next to his mother and his sisters were on his right with Huw in between and the rest of the household further down the board.

Huw's attentions were torn between Katherine's continuing assault, and the more innocent demands of Libby. He had fashioned a hat from her napkin and plonked it on her head. She laughed delightedly; her lips stretched wide as she demanded that he make one for everybody. Replete with food and wine, Huw's fingers worked deftly, the jaunty tri-cornered hats quickly emerging until every family member, even Hero, sported one. Then the minstrel's tales began; first the story of Camelot, an old favourite that was welcomed with claps and cheers.

All day, aware that she must at all costs prevent anyone from discovering their secret, Katherine watched Huw from beneath her lashes. They had not been alone together for weeks, but she knew that the time would come. She grew warm, her love for him kindling as she remembered the first time she'd seen him, naked and vulnerable upon his sick bed. The only unclothed man she had ever seen. She had instantly wondered how it would feel to touch him. An extraordinary dart of longing to trace her fingers across his hard muscled torso, twirl the hair that curled on his chest. In his unconscious state, it was not long before she found the courage to give into her curiosity and discover the secrets that lay hidden beneath the sheet.

As she came to know him better, her desire for Huw increased. She did not care that he was low born. She wanted him. At every opportunity, she sought him out and had not failed to notice how he grew tongue tied when they were alone. She'd seen his eyes lingering too long upon her body. She knew he desired her, and how close he had come to declaring it a few weeks ago when she'd led him into a small chamber. It would not be long until he finally gave in and kissed her, and when he did, she knew his pent-up passion would match her own.

Next time she would not allow him to push her away.

In her favourite saffron brocade, she knew she looked her best. Her hair was tucked beneath a high cap, revealing her elegant forehead and accentuating her eyes. She knew there was no comparison to Libby, who was wearing a red velvet gown cut in a childish style. When the music began for dancing, she turned to Huw, and demanded that he dance with her.

"Oh, I'm not one for dancing, Mistress Katherine," he cried, warding her off with both hands. "Ask your brother, he has all the elegance of leg that I most sadly lack."

The company laughed but she persisted, dragging him, protesting all the way, to take his place with her on the floor. Of course, the family saw it as a game. They laughed at him, a clumsy bear dancing with an angel.

Hampered by her impediment, Libby watched the dancers, clapping her hands and tapping her good foot upon the dais, wishing she could join in. She was unaware of the danger Huw was in. Unaware that as she watched, he was drowning in her sister's charm.

As the night wore on the revellers washed down cup after cup of wine. It flowed freely all evening, and spirits were high and morals low as they drifted off to bed. Huw's doublet was unfastened, and his fine linen stained with wine. He was drunk, drunker than he'd ever been, drunker than a Lord at a lynching. Entering his chamber alone, he pissed loudly into a pot before collapsing onto his bed. He belched and heaved himself on to his back, the room spinning sickeningly as he lapsed into snores. The room, softly lit by the candle he'd left burning, fell silent, but, just as dawn was creeping into the east, a naked foot trod stealthily across his chamber floor.

Katherine looked down at his prone body. He was snoring, his mouth open and black hair curled upon his gently rising chest. Reaching out, she gently traced the livid red scar that marred his shoulder. When she slipped into bed beside him, Huw groaned and shifted in his sleep.

Slowly and without surprise, the bowman opened his eyes and blinked at her stupidly. She was not really here. It was another dream. But she ran a finger along his cheek and pushed her body against his. Without considering the consequences, he brought his mouth down upon hers.

Revelling in his touch, the scrape of his beard on her cheek, Katherine opened herself to his ungentle onslaught, and received rather more than she had bargained for. Ignorant of the gentler aspects of love, Huw vented his soldier's lust and took her like a trollop in a tavern.

***

Libby cowered beneath the table, her hand on Hero's collar, as the voices of the two men she loved best raged over her head.

"You, Sir, are a knave and a liar! How could you seduce my sister? I should have you whipped."

"Listen, Ned, let me explain," Huw pleaded. "I never meant such a thing to happen. In fact, I didn't know it had happened until I woke in the morning. You know how drunk we all were. I would never knowingly do anything to hurt you or your family. You know that."

"Do I?" Ned scowled. "Haven't we welcomed you into our family, into our hearts? Didn't we, in a time of grief, tend your wounds and provide you with a livelihood, and a roof over your head? You have no honour, Sir, no sense of decency. To wheedle your way into a girl's affection and take advantage of her gentle heart. I was never so ill-used. Never so grieved as this …"

Huw looked at his feet. He knew there was little point in arguing; Ned was right. He deserved to be flogged. Huw remained silent, wanting to protect Katherine but unsure how. She however was defiant in the face of her brother's fury. She stepped forward, pushing past Eleanor who wept, appalled at her daughter's ruin.

"It was not Huw's fault, Ned. I did not withhold my consent. We are in love."

"In love? And does that give you the right to debase yourself? What of your status? You will never be honourably married now. You have wantonly thrown yourself away on this man."

"Then, I swear, I couldn't have thrown myself away upon a better one. You'd not find one to match him if you were to scour all England. I don't care about status or bloodline. Huw is all I desire; all I have ever desired. I know he will not dishonour me further by refusing to wed me."

Recognising the trap, Huw's eyes darted from Katherine to Ned. He knew she had won and having no choice, he nodded.

"That is true, My Lord. I will wed her if you'll allow it."

"I'm sure you will, Huw, certain in the knowledge that I will not see her starve. It's a cosy nest you've built yourself, straight from the ranks into my sister's bed. I had thought you an honest fellow. We all did."

Risking a glance at Eleanor, Huw saw she was white and shaking, unable to look at him. She closed her eyes painfully as Katherine stepped eagerly forward.

"How soon can we be wed, Ned?"

Ned looked at his sister, her radiant beauty tarnished now. He noted her lack of shame and wished he was the type of man to flay the skin from her back. His answering sigh was deep and defeated.

"You may wed him, Katherine, but do not look to me for funds. You will both be fed and housed but, by God, I refuse to spend one penny of mine in celebration of your sorry match."

***

There was no wedding breakfast and no celebration, just the legalisation of an unholy union with only Eleanor and Margery standing witness as the couple exchanged their vows. Immediately afterward Huw rode out on state business, and Katherine returned to the manor. From an upper window Libby watched them return, unsure what to make of recent events but she knew better than to ask for an explanation. Katherine had always been erratic, loving her one moment and taunting her the next, always secretive, and seldom confiding.

Although she had often felt left out of things Libby had not realised Katherine and Huw were lovers but, thinking about it now, she remembered Huw had never spent time alone with Libby. Katherine had seen to that. She was always interrupting, dragging him away, sending Libby about her business. Libby now understood why.

She knew about kissing because she had once caught a dairymaid with a kitchen boy but there seemed little connection between the scufflings of the servants and the marks she had seen on Katherine's body. In her experience, bruises like Katherine's generally denoted violence. Had Huw beaten Katherine or bitten her? Libby didn't understand but she could hardly ask. How could she? The barrier erected by her sister's status as a married woman was not easily breached.

**

Oblivious to the noise of the inn, Huw swilled the beer round his flagon. The morning's events scarcely seemed real. There was no physical mark to show he was now the husband of Mistress Katherine Thornbury, but his life would never be the same. Nothing was altered, yet his very being was changed. His daily tasks remained the same, his habits and style of dress remained simple. The only difference seemed to be that he now had the right to share Katherine's bed every night and to hump her whenever he desired. If he pleased, he could shut her in her chamber, beat her, starve her or keep her in rags and none could gainsay it.

Perhaps that was what she needed.

A trio of men, well gone in drink, began to sing a bawdy song about a ploughboy and, after a moment a fiddler stepped forward. Seeing the evening was about to erupt into gaiety, Huw drained his cup and picked up his saddle bags. His horse, still tied in the inn keeper's yard whinnied welcomingly, and Huw patted his nose before tightening the girth and hauling himself into the saddle.

The woman he loved would be waiting for the sound of his horse. Before he'd even had time to issue his orders to the groom, she would come tripping down the stone steps of the hall.

"Huw," she would cry. "Did you have a good journey?" Then she would hug him quickly before delving into his saddlebags to discover what delights he had carried home from market. His heart would lift. Her smile welcoming him home, offering momentary peace. His guilt would lift a little and, for a few short moments, all would be well.

But this woman, the woman with the sunshine smile and sloe-dark eyes, was not his newly wedded wife, it was not Katherine … it was her little sister, Libby.

***

June 1475

"Suitors, suitors, suitors" Libby stormed. "I am sick of suitors. It is all I have heard since you were wed, Katherine, and I am just not ready for marriage. They can parade as many men past me as they like but I swear, I shall not make my choice before I am ready."

Katherine, lounging on the bed, picked idly at a loose fingernail. "You are lucky to be given a choice, Libby. Many girls are wed without a by-your-leave to whoever their father sees fit. You should be glad Ned has more consideration for you than that. You wouldn't want a fat old man as husband, and if you don't hurry up and make your decision that may well be your fate."

Libby scowled at her sister. It was all right for Katherine, she already had a husband; a familiar, funny, considerate man not some gawky, half-grown neighbour with whom she had nothing in common. For weeks now they had paraded a line of young men before her and asked her to select those she would like to know better. Ned was determined not to repeat the mistake he had made with Katherine. Libby was to be married off as quickly as possible and, at fifteen, it was high time, preferably to someone of decent pedigree.

Libby waggled her good ankle, watching her jewelled slipper shimmer in the torchlight.

"Honestly, Katherine. Did you see William Throckmartin today? Oh, my goodness, what a fright. Why do you suppose he blinks like that all the time or was it just nerves? And do you suppose he really thought I should be interested in a discussion about the drapery business?"

Katherine laughed. "I have to confess the boy is a buffoon, and what about Master Stephen Wainwright? A fine leg and superbly dressed but so puffed up with is own importance. I swear I was never so bored by a fellow, there's nothing I hate more than a man who blows so loudly upon his own trumpet."

After a few moments reflective silence Libby rolled onto her back.

"Truly Katherine, I don't believe there will be anyone I wish to wed with. I begin to think that perhaps matrimony isn't for me. I should never wish to marry someone I could not like. Oh, if only I had your good fortune when it comes to picking a husband."

Katherine bridled, recalling her own man, slow to anger and quick to forgive, tender and considerate at all times; except for in the marriage bed of course and she required no tenderness there. It was no genteel union and sometimes, he grew so fierce, it was almost as if he was angry with her, although she'd done nothing wrong.

"You should remember, Libby, that when it comes to selecting a husband one should look for more than a pretty face, good manners or a heavy purse. A man needs to have passion. The best husband is not necessarily the richest. My own dear heart may never shower me in jewels but there are other compensations."

Libby bit her lip as Katherine preened herself in the looking glass.

"You are blessed, Katherine," she admitted. "It is your looks that have gained you such good fortune, but I can never hope to be so lucky. More and more these days I think of entering a nunnery, maybe I should find contentment there."

"A nunnery! God forbid. It would be all maudlin prayer and chills in a nunnery, Libby. You'd be miserable."

Libby turned away to the window.

Katherine was right. She was not devout enough; she was earthy; she wanted a home and a family, lots of dogs, and a loving man at table. Smiling unseeing across the barnyard, Libby pictured herself the wife of a kind, humorous fellow, whose wit was a great deal sharper than his knife. A fellow she could rely on to be a loving father to her children. And, as she grew warm from the thought, she pictured the scene, a pretty room, a roaring fire, children playing before it and her husband, reading by the hearth. And as she pictured it, her imaginary man looked up from his book and smiled at her, his eyes full of love. And with a start, Libby dropped her comb and tried to rub the image away, for such a thing could never be.

***

Libby stood in her mother's private chamber with her damp kerchief entwined in her fingers.

"A nunnery, Libby? Whatever do you mean? You have never once displayed the wish to devote yourself to God. What has happened to bring on this sudden change of heart?"

"Nothing Mother, except I suppose, the question of my marriage. I find I am not cut out to be a wife, the idea of a husband offends me, and I wish to make my vows to Christ."

Eleanor narrowed her eyes as she looked at her daughter's lowered head. Something had happened. Only six months ago Libby had been carefree and happy but now, she was drawn and lacklustre, and if her eyes did not deceive her, the girl was growing thin. Eleanor reached out and drew her daughter closer.

"What has happened, Lib? You can tell me. Why are you becoming a sad eyed woman? Won't you confide in me, and let me help you?"

"It is nothing that's happened, Mother. I am just growing up, I suspect. Childhood is such a fleeting thing and now it has gone, I find I miss it."

"But you sound like an old woman and are not yet sixteen. Are you sure you have not suffered some hurt?"

Libby shook her head mutely and Eleanor admitted defeat.

"Very well then, Child. I shall speak to Ned on his return and, if he agrees, we can approach the Prioress at Llanthony where I am benefactress. If at any time you should change your mind we will be only too happy to hear it. For now, My Dear, I think it best we keep this conversation between ourselves."

"Thank you, Mother," Libby forced herself to smile.

As Katherine grew larger with Huw's child, Libby retreated deeper into misery. Everyone at Thornhold was troubled, apart from Katherine whose happiness made her blind to all else. Eleanor worried about Libby, Huw railed inwardly against his unhappy marriage and Ned, far from home in Yorkshire, was suffering the pangs of an unrequited love. Faced with no option, Huw was determined to prove a dutiful husband. He owed nothing to Katherine, but he must prove himself to the other family members. Ignorant of Libby's plans to take holy vows, Huw buried himself in work, and when he was forced to spend time with his wife they spoke without conversing, smiled without laughing and lived without truly loving.

***

Huw was in the barn, polishing a piece of yew that he had cut to make himself a light bow. Unable to use the weapon in combat, he hoped at least to shoot some small game. As he worked Katherine watched him from a low stool. More and more, Huw was to be found in his workshop, preferring it to the cosy claustrophobia of their chambers.

"Oh, come along, Huw, haven't you worked for long enough. You are forever burying yourself away in here and it will soon be time for dinner. Your new doublet has arrived from the tailors, and I want you to try it on before we dine. Come along, do."

He grunted something about finishing up.

"Really, Huw," she rattled on as, scarcely listening, he continued to rub the piece of wood. "You've been out since dawn. We cannot be late for dinner for there are guests tonight. The Prioress of Llanthony is here to discuss Libby's vows…"

"Her what?" Huw put down his tools and turned to her, frowning, "Vows? What are you talking about?"

"Oh, you never listen to a word I say, do you? I told you weeks ago. Her intention is to enter the priory. She says she has no wish to be wed. I daresay it is some girlish delicacy or something. She intends to devote herself to Christ, which is ridiculous, although, to be honest, what with the babe coming, I can do with all the prayers I can get."

Huw threw down his chisel and left the workshop. After a moment, Katherine followed.

"Wait for me," she demanded, but Huw quickly outstripped her, and she was left behind. A few minutes later Katherine rushed into the hall. "Huw!" she called angrily, "Huw?"

***

Huw did not enter the house but veered off toward the gardens where he guessed Libby would be huddled in an arbour with a book. Hero, hearing his approach, barked suddenly and Libby leapt to her feet, her book falling to the ground.

"Huw! You startled me! Are you looking for Katherine? She is not here; I have not seen her…"

As his anger became apparent, her voice trailed off. For a few moments they listened to the song of a blackbird, a joy that was not echoed in their hearts. He stepped toward her, his body angled forward.

"What is this nonsense I hear about you entering a priory?"

Libby's flush deepened at the menace in his tone.

"I thought it for the best, Huw. I find no favour with any suitor that calls, and I cannot remain unwed forever…"

"That is the feeblest excuse I ever heard. If you like none of these fellows then wait until the right one comes along …and if he doesn't, well of course you can remain unwed. There is no shame in spinsterhood. Before God, Libby, you must stay here with us. I'd sooner see you a spinster than a dried-up nun, shut away from the sunshine. There's no joy in a convent, Child, and you'll be miserable. You've not a drop of religious fervour in your body!"

"Yes I have …" she began to protest but he was standing too close, trembling with intent. She wondered that he cared so much. Her voice trickled away; her argument quashed. He was right, she was not cut out to be a nun. She loved her freedom, her dogs, the garden, she loved to stuff herself with festive food until her stomach bulged, she loved bright shiny objects. But, on the other hand, she would not marry with a whey-faced boy or an elderly baronet. She could think of no alternative other than the priory. She stammered her weak defence, clutching at the one word he uttered that was not true.

"Don't call me Child. I am not a child. I am a grown woman, and I will never marry. I know that in my heart. There can be no happiness for me in that direction, and the options for a woman are few. I cannot go off on crusade to fight the infidel, and neither can I stay here."

She looked away, biting her lip to ward off tears.

"Why?" Huw's heart banged sickeningly. He gripped her by the elbows and shook her gently as if to dislodge her decision.

"You are wrong, Libby …" he groaned. "Of course, you must stay here, you are *needed* here. We love you …I love you …"

Her black eyes opened; their faces so close that she could feel his breath on her cheek. After a long moment she looked away, speaking so softly as to be almost inaudible.

"I know but, do you not see, that is why I must go …?"

The full impact of his predicament hit Huw like a wall. He released Libby's elbows so that she almost fell and, stumbling to the arbour she perched on the fragrant seat, trying not to give in to overwhelming grief. A tear dropped onto her wrist.

What was it with these Thornbury women and their incessant tears?

Libby sniffed, dabbed her cheeks.

"I know I am sinful and will probably burn in hell. Please understand that I must leave. I would rather die than be suffered to watch as you and Katherine fill the manor with children."

Huw moved beside her. "Libby," he groaned.

"Just leave me, Huw." she whispered. "There is nothing you can say. No remedy. Just allow me to do what I must."

Huw reached out and raised her chin, forcing her to look at him.

"I will do as you wish, Libby. I see you are right, but I would have you know one thing. I think I have loved you from the first moment I saw you. Your sister is nothing to me, nothing but a duty and a burden."

"Oh, don't say that …"

"I will be a good husband to her, if I can … but know this, Sweetheart. I love you and shall continue to, wherever you are, whatever you do. The feeling I had for Katherine was not love. I was a fool. You, Libby, are my best and only love, so take that with you wherever you may go. I pray that it may prove some comfort to you."

Like a cornered deer, Libby hesitated, drinking in his words as the touch of his fingers seared her skin. For a long moment, they stared at one another, the love in their eyes flooding into one another's souls. Then she fled, her twisted foot for once no hindrance to speed, and emptiness encompassed Huw like a shroud. Alone in the arbour, Huw the Bowman slumped upon the camomile lawn.

From an unlit chamber that looked south across the gardens, Katherine listened to her husband's sobs. His grief grated like barbs. For what seemed an eternity, she stared blindly across the darkening gardens before silently closing the casement.

***

Libby's hair spread like black silk across her pillow, her relaxed limbs and softly rising chest belying the turbulence through which her spirit moved. Holding the candle high, Katherine looked down upon her sister's sleeping face.

From the moment she was born, Libby had stolen an unfair measure of the love that should have been Katherine's. Even though she was unfashionably dark and misshapen their parents made no secret of the fact that Libby was the favoured child. When they were small, Ned had adored his youngest sister and even the servants doted upon Libby, feeding her titbits and seeing to her every comfort. Katherine was not even second best. For a long time, she thought she had overcome the jealousy that marred their childhood. Libby seemed to love Katherine and as long as she loved her best, all would be well. As they grew Katherine tried to be nice, tried to make their relationship special, but Libby's love was indiscriminate. She loved everyone and Katherine new she came a poor second.

The resentment lessened as they neared adulthood, and a sort of friendship blossomed. Until today, Katherine had at last found happiness. Married to Huw, she could afford to be gracious, magnanimous. She had the man she loved, and the coming child would mend the great hole that had opened at the death of her father. The future promised to be content. Ned would return home with his new bride, and the house would soon overflow with children. They'd not miss Libby once she was gone. She was no longer needed. The war was over now, and the future bright with the prospect of weddings and births, and parties. But now, the tree of contentment she had so carefully nurtured had been hewn down.

And it was Huw who wielded the axe.

His declaration to Libby had destroyed her. All along she had been second best. Nobody ever loved her best. Only Father: and he was gone.

Katherine closed her eyes, remembering the security of his knee. His face swam in her mind's eye, the safety of his big hands, his deep, kind voice. For an instant she was an infant again and Libby was nothing but a twisted monstrosity, confined to the nursery. Father was laughing as he tossed her into the air above his head, his eyes shining with love. She smiled wide with remembered joy until quite suddenly the image blurred and his laughing mouth distorted into a fly-infested gape, a maggot wriggled from his eye.

The spectre reached for Katherine in the cold darkness, calling her name.

"Katie sweetheart! I always loved you..."

Katherine dropped the candle. It guttered for a moment while she remained transfixed at the horror conjured by her own mind. Unnoticed, the flame flickered and sprang into life, finding fuel in the fabric, growing in strength until the flames began to lick steadily up the bed hanging.

Hero woke first. She shook her head, whined and scrabbled at Libby's pillow until she stirred and coughed. Rasing up on one elbow, Libby blinked in the dim light, coughed again as smoke filled her nose, trickled to her lungs. Flames leapt at the side of her bed. Suddenly wide away, she snatched off her nightcap, held it over her face as she sprang from the bed.

"Katherine!" she screamed, suddenly spying her sister. "Look out! You are alight."

Snatching up the smouldering blanket, she rushed at her sister and knocked her to the floor, dousing the flames that licked along her nightdress and shrivelled her hair. Gagging from the stench of burning, Libby raced to the door. As she opened it fresh air blew in, fuelling the belching flames. Libby screamed, grabbed Katherine beneath the arms and dragged her unconscious body from the room.

As the servants came running, Libby dumped her sister unceremoniously on the passage floor, coughing and crying, tears stinging her eyes. At the same moment Eleanor appeared at the end of the corridor, Huw rushed onto the scene, hastily tying on a robe.

Quickly realising the situation, and barking orders to the servants to fetch water, he scooped Katherine into his arms and carried her from the house. Eleanor was just behind him with Libby limping in their wake. But then, remembering her dog, she halted and turned back toward the blazing house.

As he deposited her in the forecourt, Katherine was just regaining consciousness. Without waiting to ascertain her condition, Huw turned and ran back into the fray. The house servants and grooms formed a chain, throwing buckets of water in a hopeless attempt to douse the fire. A small dog barked frantically from the upper floor where smoke was belching from the shattered window. Everyone was wailing. Huw plunged inside.

"Libby!" With his arm across his mouth, he peered through the belching smoke. "Where are you?"

"I'm here, Huw. Here, take Hero, she wriggles so." Libby thrust the small dog into his arms and together they made for the stairs, coughing and wheezing. One the lower floor, Libby darted away, disappeared into the library. "Libby!" Huw hollered, the belching smoke blinding now. When a few moments later, her blackened face appeared, he saw she clutched a coffer of jewels beneath her arm and carried her father's colours in the other hand. The great flag hampered her progress as she limped barefoot before Huw. As they staggered into the thronging courtyard, they tripped over salvaged objects scattered on the gravel and collided with the bailiff.

"I fear we cannot save this wing, Sir, but there's a chance the rest of the house can be salvaged."

"Stay there," Huw snarled. "Don't dare move!" Thrusting Hero into Libby's arms, Huw plunged back inside. Libby collapsed on the garden wall, clutching her dog to her chest and watching the flames leap like devils inside her home.

Shadows passed across the window. *It must be saved,* she prayed. *Oh God, please save Thornhold, please don't let it burn.* The faces of the household women were turned upward, watching as the old building was engulfed. As Libby looked on, a cloud passed over the moon and a brisk wind blew up, fanning the flames. While the Manor burned, The Book of Thornhold lay where it had been thrown; the glorious pages turning in the breeze.

With palpitating heart, she turned toward her mother, who knelt nearby with Katherine cradled in her arms. The moon thrust its friendly face from behind a cloud and revealed her sister's burned scalp; the skin on the lower half of her jaw was completely seared away. As they carried Katherine toward the safety of the dower house, Libby remained on the garden wall and prayed for the deliverance of her home.

Part Five
The Devil's Roar

Grant us oft times while on earth we shall tarry
To come to Hayles with most sober mode
To see and visit the precious portion of his blood
Which dropped from the wound that was full wide
Made with the spear of Longinus in His side.
(A monk of Hayles, 16th century)

Gloucestershire - September 1537

The travellers came, some walking, some riding, following the same dusty track trodden by the Thornbury children after the pestilence, one hundred and ninety years before. The road led them onward through the countryside where peasants paused in their work to watch the strangers pass. As they skirted a cluster of green hills, the pilgrims paused to admire the gentle vale of Evesham.

A scattering of small hills peppered the landscape like islands in a vast green sea; a sea that lapped the path that led through a meadow past a tithe barn. The travellers rested here, allowing their mounts to graze while they supped upon pasties and ale.

The group made a bright splash of colour on the sombre landscape, the clothing of the rich contrasting sharply with the rougher garments of the poor. While the landed gentlemen and their wives sat on the damp grass, too weary for conversation, the humbler folk clustered together, keeping their voices low in deference to their betters. The meadow ran down to a riverbank where a line of birches dipped their branches into the cool depths. The roof of a mill peeked from the canopy of the wood and, floating on the late afternoon breeze, came the outraged voice of the miller's dog.

Once the pilgrims were rested, they brushed the debris from their velvets and remounted the horses to continue on their journey, the poorer folk following at a distance to avoid the mud kicked up by the horses. As they journeyed onward, they sang a pilgrim's chant.

"A bolle and a bagge
He bar by his syde
And hundred ampulles

On his hat seten
Signes of Synay,
And Shelles of Galice,
And many a conche
On his cloke,
And keys of Rome,
And the Vernycle bi-fore
For men sholde knowe
And se bi hise signes
Whom he sought hadde"

They reached a tiny hamlet with a fine yellow-stone church and as they began to climb the sloping hillside, their breath became short, and their voices petered out. At the summit they were afforded more views of the valley and their murmured appreciation disturbed the silent hill. A rabbit darted from cover, his white tail scudding along the side of a dry-stone wall. Further along, he dashed across the pilgrim's path where the road widened into a well-trodden route, scattered with evidence of many sheep. They followed this road until a smaller path diverted them northwest toward a strangely fashioned escarpment. With dusk falling, they journeyed onward, wondering about the ancient people that once traversed these hills and, as they began the descent, the trees opened onto parkland. For the first time the pilgrims glimpsed their destination; the great Cistercian Abbey of Hayles, home of the Holy Blood of Christ.

***

Brother Thomas grunted as he reached further into the herber in search of a mullien shoot that still bore some flower. The bed was over-spilling with aromatic foliage, and pushing aside some branches of hemp, he spied his prey. With a sharp knife, the old monk cut some tall shafts and thrust them into his basket. Nothing soothed piles half as well as mullein and there was no man who needed his piles soothing as desperately as Brother Lawrence.

Brother Thomas shook his foot to dislodge small stones lodged in his sandals and continued along the gravel path; as he went he plucked a sprig of blue-flowered gentian, and some flowering heads of dove's foot, so good for colicky wind. His osier basket almost full, Brother Thomas glanced at the sun and estimated that the vespers bell would soon be sounding. He looked about for Brother Mark, a young novitiate who was undergoing training in his care. There was no sign of his off-white robe anywhere in the infirmary garden, so Brother Thomas waddled beneath an archway and into the fresher air of the orchard.

Brother Mark was energetically gathering wasp-holed apples from the grass; he looked up at the old man's approach and hurried toward him, his apron full of fruit.

"Look, Brother, so many apples were brought down by yesterday's wind! They will be good eating if we cut away the wasp holes and keep a watch for maggots."

The old monk made appreciative noises and wondered how many apples the boy had already tested for soundness. Gluttony and a loose tongue were the least of this novitiate's problems. He gestured that they should make haste and together they moved toward the infirmary door which, as usual in the warmer months, stood open. As they entered Brother Mark kept up a discourse about the orchard his family owned at Thornhold Manor.

"Such a size of apple you never did see, Brother Thomas. My mother always says that the orchard stands on the site of an old Saxon burial place, and that it is the bones of the old Saxons that unfailingly provide such a fine glut."

Brother Thomas stopped and looked down at the untonsured head of his companion.

"Brother Mark, you must learn to curb your tongue. Intemperate speech leads to intemperate action. The dispensation from the abbot was to allow us to converse while I provided you with full knowledge of herbal-lore and medicine, it was not for the indulgence of idle chatter. Quiet contemplation is the key to monastic life. Now, away to Vespers with you. I will follow at a more sedate pace."

As the boy sped off with unseemly haste, the old monk shook his head.

"What in the world is this generation of monks coming to." He wondered. There was little decorum left in the young of the day. It was all speed and no haste.

Placing the basket on the infirmary table that took up most of the stone-flagged floor, Brother Thomas passed into the under croft, on through the chapter house and vestry, and into the south transept of the great abbey church. As usual a spiritual peace descended upon him as he took his place in the quire and prepared for vespers. The late evening sun streamed through the high windows, casting God's light upon the congregation, and the bells reverberated throughout the building.

There were just twenty-one brethren left at Hayles now, not including the Abbot, but Brother Thomas remembered when the quire had been overflowing and the community prosperous. Brother Lawrence had told Thomas tales of the rich, northern monasteries where in times past the brethren had numbered three hundred choir monks alone. There had never been such numbers or prosperity at Hayles, and the monastery had always struggled against inadequate benefactors and incompetent bursars. The one thing that had set Hayles apart and fed their ever-hungry coffers was the Holy Blood, housed in its magnificent shrine in the chevet. Indeed, the most recent alterations to the east end of the church meant that the shrine was no longer central as originally planned. It sat just off centre, but its glorious canopy was not over-shadowed by the five newer chapels.

The story of how the blood arrived at Hayles had always enchanted Thomas and he never failed to send a prayer of thanks for such a gift. He made a mental note to tell the novitiate the tale when they next met.

When the abbey's founder, Richard, the Duke of Cornwall, had become King of the Romans he was accompanied to Germany by his son Edmund. There they discovered a quantity of Christ's blood, taken from his body by a Jew at the time of the crucifixion. In those days, followers of Christ were not looked upon kindly, and this Christian Jew was jeered and imprisoned, along with the blood, in a stone house outside the city. There, with no contact from the outside world, the Jew remained for forty-two long, lonely years.

Then, when the Emperors Titus and Vespasian besieged Jerusalem they discovered the Jew still alive, in his prison with the vessel of blood cradled in his lap. They questioned him in fear and wonderment and then demanded that he give them the blood. When he refused, they seized the vessel from his hands, whereon the Jew fell as dead as stone. The blood was placed in the Temple of Peace in Rome where it remained until the Emperor Charlemagne stormed the city.

In Germany, the relic became part of the ritual anointing of Emperors until Edmund begged to be given a small amount of the blood. At first, the precious liquid was kept at Wallingford castle until it was passed for safe keeping to the monks of Hayles. The relic was received amid great ceremony and for hundreds of years since pilgrims had made their way, some on horseback, some on foot, and some from overseas, to visit the Holy Blood of Christ.

***

The monks filed from the church and made their way to the refectory for collation and, as they did so, the pilgrim's bell rang at the Gatehouse. The brethren knew it was just another party arriving to see the Holy Blood but, since they were an enclosed order, they made no detour. It was the Prior's job to conduct the visitors to the shrine and offer the nobler members accommodation with the Abbot, while the common folk stayed in the humbler guest lodgings.

The monks ate a frugal meal in silence, trying not to grudge the venison and fine wine being partaken of in the Abbot's lodging. They listened as a chapter of the gospel was read to them, chewing their food slowly, and giving thanks for it. After collation there was time for a short period of scripture reading and study in the north cloister before the bell rang for Compline, the last office of the day. The monks would all be abed before eight o'clock, for sleep was precious, they'd be woken at a quarter before two to hear night Vigil.

The next morning when Mark ventured into the infirmary garden in search of Brother Thomas, a muslin veil of mist still shrouded the sun. He discovered the old monk feeding crumbs to the birds. He looked up at the boy's approach, brushed his hands and bent to pick up a basket. As they walked on, he offered it to the boy to carry.

Today they were to collect seeds for drying and storing and, as they gathered them, Mark recited the properties of each plant and its prime uses.

Brother Thomas was a kind man but one who expected his pupil to learn quickly, and Mark enjoyed his lessons for at least he was able to talk. Of all the rules of the monastery Mark found the rule of silence the hardest of all.

Brother Thomas' inner peace was infectious, and Mark felt his spirits calm as he settled down for his lesson. It was difficult to believe that anything had changed in the garden since the far-off days of the abbey's foundation. The ancient stone walls surrounding the garden were covered in cushions of moss, the walls of the monastic buildings spotted with lichen. The precinct slept in the late summer sun as it had always done, and the daily monastic round also continued unchecked.

As they passed among the St John's wort and the evening primrose, Brother Thomas plucked spent flower heads and showed Mark how to free the seeds from their pods. Some of the seeds scattered around their feet, falling on fertile ground where many would germinate and grow. Ordered, as monastic life was, the plants in the infirmary garden frolicked.

Hayles never changed, its peace unblemished by the wounded lion that roared against them from his gilded throne. But one by one the king's demands were growing more difficult to accommodate. Despite the Abbot having sworn, four years ago, to uphold the Act of Supremacy, an act that invalidated the pope and installed Henry VIII as the supreme head of the English Church, other things at Hayles continued in the old way. The monks, particularly the elder brethren, deplored this heresy but having sworn to uphold the king's will, they now wished only to be left to their prayers. Isolated as they were, deep in the Gloucestershire countryside, they buried their heads and stopped their ears against the horrific stories issuing from court.

Some said that the king had gone mad, but nobody dared to say it very loudly, for royal retribution was vicious. Henry Tudor's reach was long, and nobody was safe. They listened, disbelievingly, to tales of the terrible execution of the king's friends, Sir Thomas More and Bishop Fisher. These were men who had refused to compromise their faith and, in putting their God before their king, had chosen death above dishonour. For the sake of a proud, pretty face the King had angered Spain and put aside his Spanish wife, Catherine. On a whim, the king had entered the league of the devil, severed English ties with Rome and laid waste a thousand or more years of religious devotion.

Henry, however, had grown tired of his pretty queen and Anne Boleyn now lay headless in a makeshift tomb. That same year, the men of Lincolnshire had risen and marched against the king, but their protest had been futile and was viciously put down. The realm trembled while many a pious head was swiped off in retribution.

Visitors from the outside brought news of smaller houses surrendering voluntarily; the Abbots were pensioned off and some of the higher monks provided with livings at small parish churches. The rest of the brethren were dispersed among larger houses. When the king's men arrived at Hayles to take a thorough audit and probe intensively into the monk's discipline, the brethren were full of fear but at length, the men had ridden away, leaving the abbey unscathed.

The apple blossom was bursting from the ancient orchard trees, when two dispossessed brethren of Calder Abbey arrived. Brother Ambrose and Brother Paul spent the first few days in the infirmary recovering from the rigours of the journey, which they'd taken on foot across rough countryside. Then, with their strength regained, they regaled the brethren of Hayles with tales of the atrocities that were occurring in the outside world.

"The world has grown hostile to monks, Brothers, it is a cruel, secular world where sin creeps across the land. Preachers for the reformation tramp the English roads, denouncing monks and friars of all denominations. It is unsafe to be a man of God now, for we are branded as devils, and our abbeys denounced as nests of debauchery."

Mark let his gaze sweep across his own fellow brethren and wondered if they too would be classed as sinners. It was true that the Prior sometimes used ungodly language, but did that constitute real sin? He knew that last year the Sacrist, Brother John, had been before the abbot for displaying some un-brotherly affection for one of the novices, but he was still a good monk. Life was harsh here, and comforts few. Sometimes the warmth of another human being helped a fellow get by but that didn't make him evil.

The bursar tallied his books with a dedication far outside the bounds of duty, Mark smiled as he remembered he was gently mocked about his avarice. But he wasn't a bad man or even a greedy one, and Mark would swear, his devotion to God was unquestionable. In turn, Mark assessed his companions and decided that, although none of them were perfect, they were all good Christians. A monastic vocation was testing, and sometimes they struggled but, on the whole, Hayles was a devout community, serving both God and the king the best they could.

Trouble began in earnest when Queen Jane, the daughter of the ambitious Seymour family, died in childbed after giving Henry a son. With no devout wife to curb his excesses, the king grew evermore vengeful. He unleashed Cromwell and his hounds upon the larger religious houses, and his latest heresy was to outlaw the religious shrines and relics, upon which so many great houses relied.

September 1538

Mark sat at Brother Thomas' feet listening as his elders discussed their increasing peril. He was drowsy but prevented from sleeping by the voices of the brethren that rose higher as their agitation increased. Try as they might they could not digest the latest demands upon them.

"The abbey church is in disrepair. Abbot Sagar had promised me we could use this season's income from the shrine to repair the stonework above the quire. And the tiled floor in the porch is now so uneven it poses a danger. There is no hope of maintaining the buildings without the revenue from the Holy Blood. We will be impoverished. Barely able to offer alms or even to maintain the scriptorium. As our members age, the strain upon our purse grows, and the work force dwindles. These days, there are few new members joining us, and more and more of us take refuge in the infirmary."

The bursar sat down again and scratched his tonsure. Mark had never seen any member of the community so upset, but he guessed the bursar's duties must be taxing in these difficult times. Brother Francis, the head of the scriptorium, stood up next. He was calmer and hesitant, almost apologetic.

"Yes, you are quite right, Brother, the scriptorium is in a bad state of repair, and the damp is so bad that the books need to be relocated before the winter. It is heavy work, and I am not as strong as I once was. I need to request the assistance of a novitiate, tomorrow, if they can be spared."

"I can do that for you, Brother Francis," volunteered Mark. "If Brother Thomas will allow."

The two other novices raised their hands to indicate that they were also willing to help, and Brother Thomas nodded his agreement. As Brother Francis sat down again, Brother Jude stood up, a younger monk whose beliefs veered toward reform.

"Surely, if there is duplicity in an order and the abbot is lax, then it's the King's duty, as head of the church, to wean it out. We have nothing to fear here, for our abbey is incorrupt. In my opinion, it's not the revenue from the shrine that we will miss so much as the income from the sheep. Our flocks have halved in recent times, and the taxes upon the export of wool are crippling. Where once a thousand sheep grazed now there are but a few hundred. The tithes from the mills and lay churches are too slow to arrive, and too quickly absorbed. Perhaps at the next General Chapter meeting the Abbot should request aid from Citeaux, for Beaulieu, our mother house, has ever been willing to give aid where it's due. I pray that we can survive until the storm blows over. We must remember that God is with us, and the righteous will triumph."

The octogenarian, Brother Lawrence, staggered to his feet, and clung to the back of his chair.

"Tell that to Abbot Thirst of Fountains. It is not safe to ask for help. In this day and age to speak of injustice is to speak against the king and we all know what follows then. Torture! Death! Look at Abbot Kirby who merely questioned the king's right to supremacy, he was deposed with no trial. And those monks who were forced by the rebels to join the Pilgrimage of Grace, or see their abbey burn. Everyone was executed, and for what? Raising questions, that's all. It is a sorry kingdom where a monarch seeks to rule men's minds. Those Abbeys were true to their God yet still Cromwell accused them of manifest sin, and carnal and abominable living. It is a scandal and Henry's good mother must be shamed in her grave. Why, I mind as a lad seeing the last Plantagenet ride through the City of York. Now, he was a king to behold. The people loved that man, and his brother before him, because they were pious and just rulers. God's curse be on all Tudors…"

A murmur of discomfiture licked around the room, and to diffuse the situation Brother Thomas placed a calming hand on the old monk's shoulder.

"Peace Brother Lawrence," he soothed as he led him away. "You are over wrought; I expect it is due to the dandelion and hemlock I dosed you with. No doubt you'll be much recovered in the morning. Come, let us to bed now, and first thing tomorrow we will ease you with a bloodletting. Remember, bloodletting means you'll be given a hearty breakfast. Come along, Old Fellow, say good night and off we go."

Mark hid his face in his folded arms and grinned into his elbow, knowing full well that the old monk's outspokenness was not bred by the overuse of hemlock but from an unholy hatred of all things Tudor. Born into a freer world, he had witnessed the steady disintegration of monastic life under the Tudors and remembered with nostalgia the piety of the Plantagenet kings.

After Compline, the prior summoned Brother John to his office and Mark was asked to replace the candles before the hight altar to ensure they remained burning all night. Forgetting decorum, he scampered off to do as he was bid, passing through the empty chapter house and vestry and entering the abbey church via the south transept door. His sandals pattered across the tiled floor but, as he reached the presbytery, he remembered himself, skidded to a halt and bowed devoutly before the high cross. Murmuring a prayer for forgiveness, he checked the candles as requested and then looked about him.

Moonlight streamed through the vaulted windows, illuminating the church interior and softening the deeper shadows. It was perfectly silent. Mark was seldom in the church between services, and the depth of silence made it seem the angels were holding their own breath to allow God's voice to be heard.

Mark moved soundlessly toward the apse, where the shrine lay guarded by its five radiating chapels. He paused upon the steps behind the altar to drink in the beauty of the blue moonlight when, suddenly, the peace was shattered with a loud bang.

Mark cried out in alarm. "Who's there?"

And then, in the moonlight, he saw an angel, clad all in white, her golden hair shining, her flowing gown illuminated in the dark. She was like a sculpture, her chiselled hands cupping her face. At her feet lay a book and it was this that she had dropped. Mark shook his head, dispelling the vision. He realised it was a girl, not an angel.

Members of the laity were forbidden access to the monastic buildings, and he was quite certain that a woman would never be allowed inside. But, remembering the manners he'd learned at his mother's knee, he picked up the book and held it out to her. She dimpled a smile, and Marks fears lessened.

She was no more than twelve years old, and her feet were bare. At fourteen, Mark had seen few women, other than his mother and sister, but he smiled and rubbed the end of his nose.

"I'm sorry if I startled you," he said. "I had thought the church empty. Brother John is with the abbot. Was it him you were wishing to see?"

"No," she answered at last. "I was hoping to see the Holy Blood. I rode in with my father and a group of pilgrims this afternoon, but the roads were long, and we arrived too late to be shown the shrine today. The abbot said we should see it in the morning, but I couldn't sleep. I went for a walk and found myself here. It was so quiet, I thought I could creep in unobserved. I'm sorry if that was wrong. I have waited so long to see it, and my father says that since the days of the great abbeys are few, this is our last chance to visit the shrine."

She stroked the cover of her book and Mark saw it was a fine book of hours, a compact volume, highly decorative and small enough to be held in the young girl's hand. He risked another look at her face.

She was fair. Her eyes innocent and her cheeks plump. She was, as yet, unspotted by the world and her purity touched him. Although not entirely sure she was real, he gestured her toward the shrine. The golden canopy dwarfed them with its splendour.

"And did you see the blood?" he asked, pointing toward it. She shook her head and then leaned nearer. She was quite close to him and smelled …like his mother - of rosewater and almonds. As he lit another candle to allow her a better view her face was also illuminated. Her eyes shone, and her cheeks were tinged pink, like the palest rose. He inhaled and his senses swam. As she gazed upon the holy relic, he put his face so close to hers that his breath stirred her hair as he whispered the miraculous story of how it came to be there.

"Oh my," she breathed. "I had no idea. Thank you so much for showing me."

Mark took the candle and, placing a finger to his lips, escorted her to the north transept door. She waited while Mark opened the portal, then passed through it, back into the secular world. Then she turned to face him, the moonlight shining behind her like a nimbus and very shyly, she asked his name.

"My name is Mark," he whispered. "What are you called?"

"My name is Anne. I thank you, Brother Mark, both for the pretty tales and for concealing my trespass. Goodbye to you, Sir."

Mark listened until her footsteps ceased then, emitting a sigh, he began to walk back to the dormitory. It they had been seen, he would have been in a great deal of trouble. The church's view of women was a dim one, and he knew that, at one time, women had not been allowed to enter at all. Even now, their presence was strictly monitored, and female pilgrims were always housed outside the precinct and escorted to the shrine by both the abbot and the prior. Even then, they were only admitted at times when the brethren were safely tucked away from feminine corruption. But, luckily, he didn't feel contaminated; he didn't feel contaminated at all.

He sped back to the dormitory with his head in turmoil, recalling the sweet aroma of her hair, knowing that her glorious feminine freshness must forever remain a memory.

As the boy bent down to remove his sandals, he came to realise what a spectacle he must have seemed to Anne. He looked down at his off-white robe, stained with berries and dirt from the infirmary garden. It was caught up at the waist with a cord and the ragged hem hung unevenly. The sleeves that covered his grubby hands were in tatters and, to make matters worse, he had grown apace this season, and the robe was far too short, revealing his hairy ankles and dirty, broken-nailed feet protruding like an insult from the bottom. Mark peered into the window glass and grimaced at the scarecrow who peered back at him. His heart sank, adding the sin of vanity to his list of wrongdoing.

October 1538

October blew in bright and cold; the frigid chill chasing away the few remaining summer blooms, and forming a thick crust on the infirmary chamber pots. As the day wore on the heavy frost surrendered to the powerful rays of the sun and Mark grew warm with the exertion of clearing the gardens.

All morning he had been cutting down the woody herbaceous stalks and tidying leaves into a neat pile in the corner by the precinct wall. He was alone in the garden, which allowed worries to tumble in his head. At noon he paused his labours to rest in a niche in the north cloister wall. It was a favourite spot of his; an ivy-covered stone bench, the back of which was inscribed with the words of St Bernard:

"Bonum est nos hic esse, quia homo vivit purius, cadit rarius, surgit velocius incedit cautius, quiescit, securius, moritur felicius, purgatur citius, præmiatur copiosius"

"It is good to be here. Here man more purely lives, less oft doth fall, more promptly rises, walks with stricter need, more safely rests, dies happier, is freed earlier from cleansing fires, and gains withal a brighter crown."

Mark loved those words that celebrated the security to be found in a life dedicated to God. The seat was warm, far warmer than the rest of the garden. He leaned back, and the abbey cat leapt up beside him to rub his head ecstatically against Mark's chin. The sun was welcome this late in the season. He closed his eyes, just for a moment and let his troubles drift away. Just as he was dropping off, he jumped as if someone had shaken him awake. It would never do to let sleep overwhelm him for Brother John was not far away. He was busy in the infirmary, dosing the older brethren who were suffering from autumn chills.

Last night Brother Lawrence's recurrent chesty cough had been liberally dosed with liquorice root and maidenhead fern and he now sat up in bed, well-wrapped against the cold. Brother Thomas worried that the shortness of his breath had a more sinister connotation and had instructed Mark to search for some bryony and hog's fennel to be brewed ready for when the old man awoke. As the seasons pivoted, many of the older monks fell victim to sniffles and, in readiness for this, the infirmary shelves were well stocked with medicines.

Small white clouds scudded past the church tower and a brilliant sun smiled indifferently as the lodge bell rang out violently. Some of the brethren strayed from their allotted tasks to discover the cause of the commotion. They hastened towards the lodge, looking on aghast as the inner precinct filled with men at arms.

A leather-clad man removed his helmet, barking curt instructions to the abbot. They could not hear his words but his manner told them all they needed to know.

"It's the King's men. Come to destroy our holy shrine," they muttered.

The monks surged forward, pleading, begging to be left in peace but they were given short shrift. The king's men drew their swords and drove them back. There was nothing they could do but watch as the king's men threw open the great west door and filed into the church.

The silence didn't last. Soon the sound of splintering wood, smashing glass spoiled the brightness of the day. They clung together, their bodies trembling with unfamiliar rage. Mark thought of the gilt workmanship on the shrine and dashed moisture from his cheek. Sick at heart, for the first time in his life, he wished he knew how to wield a sword.

Cromwell's man emerged from the darkness carelessly juggling the phial of holy blood and tossed it to his master. The callous treatment of their sacred relic made the brethren cry out in horror. Latimer spun on his heel; his eyes narrowed as he scanned the faces of the congregated monks. Then he snarled at their sorry expressions.

"You fools. You've all been duped. It is nought but pig's blood. Your Sacrist replenishes it monthly. Brother Lawrence, he is named is he not? Oh, yes, we are well-informed. We know all about you." His mockery drew his fellows to join him. He pointed rudely at the monks.

"Would you look at these gullible fools? Can you credit that they really believed themselves to be the keepers of Christ's blood. Such arrogance in a house of the meek. God's teeth, if it weren't so funny, it'd make me spew."

He spat rudely, and Mark saw a great gob of spittle cling to the hem of the Prior's robe, but he gave no reaction; his inner thoughts were veiled. *Why doesn't he act? Why doesn't he fight?*

Mark narrowed his eyes, for the first time in his life feeling a simmering hatred.

No doubt the Abbot has warned him not to show violence. After all, his main concern is to keep his new post as Royal Chaplain, he thought. *But how can God let this happen?*

Further sounds of desecration issued from the church. A frigid rain began to fall, the bright skies now dark, the monks hung their heads, too miserable to even pray. The bad weather hastened their departure and, hiding his relief the abbot accompanied them to the gate, engaging them in conversation as they went. Mark watched him politely bid the man goodbye and bade him to give his regards to the King's Secretary.

It is as though they called to take a cup a wine. Mark thought in disbelief. Mounted now, the leader's grip was brutal upon the bridle. His horse pranced on the spot, churning the sward to mud until given his head and allowed to gallop away across the hills.

Mark was too stunned to move as the cavalcade dwindled away. Slowly his wits returned. It was cold, he was wet through, and realised the prime bell had not rung, although it must be long past time. The brethren dispersed slowly, receiving no guidance from their abbot who hastened back to his lodgings. Mark heard the sound of someone sobbing and he noticed Brother Francis seemed to be having some trouble moving. He held his head in his hand while his companion helped him gently along.

Another huddle of monks were engaged in earnest conversation, their arms gesticulating and their anger evident, but Brother John walked alone, in the direction of the abbey church. Mark ran after him, his footsteps loud upon the gravel. Brother John turned.

"Still running, Brother Mark? What a strange manner of boy you are. Will you never learn?"

Mark grimaced an apology, and John smiled his gentle smile before placing a hand on the boy's shoulder. "Come," he said. "We are all upset, walk with me to the church."

At first the changes inside were indiscernible. The wealthy founder's grave remained untouched and, apart from mud daubed across the aisle, all else was as it should be. But, as they moved deeper into the nave, past the quire and presbytery and into the east end, the difference was stark.

The king's men had taken no care in their task but had hacked the shrine apart to gain access to the phial. Had they asked, the brethren could have shown them how to open it safely, but they had preferred brute force. Discarded offerings and pieces of gilded plaster were scattered across the floor.

The apse seemed empty, the five splendid chapels, although still intact, seemed diminished by the loss. Mark fell to his knees and tried to cover the yawning hole, but Brother John stopped him.

"Mark," he said. "What use is the shrine without the treasure it held?"

When his tears began to fall, Brother John lifted him to his feet. "Come, boy," he said gently, "let us go from here. The others will have gathered in the chapter house, we may find some comfort there. God and all his angels must be sleeping for such blasphemy to triumph unchecked. Abbot Sagar will instruct us … that is, if he isn't too intent upon saving his own neck."

To speak ill of the abbot was akin to blasphemy and Mark was shocked by Brother John's words.

"What will happen to us all, Brother John?" he wailed as they hurried back the way they'd come. He wiped his tears on his sleeves and loudly blew his nose. "How can Hayles exist without the Blood of Christ? Will it be safe in the king's keeping? Or will it be destroyed as so much else has been?"

"I fear there is little we can do to retrieve the Blood now. We can only look to ourselves, Boy. Nothing will happen yet, and I believe we have some respite, time to make proper provision for those treasures left to us. Will you help me?"

June 1539

During the dark months of uncertainty that followed, Mark's duties increased, his strong body and agile mind ensured he was in demand. Life at the abbey carried on much as it always did, and he continued to spend his mornings with Brother Thomas in the infirmary garden. The latter half of his day was spent assisting Brother Francis in the scriptorium.

Brother Francis was in the process of redesigning the interior of the scriptorium. The damp that crept through the ancient walls had begun to seep into the fabric of the books and they urgently required relocation. The only light entered the chamber by windows, set high up in the walls, leaving the lower half uncluttered. At Mark's suggestion they relocated the desks at right angles to the exterior walls to allow the light to fall directly across the desks. This both eased the scribe's eyes and extended their working day.

Shifting shelf upon shelf of huge tomes proved a long and tiring task. He then had to relocate and clean the shelves before dusting the books and replacing them; he often arrived at Vespers coated in dust. The old monk and the young novice had worked together on the project for nigh on nine months and the task was now almost completed. It was warm work, requiring plenty of ale.

Many of the books had been printed quite recently on Master Caxton's press, but many were ancient, handwritten texts, embellished by Christian scribes long since dead. Mark loved these books the best. Each turn of the thick pages emblazoned his world; opening a book was like stepping from the darkness into the infirmary garden - a splash of colour in his grey world.

Brother Francis seemed to know the history of each and every volume; he knew who had commissioned a book, who inscribed it and who had undertaken the elaborate decoration. Such was his skill that he was even able to identify some scribes through the style of their workmanship alone.

One book in particular fired Mark's imagination more than any other. It was an old book, old beyond imagination, written and decorated long before the Normans had chased away the last Saxon king. Brother Francis believed the book was created when Christianity was newly arrived in England. He pointed out to Mark how the parchment pages were rudely fashioned compared with other books, and in places the stitched binding was loose. The ornate cover was shabby and tarnished and bore the signs of age but, inside, the leaves remained as colourful as the day they were painted.

A closed book was protected from light, which stopped it from fading and preserved an illuminated page indefinitely. Mark felt he was holding hands with the scribe from more than eight centuries ago. The most wonderful thing about this particular book of gospel was that it originated to his ancestral home, Thornhold Manor. There was no indication of how it had arrived at Hayles, or why, but the abbey records stated the book had been gifted by a son of Thornhold Manor, for kindnesses rendered.

Whenever Mark opened it, he felt a strange prickling in the nape of his neck. The text was written in an ancient Latin hand, and the margins overflowed with decoration with tiny red dots predominating the page. A few pages from the centre, the text was marred by a small red handprint, obviously that of a young child, but it had no relevance to the content, and was not a carefully made mark. It splattered messily across the page and, as he traced it with a grubby finger, Mark wondered who had owned the hand who made it. *What happened to him?*

He turned more pages, moving further into the book and, almost at once, he noted an illustration where the text had finished short of the foot of a page. It was a scene depicting a small settlement, nothing more than a circle of huts, a central pool and even a primitive church. The depicted figures were intent upon the construction of the church and the whole scene was encircled by trees.

The next page was decorated with brightly plumaged birds sitting among stylised branches, the design surrounded with further tiny red dots. But the real thrill was at the back of the book. The few lines of spidery text that enthralled him most of all were not embellished in any way, the page was mildewed but the handwriting stood out clearly. In Latin it said:

"Alric of Alricsleah in Northumbria began this book and was helped by his pupil Alricson who carried it with him after Alric's death to Lindisfarne where it was made complete."

It was astonishing to consider how the book had travelled the length of the country, from the holiest of holy islands, to an abbey in Gloucestershire. He wondered what stories it could tell if it were able.

"Who do you think could have written this, Brother Francis?" he asked for the hundredth time. "Do you think if we sent a missive to the monks at Lindisfarne they might know? It is the only clue we have to its origins."

Brother Francis distracted by his task, smiled and said, "perhaps."

Further down the page, written in a different hand Mark's finger traced another record.

Today, on this the nineteenth day of January 1069, was born to Rainald of Caen and Byrtha of Thornholding a son, Robert, an emblem of future peace.

He had heard Thornhold Manor referred to as Thornholding before but, who were Rainald and Byrtha? The date 1069 was just a few years after the Norman Conquest. Could he truly be looking at a sentence written so long ago? The ink still seemed so fresh. And the reference to "future peace," what did that mean? Could it mean that a Norman and a Saxon had reached some sort of peace at Thornholding after the invasion? It didn't seem likely, but he would never know. Brother Francis said most people weren't even literate at that time. He was convinced a monk or a priest must have written it on behalf of the parents.

The book was clearly linked to his home, but were Rainald and Byrtha his forebears? Was the name Robert recurrent in the family? He didn't think so.

Many years ago, Thornhold Manor had been partly destroyed in a great fire and refurbished just sixty or so years back. His mother said, she had been told that the orchard was planted on the site of an ancient burial site, but he had always dismissed that as a story, made up to amuse him and his sister. His taste buds swelled as he recalled the huge rosy apples he used to collect with his sister. Had they really been playing where the bones of their ancestors lay?

Suddenly conscious of his own mortality, he ran a hand over the page, his head far off in the past. A patter of footsteps brought Brother Francis. The monk clapped his hands to hasten him along to Vespers.

Mark sighed and closed the book.

December 1539

Life limped painfully through the bitterest winter, battling against cold and disease in the infirmary, and continuing the timeless round of worship, the brethren tried to ignore the ominous shadow that cast darkness over England. The Abbot's strategy continued to be one of compliance.

They were forbidden to express resentment when constrained to embrace the new laws from the king. Now, the scriptures were read in English; the tongues of the older monks stumbled over the unfamiliar words. Mark missed the rhythm of the Latin verses and often chanted them in his head as he worked in the infirmary gardens. Slowly but surely, the abbey's wealth was being consumed by the greedy king and his supporters. The abbey farm at Longborough had been taken out of Hayles' jurisdiction and was now the residence of one of Cromwell's nominees. It seemed the whole world was indifferent to the plight of the monasteries, for barely a hand was raised in protest as fifteen hundred years of worship was swept away by the vagaries of one man.

Brother Lawrence had been the sacrist for sixty-five years. He had cared for the abbey church building and all the relics and plate therein; dutifully polishing and guarding the shrine, making it gleam until he became too old, and the post passed to Brother John. Brother Lawrence was tormented by accusations of fraud and deception laid against him by Cromwell's men. On examination, the officials decided that the Holy Blood was a deception, and the Bishop of Rochester, no doubt at instigation from Cromwell, had declared from St Paul's Cross that it was, "no blood but honey clarified and coloured with saffron".

Robbed of his spirit, Brother Lawrence no longer railed against Tudor rule. Instead, he wept hot tears of ignominy. For all the care he received in the infirmary, the old man wasted away. Refusing food or drink, he wept his way to the quiet solitude of the abbey churchyard. Mark grieved for the old man, and while the weather allowed, he gathered liquorice and comfrey flowers to lay upon his grave.

In the abbey church, the shrine stood empty, taunting the monks each time they came to worship. As the community dwindled so did the pilgrims and the bell at the gate ceased to ring. They could no longer ignore that the days of the abbey were numbered. When news came of the abbot of Glastonbury, with his prior and sub prior, being dragged through the town on a hurdle to hang like felons on the Tor, the monks at Hayles knew real terror. The plugged their ears against the stories of how the brethren of Glastonbury bodies were slashed into quarters. Their heads and limbs were dispersed about the kingdom as a warning to traitors.

The monks of Hayles knew without doubt those monks were innocent of the crimes levied against them, and by the same token, understood their own purity was not enough to save them from a similar fate.

Gloom hung like thunder as the monks went about their daily duties. Brother John and Brother Francis, determined to preserve in some manner the old ways, accumulated abbey treasures and concealed them around the precinct. Items of exceptional beauty were spirited away. For two fearful days the church plate lay hidden in the leaf pile by the precinct wall before the monks found the opportunity to pass them over the wall into Brother Mark's waiting hands.

With a thumping heart, he hid them in the bottom of a shallow pit at the foot of a gnarled oak tree. For although they despaired and inwardly railed against the new regime, the brethren never once lost faith that one day God would reinstate the old ways. When that day came, one of their number would survive to restore the church treasure to its rightful place.

The three monks spent hours determining which books should be saved. They heard many tales of treasured books being distributed to the laity and some said that rich landowners even used the lovely pages in their jakes. Other stories told of religious manuscripts used to wrap groceries, or to clean shoes and candlesticks. In the days after the abbey of Winchcombe fell, Mark furtively carried several heavy tomes to his dormitory. The books were dispersed among those monks willing to carrying them away, but Mark retained the Book of Thornhold for himself.

They could no longer deny that the abbey would close but no real plan was made. It was beyond their comprehension that the day would come. Some monks would take places in lay churches, and some would accept a pension. Abbot Sagar was certain to have secured a comfortable position, but Mark wanted no blood money. If and when the day came and they were forced to leave, he would return to Thornbury Manor, where his mother would welcome him.

As winter's bite grew sharper and the monks of Hayles sang in praise of Christ's birth, Cromwell's noose tightened. With little income, food was now very scarce within the monastery and although the infirmary garden provided some sustaining soup, bread and fish was rare. The monks grew thin, their teeth came loose and those that fell sick, failed to recover. But Abbot Sagar complied with the demands of the Vicar General and grew fat and prosperous.

Christmas Eve 1539

A blanket of snow, marred only by the tracks of deer, covered the abbey grounds, and the monastic buildings sparkled in the low winter sun. Mark was in the monks' kitchen trying to dislodge the ice from the sluice when the bell at the porter's lodge rung out. Placing his bucket on the floor, he hurried through the cloister and peered across to the west range to see if he could discover who called. Few visitors came to the monastery these days and, any that did come, were not friends. Having no legitimate business in the west range, Mark tiptoed along the shadow of the wall where, hearing voices, he stopped, held his breath and strained his ears.

Abbot Sagar was in conversation with a stranger.

"It is good of you to ride on ahead to alert me. You have been a good friend in these trying times, and your loyalty will be remembered." The abbot sighed heavily. "It is harsh though that they come on Christmas Eve; the brethren are distraught enough without the most holy of holy days being spoiled."

Mark, dry mouthed in his hiding place, turned on his heel and ran back through the cloister, to the south transept of the church. He burst into a small side chapel where Brother John was in private prayer.

"Brother John," he cried, ignoring monastic etiquette "The king's men are here. I heard Abbot Sagar speaking with one who has ridden on ahead. Oh, Brother John, what are we to do?"

"Shush, child," said the monk. "Calm yourself. We must alert the others. Run quickly and summon all you can to the warming house. Remain calm; there is nothing to be gained from confrontation. Remember what happened at Glastonbury, we must be seen to comply so that we can regroup and fight the infidel another day."

Taking refuge in a disused strong room above the porter's lodge Mark felt sick as he saw Abbot Sagar meekly hand over the keys. Unknown to him, across the valley upon a vantage point, the King's Vicar General also watched from the back of his horse.

For Mark, if not for Cromwell, it was a painful scene. The precinct quickly filled with lumbering ox carts which Cromwell's men loaded with God's treasures. Armfuls of plate, reliquary boxes, vestments and heavy jewelled candlesticks were brought out and added to the haul. It required eight men to carry the two coffers which were stuffed with gold and jewels.

The vault of the founder, Richard of Cornwall, his wife, Sanchia and son, Robert, were breached and their bones scattered across the floor while the marble from the tomb was carted away.

Huge bonfires burned; bonfires that turned the burly thieves into demons as they kept the fires fuelled. The rood screen was ripped out and cast into the flames, the fine rich carving blistering and peeling before warping, twisting and diminishing in the inferno. Carved misericords upon which monks had rested during services were fed to the flames, the lead in them carefully salvaged.

Smoke billowed around the precinct, choking and blinding the brethren who knelt at the periphery and witnessed the burning of blessed saints and venerated martyrs. As the flames took hold and the vibrant paint ran like tears upon the blessed virgin's face, her patient eyes looked out through the smoke and forgave her violators even as they showed violence against her.

High up on the church roof men threw down great lumps of lead to be melted into ingots in the furnaces that had been constructed there. Without the protection of the lead, the rain would soon seep through the roof and into the fabric of the building. It would rapidly spoil the decorated plaster and undermine the floors; trees and nettles would take root and flourish where once only the feet of monks had trod.

Cromwell's men seemed to be mainly wreaking their vengeance upon the beautiful church, but Mark had heard other abbeys where the roofs had been destroyed on every building to ensure the monks could not return. He had heard that the monastic lands were gifted to the favourites of the king, and the buildings turned into private houses. He wondered how they slept peaceful in their beds. He hoped the ghostly vengeance of the mistreated would haunt their dreams.

It was no easy thing to watch the vast stained-glass windows of the church removed and stowed onto the back of waiting wagons. There was little care taken and two or three times he saw the brilliant glass shatter, cascading like broken rainbows to lie abandoned in the snow. Great boots stepped upon the Tree of Jesse, obliterating the remaining story, the twisted ironwork wrested from the damage and tossed along with the roof lead into the furnaces. His heart twisted when he realised a further furnace was being constructed inside the church, just before the high altar.

Nothing of price was spared. A cart piled with manuscripts from the scriptorium passed beneath where Mark hid. He saw the pages flapping in the wind and almost cried out in warning when Brother Francis stumbled after the cart, his arms outstretched, beseeching the men to be gentle with his treasures.

He realised now that the few items they had saved from the scriptorium were not enough. The books now being stolen were irreplaceable. His heart broke as he watched the cart roll along the road, he prayed they would fall into the hands of a scholar, be he for God or against him, for no man of learning would ill-treat a book. Pray God, the wicked tales he had heard were nothing more than rumour for the thought of some heretic using them to wipe his arse was more than he could bear.

At last, as the cart moved out of sight, his attention turned to a gang of workmen attempting to lower a massive bell from the church tower. The bell was heavy, even with the aid of mammoth ropes and pulleys, the men strained in their efforts to lower it safely. He noted their struggle, taking unholy pleasure from the pain they must be feeling as their muscles tore. The bell was less than halfway down when the weight proved too much and it fell, clanging to the ground. The impact of the fall cracked the massive shell and the huge bell rolled forlornly in the snow, scattering workmen, before settling mournfully at the base of the tower. Useless now, the bell that had called monks to prayer for time immemorial would be melted down for scrap.

Mark rubbed his arms and stomped his feet and wondered what time it was. Without the regular chime of the bells ringing out vigils, lauds, prime, there was now no way of telling one hour from another. He squinted at the pale sun, just beginning to sink into the west, and presumed it must be well past vespers. As the day grew short, feelings of detachment and unreality took hold and he suddenly craved companionship. Feeling sad, alone, and without purpose he decided to attempt a circuitous route to the warming room without being seen.

The shrinking band of monks had gathered but, in contrast to the raging flames of the furnaces outside, the fire was far from warm. They huddled over the embers, too afraid to venture outside to replenish the firewood. But, braver or more foolish than most, Mark hurried to the infirmary garden where he knew a good stock of firewood waited. Taking an armful of logs back to the warming house, he began to feed the embers. Apart from a continuous babble of prayer there was no conversation. The heart had been ripped from Hayles Abbey, and it would take more than warmth to resuscitate it.

The fire brought no comfort, for the cold they suffered clutched at their pious hearts. Mark and Brother Francis listened as the older monks reluctantly agreed to take pensions in lay churches. Brother Francis urged Mark to abandon the ecclesiastic life, but he believed the day of the monks would return. He was not prepared to sacrifice his convictions on the whim of a mad man. Instead, he deferred his monastic vocation until a later date.

As darkness fell, in the infirmary garden, two figures scaled the precinct wall. Thrust by the helping hand of his accomplice, Brother Francis reached the other side first, then the more agile figure of Mark leapt up onto the wall, hauled a heavy sack up behind him and dropped to the other side. The outside.

***

A cruel wind blasted in their faces as they ploughed their way through heavy snow. Before leaving the abbey, Mark and Francis had taken the precaution of binding their lower legs with bandages and then covering them with woollen stockings. They wore all the clothing they could lay hands on, one robe on top of another. But these measures fell far short of adequate, and they were soon soaked through, their legs and feet as cold and sore as their hearts.

Darkness hampered their progress and, forced as they were to avoid the highway, they blundered into ditches and fallen branches. The moon, that had been their accomplice at the start of the journey, retreated behind a cloud and more snow threatened.

Knowing they could travel no further until first light, they sought what rest they could and while they battled for sleep beneath a thin coverlet, penetrating cold gnawed at their bones. Neither man slept properly but drifted somewhere on the brink of unconsciousness until dawn, by which time the cold was so intense that it was more comfort to move than to stay.

In the morning, they munched on wizened apples and hard cheese but still their bellies roared for sustenance.

"We will go to Thornhold," Mark said. "Mother will welcome us. It isn't so very far."

Mark longed to see his mother. He recalled the comfort of her arms, her warm smile, her deep laugh. He imagined how she would pause in disbelief when she saw him, but her incredulity would soon change to delight, and he would be swept up in her love. The book would be safe there, and there'd be little danger of discovery.

With each step, the bundle Mark carried swung painfully against his legs, the sharp edges of the jewelled cover cutting into his skin. *Others have suffered worse than this*, he told himself, and concentrated upon Christ's path to Calvary, praying for similar forbearance.

They spoke little, only enough to point out landmarks for reassurance that they were on the right path. Occasionally they sheltered from heavy flurries or paused to pass water, and each time they stopped they breathed upon their hands and clapped them together to bring the blood back to their fingers. Then pulling their cowls low over their faces and keeping their chins tucked to their chests, they resumed the weary journey.

The December day declined early, and by dusk it was no longer possible to see a foot ahead. They were passing through a stand of beech and thought it as good a place as any to pass the night. Since they were now far enough from the abbey Francis agreed that Mark should build a small fire. It was a struggle to light the damp wood, his reddened hands were stiff, and he could barely hold the tinder but, after some perseverance, a sulky fire was persuaded into life.

While Mark coaxed the fire, Francis heaped snow up around them to form a windbreak. Soon, they were the warmest they had been in days ... and the most secure. They cooked apples on the fire and ate them hot and sticky, the cheese was gone and only four or five apples remained for the next day. As he savoured the pulpy flesh, keeping it in his mouth for as long as possible before letting it pass down his throat to his churning stomach, Mark tried to forget the joy he'd had collecting them in the orchard, just a few months ago.

As they settled for sleep, Francis asked about Mark's family at Thornhold.

"Well, my father died leaving my elder brother in charge. Then there's my mother; she's a good woman, a bonny woman, many do say. You can be sure of a good welcome, Brother, but her cooking is too tasty to be holy," he laughed, pausing for a while to recall the melting pastries that his mother baked. "It is not a grand household; it is comfortable but we've no misconceived illusions of grandeur. We live simply but well, live by the book and serve the king ... although whether it is still possible to do both I know not...Most of the house was built in the last century but it is nothing fancy. It's solid and functional, and it stands of the site of an older manor house that was burned down. Much of the old building remains and there is a mound close by the orchard that our old gardener Jacob, whose family has worked for ours for generations, swears was made by ancient people long ago."

Francis nodded, "And you have a sister, I believe. I seem to remember you speaking of her one day in the scriptorium?"

"Yes, Alyce. She is two years younger than I and is probably a beauty by now. Tomorrow, Brother Francis, you shall meet them all, for after that we need travel no more." Mark turned on to his side, his bundle serving as a pillow and, as the wind howled above them, he slept.

The next morning Mark woke in an optimistic mood. In a few hours he would be entering the gates of Thornhold, where his mother would be waiting. They trampled out the dying embers and, after collecting their belongings, made their way through the wood. As they journeyed, Mark became aware of the strange terrain.

"Look Brother," he said. "See how the land is curiously formed? It is almost as if it was made by human hands. Perhaps ancient people lived here, and this is all that's left. Look at that upright stone, standing alone over there? It looks like no natural stone I have ever seen."

They journeyed on, able now to see the earthwork of the fort that had once topped the hill. Tracks that had been untrodden for years were still discernible among the undergrowth. The descent down the hill was tough on Brother Francis, who suffered badly with his knees, and he was glad to reach the flatter land that followed the path of the river. Soon the snow stopped, and a yellow sun attempted to warm them. Mark, knowing that home was near, allowed his step to lighten and his chatter grow faster. Francis listened, grateful for his companionship. They passed close by a small copse and as they drew level saw smoke spiralling from the treetops. Mark hesitated, tempted by the promise of food, but Francis placed a finger to his lips and shook his head, his silent warning reminding Mark there were many terrors on the roads.

As they began to pass quietly by, a snapping of a twig alerted them that they had been seen. Together they turned toward the fellow traveller with a greeting on their lips.

"Good morrow. We are travelling monks on our way to help the needy."

There were two men, tattered and rough looking fellows. One carried a dagger thrust into his belt and the other held a stout club.

"Monks, is it? Well, well, I thought the days of monks was over, didn't you, Harry?"

"Oh, I did, Will, indeed I did." agreed Harry.

"From Winchcombe are ye? Fleeing with the king's loot, no doubt. What's in that bag, Boy?"

Mark thrust the bundle behind his back.

"It is the Abbot's business, not yours," he cried, backing away as the men edged closer. "And he's expecting us back, very soon. He will be sending out a party, should we be late."

The vagabonds leered.

"Now, don't take offence, Brother; we was only bein' friendly like. Just asking your business in a neighbourly way, you understand. We've got ourselves some nice rabbits over there, we have; roasting them on our fire we were, when we heard your voices. Care to join us, would you? There is more than enough for us."

The monks' stomachs growled at the thought of meat, they had barely eaten for a month or more. The two strangers were waiting for a reply. Harry began to clean his nails with his dagger. The monks were exhausted and hungry, and the strangers, now the first tension had passed, seemed friendly enough. After a moment's hesitation, they nodded and followed their hosts to the fire.

In the midst of the small copse, two rabbits were spitted over the flames. To their surprise, a slatternly woman was tending the meal, her lousy hair hanging limp and greasy about her face. She showed no surprise at the arrival of guests but silently proceeded to tear the meat from the carcass and dispense it among the men.

The sweet flesh of the rabbit hurt Mark's tongue, his taste buds bursting painfully and, as hot as it was, he swallowed it down in lumps. When it was gone, he licked the juices from his hands. Francis was slightly more delicate, savouring the unaccustomed taste. Opposite them the strangers spitted two more rabbits and set them ready above the flames.

"Will here is top when it comes to snarin' rabbits, he is," Harry volunteered, "We never go hungry when he's around."

Francis smiled. "It's marvellous, and we thank you for your generosity. We were very, very hungry and it was so well-cooked." He smiled at the woman, but she averted her eyes, nervously sucking meat from a bone.

Since the travellers only seemed to have water to drink and that probably none too fresh, Mark offered them his wine pouch and the men drank greedily. As the woman crouched before the fire, slowly feeding the flames, she kept her eye on the men, watching them keenly, as if in expectation.

"Anyway," continued Will. "What's in the bag?"

Mark licked his lips, looking anxiously from Will to Harry. Francis answered for him.

"We carry missives and paperwork from the Abbot. It can be nothing of import or they should not have entrusted it to us."

He smiled in what he hoped was a winning manner.

"If it nuffin' important, yer won't mind me lookin'. Show me," said Will. "I want to see, and I always has to have my way, don't I, Harry?"

Francis stood up.

"We were told to deliver it straight to the bishop. We must do as we are told. We cannot show you, I'm afraid."

In a single bound Will sprang across the clearing and pinned Francis to the floor, his knife pressed hard against his throat. Frozen to the spot, Mark was astonished to see a trickle of blood soak into Francis's white robe.

"Let him go," he cried. "Please! Release him and I'll give you the sack. He is a man of God; you must not harm him."

Will laughed slowly.

"Now then, my lad, first things first. You give the bag to Harry and then I'll be letting your friend go, see." He leered horribly as Mark slowly handed over the bundle. "That's it, that's it, what a fine, wise fella ye are."

The woman crouched, watching the proceedings keenly, waiting for instruction from her man. As soon as Francis was released, Mark rushed to his side and tried to clean the blood from his neck. There was no serious damage, it was just a nick in the skin, but Mark was sickened by the violence. Shakily, they rose to their feet, clinging together as one of the men drew the book from the sack. When they saw the jewel encrusted cover Will whistled and Harry looked at the monks in disbelief. The woman stood up slowly, the better to see the treasure.

Discarding the sack, Harry lost no time in helping Will lever the jewels from their gold mounts, but they soon lost patience and Will decided that it would save time to rip the covers from the pages and take them in one piece. He had no use for the pages of text. It was the treasure he wanted.

It was no easy task to tear the hard covers from the parchment and it took all of his strength but eventually the stitching began to give. Will emitted a grunt as the book parted from its cover. Then, tucking the treasure inside his jerkin, he tossed the remaining pages into the fire. Mark squeaked in horror as Will stepped closer.

"Well, Brothers, since you've been so generous, I'll spare your lives and let you go. Safe journey to you and may God keep you both."

They ducked off into the trees leaving the monks standing shocked and silent in the glade while the woman collected her belongings. Obediently, she scurried after Harry and Will but before she did so, she paused to kick the smouldering book free from the flames.

"In 'appier days, I lived close to an abbey. Me father worked the land there and more'n once we benefitted from the monks' charity." Before disappearing into the trees, she flashed an apologetic smile at the monks.

The monks prayed for a while, asking that God forgive their transgressors, and then they collected the charred remains of the book and put it in the sack. The loss of the jewelled cover did not trouble them, for they knew that the book's true value lay in its content, not its costly cover. For an hour or so longer, they tramped a road that grew slushy as the day warmed and, as that sun began to slip toward the horizon, the bristling chimneys of Thornhold Manor became visible among the trees. The windows twinkled in the dusk and its welcoming light lifted their spirits. The travellers picked up their pace.

∗∗∗

It was many years before Mark saw Hayles Abbey again. Before that day, however, fate arranged it that he should marry and make a home, raising a handful of fine children and, in time, his grandchildren were numerous. One day, as the approaching summer warmed the chill of spring, Mark asked his grandson to accompany him on a laborious journey, back through the past to his days of innocence.

They followed the overgrown pilgrim's path and travelled the verdant valleys toward the old abbey. And there, among the ruins of the bare, roofless quire, in an abandoned garden, Mark sat upon sun-warmed stone to dream where the sweet birds sang.

He took from his baggage The Book of Thornhold, now richly recovered, and opened it to the page where others had left their mark. There, he wrote in round English script, the words that had become his creed.

"It is good to be here. Here man more purely lives, less oft doth fall, more promptly rises, walks with stricter need, more safely rests, dies happier, is freed earlier from cleansing fires, and gains withal a brighter crown."

Part Six
'Duking Days'

If I could write the beauty of your eyes,
And in fresh numbers number all your graces,
The age to come would say, "This poet lies.
Such heavenly touches ne'er touched earthly faces."
So should my papers, yellowed with their age,
Be scorned, like old men of less truth than tongue,
And your true rights be termed a poet's rage,
And stretched metre of an antique song.
(Shakespeare sonnet 17)

Thornhold Manor - May 1685

The month was May and the windows of Thornhold Manor sparkled in the sun. Winter was gone, vanquished at last by spring, and the hedgerows were festooned with fresh green leaves and blossom. In the orchard, beneath lathered apple trees, a flock of Jacob sheep and lambs cropped the lush grass of the hillside. To the front of the house lay a knot garden. The exuberantly coloured beds, intersected with honey-coloured gravelled paths, provided a carpet of colour, curtailed by low, clipped box hedging. At the gate that led from the orchard to the garden, Joanna Thornbury was enjoying the smell of wild ransoms. She leaned on the gate and sighed.

Joanna was rarely content. She was an impatient and frustrated woman; her unprepossessing face was made plainer by her mood. Aware that she was not a likeable person, that she was a prickly companion, and an unsatisfactory wife increased her bad temper and sharpened her tongue. Behind her back, the servants grumbled, and Joanna was well aware that her stepdaughter's prolonged stay with a maternal aunt in Taunton had little to do with family duty but more with a dislike for her stepmother.

Ten years previously, Joanna arrived at Thornhold Manor as a young bride with little expectation of happiness. Her husband, the master of Thornhold, was thirty-five years her senior who, on finding himself a widower with a small daughter to raise, had made the hasty decision to wed the un-dowried daughter of an old friend. Within two hours of being handed into his custody, Joanna knew that she would never be able to like, let alone love the wheezing old man she was to call husband.

After the wedding, they spent a fortnight visiting various of his fat, bucolic relatives, a family in whom Joanna failed to find any redeeming qualities. And, also during that time, James was delighted to discover his bride had an unexpectedly luscious body. Nightly, he exercised his marital rights upon her, never once asking for her consent or enquiring as to her comfort afterwards. To Joanna's dismay, his attentions were both thorough and prolonged. James was not only an unskilled and inconsiderate lover, but he was also a prosaic bore and a bully and Joanna sensed that, if she disobeyed him, retribution would be swift and thorough.

It was not a happy bride in the claustrophobic carriage as it travelled the rutted road to Thornhold Manor but as they approached the honey-coloured walls of her new home, her spirits lifted – just a little.

The house seemed to have sprung from the terrain around it; the curiously ridged green hill rising just beyond, the walled gardens and church seemed to be part of an older, kinder world, a world that held a welcome for a plain, unhappy bride. Joanna knew instinctively that this was a place where given the chance, she could be happy. Here she would learn to be a good mother to her stepdaughter and raise some children of her own.

She pictured them at her feet, saw their eager faces looking up at her as she read to them. Oh, yes, here at Thornhold, she could grow into herself and become the woman she had always planned to be.

The Thornburys had lived at the manor for generations. James and his sister spoke proudly of a lineage that stretched beyond the conquest. He heaped scorn upon Joanna's own lack of pedigree. A Thornbury had come over with the conqueror, and another had died fighting for King Richard at Bosworth. As he boasted of his family's longevity, Joanna thought sourly that their long proud lineage had not raised them far, for as she understood it, her husband was only modestly rich. Perhaps it was just bad luck, or perhaps the Thornburys lacked the necessary guile required to rise really high.

The coach swept into the drive and the servants appeared, taking charge of the sweating horses, opening the carriage doors. As she placed her foot on Thornhold soil and smelled for the first time its own peculiar smell, Joanna's lips curved upward.

But that was ten long years ago and Joanna grimaced to recall her crass optimism. Before the week was out, she had been rudely kicked by her six-year-old stepdaughter, subjected to her husband's attentions on a nightly basis, and informed by the housekeeper that since she had run the house successfully for so many years, she saw no reason why that should change. Other disappointments followed, and it took several years for

Joanna to be reconciled with the fact she would never become a mother. Not one of her babies lived longer than a day.

She had become quickly pregnant and born the discomfort of gravidity well. But, after a prolonged and painful delivery her first-born son had lain in her arms for just a few hours before his faltering breath ceased. Within days he was placed, cold and alone in the churchyard, leaving Joanna to her grief.

In the following nine years Joanna bore James six more children, each time watching life flicker briefly before they died in her arms. As her body grew tired, her mind grew bitter. It was no excuse, James shouted at her, she wasn't alone; most women lost babes. Her own mother had buried three before giving birth to Joanna and her brother, and even royalty was not exempt from disappointment. Queen Catherine had suffered miscarriage after miscarriage while Charles begot fourteen bastards on his court favourites. But to Joanna it just wasn't fair. Her bitterness increased every time a tenant produced yet another brat to be raised in squalor. There seemed little justice that a rough, lousy cottager could produce a child every year, acquiring families too large to be loved or nurtured, while she pined for just one tiny hand to hold in her own.

Now that her husband was enjoying the favour of the newly crowned King James, Joanna was left alone. She spent most of her days in the garden at Thornhold, feeling almost happy as her skirts swept the honey-coloured gravel. With her dog at her heel, she moved among the flowerbeds, snipping heads here and prizing weeds from the soil, there. It was the closest she ever came to contentment. There was something about the droning bees and the ecstatic birds that soothed her spirits and eased her pain. Only on the harshest of days was she to be found within doors, she would brave the wettest weather, bundled in an old coat to wander about the winter walks in search of spring. When really heavy rain kept her inside, the servants had learned to pass their mistress's chamber with a soft tread.

The only member of staff Joanna liked was old Jonah Gardner. She would often summon him to the library, to seek inspiration for a new planting scheme. Uncomfortable in the sumptuous room, his gnarled fingers would pull at his forelock before he stepped forward to share knowledge that had been handed down from father to son for generations. At first Joanna had been dismissive of his more obscure lore but experience had proved that nine times out of ten, he would predict inclement weather or a glut of apples with singular accuracy.

Together they had extended the area of garden, incorporating new beds and re-gravelling the paths. At her insistence, a sandstone sundial had been placed in the centre where the four pathways converged. Her gown was often muddy, and her hands callused, but she was invigorated by the garden, and almost happy.

Sometimes she unearthed curious items, and she took them into the house to be cleaned and examined more closely. One such find was the remains of a child's shoe, the lacings had long since perished and the leather was stiff, but Joanna treasured it and whenever she looked upon it felt a sense of curiosity about the tiny foot it had once enclosed. She wondered if the child had played in the house or beneath the trees in the orchard? Sometimes she imagined she glimpsed a fair head bobbing along between the beds in the knot garden.

On seeing her interest, Old Jonah began to bring his own finds to her, and she now had a clutch of coins and a buckle, curiously wrought that looked as though it came from the harness of a horse. When the earth was washed away from the surface the figure of a leaping deer emerged. Intrigued, Joanna laid it on the library shelf alongside the coins.

Every spring the orchard was devastated by moles as they excavated more tunnels, and sometimes they turned up bits of thick, roughly cast clay pottery. On careful examination it was possible to make out geometric markings on them. When she trawled through the Thornbury estate records it showed that the orchard stood upon the site of an ancient burial ground. Old Jonah said that the prize-winning apples grown at Thornhold was thanks to the festering Saxon bones beneath. When she questioned the source of his knowledge, he scratched his head.

"I'll be beggered if I know, mistress. I suspect my mother tole me."

There were many stories connected to Thornhold Manor and Joanna learned via servant gossip that nine times out of ten, it was not just the wind sighing and whispering in the branches, but the voices of the dead.

Supressing a superstitious shiver, Joanna wondered about the people who had lived in the house before her. She did not bother asking James for she knew he would scorn her. She had found old papers in the library that bore out some of the servants' tales. Foraging among yellowing rolls and dog-eared accounts she found that there had been Thornburys at the Manor for longer than anyone could precisely tell. The stones in the churchyard bore the name for centuries past and according to the priest, just to the right of the church door, was the pit containing the remains of victims of the first black death. This last story made Joanna shudder for the danger of plague was still very real. Just twenty years ago London had been struck with a virulent attack and hundreds of people had perished. But her most marvellous discovery was undoubtedly the book she had discovered among the oldest items in the library.

The family referred to it as, The Book of Thornhold; it was very old, handwritten, so they said, by Christian monks. The detail and design was primitive yet beautifully wrought, and the spiritual devotion of its maker spoke as loudly from the decorated margin as the sentiment of the Latin text. Some later inscriptions had been made on the last few pages. The first was by a man named Alricson, who claimed to have made the book in 793, and the second celebrated the birth of a child. A religious poem came next, a verse Joanna had never heard before, but the words evoked great emotion in her, for poetry was a thing she loved almost as much as her garden, and the lines celebrated both.

"It is good to be here. Here man more purely lives, less oft doth fall, more promptly rises, walks with stricter need, more safely rests, dies happier, is freed earlier from cleansing fires, and gains withal a brighter crown."

From the wear and tear of the pages, the book was ancient. It was stained with water, scorched, and one page was marred by a red handprint. The pages smelled musty, like a church, but it was clear the book had once been a costly attribute. Now, although its monetary value was small, it was invaluable to the Thornbury family. Even James saw its worth and had sent it away to be recovered in a fancy cover with a heavy gold fastening and a chain and key to secure it to its stand. His pleasure in her discovery was the only favourable thing to come out of the marriage so far.

Joanna often stood at the lectern, slowly turning the pages to absorb its peace, and ponder on its past. The book had been in Thornbury hands for so long, passed from generation to generation, valued and revered until now, 1685, when for the first time there would be no male heir to inherit it.

Joanna didn't care about failing to give James an heir. He had his daughter after all and Hope may have a son one day to continue the bloodline but, oh, it cut like a knife that she did not have a son of her own to safeguard the book and the manor when she was dead.

Now, at the orchard gate, inhaling the tang of the ransoms, Joanna shook herself from her reverie and peered up the valley where a cloud of dust in the distance told her that her peace had ended, for James and Hope were home.

Joanna raised a cynical eyebrow at the girlish enthusiasm that bubbled from her stepdaughter's lips. She listened to Hope as she dipped a spoon into her soup, and wondered what had brought about the change in a girl who was usually not in the least friendly or forthcoming.

Hope presented a pretty picture, adorned and trimmed with rose coloured silk and ribbons. The candlelight illuminated her skin and tight ringlets that bounced neatly on her shoulders but there was a new vivacity that spoke of inner change. When she had left for Taunton barely nine months ago she had been a rebellious child but now she had matured into a young woman. Joanna had noted her newly acquired sensuous grace straight away.

Hope proffered her wine glass for a refill and Joanna sensed again her barely concealed excitement. She pondered upon possible reasons for the transformation of the plump, spoiled child and watched Hope languidly caress the rim of her glass. Her fingers were perfectly manicured and the sight of them made Joanna hide her own snag-nailed hands guiltily in her lap.

Hope barely touched the main course but pushed the food disinterestedly about her plate. She chattered about her uncle's home and how different their rambling, overcrowded household was to Thornhold.

It was never silent in the Oswald house and the small children were allowed just as much freedom of speech as their elders. Her female cousins, Meg and Annabel, with whom she attended school at the Misses Musgrave and Temple's establishment, were encouraged to air their views upon everything from fashion to politics so that the dinner table was often a place of vigorous debate. Aunt Carrie had been raised in the Catholic faith, but her religious leanings were not strong and, much against her father's will she had married an impoverished Protestant, whom everyone called Uncle Leo, whether they were related or not. The children of the union were raised in the Protestant faith, and it was testament to Uncle Leo's good nature that he welcomed contact with his wife's Catholic relations.

Leo and Carrie were lucky, for of all the fifteen children born to them, they had lost just two. Their household was both a raucous and a happy one, and Leo Oswald was well content. With his eldest son already wed with small children of his own, his second son away at college, and the third destined for the church, the future of the family was good. His older daughters were fast approaching marriageable age and the nursery still replete with young Oswalds to enjoy. Joanna could not help but be envious.

The bright happiness of the Oswald's home provided a sharp contrast to the empty parlours and cradle at Thornhold Manor. Their overheated, overpopulated, cluttered house showed Hope for the first time what the word 'home' meant. It was a place where cushions were crushed, books left upon tables, shoes were kicked off anywhere, and boisterous laughter rang to the rafters. As she became accustomed to their free manners, so she absorbed their differing political leanings and theological beliefs.

Hope had never questioned the teachings of the Catholic Church, but she was not devout. Her mind wandered during church services, and from Sunday to Sunday she entirely forgot about God or matters of faith. She saw little point in pondering unanswerable questions when there were outings to plan and parties to attend. But as an astonished witness to the impassioned discussions during suppers at her cousin's house, Hope began to realise that, perhaps, there was more to life than fashion.

The thrust of the argument was above her head but, entirely receptive to the impassioned blue eyes and long tawny hair of Beatrice's elder brother, Samuel Trelask, a new interest germinated. As Hope tried to sleep that night, the firm line of Samuel's jaw, and the way his hair fell upon his neck lingered, making her fidget. Samuel Trelask had continued to intrude upon her thoughts ever since.

James was delighted with the effect Taunton society had upon his daughter. As he forked food steadily into his mouth, he listened to her half-formed arguments, nodding and murmuring agreement in the appropriate places, besotted by her charm. He leaned over to splash more wine into Hope's glass, beaming across the table in fine spirits but, when he moved to replenish Joanna's, she shook her head, declining his offer. James shrugged and gulped his own wine, swilling it inelegantly around his mouth to remove pieces of chicken that clung to his teeth.

"And what about school, Hope? What's that like, eh? Those women aren't filling your head with a lot of nonsense I hope, what?"

"No, Father. Miss Musgrave and Miss Blake are intent on turning their girls into the most attractive marriage prospects. We speak of domestic things as we stitch at our embroideries, and we have lessons in housekeeping and then, of course, there is the social gossip. We also have lessons in needlework to ensure that all our outfits are a la mode. Beatrice is a marvel at turning a frowsty old frock into the latest thing. Her family live just a few doors down from us … the Oswalds that is. Her elder brother, Samuel, is fun and has some interesting friends. Beatrice says he was sent down from college for writing a dissentious pamphlet. Now he is home, he spends most of his day sleeping, and all-night drinking and gambling. Beatrice says he is always in trouble with her father because he speaks unwisely about the King … you know, because the king is a Catholic and all, and she says her father has threatened to send him into exile if he misbehaves again. From the country you know. He cuts quite a dash; I can tell you. One afternoon he came galloping through the town on his big black stallion and fairly bellowed up at the schoolroom window to attract Beatrice's attention. My, but you should have seen her blushes. Miss Musgrave is very lenient, too lenient in many ways, and let us all go to the window and when he saw us all looking down at him he blew us all a kiss. My! It was a lark, but Miss Blake came in. She is far stricter than Miss Musgrave, and she was furious, and ordered us all back to our places. And then, right in front of us, she took poor Miss Musgrave to task. We all bent our heads over our stitching for fear of a row too, but it was so hard to suppress our laughter. My, but it was a lark!"

Her laughter jangled. James coughed and assumed a stern air, leaning back in his chair and patting his belly.

"Hmmm, well, it may have been a lark, but mind you behave yourself. Your mother would be mortified should you turn out to be anything but a lady. Fine woman, your mother. A fine woman …"

Joanna looked down again at her nibbled nails and wondered if the day would ever come when she was described as a 'fine woman'. She was quite certain Hope's mother had never come to the table with dirty hands. She felt no jealously toward James' first wife, in fact, she wished wholeheartedly that the woman had been spared so as to avoid her own present misery. Glancing up, she saw James was watching her. He belched discreetly, smiling at her over his kerchief and, as the servants came to take the plates away, dread began to ferment in her stomach as it always did when he was home, and the evening was drawing to a close.

"There is a fire in the other room," she said, rising from her seat. "Shall we withdraw to the parlour?"

Leaving her to her own devices, James took Hope's arm and paraded with her toward the drawing room. A subtle fragrance wafted from Hope as she rustled across the carpet making Joanna, in her frumpy blue, feel like a maidservant in comparison.

Determined to make an effort Joanna perched upon the edge of the settle and forced a smile to her lips.

"It sounds as if you are enjoying life in Taunton, Hope. We must seem very dull here after that lively household."

Hope tossed her ringlets and lifted her chin, exposing a length of unblemished neck. In the firelight she looked darker, almost swarthy and the whites of her eyes glistened like a gypsy's. Tucking her chin down, she regarded her stepmother for a moment before responding.

"Thornhold is so old fashioned. The house, the grounds, the furniture, the tenants, the way of life. Nothing ever changes here. People at Taunton seem to be more alive somehow. They are full of passion. Anyone you speak to there tell stories of siege and rebellion and action. Most of them are not happy with the King and think he will promote Catholics on the strength of their religion rather than their political worth. Many of them think King Charles' son, Monmouth, should have inherited the throne for all that he's a bast… illegitimate, and they will fight for their beliefs too, given the chance. The people there are not complacent. Oh, I declare nothing has ever happened at Thornhold, of that I am quite sure."

Joanna looked toward the window, too unsure of herself to offer a contradiction but certain, in her own heart, that Hope was quite wrong. Sometimes she could almost feel the things that had happened at Thornhold Manor; it was as if the old inhabitants were in the next room. James stroked his beard, startled out of his indifference by Hope's slur on his history.

"Oh, I think things have happened here, but don't ask me what. I believe, way back, a Thornbury fought at Tewkesbury, lost his head over it, so I'm told and, the house deeds trace back as far as the conqueror …although I haven't checked that out myself. Erm, Joanna, isn't there a story or something about the orchard being on the site of a Saxon burial ground? Presumably they would have been Thornbury Saxons, wouldn't they?"

Joanna's reply was cut off by a trickle of laughter from Hope.

"Oh, Father, really! I meant real things, things that matter. Not things of no consequence that happened ages ago. Anyway, I am quite fatigued from travelling, I think I shall retire. Good night, Mother." She stood up, rustled across the room to place her lips upon Joanna's cheek. "Good night Father". And then she was gone, the draught from the door guttering the candles.

Joanna and James were left in awkward silence. Joanna focused on the fire crackling in the grate until James tapped the tobacco from his pipe and placed a hand on each knee.

"Well, we might as well go up too, what? It's been a long day. I can't tell you how I welcome the idea of a soft mattress and well-aired sheets. The conditions at some of those posting houses were appalling, not fit for a gentleman. Come along, wife, up we go."

Hope, meanwhile, lay upon her pillow reliving, in minute detail, her few encounters with Samuel Trelask her mind far away from Thornbury.

She had been excited by the invite to dinner at the Trelasks, but the first course was already under way when Samuel arrived late. Fresh from a brisk canter from Exeter, still dusty and smelling strongly of the stable, he had joined them at table with a breezy apology and immediately fallen upon his food as though he had not dined for a month.

Hope watched him rip into his bread; Fascinated by his strong teeth, the way his Adam's apple bobbed slowly as he gulped down glass after glass of wine. For the first and second courses, the conversation remained light-hearted but, as the covers were removed for the sweet course, the gentlemen turned to politics, initiating an abrupt change of mood.

Mr Trelask agreed with Samuel that King James was promoting the Catholics at the expense of better Protestant men but did not extend this belief to the extremes his son took. Unable to comprehend a peaceful way of dealing with the matter and, believing that England already had seen too much war, did not agree that arms should be taken up again. Growing quickly impatient with what he termed his father's 'feeble restraint,' Samuel struggled to keep his temper. As the conversation grew more heated, Hope's head turned one from the other until Sam banged his fist on the board, making the wineglasses tinkle and the women gasp in surprise.

At nineteen, Samuel believed it to be the duty of every Englishman to fight for what he believed in. Only a coward would sit by his fireside while his fellow countrymen fought for justice. As Hope quietly observed Samuel's flushed face, his piercing blue eyes and firm jaw, she felt something shift slightly within her, a tiny jolt that marked her transition into womanhood.

Making no contribution to the conversation, she silently agreed with Sam. Even though she was of the Catholic faith she clearly saw the justice of his argument. Why should good Protestants like Sam be overlooked just because the king favoured Catholics? Should a man not be judged on his political worth instead of his religious leanings? Samuel's jaw was clenched, and his lips stretched across his teeth as he fought to rein in his anger. He was full of passion. Hope wondered how it would feel to be kissed by a man like Samuel Trelask.

The day he rode his horse straight from the tavern to the steps of the academy was the second occasion that their paths crossed. She had rushed excitedly to the window with the other girls and perched on the windowsill to see him. The girls waved boldly, giggling louder when he swept off his hat and executed a bow, blowing a kiss up to them. Hope was sure his gaze lingered upon her and, certain that he had recognised her, she made bold claim to the proffered kiss.

Afterwards, it seemed an age until Hope's pulse returned to normal. She answered her fellow classmates absentmindedly but, to her surprise, nobody appeared to notice. Her very soul seemed to tremble with the conviction that their union was predestined.

Two days later, Hope received a letter from her father informing her that he would be passing through Taunton to take her home to Thornhold. Dismayed at this turn of events and desperate to see Samuel again, she asked permission to run down to Beatrice's house to tell her the news. Fastening on her bonnet and briskly walking three doors along the busy street to her friend's home, she was shown into a side room while Beatrice was fetched from within. She moved to the window and was startled when the door behind her was thrust open. She turned, her heart leaping when she found not Beatrice but her brother, Sam. He stopped in surprise but, recovering himself quickly, he bent over her hand and placed his lips upon her wrist.

"Mistress Hope, you find me enchanted," he drawled.

Hope smiled blissfully into his blue eyes and acknowledged privately that he had remembered her name. She swallowed, fumbling for words as she reluctantly retrieved her hand.

"And you find me enchanted also, Mr Trelask."

He laughed at her.

"So formal, Hope? My name is Sam, as well you know. I take it you are come in search of my little sister. I believe she is helping Mother with the arrangements for a small gathering we are having this evening. Come, I will take you to her."

He held out his arm and she grasped his velvet sleeve and a few moments later when a bewildered manservant came to tell her that, unfortunately, Miss Beatrice seemed to be from home, he shrugged his shoulders in the empty room.

As Samuel squired Hope around the spacious house, bursting into empty rooms and loudly calling his sister's name, he regaled her with conversation. He told her about his determination to rendezvous with Monmouth should he invade. Hope said little but she looked a lot, and her stammering blushes left Sam in little doubt that her shyness denoted fondness. He was intrigued by her dusky looks and lips that were made for kissing.

The reached the nursery at the top of the house, where no one seemed to have been for a very long time and paused to look from the window. Samuel stood slightly behind her, she could feel his breath on the back of her neck, sense the racing of his heart. Certain he was going to put his hands on her shoulders and turn her around for their first kiss, she closed her eyes.

"There, in the garden!" Sam's voice was loud in her ear, making her jump. He grabbed her hand and ragged her from the room. Hope gasped for breath as they ran helter-skelter down four flights of stairs, along the dark passage that led past the kitchens and tumbled out into the verdant green.

It was quiet. The aroma of warm flowers lay heavy in the air. Hope, battling to regain her breath and dignity, finding her bonnet had slipped over one eye, removed it and smoothed her hair.

Still hand in hand, Sam led her between low, clipped hedges to a rose arbour at the far end of the path.

"I swear I saw her here, not five minutes ago." He scratched his head, and sat down, indicating that Hope should sit beside him. Silence fell, as they admired the garden but after a few minutes, Sam broke the silence.

"I'm afraid to go to war of course, Hope. I have no skill with powder, I'm a rotten shot and I have little training with a sword; I swear, I can shoot a cross bow no further than you could."

"Oh, Mr Trelask," Hope ventured, extending a hand to his velvet sleeve. "Maybe it will not come to that, maybe Monmouth will not come."

He stood quickly, and Hope followed. He ran a hand through his hair, and turned, taking hold of her shoulders so suddenly that she dropped her hat.

"Do ye think that's what I want? Do you think me a coward? It isn't that at all. Men like me have no choice. We have to fight. My father is against it, and I know I owe him obedience, but the country will go to wrack and ruin under James. At least the old king had the sense to realise the mistakes that led his father to the scaffold, but James is an idiot; an idiot with all the makings of a tyrant. We *must* fight, and I *want* to fight and … but a chap would be a fool not to be afraid."

Ruffling his tawny hair again, he gazed across the gardens, avoiding her eye. Hope ventured, "I don't believe you're afraid of anything, Sam."

He smiled and dropped his head, the tension relaxed, and he reached out gently to twirl a strand of her hair in his fingers. She held her breath, his eye fastened on hers, like a stab in the heart.

"You are a sweet girl, Hope. I thought so the first time I saw you at dinner, and again, when I saw you at the schoolroom. Do you know, I believe it would give a man strength if he had a girl like you waiting for him to come home." He took both her hands and edged a little closer. "If I had Hope, I swear I'd fight like hell to come home."

Unaware that her eyes were like torches, she did not resist when he drew her into his arms, instinctively she opened her lips, reached up to touch the back of his neck and closed her eyes.

Now, lying in her bed at Thornhold, she toyed with the token of his love that hung about her neck. It is not long until her return to Taunton, and when that day came, their union would be made absolute … whether her father liked it or not.

***

For Joanna, the next few weeks were fraught with conflict. Her accustomed peace smashed. Hope's complaining voice drifted to where Joanna was snipping sprigs of lavender in her garden. The girl found fault with everything, the servants, the food, the weather. She demanded that a fire be lit in her room at all times and then complained that it was too warm and threw open the casements. Hoping to appease her, Joanna offered her the use of Maud but Hope, grown used to the skills of the maid she shared with her cousins, despaired over Maud's attempts to serve her and had twice reduced the girl to tears with her rude tongue.

Her strident tone disturbed the dogs who barked each time she raised her voice, or impatiently threw down her needlework. It was a trying time, the only consolation being that James was often away from the house visiting his tenants and sometimes, Hope rode out with him. His only real contact with Joanna was during dinner where his dull droning voice formed a backdrop to her private thoughts and dreams. One evening, as they finished the last course James opened a bottle of port and cleared his throat.

"An acquaintance of mine will be arriving in the next few days."

Joanna raised her eyebrows and was preparing to ask the name of the guest, but Hope forestalled her.

"Who is it, Father, anyone we know? Oh, I suppose it's some prosy old bore from court. Do you not know anybody interesting? I declare I could die of boredom, buried away here in the country."

"His father, Robert Grey and I were at Oxford together. Robert is ailing and likely to die soon. He has sent his son with some papers he wishes me to sign."

Hope pouted. "There you see, prosy and dull, just as I suspected." She pushed herself back in her chair and folded her arms, an action which, to Joanna's surprise, brought down the wrath of her father.

"Hope! You will mend your behaviour while my friend is here, and if he should, in any way, suspect that you find his conversation dull, I shall lock you in your chamber for a week. And you Madam." he turned his anger on Joanna. "You will make yourself available at all hours of the day, no skulking around in the garden, and you are to be dressed appropriately at all times. I will have no more dirty fingernails and straggly hair at my table. Do I make myself clear? Thornhold Manor is a respectable household and, for once, we will all be testament to that fact."

The women said nothing. Joanna reached for her glass and refreshed her dry mouth while Hope glared. It was clear that she had plenty to say but knew better than to do so. The evening was spoiled, and conversation became so stilted that they were all relieved when it drew to a close.

Visitors came seldom to Thornhold Manor. Joanna believed shame of the empty nursery disinclined James to invite his acquaintances to stay. The guest chambers had been unused for such a long time that they required a thorough cleaning. She set to work at once, ordering the hangings brushed and the bed linen purchased.

"His name is Simon." James told her. "He is a good Catholic like his father and now that Catholic fortunes are on the increase, he is pressing for a place at court. Since I have the ear of the king, I have promised his father to do what I can. We will travel to Greenwich together when I return. He is a good sort, well read and congenial; I believe you will find him tolerable company."

If James' other acquaintances were anything to go by, Joanna very much doubted it. Looking out across the garden, she sighed, knowing that for the time being she must leave the garden in Jonah's capable hands. The box hedging was due to be clipped and the gravel paths needed weeding and raking but thankfully the twice-yearly task could easily be left to the gardeners. She had hoped to pot on her lavender cuttings into a sandy loam for she enjoyed the solitary, repetitiveness of the task. She should have a day or two's grace before Mr Grey arrived, maybe she would have time to sneak out and attend to it.

A few hours later when Simon Grey leapt from his hired hack, beating the dust from his clothes with his hat, he found his hostess waiting quietly, her hands clasped tightly at her waist. Immediately he broke into a torrent of lively conversation.

"Ah, Lady Thornbury; I am so glad to meet you. What a journey! The coach I took was infested with fleas! It was so intolerable I decided to hire a horse for the latter part of the journey. You can see the countryside so much better from the saddle."

Murmuring sympathy, Joanna ushered him toward the house but as they reached the gate to the gardens he paused and turned in a circle surveying his surroundings.

"But I had no idea Thornholding was so splendid," he cried. "The house seems to have grown among the knots of flowers; see how the yellow walls seem to melt into the shrubbery. Oh, and the scent of this honeysuckle. I declare, Mistress Thornbury, you must have a treasure of a gardener hidden away here. It makes my father's place look like a patch of muddy scrub in comparison."

Delighted at such praise of her precious garden, Joanna's smile stretched into genuine pleasure. "Perhaps I can show you round after you have settled in. I am sure James will find the time."

"I shall look forward to it, indeed I shall."

While they waited for refreshments, he kept up a steady stream of light-hearted conversation, so much so that Joanna had difficulty in finding a convenient pause to inform him that Sir James was from home.

"No matter, no matter," he replied when she had eventually filled a brief pause. "I find the present company pleasing. Tell me, Mistress …" He paused, held up a finger. "I thought I heard a child crying, your son or daughter perhaps?"

Joanna's throat closed; she looked down at her clenched fingers and shook her head. Realising her distress, Simon was instantly on his feet.

"I've always been a blundering, inelegant fool. I do hope I haven't spoken out of turn. Do say you forgive me and, here, please use my kerchief and we'll talk of something else."

Joanna sniffed and even managed a shaky laugh, begging his forgiveness in turn. Conversation turned to safer things while Simon told her of the exotic gardens he had seen on his travels.

"Had I known of your interest, I should have brought you some roots to transplant into your own garden. I think I noticed a strong feminine influence out there; tell me, is that so?"

As Joanna opened her mouth to reply Hope came tripping down the stairs and, halfway down, appeared to notice Mr Grey for the first time. She paused for effect, lifting her chin in feigned surprise and squinted elegantly down her pretty nose. Simon rose and assayed the most stylish of bows and, somehow certain there was mockery in it, Joanna hid a smile. A short time later when James returned, he discovered both his wife and daughter captivated by his guest.

Joanna's early suspicion of Simon soon melted, and she began to enjoy his company. His lively conversation made a welcome change to the prosaic ramblings of her husband. Simon was educated yet never preachy and his political viewpoints never radical enough to offend anyone, not even James.

No one in the Thornbury household was musical but, robbed of its dusty cover, the spinet that had stood for years, unused in the corner, wheezed into life under Simon's ministrations. Some old broadsheets were produced and, much to her own amazement, Joanna found herself accompanying Hope, singing along as Simon played. Owing more to enthusiasm than skill, the sound of the old instrument filled the house, making the servants pause and look at one another in surprise.

It was many years since Joanna had laughed properly and it transformed her face. When she slipped between the cold sheets at night, instead of thinking of the cold graves in the churchyard, she thought back on the pleasant evening and anticipated the arrival of the next day.

Simon was an early riser, and once or twice Joanna bumped into him as she emerged from the still room.

"Good morning," he whispered, careful not to disturb the slumbering household. 'shall we take a turn about the gardens."

Lured from her duties, Joanna followed him. Together they moved between the flower beds, climbed up the hill to the orchard and, when the dew had dried, sat in the grass while he gently prised beneath her reserve to discover her secrets, her dreams …and disappointments.

Within a matter of weeks, she found herself telling him private things; the despair of ever bearing a living child, of her loneliness and lack of fulfilment. He listened quietly, his answers gentle and, to Joanna's surprise he tried to find small ways to increase her happiness.

James had never offered her solace for their loss and never appeared to mourn the children at all. It was as though he was personally affronted by her failure rather than grieved by it. His lack of an heir was a slur on his spotless reputation, it did not touch his heart. Somehow, sitting in the long grass of the orchard, she felt at peace and able, for the first time, to speak about her bereavement.

Sometimes, after supper, Simon suggested they all walk in the garden and, as the sun sank behind the house, the four of them would wander among the flowerbeds. They stopped beneath the bower where Hope and Joanna perched upon the camomile seat; a light breeze was stirring the newly formed rosebuds, which spurred Simon into spontaneous poetry:

"Rough winds do shake the darling buds of May.
and summer's leaf hath all too short a lease..."

The poem triggered something in Joanna's memory and her laughter stilled as she turned to him.

"That is by Master Shakespeare, is it not? I remember my father reading something similar, but I had long forgotten how it ran. He could recite many, many verses but, sadly, I lack the same skill. It is lovely, Mr Grey, the words are chosen quite perfectly, no others would do so well."

Disinterested, James and Hope moved on, eager to end the promenade as soon as possible and return to the comfort of the parlour but Joanna and Simon lingered. As James' hectoring voice faded away, Simon reached up and plucked a cluster of hard green rosebuds and pressed them into her hand. As she smiled at the gift, he murmured so his voice did not carry.

"Shall I compare thee to a summer's day?
Thou art more lovely and more temperate:
Rough winds do shake the darling buds of May,
And Summer's leaf hath all too short a lease:
Sometime too hot the eye of heaven shines,
And oft" is his gold complexion dimmed,
And every faire from faire some-time declines,
By chance, or natures changing course untrimm'd:
But thy eternal Summer shall not fade,
Nor loose possession of that faire thou ow'st,
Nor shall death brag thou wandrest in his shade,
When in eternal lines to time thou growest,
So long as men can breathe or eyes can see,
So long lives this, and this gives life to thee,"

Joanna blinked tears from her eyes as, murmuring her appreciation, she hurried in pursuit of James and Hope, her heart beating like a rabbit's. Quickly catching up with them, Simon acted as if nothing had happened, and as the walk continued, he commented upon Shakespeare's use of language and the poet's certainty of his poem would prove to be immortal.

Joanna began to relax again. Maybe she had imagined the intensity of feeling that sparked so suddenly between them. The absurdity of the idea that she might hold attraction for a young man like Simon convinced her that she'd imagined it and, by the time they passed back into the house she was laughing again. James paused to remove his muffler, and turned suddenly, drawn up short by the vision of his laughing wife. The evening breeze had loosened her hair from her cap, and it framed her face. She was flushed and glowing and looked almost pretty.

As summer began to take hold in the gardens, there were many extra tasks and only one man to carry them out. Noting Jonah's bent back and increasing rheumatism, Joanna decided it was time for Jonah's grandson to learn his trade. George proved an enthusiastic worker and was soon struggling about the garden with barrow loads of clippings.

"We are a little behind this year," she explained to Simon as they watched the boy hurry back for a fresh load.

"I hope it isn't my fault. I would hate to have hindered you in any way. You are so lucky to have the garden. Working at something you love is a privilege indeed, and I imagine the garden offers you solace for …other disappointments."

Joanna brushed an imaginary fly from her face before smiling up at him, refusing to acknowledge that his eyes were the same blue as the sky.

"You're right, Master Grey, it is the place where I feel the most content. I think we were originally put on earth to cultivate the land and that's why it feels so right. All …most of my unhappiness melts away after just a few moments of being out here. Sometimes … and you will think this silly … it is as if I can feel the people who were here before. Perhaps one of my forebears was a peasant farmer or something, I know I am more at home in the garden than I am in the drawing room."

Simon laughed. "Well, one would never know it." His smile faded. "You know, I am leaving soon. I am travelling with your husband and Mistress Hope, first to Taunton, and then on to Greenwich." He paused, looking about him and licking his lips which had apparently become very dry. "I don't know if I will ever return. Joanna … Lady Thornbury but I'd like you to know how much I value our …friendship."

Joanna tried to speak but found she could only croak. She coughed to clear her throat that seemed to be closing up. At length, regaining the use of her voice, she said,

"Oh, I think I do know, Master Grey, for I value it equally, and I thank you for bringing happiness to Thornhold, albeit briefly. None of us shall ever forget you."

Blinking away tears, she looked across the gardens and shivered, the sun seemed to have gone in for she was colder than before.

"Joanna, I want you to have this, in memory of me. I know it is improper for me to offer it but, since our friendship is to be cut short, I thought you might forgive the impulse."

He was holding something wrapped in velvet cloth and taking it from him she untied the ribbon fastening and drew out a slim volume of poetry and turned it over.

"Master Shakespeare, 'she exclaimed.

"It was my mother's," he said. "I would like you to have it in remembrance of me." Joanna was barely able to breathe; a tear fell onto the calfskin covering and seeing it, Simon's hand shot out to grip her wrist.

"Joanna!" he groaned as she wrenched herself from him and ran away.

***

It was a difficult leave taking. Joanna, still battling with disgust at James' attentions last evening, wrestled with the pain of parting. Unable to look at him, she ate her breakfast without tasting it while Hope maintained a stream of excited babble. Nobody replied, Joanna and Simon were too torn with emotion, and James merely grunted disinterestedly at appropriate intervals.

Hope didn't notice. She was in a fever to return to Taunton and rudely declared she had never been so dull in all her life as she had been the last few weeks. Thornbury Manor had been fine while she was a child but now that she was a woman, she required more. A girl of her age needed to be among friends. Joanna couldn't agree more and acknowledged that now Simon was leaving, she wouldn't have a friend in the world.

As the covers were removed, James complained loudly at the state of England's roads. Simon, only half listening, flashed a glance at Joanna. She looked plain this morning; her face was pinched, and her hair pulled into a severe knot at the back of her head; the stiff ringlets framing her face were limp and lustreless.

Although she could feel his eyes upon her, Joanna did not dare look up. Hoping that the livid reminders of James' lust were hidden beneath the lace of her collar, she kept her eyes on her plate, taking only small bites because her food tasted of ashes. Although she chewed for an age, it remained obstinately in her mouth until, at last, she managed to swallow it, almost whole.

Joanna could not imagine resuming the friendless state that was once her normality. Simon Grey had changed everything; he had shown her how precious life could be …in the right company. She peered from beneath lowered lids and saw that his face was pale, as if he too had spent the night in dread.

"Come along, or we will be on the road all day." Hope, breaking into Joanna's misery placed a perfunctory kiss on her cheek. "Perhaps I will come back for Christmas, if the Oswald's don't ask me to stay."

Before he boarded the coach, James planted a wet, meaningless kiss on her cheek and climbed into the carriage. As they settled, Joanna could hear Hope complaining stridently that he was sitting on her skirt. A footstep sounded on the gravel beside her, but she didn't dare look up. He must not guess her grief. She felt him take her hand, lean toward her and she opened her eyes to see his fair head and feel the touch of his lips upon the back of her hand. Then he stood up, and she found she could not look away. Although he smiled she felt no comfort. Her eyes stung with unshed tears, the pain in her chest akin to swallowing a stone, but somehow she managed to smile back.

Please God, let him understand my lack of words. She stared deep into his eyes, drank in his image as if trying to quench her thirst. James poked his head from the carriage.

"Come along, man, we must make Stroud before dusk, or the inns will be full."

Simon gave her one last crooked smile before turning away and, as the horses passed beneath the barton gate, he leaned from the window to raise a slow hand in farewell.

Late May 1685

The dull contentment of the days before Simon's arrival did not return. Now the peace was like a shroud, a dark, glooming, suffocating misery that would not lift. She was haunted. His shadow remained in the barton where they had met, the dining room where they had laughed, the parlour where they sang, and the garden where he had almost pledged his love. Although there had really been nothing more than friendship, no inappropriate behaviour at all unless one counted the gift, or his lips upon her bare wrist, she could not forget him. His behaviour could be construed as those of a lover, but his affection had been expressed only in the simplest terms of friendship. Perhaps she was mistaken. Perhaps her loneliness had made an icon out of clay for wasn't it inconceivable that a man of his calibre could form an attachment for a woman like herself?

Joanna could not get warm, ague seeped into her bones and would not shift, and even the huge fires she ordered lit ceased to warm her. One rainy afternoon while she was huddled before the hearth, she received a letter from Hope. She tore it open, scanned Hope's wide round handwriting. Characteristically the letter omitted any enquiry into her stepmother's health but plunged straight into Hope's news.

"Oh Mother," she wrote. "You would not believe the excitement here in Taunton, the whole town is in a fever of activity. There is scarcely a family in the whole town that doesn't support Monmouth, and at school we girls have been making flags for him to carry into battle. What fun to think of the future king bearing colours made by my own hand. I do hope he picks mine to carry, for it is quite the best, although Beatrice's is nice too.

There is to be a procession and all the bells will be rung in welcome. Beatrice's brother, Sam, I think I spoke of him before, was too eager to wait for the Duke to arrive in Taunton so he has ridden off to the muster near Ilminster. Sam says that the Duke is sure to win, and that as he moves across the country, the whole population will rise up to join him. There is not a soul in Taunton that has a single good thing to say about King James. They say he is cruel and falsely promoting the cause of the Catholics to the detriment of the Protestants.

Now, I know I'm a Catholic, Mother, but I cannot fail to see that these people may have a point. If a fellow is efficient at his allotted task, then surely, that is all that should matter. I don't see why anybody should be given a position of authority solely because his religious beliefs match those of the king.

I have heard rumours that King James plans to force all men to become Catholics again, and really, that can do no good at all. Look what happened to his father. After all some things are better left to a man's conscience, don't you think?

Beatrice and I were at the milliners on Tuesday, and I have ordered a gown, all in yellow silk. The neckline is rather daring but I have chosen a sumptuous cream lace fichu for decencies sake, and the seamstress promises it shall be ready to wear on the day the Duke comes to town. They say he is awfully handsome, charming like his father and very, very gallant, and all his followers will be with him. They will come marching right up the high street, making a fine sight. They say he has an eye for the ladies, and I should so love to be noticed by the future king. And besides Sam will be riding with him and I long to see him again.

I probably should have told you while I was home that I've formed an attachment for Samuel Trelask, but Sam thought it best to wait until such time as he can speak to Father formally. Oh, Mother! He is so tall and handsome, and come from a very good family. He doesn't mind about me being a Catholic, and will speak to Father just as soon as the battle is won so, please, Mother, will you keep my secret until such time?

I cannot wait to become Mistress Trelask. I am so happy when I am with him but when he is gone from me, all is misery."

Joanna dropped the letter into her lap, the last line echoing in her head, she could relate to that sentiment very well. She had been right to suspect that Hope had formed some romantic attachment and wondered what Samuel was like. He was close to Hope in age at least, perhaps love would calm some of her stepdaughter's fierceness. That is, if they could convince James to agree to the match.

June 11th, 1685

It was hot. Joanna could scarce credit that so short a time ago the countryside had foundered beneath four feet of snow. From November to February the rivers had been frozen and the water in the garden barrels, impenetrable. Young and old alike had perished, victim to the cold and hunger. Sheep were found frozen stiff in the byre, and the number of rooks tossing about the pale skies dwindled before the thaw set in. Joanna, trapped indoors by the vicious wind, had chaffed at the inactivity. Despite the huge fires roaring up every chimney, the ice remained thick on the windowpanes until late in the day. The frigid loneliness seemed endless, yet here she was, not five months later, so hot she could scarcely draw breath.

She breakfasted on the terrace looking out across the garden. It was going to be hot again, but the roses could be ignored no longer. She was determined to remove the spent heads before the sun rose too high in the sky. Scandalising poor Maud, she went upstairs and discarded most of her petticoats. The thought of all those layers was too much and, rejecting her severe black workaday dress, she donned instead a simple afternoon gown with just one petticoat for modesty. She would dearly have liked to have left off her stockings, but Maud's would probably have burst a blood vessel, so she put them on and tied the garters just above the knee.

The last few months had been hard. The days longer and lonelier than they had ever been but determined not to be vanquished by loneliness, Joanna immersed herself in the garden and found that working until dusk not only helped the day to pass but ensured that she slept soundly. There was no good dwelling on the past or the what-might-have-been, and at nighttime she emptied her mind and willed herself to go to sleep. She refused to think of the future stretching like an empty road before her, until old age chased her to her grave. She took one day at a time, not expecting happiness and concentrating all her energies upon each task as she came upon it. Her servants found her softer, less rigid but they did not see the tears she did not let fall.

George was weeding among the lettuces but as soon as he heard her step he scrambled to his feet.

"Good morning, George, I cannot see Jonah anywhere. Do you know where he may be?"

"Yes'm, Milady," he replied, tugging his forelock. "Him be sick abed with the ague, Milady. Too bad to rise, so Mother do say. Jonah says I'm to get on with pulling these weeds."

"Yes, George. Yes, you do that. You are doing a fine job."

She swept along the path toward the stillroom, and after collecting a few things, she set off in the direction of the gardener's tumble-down cottage.

The nettles and foxgloves that straggled along hedgerows petered out as she reached the tiny plot of land that enveloped Jonah's home. In his tiny plot of garden there were neat rows of cabbages, lettuce and leeks. A well-used spade leaned near the porch and Jonah's boots were neatly tucked beneath a bench. The door was open, and a tabby cat was cleaning its paws on the step.

Knowing Jonah was very deaf she rapped loudly, trying not to look inside but, as she waited for a reply, she couldn't help noticing a chicken on the kitchen table. It was scratching about, pecking the crust from a half-eaten loaf of bread. It was some time before Jonah's daughter emerged from the gloom. She stopped abruptly when she saw the visitor and, bobbing a hasty curtsey, asked her in.

Joanna put her basket on the table.

"Good morning, Dorcas. I wondered how your father is. George told me he is ailing so I thought I'd bring him some physic."

Dorcus sniffed and began to rummage in the basket.

"He isn't sick unto death, Milady, just ailing a little. Put it down to the weather I do. It is terrible hot. We was all surprised when he made it through the winter, it were that harsh. You can see him if you've the mind to".

The old man's sleeping place was tiny, with no window to allow either light in, or heat to escape. Jonah was propped on an ancient pallet, and with one foot he rocked a cradle, but his ministration seemed to have little effect on the bawling infant within. Jonah's face opened in astonishment when his mistress ducked beneath the entrance.

"Why, Milady," he wheezed, trying not to cough. "It's good of you to call. I'm none too gradely, as ye can probably tell, but I'll be up an about the morrow. We must be netting them peas afore the pigeons have them."

Joanna looked around for a chair but, after some hesitation, decided to remain standing. "You will remain here until you are quite well, Jonah. You are no use to me if you're unfit. Young George and I will cope on our own but let us hope it doesn't take too long or the garden will miss your skilled touch."

"It is just this heat, Milady. I'll be up an about in no time just as soon as this weather breaks but us must hope it won't bring heavy rain or the garden will be battered."

As Jonah struggled to sit up, the babe whimpered fretfully, and Joanna resisted the impulse to pick it up. She wondered how long the poor thing would survive with little maternal attention or proper nourishment. It was stifling in the cottage, and the stench of onions and chickens nauseating.

"I've brought some things to aid your recovery. There's some marigold salve for your joints, and some Echinacea for your chest. Ask Dorcus to come to the kitchens and cook will give her some bones to make a broth. "

Seeing Jonah so frail made Joanna suddenly afraid of losing another friend. She was used to seeing him well-wrapped in all weathers, and he looked different with his shirt unbuttoned and his feet bare. Realising he was the closest thing she had to a friend now, she moved a step nearer the bed.

"I'm sorry to see you so low, Jonah. You must hurry up and get well."

Dorcus, coming upon her mistress as she left the cottage was surprised to see her wiping away a tear.

"Goodbye, Dorcas. Look after him, won't you? I will return tomorrow to see how he is. Don't let him get up too soon."

Back in the garden, Joanna moved slowly among the roses, snipping off the spent flower heads and tossing them into a basket. As the hours ticked by the day grew more and more oppressive, the heat bouncing back off the gravel until Joanna felt as though she were baking in a kiln. Abandoning her labours, she wandered off in search of shade, passing George who wielded a large basket of vegetables. He nodded to her, trying to pull his forelock as he had been taught until Joanna shook her head to indicate that it did not matter.

"Are these for the kitchen George?" she asked, picking up a carrot holding it to her nose. Earth still clung to the root, but it smelled so delicious her mouth began to water.

"Yes, Milady. Cook 'as give me a whole list for the table and says she'll brook no delay."

"Very well then, George, I'll not keep you from your chores. May I keep this carrot and have it for my luncheon?"

Hitching up the basket, George looked bemused.

"Course you can, they're your carrots, ain't they?"

Joanna was still laughing as she headed for the shade of the old churchyard where the grass was lush underfoot. Cow parsley bordered a bright carpet of grass where gravestones sprawled like an old man's teeth, some leaning and some long since fallen. Joanna moved among them, trying to figure out the mouldering writing and wondering about the people that decayed beneath her feet. They were the same people who had worked and lived at the manor, the same people whose possessions she sometimes unearthed from the soil.

A robin hopped onto a stone, his head cocked, hoping for a crumb, and as she moved away he flew to a low branch to let loose a burst of song. At the Thornbury vault, she read the plaque as she had so many times before. It was a simple memorial and plainly wrought. The words were cut deep, straight and legible, although they had been carved over three hundred years ago.

Here lieth
Sir Henry Thornbury
Lady Isabella Thornbury
Arabella Thornbury
Thomas Thornbury.
Dead of the pestilence in the year of our lord, 1348

Joanna stood quietly, wondering about these people; members of the family she had married into. She speculated upon the ages of the children of Sir Henry and Isabella. She guessed Isabella had been the mother and her daughter, Bella, named for her. What had Bella and Thomas been like? Naughty or good? Sickly or hearty? How sad that pestilence had wiped out this happy, thriving family, although, of course, they may not have been happy, but she liked to imagine them so.

The plague still reared its ugly head from time to time, cutting a swathe through the population, taking rich and poor alike. Wives were made widows, mothers and fathers left childless, children left without parents, sweethearts left broken hearted. She wished she knew which of Henry and Isabella's children had survived, ensuring the name Thornbury lived on. She began to count back the generations …As the spectre of death moved closer, Joanna forced herself to take another path, one that led to the most difficult place of all.

Inside a low picket fence, where daisies were scattered like stars across the grass, eight tiny stone crosses bore witness to the brief lives of her children. She did not need to read the names for they were branded into her soul. James, May, Elizabeth, Katherine, Thomas, Charles, Anne, and Edward Thornbury.

Only the droning of a bee disturbed the silence in this place where Joanna rarely came. It was a place she could not bear. A place that marked the death of her dreams, her hopes and happiness. With all her children gathered in the shady quiet, she felt so lonely she wished she could simply lie down with them and wait to die.

But she did not tarry long, the pain drove her away. She moved on through long, lush grass and on impulse she knelt down and slipped off her shoes and stockings. There was nobody to see and fewer who'd care.

She felt like a peasant girl as she walked through the cooling grass, up the steeply sloping hill and ducked beneath the limbs of ancient fruit trees clustered near the summit. The cow parsley was more rampant here than in the churchyard, and bees blundered drunkenly in search of nectar. The coolness underfoot soothed her and spiritually calmer but a little breathless, she flopped onto her back and threw out her arms, sending up a skein of flying insects.

She smiled wryly, imagining James' horror were he to see her lying like some ditch drab in the undergrowth. Her skirts were hitched to her bare knees, but it was too hot to matter, and there was no-one to see. She stared at the pattern of branches against the cloudless sky, enjoying the feeling of freedom and, far up, close to heaven, watched tiny birds wheeling in the air. She squinted up at them for so long, her eyes became heavy and after a while they closed.

She dreamed of Simon Grey. They were walking through a misty white world, their arms were linked, their heads close in a misty white world, and her dreaming self was laughing. She knew herself to be beautiful, and she knew herself to be loved. And as she slept a shadow crossed the sun, breaking into her dreaming.

Still half in her fantasy she murmured, 'Simon?" and passed the back of her hand across her damp brow.

"Joanna?" All at once her eyes were open, blinking stupidly into the sunlight. "I didn't want to wake you, you looked so peaceful."

It was no dream. He really was there, sinking to his knees in the long grass beside her. He was dusty and a little sweaty in his brocade coat, but he really was there. Letting out a sob, of half grief and half joy, she launched herself into his arms.

"Oh Simon!"

He buried his face in her neck, breathing her in. He had travelled for many days across a country shrivelled by the heat and, knowing that his coming broke all the rules, he had been tempted many times to retrace his footsteps. Only the urgent need to see her again drove him on. He had prayed she would understand and scarcely able to believe his luck at such a welcome, his arms locked about her. Her un-corseted body was flattened, tight against his chest and when he brought his face slowly down to meet hers, they both knew it was too late to turn back.

***

The sun was sinking, blessedly cool after the heat of the day. Joanna sat up suddenly.

"Sshh," she placed her finger to her lips and they both listened to the voices floating from the foot of the hill "It's Maud and young George calling me. I must've been away for hours."

She turned to Simon in the grass beside her, looking much younger than his twenty-three years. His brocade coat was discarded upon the grass and his shirt unlaced to the navel. Joanna could not resist reaching out to stroke the down of fair hair that dwindled into a point below his breeches.

"I must go, Simon, before they come looking. Can you help me dress?"

Her hair was full of grass seed, her breasts tumbling from her open bodice. Simon groaned and reached for her, pulling her back down, nuzzling her neck.

"Must you go? Right now?"

"Yes, right now. Maud is looking for me." She wrestled with him playfully. "It will never do to be caught like this. I shall have to make up a story as it is. At least I can be quite sure that none of them will suspect I've spent the afternoon with my lover. Since it is not my general habit." Sobering suddenly, she dropped her head. "Simon, I can't bear for you to leave like this. Where is your horse? Can you not ride off quietly, and then return like a regular visitor? I can feign surprise that you've called and invite you to take tea in the parlour. Then I can invite you to stay on... please?"

He smiled, and began to help her dress, shaking her breasts back into her bodice and pulling the lace tight.

"Of course, my darling, I am your servant and will do whatever you wish. I tethered my horse in the cool of the wood. I shall ride quietly away and then return in an hour or so to defray any suspicion."

"Oh Simon!" Joanna murmured biting her bottom lip. "Are we quite mad?"

"Probably," he smiled, as he fastened his breeches and pulled on his boots.

When Joanna strolled casually into the barton a short time later, she found a crowd of servants preparing a search party. As they became aware of her, Maud gave a shriek and detached herself from the crowd.

"Oh, My Lady. There you are. We've been that worried, looking all over for you and calling and calling. Didn't you hear us? Look at you, your gown is all besmirched. I'll draw you a bath, shall I, Madam, and bring a tray to your chamber?"

Joanna smiled more warmly than ever before, looking as if a candle had been lit behind her eyes.

"That will be lovely, Maud. Thank you, and bring plenty for me to eat, I find I am quite famished. I fell asleep in the orchard and haven't eaten since breakfast. Perhaps an infusion of ginger and camomile too, for I feel a headache coming on. I fear I may have taken too much sun. I'll await you in my chamber."

As the tray was taken away, and Joanna pretended to prepare for bed, a servant arrived to inform her that Master Grey had arrived with messages from London town. Feigning surprise, Joanna smoothed her hair and descended to the parlour to entertain Master Grey with tea and cake. After an hour or so he agreed that he would be delighted to stay the night if she were sure it would be no trouble, and Joanna rang a bell and ordered the blue room to be prepared.

"Would you like to take a turn around the garden?" she asked, with the smile she kept just for him.

Much later, when the sun at last disappeared over the horizon, its reflected glow still burning in the sky, Simon opened his chamber door and listened. The night was warm, an owl hooted in the garden but all else was silent. Closing his door again, he crossed to the window and climbed out onto the terrace. The gravel crunched at every step as he worked his way around the house to the sunroom. The porch was in shadow, and for one heart-stopping moment, he stopped sharply, mistaking the bay trees flanking the door for people. Smiling at himself, he placed his hand on the handle and entered the house without a sound.

Simon began the ascent to the top floor. He crept along a corridor, past Hope's chamber and on to Joanna's, which she had told him lay at the far end. Looking furtively around to ensure he was not seen, he reached out and grasped the handle.

Joanna was waiting and, as soon as she heard him, she wrenched the door open and pulled him inside. Quickly, she barred the door, her heart hammering.

"Oh, my god, I can't believe we are doing this."

Alone again with his lady, he was suddenly shy to be there.

Although the casements stood open to the night air, the chamber remained airless, the moon making Joanna's thin shift transparent and clothing her limbs in light. She smiled over her shoulder as she poured him some wine which he accepted with a salute.

"You can't be thirsty," she laughed. "For you certainly made the most of the wine at dinner. I was beginning to think you were in search of courage."

Wiping his mouth on his embroidered sleeve, he countered, "And I needed it, creeping through the house like a thief. Burglary's a felony you know. You could get me hung. And what was all that, "Master Grey," business at supper? You've been addressing me as Simon in front of the servants for months now."

"I was trying to make a good impression," she retorted. "Goodness knows, one of us had too, you were making cow eyes at me right under the footman's nose."

Putting down his goblet, he grasped her wrist and pulled her toward him.

"Mmm, you smell good."

"Better than earlier, I'll be bound. I have taken a bath and changed my linen and brushed my hair. It is not often I go to such trouble. I've often heard that romance begets vanity, but I'd never believed it before."

"Shush," he said, struggling to undo the ribbon that fastened her shift. She let him wrestle with it for a while until, taking pity on him, she offered help.

"It is the end you need, Simon. Grasp the end of the ribbon and pull, and all will be well."

He pulled firmly and felt it give. The gathered neck of the garment loosened, exposing her shoulders but lodging just above her breast, exposing a generous depth of cleavage. Suddenly impatient, he tugged the chemise and let it fall to the floor and stepping from the ring of fabric and taking his hand, Joanna led him to the bed.

August 1685

Joanna retched helplessly over the chamber pot, her empty stomach churning in revolt. Slumping back on the pillows while Maud hurried in with clean linen, she cursed herself for a fool. Hot tears began again as her belly growled, calling for food but she ignored it, knowing the futility of feeding a stomach incapable of accepting nourishment. She had recognised the symptoms straight away and did not need to be told that the onset of queasiness betokened another fruitless pregnancy.

She did not inform Simon of her fears but let him ride away knowing that this time, they would never meet again. After his departure the sickness increased until constant nausea and violent biliousness forced her to confess her condition to Maud. The maid was delighted.

"Oh, mistress that's rare, good news. And there was I thinking you'd been taken down with some malady. This time we'll make sure things are different. My granny was a rare hand with the childbearing, and they do say I've took the gift. Why, the master will be right pleased, after all this time."

Joanna took great gulps of air in an attempt to quell the rising tide of nausea as her world fell further apart.

While Joanna was still suffering, a letter arrived from Hope.

"Oh Mother," she read. "Taunton is a sorry place to be right now. Our dear Duke was seized by the king's men and executed at Tower Hill. The scandal mongers say that it took five swipes of the axe to take off his head and that he debased himself at the last, sending begging letters to King James, betraying some of his most loyal supporters. I cannot believe such a thing of him, for surely he was the handsomest prince to ever grace our shores.

Everyone here is full of fear. Aunt Carrie is quite beside herself with worry for Edward for we have no idea where he is. Everyone knows the Royalist troops were ruthless after the battle at Sedgemore Plain. It's said that they pursued our soldiers across country, hanging those they didn't put to the sword and now the lanes are cluttered with corpses. It may be just hearsay, but we cannot know for Uncle Leo will not let us leave the house. We cower here in fear, waiting for God knows what. Those that were spared are being brought to Taunton Castle for trial, but we all know that the trial will not be justice.

Oh, Mother, what can I do? I am so afraid of what will happen. We have seen not hide nor hair of Edward and Sam since they marched off to Illminster, and all our attempts have failed to discover whether they are captured or in hiding. My instinct is to run home to Thornhold, but I must stay, Mother, Aunt Carrie needs me, and I cannot flee when my dear Samuel is in such peril."

Joanna wrote to Hope straight away, ordering her immediate return but, fearing Samuel hung or slain on the field, Hope refused to leave. Wanting to offer comfort to her uncle and his family, she remained in Taunton although the atmosphere was dire. Every family had lost, or were in danger of losing, at least one family member. There was widespread resentment against the crown, but the West Country was helpless, caught in the vice-like grip of King James' vengeance.

Joanna read all this with horror. While she and Simon had been revelling in each other's arms, the country had lurched into chaos. Dashing off a hastily scrawled note to James in Greenwich, she gave herself up to the miseries of early pregnancy.

She could barely set foot on the chamber floor without an immediate attack of vomiting. She knew she should write to James to inform him of her condition. She could only pray he'd assumed the child to be his. Surely, if she were vague about the due date, he would not suspect a thing. Besides, it was not as if she was likely to carry the child to term and knew it was not possible, even for a doctor, to tell if an aborted foetus was a few weeks younger than it should be.

She had no doubt the baby was Simon's, and she wondered that they failed to consider the possibility of pregnancy. Now she was fated to spend the next few months suffering, unwittingly forming affection for the tiny spark of life within her, only to produce a dead child at the end of the term. She felt so ill she almost regretted her behaviour but, by the end of August when she could just about stand without vomiting, and even swallow a little dry bread, some of her spirit began to return.

When she could bare to look, the mirror showed a wan face, her hair lay limply on her shoulders, her clothes so loose they could have been made for somebody else. Joanna, unable to take interest even in her garden, merely wanted to bury her head beneath the tester.

In the autumn, news reached Taunton that Lord Chief Justice Jeffreys was on his way to conduct the trials of the rebel prisoners. He was reputed to be a ruthless man, dispatching his version of justice with dispassion. At Winchester in late August Dame Alice Lisle was arrested for harbouring the king's enemies and, despite her plea that she had not known the two men she gave shelter to were fugitives, Jeffreys condemned her to be burned. After an appeal to King James the penalty was commuted to beheading; in every west-country town the people growled in corners and, when the deed was done, the news of her brave end lodged deep in the public imagination. Joanna was not the only one to weep.

Deprived of the burning, fuelled with retribution, the Hanging Judge Jeffreys, journeyed across the country, issuing a swathe of rebel executions. His involvement, more than anything else, convinced Joanna that she must travel to Taunton and force Hope to come home.

It was a nightmare journey. The coach lurched into potholes and skidded off stones, throwing the women about as though they were rag dolls. Maud clung to her mistress's arm, afraid in equal measures for their safety and that of Joanna's unborn child. Clouds of dust billowed through the leather window blinds, making them cough, and twice Joanna vomited into the earthenware bowl brought along for the purpose. Sleep was impossible and their world shrank to the confines of the lurching coach interior. After such a day, the lice ridden accommodation at a wayside inn seemed a welcome luxury, where the two women, drawn together by homesickness, fell straight into an exhausted sleep.

The next day the torture resumed, and it wasn't until the day after that the driver knocked on the roof to alert them that they were finally approaching Taunton. The town was in sight and Joanna, struggling from her seat to throw up the blind, recoiled in horror. She had expected to look out at a tranquil country lane. Falling back to her seat with her hand across her mouth, she gaped at her maid.

"No, don't look out there, Maud!"

But her warning was too late, for Maud was already poking her head from the carriage. Instead of a rural idyll, she was confronted by bodies hanging from the roadside trees as a grotesque warning to other rebels.

As the coach passed the fly-encrusted corpses, clouds of carrion flew up, their coach filled with flies as they arrived in town where the once-rampant flag flapped raggedly in a lazy wind. The usually heaving streets were empty, the local population cowered in their homes, not daring to venture forth. The two women peeped white faced from the window as the coach clattered through cobbled streets to the inn door.

As Joanna gathered her skirts and prepared to alight, a groom shuffled forward to take charge of the horses, leaving the women to find their own way inside. It was as if the town was holding its breath, waiting for retribution. With a deep, strengthening breath, Joanna opened the door and went in search of the innkeeper.

As soon as she was settled in her room, Joanna dashed off a note to Leo informing him of her arrival and asking if she could call. When she handed the letter to the innkeeper, he glanced at the addressee and scratched his head.

"It's a bad business and no mistake, Milady. They're a good family, like the rest of us, just trying to get by like. That fine woman, Mistress Oswald, she don't deserve this and that's a fact. Young Edward is just a lad, into mischief like any other, but they're giving no quarter, that's the trouble. Out to make an example of us Tauntonians and that's just not fair, in my opinion. Just not fair …"

Frowning as she groped for understanding, she interrupted,
"But tell me, please, what has happened?"

"Oh, don't you know? 'Tis a bad business and no mistake, but young Master Oswald, Edward that is, and the young Trelask boy, Samuel, they've been locked up with the rebels in the castle. Brung them in last night, they did. I reckon they'll hang too if that devil Jeffrey's has his way. Oh! Ma'am!" he cried, grabbing her arm to prevent her from falling. "You're not acquainted with the Oswalds are you? Not kin, are they?"

Breathing deeply to quell the tide of nausea, Joanna replied,
"Yes, they are kin of a sort. I am Lady Thornbury; Mr Oswald is my husband's brother-in-law. My stepdaughter, Hope, is staying with them. I have come to take her home."

"Oh, I know Mistress Hope, Milady. A fine young woman, she's up at the academy with the Misses Musgrave and Blake. They put on a great show for our Duke, a fine parade, made him most welcome. Anyways I'll be sending your note round right now. Shall I be sending you in some more fruit cordial?"

Joanna sat in the sombre parlour at the Oswald's house and wished desperately to be home at Thornhold. The room was stuffy and overcrowded and she wasn't good at offering comfort. While Hope was sent for, Carrie griped her hand, her polite conversation hampered by the lump in her throat and, while they waited, Leo implored her to take the girl home straight away.

"Taunton's no place for a girl, just now, Joanna and things might yet happen that no young woman should bear witness to."

"Perhaps all the girls should come home with me," Joanna suggested. "I'm sure they'll be safer far from here."

But Leo shook his head. Although there was little hope of reprieve, they all felt they had to stay because of Edward. As an officer in Monmouth's army, Edward could be condemned to a traitor's death. As he explained the situation, Joanna clung helplessly to Carrie's hand, sharing her suffering. Perhaps it was better to lose your children at birth than after years of getting to know them and accumulating happy memories.

Hope's quick footsteps in the passage brought Carrie's head up and she fumbled for her kerchief. By the time her niece burst into the room, she was wiping her eyes. Seeing Joanna sitting on the sofa, Hope let out an impassioned cry.

"Mother!" She launched herself onto Joanna's knee.

It seemed that, for once, Hope was glad to see her, and Joanna smoothed her hair, trying to calm her.

"Hush," she murmured. "Hush, it will be alright, Hope. I have come to take you home."

"Home?" Hope sat up again and wiped her wet face. "Don't be silly, I can't go home! Not now with things the way they are. Don't you know Edward and Samuel are likely to be hanged! I'll not set foot out of town until they are free. I had thought, when I saw you, that you brought good news. Father has the favour of the king, surely he will not let his own kin perish for what was little more than a prank."

"I wrote your father when first I heard but have had no reply. I knew nothing of what had befallen Edward and the other boy until I arrived in Taunton this very afternoon. There is nothing we can do, Hope, without endangering ourselves and everyone else around us. Judge Jeffreys is a dangerous man; it would be foolish to antagonise him, surely you must see that. We must get you home to safety."

Hope stuck out her chin, reminding Joanna of her father.

"I will not go with you, Mother. I must wait here and see what befalls my cousin and my betrothed. I suppose you had forgotten that I am betrothed. It is my duty to stay here, surely you must see that, Mother?"

Helplessly, Joanna looked to Leo for support, but he simply smiled and shrugged his shoulders. His son could well be hanged, nightly they prayed for a miracle. Sometimes a death penalty was commuted to transportation and, although it would be dreadful to lose Edward to the colonies, at least he would be spared his life. Conditions were harsh in the New World but there was a chance of prospering, a chance for life, whereas hanging would spell the end for all of them. Should it come to that, Carrie would never recover.

"I think we should sleep on it and talk again tomorrow. We are all overwrought and, truly, Hope, you can do little good here. It would be better for you, and your mother, if you went home but… I do not feel we can force you. I appreciate your loyalty to your cousin, and to young

Trelask and I know they will be touched by your support, too. Come, my dear, say good night and try to get some sleep, things will look brighter in the morning. They always do."

It was a sombre evening. Joanna watched as Carrie's children clung to her skirts, and her elder daughters, deferent and concerned, bid her a gentle goodnight. She, who would never feel the tenderness of a child's needy hand, bit her lip and tried not to fall victim to the sin of envy.

When darkness fell, Leo accompanied her back to the inn, apologising that the inconveniences of their overcrowded terrace meant that they could not offer her hospitality. In a way Joanna was glad of the impersonal surroundings of the inn where she could forget, for a while, the semi-smothered terror that beset the Oswalds.

She longed for the familiarity of home and when sleep evaded her, she imagined she walked among the flowery beds of her gardens with the earthy sweet smells rich in her nostrils. But, when Simon Grey intruded upon her dream, she did not allow him to stay but turned sharply from him and took a different path.

The next morning, either from the effects of the hot weather or the infesting posting houses, Maud had come out in hives. The poor girl's face and body was covered in red and itchy swellings and, stupidly, Joanna had not thought to pack any salves or ointment for the journey. Taking pity on her, she left the girl at the inn; promising to call at the apothecary for some ointment and return with it as soon as she could. Then, quelling her own gestational upsets, she engaged a link boy to escort her to the Oswald's house.

The maid was clearing the untouched dishes from the breakfast room when she arrived, and she was shown into a room where Carrie was shredding a lace handkerchief on her lap. Leo stood a little apart, gazing from the front window. He turned when she entered and, going forward to greet her, offered her a seat. She could tell at once that they had received further ill news and, her legs suddenly refusing to hold her, she sat in the closest chair and waited to be told.

Leo cleared his throat. "You find us with a fresh worry this morning, Joanna, for we have had news that typhus has broken out at the castle gaol."

Joanna started up from her chair, her hand to her mouth. "Oh, my Lord, Leo. Whatever next?"

His reply was forestalled by Hope, who appeared in the doorway.

"Next, Mother, they will probably perish but no doubt 'tis a nobler death than hanging."

She flounced into a chair, her tear-streaked face belying her flippant tone. Hope looked as though she had scarcely slept; her hair was unbrushed and her gown creased. At her side Beatrice slid her hand into Hope's palm and whispered, "Don't give up, Hopey, we must pray for them. It will take more than gaol fever to see my brother off, of that I am sure. The worst thing about it is that we cannot now visit to take them medicine, blankets or food."

Hope, ever renowned for speaking truths others left unsaid, shook off her friend's hand and turned on her. "The worst thing, Beatrice, is that they are sick! Have you not heard of the stench and misery in those places? At the best of times, gaol is a hell on earth but now, when the cells are overfilled, the rats are biting and sickness if rife, and they have little or no chance of survival. Hanging could prove to be a mercy killing. Ooh, if I were a man I would storm the place and set them all free. I hate this inactivity. There must be something we can do. Have you sent to Father yet? Does he even know what is happening?"

Joanna, taken by surprise, gaped helplessly and shook her head.

"I have sent no further news, other than to inform him that I am here but I think you overestimate his influence. I suspect he might not be in the country, or we should have heard from him by now. Anyway, I believe there is little he can do to sway the king without risking his own neck, any seeming show of sympathy to Monmouth's cause is sure to court danger."

The expression in Hope's eyes suggested that it was perfectly reasonable for James to risk his neck for the sake of his daughter's lover. Refusing to see her stepmother's common sense, she leapt up. "I will write to him myself, then, and demand that he do something."

James had never refused Hope anything, and she failed to see why he should start now.

***

The trials of five hundred rebels began at Taunton castle on the seventeenth of September; the room, packed with officials and spectators, was oppressive. A warm sun filtered through windows set high in the vast stone walls, throwing a little daylight on to the scene. The heavy beamed ceiling seemed to press down on the proceedings. The crowd was subdued, the low rumble of their conversation rising and falling as they waited for the trial to begin. When the door opened and the judges filed in, a buzz of apprehension spread across the room, quenched abruptly as the men took their places at the far end of the hall.

The judges looked down supercilious noses to where the townspeople were gathered on benches, hastily made of scaffolding and board. In an attempt to stir the fetid air, the ladies fanned vigorously while the simple folk sweated and coughed at the back of the courtroom. Somewhere in the crowd a woman was weeping.

It seemed an age until the prisoners were brought in, twenty or so at a time to stand defeated, before the judge. There were many prisoners to be dealt with in so short a time, and Jeffreys dealt with the matter promptly, dispensing with their lives with no more compassion than one would show a troublesome fly.

Some were sentenced to hanging, and some to transportation but there seemed to be little method to his system, but none were found innocent, or shown leniency. With each penalty the simmering resentment in the crowd increased. The peasants were dealt with first, the higher-class rebels, those who had taken commissions in the Duke's army, saved until after the morning break.

Joanna was already nauseas before the judges withdrew for comfort and refreshment.

"Would you like to take some air?" Leo suggested. "There is time to go outside."

She was tempted to accept but Hope refused to budge, fearing that she would lose her seat, so Joanna remained with her, although her bladder was full, and her mouth horribly parched.

"I will find us some refreshment then," Leo, reluctantly leaving the women alone fought his way to the street and bought a flagon of ale and some pasties from a one-eyed hawker.

Joanna drank gratefully, inelegantly swilling the liquid around her mouth before taking a bite of the pasty. As she passed the flagon to Hope, Leo nudged her to alert her to the prisoners shuffling back into the courtroom.

The accused men stood before the judge, Edward among them and when Carrie saw his matted hair and scrubby beard she began to sob quietly. He did not look up but kept his eyes fixed upon the floor. The truth was that, with the fever upon him, he had no idea what was happening and cared little.

"Edward Leopold Oswald," bellowed the judge. "You are brought before us charged with treason, rebellion and insurrection. How do you plead?"

Edward made no answer, and, after a brief pause, the guard kicked the back of his knees. Carrie cried as her boy crumpled and fell heavily onto the rushes. Leo gripped her arm tightly as Edward was hauled to his feet and his head pulled back fiercely. It was plain to see he was sick, his face was covered in sweat, his eyes turned back in his head.

"Oswald, I repeat. How do you plead?"

There was no response.

"You took a commission in the rebel army, is that not so?"

An unintelligible sound issued from the prisoner's mouth before his head flopped forward, his filthy hair once more concealing his face.

"Oswald, you will answer the court." Jeffreys was riled. His chin thrust forward, and his eyes slit. The silence was absolute, resentment for the judge jangling.

"This one's been crook all night, Milord," volunteered the guard. "Raving, he was earlier. I reckon it was "guilty" he answered, Milord, but I doubt he'll make it to his hanging."

Jeffreys looked down at his papers.

"Thank you, gaoler. Edward Leopold Oswald, I sentence you, in the name of the king, to be hung by the neck until you are dead. May God have mercy on your soul. Bring the next prisoner forward."

As Edward was led stumbling away, his sisters screamed and wept while Carrie turned into the circle of her husband's arms. Hope, with tears standing upon her lashes, waited unmoving with Joanna's hand clenched in her own and, as Samuel shuffled forward to take his place in the makeshift dock, a sob escaped her rigid lips.

Gone was his jaunty smile. It was a hollow-eyed stranger who glanced briefly at the gathering, a flicker of recognition flashing across his face when he spied Hope waiting in the crowd. Until now his natural optimism had convinced him of reprieve but after hearing Edwards's sentence and seeing Hope again the full force of his plight hit him like a wall.

Shocked by the fear in Hope's eyes Sam was persuaded that he must make some attempt to save himself. He realised for the first time that she represented all his dreams and, even though it went against his principles to, he realised that he must at least try. He looked upon the stony judge, and saw with dreadful clarity the hanging, the butchery and the agony that was to follow. To hell with honour, this was his life he was fighting for.

Hope's throat ached. In the months since she had seen him her burgeoning love had swollen into a torrent and witnessing him at the mercy of the killing judge, she felt she was drowning. Hardly breathing, she raised her gloved hand in greeting, absorbing every detail of his face. He seemed relatively healthy and, apart from some sores on his chin, he displayed few of the infirmities of Edward. He had lost weight and grown a shaggy beard but just possibly, given the chance, a good meal or two and a hot bath could restore him. If only he could be gotten to safety.

The courtroom was stirring.

'Samuel Trelask, you were an officer in the rebel army, Sir?"

A brief pause while the prisoner cleared his throat,

"No, Milord, I was not. I was just an ordinary foot soldier, Sir."

Hope's head shot up, knowing this to be untrue for she had sewn his colours herself. *What was he thinking? Was it wise to lie to this judge, of all judges?* Her eyes darted feverishly from Sam's face to that of Jeffreys.

"That is contrary to the information I have before me, Sir".

"Then your information is faulty, Milord."

A murmur ran about the court bringing sharp looks from the bench.

"You know the penalty for deceiving the King's court, Sir?"

"I do, Sir, 'tis the same as that for rebellion and sedition."

Jeffreys raised his head from the paper before him, his eye fixed upon the prisoner.

"Don't try to be clever, Sir. You were taken at Sedgemore, were you not, wearing the colours of an officer of Monmouth's army?"

"I was not, Sir. That is incorrect. I was taken in flight, about a mile from the field, in the breeches and shirt I have on now, Milord. I wore no colours, Sir."

The courtroom held its breath while Jeffreys peered down his long nose at the script in his hand. After a pause that Hope thought would never end, he turned his attention back to the felon. He looked at the boy who, despite his bedraggled garments and lousy hair, stood arrogant before him.

"Are you repentant, Trelask?"

"Oh yes, Sir, for I was led astray by lies and trickery, Milord. I'm for King James now and always will be, Sir."

The grumble of disapproval from Monmouth's supporters was not echoed in Hope's heart, and she prayed that his duplicity would work. She felt no shame for him. Monmouth was dead, so what good were foolish loyalties now? Her heart hammered as her eyes darted rapidly from one face to the other. Jeffreys wore an unconvinced expression, while Sam's was open but unreadable.

"I think you lie, Trelask," he said. "Or at least are being economical with the truth."

Jeffreys paused again, the pain in his gut biting deep as he contemplated the sentence. The courtroom held its breath.

"However, in the light of the situation, and the sheer quantity of justice I must dispense this day, I commute the death sentence to transportation for ten years. You will be taken down to await shipment to the colonies. Bring forward the next prisoner!"

Hope sat down abruptly and bit her clenched fingers. She should be thanking God for answering her prayers, she should be dancing with joy, but all she felt was a wrenching sense of loss. Tears hot on her cheek, she turned to see Beatrice holding her mother in her arms.

"Transportation is good, Mother, better than death," she was saying but Hope remained uncomforted. "Ten years is not so long, is it?" Beatrice continued. "He will come home, once he has served out his sentence." But when her eyes met Hope's over her mother's head, her optimism was qualified by three unspoken words, "…if he survives."

"Father will just have to buy his freedom. After all, slaves are bought and sold all the time. I can go with him, work alongside him until we can afford a passage home."

Joanna, worn out by pregnancy and the stress of the last few days sighed. The difficult thing would be locating James in the first place. He was after all unaware of his daughter's attachment for Trelask, let alone prepared for her to take passage to the New World to be with him. She tried to dissuade Hope but that night the girl composed a letter explaining the attachment she had formed for Samuel and begging that he help them to be together. Unfortunately, Hope was overlooking two things; her father's desire that she marry into a good Catholic family, and Judge Jeffreys, who lurked, like a venomous spider, at Taunton castle.

Jeffreys studied the report that described the lavish street decorations and crowds of jubilant townspeople who had turned out to welcome their "Darling Duke". They had proclaimed the man king and the pupils of a local girl's school had presented him with flags, sewn by their own hands, to carry into battle.

He threw the paper onto his desk in disgust. It was incredulous that one small town could contain so many rebels; the infants here must suckle sedition from their mother's dugs.

Scowling into his ale, his kidney stones stabbing like a blade, Jeffreys determined to wreak vengeance upon these people. He would make an example of the town and summon these sisters of Satan into his court. If he could find no way of hanging, burning or flaying them, then he would hit their families so hard that the town would never recover.

***

Edward died that night of the typhoid fever. The Oswalds were still reeling from his loss when they heard of the imminent arrest of the girls from the academy. Word spread quickly across town that Miss Musgrove and Miss Blake had already been taken to the castle and, although their poverty was well known, their liberty was subject to the payment of massive fines. The terrified women, overwhelmed by the threatened violence, were even now providing Jeffreys' clerks with the names and addresses of every pupil who had taken part in the Monmouth celebrations.

Carrie sat in trembling silence as Leo launched a fevered investigation into how much cash could be raised to secure his daughters' freedom. Their grief for Edward momentarily put to one side, their thoughts turned to self-preservation. The girls huddled together in the parlour. Only two of them were pupils at the school, and Hope of course, but Leo could never raise enough money to keep them from gaol. The thought of Taunton prison, where fever claimed as many victims as the hangman, swung like a noose in their imaginations.

Spurred out of sickness, Joanna sent a frantic rider to Thornhold Manor with a message for the bailiff to raise all the ready cash he could. Another messenger was sent post haste to Greenwich with orders to search for James until he was found. But Jeffreys moved swiftly and, early the following morning the maids of Taunton, with Hope and her cousins among them, were rounded up and herded through the town to await the justice of the hanging judge.

The streets thronged with weeping parents. Those with the required resources were released immediately, but Leo's financial affairs were as chaotic as his household, and Hope and her cousins could not expect an early release. That night, after Hope's arrest, Joanna tossed sleepless on her mattress while Maud, her blotchy face creased with anxiety, attempted to soothe her mistress's ills. The unborn child lay like a stone in Joanna's womb, sapping her energy but, sick as she was, Joanna knew there was just one course of action she could take.

Early the next morning her knees trembling, Joanna donned her best clothes and ordered a chair to carry her to the castle. As she was transported through the streets of Taunton, the soft rain turned heavier, and rivulets of water were soon racing down the road that led to the castle. She shuddered as the grey walls of the keep swallowed her, and when she climbed from the chair, a surly porter appeared and rudely asked her business.

***

The judge breakfasted well before turning his attention to the day's business. There were papers to sign, letters to write, reports to dictate. He glanced at the clock, anticipating a rare afternoon of relaxation and was displeased to be told that a lady was below wishing to speak with him privately.

Jeffreys did not like women. He barely tolerated his wife, who at least knew when to hold her tongue; usually he avoided other women at all costs. On his enquiry, he was told the lady in question was a Lady Joanna Thornbury. He squinted into the fireplace trying to recall if he had previously made her acquaintance. He dimly recalled meeting a Lord Thornbury at court; an oily, objectionable bore but one who must not be offended as he was favoured by the king.

Nervousness did nothing to enhance Joanna's appearance, and the judge did not hide his irritation at the whey-faced creature who was shown into his presence.

"Lady Thornbury?" he bowed coldly in response to her elaborate curtsey. Joanna adopted what she hoped was a confident, winning air.

"My Lord Judge," she smiled as she took the seat indicated and arranged her hands in her skirts, so her grubby fingernails were not in view. "I have come to you because there seems to have been an error of which I am sure you are unaware. It concerns my stepdaughter, Mistress Hope Thornbury. I think you are acquainted with my husband, Lord James Thornbury?"

Jeffreys took a pinch of snuff from his box.

"Indeed, I am, Madam, but, I confess I had not thought to encounter his wife in this hotbed of intrigue".

Joanna summoned some dimples and tossed her damp ringlets. She continued brightly.

"I am here to collect my daughter, my stepdaughter I mean, Hope Thornbury, who has been staying with her cousins in Taunton for a while. My husband is at Greenwich, as you know, and I have been, well … I have been unwell and had no idea of the events taking place here, closeted as I was in my chamber. Of course, as soon as I heard of the treasonous crimes against our anointed king, I came post haste to remove Hope from the influence of this horrid town. As you know, the Thornburys are good Catholics, My Lord, and would never countenance disloyalty."

She smiled at him again, but he merely raised an eyebrow.

"And how can I be of help to you, Madam?"

While Joanna fiddled with her handkerchief, he took in her pale, shadowed face, her unprepossessing mouth and thought how he detested plain women. They should all be whipped. "Come along, madam, I am a busy man. I can spare but five minutes more."

"Yes, My Lord, of course. I do apologise for keeping you, but my stepdaughter appears to have been mistakenly placed under arrest with the young women from the academy. I request a letter of release so that I may take her home."

She had his attention now. He was interested but puzzled, he raised one eyebrow.

"Arrested madam? How can that be? Does she have anything to do with the dissidents?"

"Well, Sir, yes, I suppose she does, but an innocent connection. She is, by chance, cousin to some of the girls involved, and was mistakenly in their company on occasion…"

Jeffreys cut across Joanna's carefully rehearsed explanation. "And would that occasion happen to be the welcoming committee for the traitor Monmouth?"

Joanna could contain herself longer and, to her shame, a tear dripped from her eye. She wiped her nose miserably and nodded her head, her tears gathering pace and washing down her cheeks. Spittle clung to the corners of her mouth as, surrendering all pretence, she wailed,

"But she is an innocent, My Lord, a good Catholic girl. My husband is the king's loyal servant, and we are a family of unspotted reputation. You will do the king ill if you offend my husband."

Jeffreys curled a lip, offended by her attempts to win his favour, disgusted by her snotty red nose. She could go hang with the rest of them and God damn Thornbury.

"She will pay for her crimes with the rest of them, Madam. If I had my way they'd hang. The fine has been set. You can take your rebellious spawn home when, and if, the sum has been paid in full. Now good day, Madam, I have important business to attend to."

Disbelievingly, Joanna stared at him. Clinging to her temper she cried, "She is a child, Sir. What sort of man wreaks vengeance upon children? I have sent for my husband, and he is on his way. What do you imagine the king will say when he hears of the treatment our only daughter took at your hands. You will be punished, either here or in the hereafter."

Jeffreys looked at Joanna as though she had crawled out of the moat. Her chest heaved, her ringlets were slipping from their bands, and two spots of colour blazed on her prominent cheekbones. Her eyes were slanted, glinting with anger. Jeffreys stepped away. He had read about witchcraft and knew they had the ability to strike a man down from some distance. He watched from the corner of his eye as she wrestled with her rage.

Joanna knew she was going to faint. Pinpoints of light danced behind her eyes and her ears rang loudly. Swallowing the phlegm in her throat, Joanna breathed deeply, and when she was able, she spoke again, more quietly this time.

"Have pity, My Lord? She is a child, a good Catholic girl. Release her, I beg of you, we will pay whatever you ask. I will give you my written oath on it, but I cannot pay until my husband arrives with the money. Let me take her home now and I swear to you, I will keep her out of trouble, and you will never hear her name again. You have my word as a dutiful Catholic. Let me take her home…"

Jeffreys, suspicious that he was somehow being threatened, let out a long breath and sat down to ease the pain in his side. He wanted rid of this woman. Drawing a sheet of parchment toward him he scratched upon it for some while before thrusting it unceremoniously toward Joanna. She took it in her shaky hand and read his spidery scrawl.

I, the undersigned, Lady Joanna Thornbury of Thornhold Manor in the county of Gloucestershire, in the absence of my lord husband do undertake to pay the fine of £200 levied upon one Mistress Hope Thornbury, guilty of fraternisation with rebels and spies against our King James the second. My liberty is my bond.

The journey home was long. The hot weather having receded into steady rain, the coach skidded and lurched into puddles, several times becoming mired in the mud. The three women hunched miserably within, the damp seeking a way in, keeping their spirits low. Hope, shaken and exhausted by her experience, curled in the corner. Joanna was certain she merely feigned sleep but left her to her misery. Joanna knew her pregnancy would terminate soon; the hot water bottle she clutched beneath her clothes did nothing to relieve the dragging pains in her stomach.

Maud stared miserably through the window, the blemishes on her face enhanced unkindly by the daylight. They dined at posting houses, the mood sombre and Hope retired directly to bed without speaking. After her release she had clung to Joanna, shaken from resentment by gratitude but now her safety was assured, she retreated once more into silence.

Joanna prayed James had received her letters and would be waiting at Thornhold so she could hand over all responsibility and relapse into her own private misery. It was late on the third day, when the twinkling lights of home appeared in the distance. The servants hurried out to welcome her, but the master was still from home. Her duties could not be relinquished yet.

***

Joanna was breakfasting upon coddled eggs and feeling better than she had for some time when a letter arrived from James. Opening the seal, she found a reassuring message but no word of gratitude. He informed her the fine had been paid. The affair was over. He had raised enough capital to provide Leo with a loan, repayable over ten years, but although his daughters were freed, he feared that Leo was a broken man. James went on to say that the King had strongly advised him to marry Hope forthwith to a law abiding Catholic. It seemed James intended to lose no time in doing so.

"I shall be returning in time for Christmas and will bring with me one whom I believe will provide Hope with the guidance and stability she requires. I charge you, Wife, with the duty of conveying my wishes to her, and to ensure that she is provided with all the regalia required for the ceremony. Procuring a trousseau should prove a welcome diversion. We expect to arrive at Thornhold around the second week of December, in good time for the festivities. Look to yourself, Wife, and to the unborn child with whom the good Lord has seen fit to bless us."

"Pompous old fool," muttered Joanna as she thrust the letter into the pocket of her housecoat. She sighed and glanced across at Hope who was dabbing her spoon in a bowl of porridge. It was too soon, far too soon. The girl had given no sign of recovery but spent her days, meandering dismally around the house, with her clothes creased and her hair not properly brushed. When she learned of Joanna's pregnancy she greeted the news listlessly, as if it was none of her affair. But, in many ways this new Hope was more likeable than the old, she was certainly easier to live with.

Like a coward, she postponed telling Hope about James' plan; she quailed at the thought of the stormy reception such unwelcome news would be met with. Instead, she escaped to the bare borders and colourless walks of the garden. As the weeks and months passed, and the child grew heavy in her womb, she paced the gravel paths, watched the cloudy skies, and tried not to think of Simon.

Each night before she climbed into bed she looked down at her swollen stomach and marvelled at the size. She'd abandoned her corsets long ago. Counting on her fingers she tried to calculate the due date and arrived at the same conclusion, the child would come in early March, yet the size of her belly betokened a much sooner delivery. Never, in all her pregnancies had she been this big so soon.

December 1685

Belying the mood of the household, the scene in the great hall was festive. Jonah and George had brought in great swathes of greenery to thread along the railings of the minstrels' gallery and draped above the fireplace. In the grate, the Yule log was waiting to be lit. Joanna left the servants to carry on and, untying her apron and smoothing her hair with both hands, she hastened to the door to greet the new arrivals. Her heart sank but she forced herself to smile as James lumbered from the coach. He turned to retrieve his bag, talking all the while to his companion who was still inside. Two months or more of his company was not going to be easy. James stretched his arms, and looked about his dominion, taking as much pride in the neat borders and swept paths as if he'd laboured over it himself.

He signalled for his man to take the small valise before turning to assist his companion from the coach. A young man, lighter and younger than James, stepped down onto the gravel and Joanna's blood froze.

Surely fate could not be so cruel, even to her.

"Ah, Wife. There you are. How are you, my dear? You remember Master Grey, do you not? Let us in, Dear, we have no wish to linger here on the doorstep, what?"

She stood like a statue to allow them pass, her head swirling; she had prayed nightly to see him again but not like this. *Never like this.*

Following them into the hall and knowing that her complexion was washed out and her body was bloated, she summoned a valiant smile and managed to greet Simon as though there were nothing between them.

"Master Grey, how nice to see you again. I'm afraid the servants are busy in here. Shall we retire to the library?"

James was already making his way on his sturdy legs and Joanna gestured with a hand for Simon to follow but he did not move, his eyes were fixed on her belly. Unsmilingly, she answered his silent question.

"Yes, Master Grey, we expect a new arrival in March, and pray all will be well this time."

Banishing all tenderness from her face, she met his gaze.

"March?" he repeated uncertainly. "H-how splendid, I wish you well, My Lady."

Before he could say more, Joanna turned sharply and followed James into the library.

"So, Wife. How are you feeling and how did young Hope take the news of her forthcoming nuptials, what? She couldn't wish for a better fellow. Where is the girl?"

Settling into a chair, Joanna swallowed and looked down at her roughened hands.

"Indeed, but I confess I have not yet told her. She has not been well and I myself have been incommoded of late. I'm afraid I've left it to you, James, the news will surely come better from her father."

"Not told her, Madam. God Lord, it is weeks since I wrote to you of it. Can't I rely upon you to do anything?"

Simon was examining the books on the library shelves, trying not to recall other evenings spent in the room. Joanna lowered her voice.

"I must warn you, James. Hope is not well. She took the loss of the Trelask boy very badly and feels her heart is broken. We must go gently with her, My Lord, she is young and has suffered much. The shock of her cousin's death, and the loss of Samuel Trelask, and then to be thrown into gaol like a common felon has taken its effect. I expect she may require many months to fully recover. And, if her heart is truly lost to this boy, it is possible she never will."

"Nonsense. Marriage will solve all that. Go forth and call her; I will break the news gently; never fear. Master Grey, perhaps you would grant me a while with my daughter alone. My wife will show you to your chamber."

Assuming a graciousness she did not feel, Joanna stood up and ushered him from the room. Scarcely able to believe he was here in the house again she clenched her fingers tight in her palms and prayed he would keep his distance. It would be impossible to resist if he made advances.

She had ordered his things to be taken to the Blue room on the first floor, not far from the master bedroom. As they reached the top of the stairs, Simon grabbed her arm and turned her roughly to face him,

"The child is mine, isn't it, Jo? It is mine?"

"Hush," she hissed, snatching her hand away. "Are you a fool? Do you want to be overheard?"

Continuing along the passage and flinging open the chamber door, she said loudly for the benefit of any who may be near, "I've put you in here, Master Grey. There is a lovely view over the gardens. I'm sure you'll be comfortable."

"Joanna!" He followed her into his chamber and threw his valise on the bed. "Tell me, it is my child you are carrying. How could you not let me know?"

Joanna paused, gazing at him miserably for a long moment.

"How could I have let you know? I thought never to see you again, Simon, and anyway, it seems you are to marry now. You're soon to be my son-in-law and soon will be providing my child with a little nephew …or perhaps a brother!"

She tried to leave the room, but he pulled her back,

"I didn't look for this wedding, Jo. How can you think that? What was I to do when Sir James approached me? Tell him "Oh no, I'm sorry, Sir. I must decline from wedding with your daughter for I'm in love with your wife. God's teeth, this is a nightmare." He ran a hand through his hair, the degree of his shock evident in his face.

"It is such a mess, Jo; I grant you I see no way out. Oh, why did you not let me know?"

Joanna, exhausted by the sudden emotion, slumped.

"To what avail, Simon? I am a married woman, and you are lost to me. We had agreed never to see each other again. If I can only bring the babe forth safely, I will have a little happiness. He is all I have. I never imagined you'd turn up again like this, out of the blue, expecting to marry my stepdaughter. What on earth were you thinking?"

Joanna began to weep.

"Shush no, don't cry, Jo. It will make the others wonder if they see you with red eyes. We will think of something, never fear, perhaps I can behave so obnoxiously Hope will refuse me."

Drawing her into a swift embrace, his lips brushed her forehead, before he released her again. Then glancing about to make sure they were unobserved, he whispered.

"Go now, Sweetheart. I will be down as soon as I have freshened up."

James' bluff mood contrasted sharply with the rest of the company, but he blundered on, unaware of any tension in the room. Throughout the meal, Hope glared at Joanna with her eyes blazing. She had taken the news of her betrothal badly and seemed to hold her stepmother entirely to blame. Joanna didn't know what to think, but she wished Simon had never come. The false security she had built out of the ruin of her life was crumbling again and, as James revealed the details of his plans, the future seemed impossible.

"You and Hope will live here, of course Simon. So you can learn the running of the estate and the tenants can get to know you. Thornhold Manor will someday be yours …unless of course, this child my wife is carrying turns out to be a boy …in which case, things would have to be reconsidered."

He chewed for a while on a stubborn piece of mutton, swallowed audibly with little apparent hope of a live heir.

Joanna kept her eyes on her food but could feel Simon's eyes were often on her. She did not know how she could bear to have him and Hope living here, loving here, raising their children. There would be no way to avoid them, and she had no wish to watch as he fell out of love with her. How could she possibly undertake the role of grandmother to Simon's future children? Valiantly fighting down panic, she kept glancing at Hope who refused to break her stony silence. Everything was in Hope's hands. She must be persuaded to refuse to marry against her will. It was the only way to free them all from certain disaster. But how could she explain why it was so imperative?

Tired as she was, Joanna waited for the house to fall silent before tiptoeing along to Hope's chamber. There was no answer to her discrete knock but, taking her courage in her hands, Joanna pushed open the door and stepped inside. It was dark, only the fire in the grate illuminating the room but a hump on the bed revealed that Hope had retired for the night. Joanna knew she was not asleep and crossed the room to stand beside the bed.

"Hope?"

"What do you want?"

"Just to apologise for not telling you sooner. I didn't know how to, knowing how badly you felt and all. I'm sorry. Look, why not let me help you? Why do you always shut me out? I am on your side Hope. We could be friends!"

Scrambling to sit up, Hope said quite calmly.

"There is no help you can give, Mother. There is nothing that can be done. Samuel is gone, dead for all I know. I hate Father for this, and I always will but I suppose he must have his heir. Simon is a good man, so it may as well be him as anyone. I may as well give in and do as father wishes. Nothing matters anymore, not if I can't have Sam. I don't have the strength to fight, Father always has his way in the end. Why go to all the trouble of being locked in my chamber, or whipped until I give in. I may as well concede defeat now."

With her head hanging and hot tears falling, Hope looked like a small child. Joanna groped for her hand.

"Hope, there may be a way, if you were able to trust me. If I could be sure that your need to be with Sam would ensure your utmost faith and trust in me and your absolute discretion, there might be a way."

Hope sat up. Rubbing the tears away, she gripped Joanna's wrist like a vice.

"I would help you commit murder, Mother, if it meant that I could be with Sam."

Joanna, seeing her set white face and trembling chin, fell onto the bed where they wept together, allies at last.

***

Too sick to attend Hope's wedding and claiming the inconveniences of pregnancy, Joanna kept to her chamber. At the church, hastily sewn into her mother's wedding gown, Hope swore dispassionately to love, honour and obey Simon Grey until death. The bells rang out in celebration and, as they stepped out into the cold morning sunshine, James kissed the clenched lips of his daughter, and shook his new son-in-law heartily by the hand.

He did not notice any lack of joy on the part of the newly-weds. His daughter was wed to a man he respected and the heir as good as in the cradle already. Joanna watched the party return from her chamber window. It was easy to read the fury in Hope's face, but she searched in vain for a clue as to Simon's feelings. His face was open and as seemingly pleasant as ever, as he listened politely to his father-in-law's discourse.

James' bellowing voice drifted up the stairs as they passed into the hall and, after a short while, Maud came tapped on the door.

"Oh, Milady" she said, bobbing a quick curtsey "Sir James is asking for you to join them in the dining room."

She was met at the door by James who offered her the glass he was carrying.

"Ah, here you are, my dear, we are just about to toast the bride and groom. Come along and join us."

Her hands shook, threatening to slop wine down her gown but she somehow managed to make her way to a chair near the fire. She glanced up, catching Hope's eye, who flashed a conspiratorial smile. Maybe it would be all right after all. Joanna raised her chin and pretended interest in James' speech.

"Hmm, well, what can I say? A fine day for a fine wedding, and you are the most beautiful bride I've ever seen. Welcome to the family, Simon, and congratulations, my dear."

He raised his glass, and the others did the same.

"Yes." Joanna coughed to clear her throat. "Congratulations, Hope and Simon. I hope you will be very happy." Then, bowing her head, she placed her lips on the glass, but she did not drink.

James' conversation dominated the meal that followed. Joanna, unable to look at Simon for fear of what she may see, couldn't help imagining what might take place between them after dark. For the first time since she had hatched the plan, a worm of distrust nibbled at her complacency. The wedding breakfast was only the beginning of a long and difficult day.

"Thornhold is all very well," blustered James. "But it needs updating. We are still in the dark ages here. Look at all that stone wall, and tiny windows. We need some light airy chambers with decent fitting windows. I swear the casements in my bedchamber keep no cold out at all. You should see some of the innovations at Greenwich. If we were to build another wing here, it would get the sunshine all day long. At my time of life, a fellow starts to look for warmth and comfort if he can get it, what?"

"But, Sir, what about the gardens?" asked Simon, indicating Joanna's clipped hedges and tidy winter beds. "It would seem…"

"Oh, we can do away with those. Gardens can be made anywhere, and I fail to see why they should take up valuable building space."

Simon and Joanna exchanged fearful glances, and with an imperceptible shake of her head, she indicated that he should just allow James to ramble on. As the men moved on ahead, Hope and Joanna walked side by side, the girl linking her stepmother's arm with an encouraging squeeze.

"Don't worry so, Mother, it will be fine I promise. Simon and I are determined." Turning to her father, Hope interrupted his flow. "Father, Mother is looking very pale. I think she should lie down until dinner."

James looked toward his wife.

"Is she? I hadn't noticed. Just as you like, my dear, just as you like."

Immediately he turned back to his conversation while Joanna crept gratefully away. She lay on her bed allowing the tension to seep away and, although she expected the trauma of the day to keep her awake, she slept until mid-afternoon.

Maud hurried to her summons and helped her into an afternoon gown before she went downstairs. The house was quiet and, guessing the others were still dressing for dinner, she crossed the hall, climbed the four stairs that led to the study and opened the book upon the lectern. As she was turning the pages, the terrace door opened, and Simon came in.

"Jo!" he whispered. "I was so worried for you this morning. Please don't fret, my love, all is as it was before. The ceremony was a sham, and all involved know it ... apart from James ... and God, I suppose."

"Simon, don't. Don't ever mock God. What we are doing is terrible, and I am sure we should stop while we still can…"

"Well, we have to do it now, don't we? I don't want to stay married to Hope, and she doesn't want to stay wed to me. We would both be driven mad."

They stood in the light of the terrace doors with her hands in his. She bowed her head and said quietly, "I wonder if we are not a little mad already, my love."

Simon lifted her chin and brushed his lips lightly across hers. "Shush, think of our child." He placed a hand upon her distended belly. "Think of little Master Grey."

A sharp cry brought their heads around, and they saw James hovering in the open doorway. His chins trembling in agitation, he took a step toward them, pointing a finger, the realisation of the awful truth written clear across his face. Transfixed, Joanna and Simon watched him take an unsteady step toward them, his eyes accusing, as he uttered incomprehensible sounds and little explosions of breath. His eyes bulged and there was spittle on his lips.

Simon thrust Joanna behind him.

"James, you must try to understand …" he began but James cut him off. Ignoring Simon, he jabbed a finger at Joanna, and screamed,

"YOU! Y-y-you …" He clutched at his chest, his face turning blue, "…bastard!" he cried, before crashing like an oak, to the floor.

***

April 1586

Life was strange but few people's lives were as strange as Joanna Thornbury's. After years of loneliness, she now possessed all she had ever asked for …and more besides. Just a few weeks ago, after a troublesome nauseous pregnancy and a traumatic birth, she had produced lusty twins, a boy and a girl. At first, expecting them not to live, she had resisted motherhood, refusing to note their tawny fair hair and bright blue eyes but as their hold on life strengthened she began to have some tentative belief that God might bless her after all.

Now, she spent most of the day in the nursery, gloating over their perfection and laying down plans for their future. She embroidered tiny gowns and knitted lace trimmings, presiding over their feeding and nursing them into the night; spoiling them, so said the nurse, but Joanna called it mothering.

For the first time in years, she delegated the care of the garden to Jonah and George and left the day-to-day running of the household in the hands of the housekeeper. The servants forgot they had ever dreaded the sound of her footstep and smiled to hear her laughing and singing. Thornhold was fast becoming as loud and rambunctious as the Oswald's home, the only time anyone crept around these days was when passing the master's chamber for incapacitated as he was, James still had a way of making his displeasure known.

Eight weeks after the birth, she wandered into the garden and found her son-in-law, Simon Grey, discussing plans with Jonah for a new garden at the rear of the house. He smiled when he saw her, removing his hat.

"Ah, Lady Joanna, would you care to join me. I was just about to admire the daffodils and hellebores that are so remarkable this year."

Her face glowing, she accepted and slipped her hand into the crook of his elbow.

"How are the twins, this morning?" he asked, helping her to circumnavigate a wheeled barrow that was blocking the path.

"Very hungry, this morning but in fine health. You should visit the nursery later on today…"

"I shall be glad to." He said, stooping to snap off a spent daffodil head.

"And how is Lord Thornbury, my Lady?" asked Simon, sobering suddenly.

***

Nobody had been more relieved than Joanna and Hope when James' affliction removed the need for their plan to be carried out. In retrospect it had been a mad idea. Joanna looked on it as God's intervention for he had shown them another way. Of course, it was tragic that James had been confined to his bed since the day of Hope and Simon's wedding; unable to speak or to move, his left side was completely paralysed. The servants whispered he had been cursed, a cruel blow. Life was harsh. Other believed he got his just deserts.

Joanna paused to remove a stone that was lodged in the sole of her shoe, gripping Simon's sleeve for support. His hand came down to rest upon hers and she let it remain there until she had regained her balance. They continued along the path, stopping to examine emerging shoots here and there, and concocting planting schemes for the coming season, until they reached the manor house and entered the old hall.

Maud came bustling toward them bristling with self-importance. "A letter has come, Sir, from foreign parts so we believe. Here it is, Sir; would you like some refreshment, Milady?"

Joanna shook her head, and Maud placed the letter on Simon's desk and, bobbing a curtsey, left the room. Simon examined the envelope, turning it over and over in his hand.

"That envelope won't tell you anything, Simon. Open it up, for Heaven's sake."

He laughed and, slicing open the seal, unfolded a single sheet of paper.

"It's from Hope," he said. "As we suspected. She has landed safely in the West Indies after what she describes as 'a perilous voyage.' After much difficulty, she has discovered Sam's whereabouts. The slave owner is willing to sell his bond but at a hefty price, and she requests that we forward the money straight away. She threatens that if we delay she will return home and take great pleasure in spoiling things for us. Oh, and she sends her love…"

Their eyes met as they laughed quietly together. Joanna took the letter and after scanning the page, placed it on the desk. Then, moving to the lectern, she opened the book.

Simon watched her for a while before joining her. Together, they enjoyed the richness of the illuminated pages. Joanna paused from time to time, indicating the various marks and signs of wear and tear until, near the back of the book, she paused at an undecorated page and dipped her quill into the ink.

"To Joanna Thornbury, on the seventeenth day of March 1686, was born Joseph James, an heir to Thornhold Manor at last, and his twin, Margaret May Thornbury."

Part Seven
The Gardener's daughter

There has fallen a splendid tear
From the passion-flower at the gate.
She is coming, my dove, my dear;
She is coming, my life, my fate;
The red rose cries, 'she is near, she is near;'
And the white rose weeps, 'she is late;'
The larkspur listens, "I hear, I hear;"
And the lily whispers, "I wait."
(from Maud (Part I) Alfred, Lord Tennyson)

Thornhold Manor - September 1853

Melissa Thornbury swept into the hall, pulling off her gloves and tossing them onto the hall table. Her butler, Soames, waited for her instruction.

"Where is Master Jamie? Has he returned from his morning ride?"

"No, My Lady," replied Soames. "The Master is in his study, and Miss Lydia and Miss Rose are in the conservatory. A letter arrived with the carrier. I placed it on your desk, My Lady."

"Thank you, Soames." Melissa sailed across the old hall in the direction of her husband's study. "Have some refreshments sent up, would you?"

Melissa Thornbury never walked anywhere; she marched, or paraded, or swept as the situation demanded. A draper's daughter, Melissa had done extraordinarily well to marry into the ancient Thornbury family, immediately putting to good use her years of intensive schooling. Melissa was a snob, her haughty manner defying anyone to recall her humble origin, and she spent much of her time scolding, spanking and bullying any vestige of vulgarity that dared to surface in her family.

Hampered by her husband's upper-class disregard for good manners, she had made a reasonably good job of raising his children. Her two shallow daughters were a credit, and both were certain to secure good marriages. However, the son and heir of Thornhold had not proved so easy to tame. Jamie was a rebel, viewing his expensive Oxford education solely as an opportunity for debauchery. Two years before he should have graduated, the proud parents humbly settled his gambling debts, paid off the family of a young girl he'd ruined, and brought him quietly home to Thornhold.

Lord Thornbury belched loudly. Melissa paused and closed her eyes. Gentility had come at no small cost, and she sometimes wondered if twenty-five years with Henry had been too steep a price to pay. Especially as she was forced to spend more than half a year buried alive in the Gloucestershire countryside while he hunted. She far preferred life in London. Henry looked up but made no attempt to rise.

"Ah, there you are, my dear," he said, suppressing another belch. "How was your walk? The exercise has put a little colour in your cheeks."

"My walk was adequate, Henry. Now where is Jamie, have you seen him? I made it quite clear that we needed to see him this morning, and it is already close to noon. Really, Henry, I wish you'd be firmer with him. He leaves for Africa in a few weeks and there are people coming from far and wide to bid him farewell although he shows as much enthusiasm for the party as he would a funeral."

Henry heaved himself from his chair.

"Melissa, my love, he is young. He needs to run wild a bit, that's all. In a few weeks he'll be facing a hostile army, and war is no picnic you know. He'll have to knuckle down then. Let him sow some wild oats while he can."

"Surely the oats he has already sowed are more than adequate."

Melissa marched across the room and sat at her desk. Picking up a letter, she examined the fine copper plate handwriting before slicing open the envelope. She kept one eye on her husband as he rubbed his overfed belly and winced as a dart of wind struck, just below the heart.

"I still say you are too lenient. He needs discipline and to realise the sun doesn't shine in the sky simply for his convenience."

She scanned the single page of script. It was from her sister, Evelyn. Evelyn had married badly and was now the wife of a tradesman with a dozen small tradespeople to wait on. Her letter was full of the sort of triviality such people found important; Melissa read it through quickly, disinterested until she reached the last few words which wished her nephew well in the coming conflict.

"It is from Evelyn, she wishes Jamie well," she said, tossing the letter onto the desk. "Oh, Henry, where can he be?"

She strode across the room and looked from the window, hoping to see her son dawdling across the lawn. "God knows what he is up to. If he is playing the same tricks as he was at Oxford he will be ruined this time. He wouldn't though, would he, Henry? I mean one doesn't, does one, not on one's own doorstep?"

***

Jamie Thornbury ran across the road and ducked into a small wood. Newly commissioned as an officer into the 11th division of the Hussar's regiment, he had been enjoying some well-earned relaxation before embarking for the Crimea. Since being sent down from Oxford, he spent most of his time avoiding his mother, hunting during the day and dining with friends most evenings. His companions consisted of young men, most of whom had a steady hand on a shotgun and a keen eye for a pretty girl.

In Gloucestershire, the women of his own class were guarded closely by their mothers. It was impossible to get near them. He knew of a certain tavern where one could exchange a few pence for a couple hours of fun but, since his unpleasant experiences in Oxford, where the whores were as vicious as they were greedy, he had been wary of purchasing pleasure. Lately life had become overwhelmingly dull until a few days ago when he'd discovered a new interest.

***

"I remember you," he said when he encountered her in the wood. "You are Lily. I remember the village children teasing you when we were small. You never fought back; you always ran away."

The girl stared at him with wide eyes.

"Don't you remember me, Lily? I'm Jamie Thornbury, from the big house? Do you remember when that boy, what was his name, little fat fellow … Barnabus! That was it. Do you remember when he stole your bonnet and hung it on a high branch, and I climbed up to fetch it for you?"

After a moment Lily nodded. James prodded his chest with a forefinger.

"That was me, Lily. We should have been friends then, but I had to go off to that dratted school."

She looked down, fiddled with the tassel of her shawl.

"Why don't you ever speak? Is there something wrong with your tongue?"

Mischievously, she stuck it out at him to prove there was nothing amiss with it. Then she was up and running away, laughing over her shoulder at him. Jamie smiled, entranced by the fey, gilt-haired creature, timid as a young deer, and allowed her a few minutes head start before pursuing her.

It took no effort to catch her. He grabbed her hand, and she stopped, bent over, panting loudly, her bonnet dangling, her face pink with the effort of running. As Jamie drew her close, he somehow knew he must treat her gently lest she shatter into tiny pieces.

***

Thornhold Manor was preparing for a ball; servants scurried about with floral arrangements and chairs, while musicians practised and tuned their instruments in the gallery.

"Jamie dear, there you are!" Melissa said, accosting him in the hall. "Now, have you had your valet see that your dress uniform is adequately sponged? Oh, and for goodness' sake, do something with your hair, it is almost touching your collar."

Jamie raised his eyes to heaven, trying to sidle away before she noticed anything else that needed trimming or polishing. Honestly, such a fuss for a party he did not even want. The idea was more than he could stand, and he was pleased when his sister Lydia arrived and drew away his mother's attention.

"I'm sure Rose has my gloves, Mother, for do you remember she soiled hers at Lady Welling's party on Sunday last? She was pestering for a new pair but now she has stopped, and I'm sure it is because she has mine. I wish you would speak to her; she is always taking my things." Jamie edged away.

Before dressing, the family took light refreshment separately in their rooms and, despite the warmth of the day, a fire roared in every grate. Melissa was always complaining that the sun never penetrated Thornhold's thick medieval walls. She would love to have the whole house demolished and rebuilt in the modern style, but their pockets wouldn't stretch to that. She had suggested they simply build one new wing or refurbish the existing building but since complaining was second nature to Melissa, Henry never heeded her.

Jamie lounged close by the window and blew a ring of cigar smoke into the air; he felt irritable and unsociable. Why should his last night in England be spent at some stuffy party simply to please his mother? He'd far rather be with Lily. As the first carriages began to roll up the drive, he shrugged himself into his braided jacket and stubbed out his cigar.

"Bertie!" he cried as he entered the hall. "How are you, old man?" He had no time for Albert Wellings, who was an earnest, old-fashioned bore but he was soon engulfed by other acquaintances for whom he had no time.

The dinner went well enough until it was time for the women to withdraw, and the brandy and cigars came out. The conversation turned to war, as it always did when old men got together. Jamie had no interest in either war or politics; he was going to the Crimea solely to avoid debtors, and get away from his mother, not from any ill-found sense of duty.

When the bewhiskered old soldiers arranged the salt sellers and teaspoons into platoons his heart sunk. They would be here all night. He lit another cigar, allowing his mind to wander, and it was not long before he found he was thinking of Lily.

There was something about her. She was different from other girls. He wondered if he was in love with her. He had tried to explain why he was leaving but wasn't sure she understood. Her silence was difficult; he never knew how she felt about anything. Only her response to his love making confirmed that she loved him. He longed to break the barriers of silence and hear her say the words. He wished he were with her now, instead of here with these suffocating people.

He watched his father belching quietly into his beard as he listened to Colonel Beaufort banging on about strategy. The old man's whiskers shook as he thumped the cloth vigorously with his spoon, capturing the attention of the other diners. Jamie turned toward the window and formulated a plan of escape.

Soon it would be time for the dancing to begin. His mother would hang on his arm, making a big fuss about his departure, boasting how handsome he looked in his uniform. He had to get out. It would be worth the consequences to lay with Lily once more and taste the sweet uncertainty of her lips.

As the band were warming up their instruments, Jamie strolled onto the veranda, puffing his cigar, his silhouette outlined against the night sky. In the great hall, the company were noisily sorting themselves into partners for the first country-dance and no-one noticed when he leapt the balustrade into the garden. Doubled over to avoid smacking his head on overhanging branches, he kept under cover before sprinting across the lawn.

***

The ancient strip of woodland at the bottom of the valley was a timeless place, smelling of damp and decay. Toward the bottom of the hill, where even the birdsong was hushed, the tangle of trees thinned to make way for the rushing river. Sitting on a footbridge, throwing sticks into the foaming waters, Lily waited.

The water was icy. With her skirts bunched about her thighs, Lily trailed her feet in the water, and looked into the depths. Her hair fell forward, shielding her face and obscuring the clarity of her eyes. Her mind was far away but the sound of a snapping twig brought her head up and she saw Jamie blunder from the wood. When he saw her he pulled up short and moved quietly.

He had learned to tread warily with Lily; one false move and she would run. He sat down beside her. She wiped her eyes on the back of her hand.

"Lily?" he whispered. "How are you, girl? Not weeping for me, are you?"

He reached out and placed a finger beneath her chin, but she shrugged away and resumed her study of the murky depths where weed clung to the rocks and swayed in the current, like a woman's hair.

She did not speak but, encouraged by an emerging dimple beside her mouth, Jamie continued, as if he were addressing a small child.

"You know I have to go, don't you, Lily? I can't help it. Do you understand that? I hate to make you sad, but those Ruskies have to be taught a lesson. I'll be back though, I swear I will, just as soon as it's all over. You'll wait for me, won't you, Lily, my girl?"

Lily's cheeks dimpled. As Jamie climbed to his feet, she wiped her face on her sleeve. He looked down at her, sitting with her bare limbs in the water and her hair loose about her shoulders, and suppressed a twinge of guilt. Holding out his hand, he asked, "Come with me for a walk?"

Clutching her woollen shawl about her shoulders, Lily followed him into the wood. The suffused light filtered through the treetops; the birdsong hushed. Jamie stopped near a fallen log where the evening sunshine flooded through a break in the canopy.

Lily was just as sweet as he recalled. She did not resist when he unbuttoned her bodice and slipped it from her shoulders. Discarded in the undergrowth, the sleeves of her dimity gown entwined with the fine braided sleeves of his Hussar's jacket. Jamie wrapped Lily in his arms and tasted her sweet uncertainty.

Lily was not like other girls.

He had no time for women of his own class, whose lips were tainted with scandalous gossip. She was not like the bold-eyed guttersnipes he had visited in Oxford, whose painted mouths teased and titillated with whispered obscenities. They had obsessed him for a while until they had emptied his purse and hastened his disgrace. Lily was his salvation.

She was pure, she was sweet, and she was silent; a perfect angel who gave herself unselfishly. Lily had turned a philandering drunkard into a slave.

When he withdrew, he saw she was weeping again; he fumbled for a kerchief and mopped her eyes. "Don't weep, My Lily" he said. "Don't spoil our last hours together."

Obediently, Lily swallowed her tears, regarding him silently as she listened to his voice. Jamie propped himself on his elbow, cupped her breasts as he spoke about his next few months abroad. Lily lay lazily, admiring the way his hair flopped across his brow. When the night grew cool and she reached for her petticoats to cover her nakedness, he stilled her hand. "No, Lily, let it be. I want to look at you."

The night air sprinkled her flesh with goose pimples as he studied her, and before morning came, he took her again. She clung to him, her hands gripping tightly, and when Jamie cried out in ecstasy, Lily cried out in suffocating grief.

***

Flora wrapped her shawl tighter about her shoulders.

"Lily!" she called again. "Lily, child. Where are you?" Her face lined with anxiety, she cried, "Oh Bert, where can she be? It is so unlike her to be staying out."

"I've told you so many times not to be letting her run wild like she does, but you never listen. I'll get Joe to come help me search the woods and ask Eliza to come sit with you. In future, Flora, she's to stay home. She may not be all there but that's no excuse to be letting her run wild. Stay by the fire, woman, I'll bring her back to you."

Flora sat by the fire; her teeth dug into her bottom lip as she prayed that no harm should befall her child. Lily had never been right since her mismanaged birth; a labour that had seen an end to both Flora's fertility and Lily's potential.

"Oh, Liza" she wailed. "What will I do if my girls taken some harm? She is special, my Lily!"

Eliza sighed. "Don't start fretting before you have to, Flora. Chances are she's fallen asleep or some such nonsense, up there in the woods. Your man will find her and bring her home, you wait an' see."

"She's such a good girl, my Lily, from the very first days. I never had to tie her to the leg of the table to stop her from reaching for the fire. Even as a wee baby, she was sweet and biddable. The perfect child."

Not that perfection had done Lily much good, thought Eliza as she began a new row of her knitting. *The village children shunned her and made her a figure of fun. And that silent tongue of hers, it was uncanny*, thought Eliza, shivering suddenly. In the thirteen years she had known Lily, she had never heard her utter one single word.

"Did they never tell ye why the child doesn't speak, Flora, did ye never take her anywhere?"

"When she was five or six, we realised finally that she were never going to talk, and we saved our pennies and took her to a doctor in Stroud. He said there weren't nothing wrong to stop her from speaking; it was just that she didn't care to. He said she'd talk when she were ready, but I can't see that happening now, can you, Eliza?"

"Much as you yearn for it, no, Flora, I can't, but there are other things to make up for it. I've never seen anyone to match your Lily in beauty."

Flora smiled in the firelight.

"She is a beauty and she's a good girl too but sometimes I fret about what'll become of her when I'm gone. I can't see how she'll ever catch a husband, for she don't stop in company long enough to attract a man."

"Aw, she's young yet, Flora. What is she thirteen? Fourteen? Someone will happen along and take a fancy to her, then her silence won't matter at all. Most men would say it's a blessin'."

***

Flora peered from the window for the umpteenth time but there was nothing to see. She threw another log on the fire. It was an extravagance in the summer, but the night was chilly, and Flora wanted the house warm for her girl's return. There was small comfort in the leaping flames as the two women waited through the long dark night. As the new day broke and a faint light showed beyond the wood, Flora rose stiffly from her chair and opened the front door. The women stepped out and stood listening to sounds of the early morning.

The rising sun illuminated the contours of the ancient hill and the roof of the manor house, and far off, a dog barked.

Thinking she saw something, Flora peered harder into the gloom and slowly a flickering of torchlight betokened someone's approach. With a squawk of anticipation, she ran toward it, her feet slowing as Bert emerged from the gloom. Lily, her hair loose and her bare limbs hanging limply was carried in his arms.

"Oh, sweet Jesus, Lily! My Lily!"

"Lay off, she's alive, but someone's been at her for she's half naked, as you can see. She was hiding in a clearing in the woods, sobbing like one demented. She's freezing cold too, but at least she is calm and sleeping now. Get out of my way, woman, and let me get her into the house."

Lily had indeed been "got at" and Flora wept into her apron at the state of her girl lying like a cut flower on the settle. She warmed water and washed the mud from her body and brushed the leaves from her hair. Ruby beads bubbled from bramble scratches, but Lily made no response when her mother dabbed them with stinging iodine.

While she worked, Flora questioned her gently, knowing that she could not answer.

"Oh, Lily, I'm sorry. I'll never forgive myself for this, I swear." Flora wept and Lily wept too.

Several weeks passed before it was clear there would be consequences. Her parents spoke in whispers about the unforgivable shame of bearing a child out of wedlock, but Bert and Flora knew they would bear it.

"Oh, Bert, I'm glad my mother never lived to see this day. It would have broken her heart to see our Lily brought so low… just as it's breaking mine."

"Come, lass, don't take on so. It's not the end of the world, and she's not the first lass to be taken down. It's no shame. It's not as if she were willing. You are to hold your head up and walk proud, do ye hear me? Our Lily has done no wrong. But, God mark my words, if I ever find out who has done this, I swear I'll slice off his balls."

Lily became the talk of the town; the delight of the gossips who gathered about the village pump to speculate on the identity of the father. Bert knew what they were saying. The men of the village avoided his eye, afraid of being blamed. There were few men in Thornhold village who had never looked admiringly upon Lily Gardiner.

June 1854

As Lily's belly grew she could no longer run and as the inexorable seasons swung, she was seen less and less in town. Ignorant of what was happening to her, and longing for the freedom of the woods, she waited patiently for Jamie to come. She knew he would come for he had said he would, and then they would go walking in the woods. There, beside the rushing river, they would cast off their clothes again.

Lily did not know the cause of her discomfort. She had no understanding of the changes in her body, or that they had anything to do with Jamie. Her breasts ached, her dresses grew tight, and her feet swelled in the evenings. She did not know why her mother wept so much and lacked the words to ask.

Lily was polishing the brass candlesticks that had been passed down the female side of the family for generations. Flora turned the cuffs on one of Bert's shirts. As Lily worked, she listened to Flora's tales of her great grandmother and grandmother.

"Eh, strong women they were, Duck. Ordinary in every way but they were tough. I suppose they had to be, what with the poverty they lived in. Even up at the big house the wages weren't much, not like they are today. Your grandmother would have been glad of your father's sixpence a week I can tell you. And your great grandmother, well, I think my mam told me she raised fourteen young'uns without losing one of them. That was no mean feat in them days. I tell you, Lily my girl, we have it easy today. It's like a walk in the park in comparison, just so long as we can avoid the typhoid."

For some time, Lily ignored the tightness in her belly, but after a while, she went to the outhouse. When the pain came, she was quickly drenched in sweat and wondered where she had picked up the flux. When the spasm passed, she reached for the candle but as she did, so she was gripped with pain again. She doubled up, crying out for her mother and dropped the candle, leaving herself in the dark. Lily staggered blindly up the garden path, feeling her way along the picket fence. She burst into the kitchen, falling to her knees.

"Lily!"

Flora leaped to her feet, spools of twine scattering across the floor. Bert, who had just come in, guessed what was amiss, fumbled for his cap and quit the kitchen.

Struggling with the girl toward the bed, Flora felt beneath her petticoats and laid her hand on her stomach. It was rock hard. Lily pushed her away and writhed on the mattress, her teeth clenched.

"I'll just fetch Eliza. I will be quick as I can, Lily love, stay there."

She fled the cottage. Lily could hear her yelling Eliza's name and realised she must be mortally sick. Flora wasn't gone long but when she returned the questions in her daughter's eyes couldn't be ignored. *How could she explain?*

Helplessly, Flora dabbed her forehead with a damp cloth.

"It's your baby coming, Lily love. The pain might be bad, but it will stop soon enough. I'm here to help you but you must be brave and do as your told, do you hear?"

Lily screamed as she wrestled against the forces bearing down upon her. The long travail was hindered by her ignorance, and Eliza and Flora watched helplessly as she struggled all night and into the next day.

Lily, hampered by the weakness of her mind, fought against the labour instead of working with it. At her wits end, Flora was certain Lily would not survive the night. All she could do was bathe her forehead, change the soiled linen and pray the child would come quickly ... and safely.

At noon the next day, Flora had fallen into a restless slumber. The moment Eliza nudged her with her foot, she sprang back to reality. "Lily!" she cried, before she was properly awake. Lily sat up, threw back her head and yelled like one demented as instinctively she mustered all her strength to expel her child.

The infant flopped lifelessly onto the sheet and Lily, taking one horrified look at the bruised and bloodied creature, resumed screaming. Flora grabbed at her hands, frantically trying to calm her but Lily could not be comforted. Her mother had told her there was to be a child, but she had imagined a bonny, fat babe swathed in white linen, not the bloody skinned rabbit she had birthed. While the girl continued to scream, Eliza cut the cord, swept up the child and removed it from Lily's sight.

***

Lily would neither acknowledge nor look upon her tiny son. Flora named him Tom and performed all the tasks a mother should but, every morning and evening she insisted that Lily allow her to express milk from her swollen breasts so that the baby could be fed.

As soon as she was able, Lily dressed herself and, wrapping a shawl about her shoulders, set off toward the village. Flora and Bert did not try to prevent her, and nobody else dared approach but the villagers watched from a distance and whispered.

"I always said she was crazed. I never did like her strange ways," they said as she hurried by.

Lily did not look up until she came to the junction where the three roads met, the place where the coach from London set down its passengers. She waited there every day until nightfall, and when dusk fell, Bert arrived to fetch her home.

***

The Thornbury coach lumbered along the uneven track and came to a halt outside the Gardner's cottage. The villagers peeked from their windows, curious to see the lady of the manor arrive.

Brushing the proffered chair with a glove before she sat, Melissa asked to see the baby. Puzzled, Flora brought out the bundle and allowed Lady Thornbury to peer at the red face.

"A fine-looking child." Melissa glanced toward Lily. "Now, Flora, a purse will be made available to you until such time as the child comes of age. We will ensure he has all he needs but no further contact will be permitted with the family, even after Master Jamie returns from the war."

A tiny light ignited in the back of Lily's eyes at the mention of Jamie's name. Flora gaped at Lady Thornbury, hearing but not quite understanding the implication of her mistress's words. She clutched the purse of money that, by its weight and size, promised to hold more than Bert had earned in a year. Bert scratched his bald spot, screwing up his face in an effort to understand but neither he nor his wife dared ask for clarification.

Melissa rose and took her leave and, as she reached the door, Lily rushed forward awkwardly and took hold of her velvet sleeve.

The poor child is crazed, thought Melissa. *It's true what they say.* Lily's face stretched, her mouth distorted, her face working, her eyes burning with effort. Then in a voice both thick and strange, Lily spoke her first words.

"Jamie? When Jamie come home?"

Bert and Flora were stunned by the sound they had longed for. But their joy was quickly doused as her first words tolled her shame.

November 1855

Winter held Thornhold in a relentless grip, the branches in the orchard stood bleak against the dour skies, and the frost that rimed the cottage windows did not melt, even at mid-day. Life in the village was grim. Food was scarce and even with the bed heaped with all available blankets and clothing, the penetrating cold crept in. Flora took baby Tom into her bed, his scrawny body, both providing and receiving, extra warmth, but Lily shivered beneath thin blankets, chilled as much by Jamie's absence as the winter cold.

He'd been gone for more than a year, yet he had not yet sent word. The gossips said that he was betrothed to the daughter of a rich merchant from London, a girl with no breeding but plenty of money. Lily refused to believe it. She knew that Jamie loved her. He had told her that when he came back, they would be married.

They thought she didn't know how everyone whispered about her. They thought she was unaware of the shame she had brought to her parents. Since she has spoken, Flora persisted in tempting Lily to speak again but Lily withdrew deeper into herself.

Flora chipped the ice from the top of the water jug and tipped it into the kettle. It took an age for the water to heat up enough to prepare tea, made from the scrapings of the Thornbury pot. Just as it was beginning to sing, Eliza burst through the kitchen door, clearly brimming with news. With a glance toward Lily, she dragged Flora off to the parlour. Clasping her teacup in both hands, Lily followed and pressed her ear to the door.

"Get away from the door, you ill-mannered lass," said Bert, as he stirred his weak tea, but Lily ignored him, concentrating on Eliza's voice.

"It's all over the village, Flora; the young Master's gone and got himself killed in that heathen country. They say there's no comforting the missus, and the master is at his wit's end but it's Lily you must worry about. I can't see her taking the news calmly. If ever a girl was smitten on a man, it's your Lily on young Master Jamie."

***

Lily walked through the winter wood. Brambles caught at her clothes, holding her back. When she stumbled into the clearing, the birdsong ceased. The glade was bare, the ground churned to mud and the fallen log where they'd made love spewed its white intestines into the earth. In the distance, her father was calling but Lily paid no heed. Below the bridge, she walked into the angry river, her dimity frock growing darker and heavier until it spread out on the surface and the current drew her down. Lily did not flinch from the icy cold, or react when her mouth clogged, and her throat began to fill. Jamie was gone. Lily wanted to be gone too. Swiftly, the swollen waters did their work and Lily danced a last, melancholic dance, her silver gilt hair like river weed in the current.

***

Thornhold Manor December 1855

Melissa Thornbury, wrapped in an embroidered dressing gown, sat in her chamber. Before her was the open Book of Thornhold. Unseeing, she turned the beautiful pages, untouched by their splendour, until she came at last to the required page. There, she traced a trembling finger along the ancient text and read again the ancient record of Thornbury Manor. The death of Alric who had made the book; the birth of a son to Rainald and Byrtha; a religious poem, and the birth of twins to a woman named Joanna. The book was ancient, its pages testament to the changing tide of Thornbury fortunes and the time had come for Melissa to make her mark alongside the others.

The news of Jamie's death had forced her to acknowledge the triviality of her existence. Henry, doing his utmost to shield her from the sympathy of outsiders, sat with her each day since the news arrived. Mostly they sat in silence, through each dark day and interminable night, he put aside his own grief to offer her strength when her own failed. She realised she had underestimated Henry. Perhaps it was not too late to make things better. He stood beside her now, his steadying hand on her shoulder. Melissa, humbled by grief, pondered upon Jamie's memory before dipping her pen into the ink.

"Our son and heir, Jamie Stuart Thornbury, was slain in battle in October 1854. His body lies close to where he fell but those of us at Thornhold Manor, who loved him, will remember and keep him safe forever in our hearts."

Part Eight
The Link

If you listen you will hear them
If you linger you will see
The shadows in the garden,
shades of you and me.
A footstep in the courtyard,
Painted portraits on the wall
Forgotten memories; long passed moments,
ghostly voices in the hall.
The blueprint of our psyche,
The catalyst of our minds,
Born of long dead battles
fought by those we leave behind.
Long passed pain
And long stilled laughter
Mouldered and decayed,
the foundation of the future
created by today.
A silver link of hands
Stretching through all time
Blood of Saxon, Dane and Briton
Diluted to make mine.
(Judith Arnopp)

September 2004

The woman wouldn't stop staring and, trying to avoid eye contact, Laura looked down at her lap and fiddled with the tassel on her bag. It was sweltering on the bus, and the diesel fumes a noxious insult to a country girl. She'd asked the driver to let her know when they reached the British Library, but the journey seemed interminable, and Laura wondered if he'd forgotten. As the bus slowed again, the woman sniffed and jerked her head away. A teenage mum struggled from the vehicle with a toddler and a pushchair, and when Laura leapt up to help her, she smiled her thanks.

As the journey resumed the woman's eyes absorbed Laura's torn jeans and heavy boots as if she'd never seen the like. Such clothes were acceptable in Gloucestershire where she had lived and worked since birth but perhaps in London, it wasn't so. At Thornhold, people were used to her; she was just plain old Laura Gardner, and every cottage opened their door with a welcome and a cup of tea. Here, she was nobody and her scruffy clothes and piercings were taken as a mark of aggression, her style a badge of insurrection rather than a mark of individuality. Belatedly realising this, Laura hoped the British Library didn't have a dress code.

She hadn't thought to ask.

Ignoring the woman as best she could, Laura tossed back her hair, craning her neck to catch the driver's eye. He winked at her in his rear-view mirror, and she got to her feet, swinging her backpack over her shoulder and preparing to disembark.

Laura was almost nineteen and in London for the first time. Most of the girls she had been to school with found the lure of the capital irresistible. The flashy shops in Oxford Street and the King's Road, together with the thrill of a hundred bars and clubs were too much to resist for those looking for exotica. But Laura was not like other girls. She liked the slow pace of the countryside and preferred to be at home. There was only one thing that could have dragged her away from Thornhold to this place of din and dirt.

The Gardner family had lived and worked at Thornhold Manor since before the records began, and her father and grandfather and, probably his father before him, had tended the gardens there. During the two world wars, when the house was turned into a hospital, beans and cabbages were grown in the gardens, but when the bombs had ceased to fall the manor was returned to its former glory; and this had been undertaken by a Gardner.

Thornhold Manor was now open to the public every afternoon except Wednesdays and the winter bank holiday, and there was only the old lady and her companion in residence now. Old Lady Thornbury occupied a few rooms on the first floor. Old Lord Thornbury had died a few years previously and his heir was abroad, reluctant to claim an inheritance that could only prove to be a millstone.

From an early age Laura had helped her father in the manor gardens; her first job had been gathering soft fruits to be turned into jam and sold to the summer visitors. She had realised long ago that she was a small link in a chain that stretched back into time and had always been aware that others had lived there before. Sometimes she heard, or thought she heard, footsteps on the gravel that ceased the moment she turned her head. As she played beneath the trees in the orchard, the whispering voices she heard could have been the wind in the branches, but it sounded like somebody calling her name.

Gran always claimed Laura was "a little bit psychic" and that a "weird streak ran in the family." She recalled falling over once, when she was very small, and an old man helped her up. He had wiped her tears and picked gravel off her knees. He was a nice man with a kindly face. "Run along now, Miss Margaret" he'd said when she'd stopped crying.

At the age of nine or ten, venturing into the graveyard, looking for thrills, she learned the names of the Thornburys who lived before; and those names were now as familiar as her own. Sometimes when she glanced up at the twinkling windows and glimpsed a face peering back at her, it was probably only Lady Thornbury's ginger cat but ... she couldn't be sure.

***

As she grew older Laura was promoted to waitress in the small cafeteria. With a tray of scones and coffee balanced on her hands, she manoeuvred through a maze of chairs and handbags.

"Excuse me, Miss, could I have some sugar? This pot seems to be empty."

"Yes, Sir, of course. I will be with you in one minute."

"Excuse me, Miss, but I asked for a scone, and you've given me a teacake".

"One moment, Madam, and I'll change it for you, so sorry, Madam."

It was hectic in the teashop and Laura was glad when she reached the age of sixteen and was trusted enough to work in the house, polishing the dark oak furniture and vacuuming the heavy drapes and miles of carpet. She thought it a shame that so many stately homes in England had mouldered into decay and thought it paramount that Thornbury Manor was preserved. On finishing college, she applied to take a degree in Heritage Management to enable her involvement in the preservation of Thornhold to continue.

"Laura, we must sort out some of these attics. They are full of old documents, and some of them may be important. I've set aside the use of the study for you and thought you could try to make head or tail of them. Look, there are old photos, certificates and journals."

Laura took the large box of papers from Lady Thornbury and knelt on the floor among the piles of other boxes. It was a dull job sifting through yellowed papers and receipts but one day she opened a battered box that she had found lurking right at the back of the attic.

After wiping away the worst of the dust and opening the lid, she examined the contents with great interest before taking them to show Lady Thornbury. The old lady was as intrigued as she at the strange collection of objects. There were pieces of a child's shoe, very stiff, battered and rotten. There were also a number of buttons, a small hoard of coin, a few pieces of pottery, and a rusty buckle from a horse harness with the symbol of what looked like a leaping stag.

"It's a shame there is nothing to prove they belong here, but I suspect they were found in the grounds; look, there is mud ingrained in them. Why else would they have been kept? Lady Thornbury, look at this sherd of pottery, I reckon it's Anglo Saxon."

"Oh, how lovely, dear," the old woman enthused, taking the box. "I say, look at this tiny little shoe, I wonder who wore it. How intriguing it all is."

Laura sat back. "Lady Thornbury," she said. "What if we were to start a museum about the history of the manor. We could display bits and pieces like this, and some of those lovely costumes that belonged to your grandmother. It shouldn't cost very much, and I'm sure with a small entrance fee, we could recoup more than we spend. I'd be willing to do the research and put in some of my free time. It is so important that Thornhold's past is not forgotten. We should try to preserve the memory."

The old lady rang for tea.

"What a lovely idea, Laura, I will write to William at once and see what he says. I know he pretends I can run the place as I see fit, but he still likes to be consulted. Ooh, and I've just remembered, he has some old pistols and things somewhere that might be worthy of a place in your museum, an old flintlock and a rusty sword, as well as a few old arrowheads. Fetch me my writing things and I'll write to him now, while the idea is still fresh in my mind. Thank you, dear, that's lovely. Yes, I will see you later on."

Laura and Old Lady Thornbury begun to research the family tree. There was no order to the records; family birth and death certificates were jumbled into large boxes along with household accounts, old journals, letters and photographs, many undated. Desperate to read them, but determined to approach the research methodically, Laura tried to organise the papers into chronological order.

The most recent records began in 1902 and receded into the past. Forgotten names recorded in fading ink on yellowing paper by an unknown hand. Turning page after page of domestic expenditure was dull until, leafing through an account book for the year 1854, she noticed a payment to a Lily Gardner. The name, so similar to her own, seemed to jump from the page and, working back on her fingers, Laura figured that Lily might have been her great, great, great grandmother, or maybe an aunt. She wondered why the Thornburys were paying an allowance to their gardener's daughter and delved deeper into the box. It was much later in the day when she discovered a journal made by a Lady Melissa Thornbury.

Opening it carefully, she jumped as a few pressed rose petals fell into her lap, and putting them carefully to one side, she flipped through the pages. Most of the entries were dull, trivial luncheon dates and doctor's appointments but the entry for June 1854, was significant.

I called at the Gardner cottage today and asked to see the infant. They could scarcely refuse. The child is bonny, very fair like James, and they have named him Tom. I held him for a while and assured the girl's mother that he should want for nothing. Honestly, they all stood staring at me with their mouths open, as if they had no idea what I was talking about. She, the girl, didn't speak except to enquire when Master Jamie is due home, but I didn't tell her. The cheek of it.

I long for Jamie to come home but, when he does, I shall not allow him to return to Thornhold but will keep him in town. It will never do to rekindle his attachment to the Gardener girl. I am prepared to bend to Jamie's wish that we look after Lily, and I suppose that must extend to his son, but London will be a far healthier environment for my son. The sooner he is safely married the better. Jennifer Merchant will bring much needed money, and he will be able to offer the prestige of the Thornbury name in return.

I have nothing against the Gardner girl apart from the obvious problems of class, but I very much doubt it was her intellect that attracted James. She is undoubtedly very handsome, too good looking for her own good, in fact. I left them a purse of money but received no thanks for it, and I have arranged with our solicitor, Banks, to make them a monthly allowance until the child is of an age to work. The Gardners understand there is to be no further contact. They are to raise the child and the mother is to be married as soon as a suitable young man can be found.

In the afternoon, I took tea with Penny Troughton, the vicar's wife, it was a pleasant enough way to spend the afternoon and got me away from this house which I find oppressive at this time of year ...

The entry tailed off into inconsequential gossip. A frown creased Laura's forehead as she struggled to understand what she had just read. It sounded very much as if her great, great, great grandfather had been a Thornbury bastard. The family had kept that quiet for she'd never heard so much as a hint of it before. That must have caused a scandal, a Thornbury mating with the gardener's daughter! What a laugh.

She skipped down the stairs, full of glee at her discovery and, moving quietly past the old Lady's door, hurried home to tell her mother.

"Are you sure, Pet?" Mother squinted over her glasses at the spidery scrawl. "Your great, great grandfather - a Thornbury flyblow? I've never heard the like."

"It's what it says here, Mum, and what's more, they paid him a tidy sum too, regular every month until he was old enough to work. It's the classic tale of the gentry taking down the peasant. It wouldn't surprise me if Lily's reputation was ruined."

"You've been watching too many TV dramas." Mum laughed, starting to wipe the dinner plates and set them on the table. "Well, I never, who'd have thought it? Hey, I've just realised! I suppose that means you and your dad are Thornbury's too. I mean blood's blood, isn't it? I tell you what, Pet, your dad always said he was too good for the likes of me. Maybe he was right all along."

When the door opened on cue, their laughter increased and Dad, throwing his hat on the settee, asked what the joke was.

"Well, come in My Lord, and we shall tell you…" Laura took her dad by the arm and escorted him to an armchair.

Later, Laura said, "Course it's funny to us now but at the time, it would have been awful. Scandalous. I wonder what happened to her. Have you never heard anything about a Lily or Tom Gardner, Dad?"

"No, Pet, I haven't. Only my mum of course, she's called Lily, too. Maybe you'd do well to pop and see if she can remember any old stories. Only … I'd not tell her this bit of scandal, if I were you, it might upset her and she's getting old you know. Just say you're writing a thing for college. It wouldn't be a lie after all, would it?"

As Laura lay in bed that night her Thornbury ancestors pressed close. Their whispering voices haunting her as she tried to mentally trace back the dual line of the families in her head. It didn't seem fair that while her great granddad had been through hell in the trenches, his Thornbury cousins had been officers, safe behind the lines. And while her ancestors had struggled for survival in a squalid cottage with no indoor plumbing, their Thornbury cousins had been living the high life up at the manor. God! It was like something off the telly. The gentry imposing manorial rights over their own kin but when she remembered playing around the gravestones in the churchyard, it made her shiver a little, as she recognised a connection had been there all along.

A tap on the door and mum popped her head into the bedroom.

"Hello, Sweetheart, I thought you were still awake. I've brought you some hot milk." She placed a hand on Laura's forehead. "You look peaky, are you sure you aren't over-doing this family study? You will need to be fresh when you go off to University, and at this rate you'll be burned out before you get there. Maybe you need a break from it, get yourself down to the coast or something for a bit of a holiday."

"No, mum, I can't. I'm crazy to discover more, it's as though they are here with me now, all talking at once, trying to tell me something that I can't quite hear."

"Hmm," replied Mum, "It's lights out for you, young lady, and no more books until tomorrow. You go to sleep now. All this nonsense about ancestors, I don't know, when I was your age I had no time for books and studying. I was too busy looking about for a good husband … I found one too. Until now, I didn't realise how good a catch he was!"

She winked, snapping out the light and closing the door.

Laura pushed off the duvet and stood at the cottage window, looking across the moonlight flooded garden, the rows of vegetables, the shed at the end. She couldn't remember seeing a gravestone for Lily Gardner in the church yard. There were plenty of other Gardners but no Lily, as she recalled. First thing tomorrow she would go and look, maybe her stone was overgrown, and had gone unnoticed, or maybe Lily hadn't been rich or important enough for a memorial stone.

Grubbing about in the churchyard the next day, Laura had no luck. She had just about decided that Lily must have gone away to be married when it hit her. Stunned at her own foolishness, she suddenly realised that Lily Gardner might be buried under her marital name. Back she went, examining all the graves again, looking for a Lily of the right period but, although there were Lilies aplenty, none were of the correct date. Frustrated by failure, she decided she'd had enough for one day and made her way toward home.

In the far corner of the churchyard, close to the picket gate, she stopped before a cluster of stone crosses marking the resting place of the Thornbury babes. Laura had often looked at them. There were eight graves, the markers mossed over now and the names indistinguishable. She had always thought it a desperately sad little corner and often picked wildflowers to lay on the tiny mounds. Close by, were monuments to James Thornbury who had died in 1688, and his wife Joanna, who had died in 1760. There was also a Joseph, son of James and Joanna, departed in 1740. It pleased Laura to think that James and Joanna had safely borne at least one child and raised him to maturity; he'd have been about fifty-four when he passed away.

Counting on her fingers, she worked out that Lady Joanna had been one hundred and two. Wow! That was a remarkable age. It was sad to think of her living on, a widow for so many years, watching while those about her died, even her son Joseph had predeceased her by almost twenty years. Set a little apart from the family, but still within the boundary of the rusty fence, was another grave, the stone was broken and the mound sunken and crooked. When she cleared away the ivy, the mouldering words informed her that here lay Simon Grey – 1662 –1724. There was no clue as to his role within the household; maybe he was an adopted son, or a penniless relative? A servant of the house, perhaps? Laura supposed she would never know but she left him a posy before making her way to the church in search of the vicar. The church records might be able to shed some light on the whereabouts of Lily.

Laura found him tending his garden, and he started up in surprise when he heard her step. He was an apologetic man, his short-sighted eyes continually blinking behind the thick lenses of his spectacles. When he learned her quest, he brushed the mud from his knees and ushered her into the vestry. The books he brought out were heavy and dusty, and Laura felt a twinge of guilt as the old man staggered with them toward the table.

"Here you are, my dear, records from 1850 through to 1880. That should be enough to keep you going for a while. You know, you are lucky they are still here for all records are soon to be moved to a central office so that historians can access them all in the one place."

Laura opened a black leather cover and began to turn the thick gold-edged pages, a musty smell of age assailing her nostrils. She knew that Lily's child had been born in 1854 so that seemed the best place to start.

"I suppose it makes sense to keep them all together, and I expect they will be in a specially controlled environment at a constant temperature. It is important to preserve them."

The vicar pushed his glasses further up his nose and shook his head sadly. "I can't help but think of the Cotton Collection though, my dear…"

Laura looked up at him, flicking her hair back from her face. "The Cotton Collection? What's that then? Sounds like a new range at C&A."

"No, no it's something quite different. Sir Robert Cotton, I think his name was, after the dissolution of the monasteries, salvaged a lot of manuscripts that were due for destruction and over the following years built up a priceless collection. After his death, his family continued the work. They donated a lot of stuff to the Bodleian Library when it was established and, I think it was Sir John Cotton who finally passed the entire collection of manuscripts over to the nation early in 1700. Thirty years or so later, while they were being stored in the King's library at

Ashburnham House, many manuscripts were destroyed in a great fire and many treasures lost forever."

"Blimey!" whispered Laura, shaking her head. "How awful. Think what those books might have told us."

"And one can't help but wonder if centralising records is a good thing. Even if they are digitalised, the originals remain irreplaceable."

"Oh look..." exclaimed Laura suddenly, breaking across the vicar's train of thought. "Tom's birth record is here, in June 1854. It says father unknown. What a cheek..."

She pointed out the entry to the vicar, and he leant over the page the better to decipher the fading spidery handwriting. Marking the page, she flicked onward looking for a marriage entry for Lily but there was none, and neither was there an entry for her death. Puzzled, Laura sat back and screwed up her face thinking.

"I could understand no marriage record if she remained single but no death record? That makes no sense at all ... does it, vicar?"

Shaking his head, the vicar concurred.

"None whatsoever, none at all. She may have gone away, married or died in another parish. Have you tried the internet? I'm told they have remarkable resources online. Unfortunately, I myself don't know one end of a computer from another."

"We don't have a computer at home, but I can try that when I get to university. I thought I'd start here and was pretty certain I'd find something because we Gardners don't tend to roam far. I won't give up though. Do you mind if I keep looking through these? I might find something else relevant."

"Please do, my dear, but I must get back to my garden if you don't mind. I have peas to harvest before supper. It's a shame The Book of Thornhold is no longer with us, it is such a good source of family history as I recall, and dates from way back too."

"The Book of Thornhold? I've never heard of it. What is it, and where has it gone?"

***

When questioned, Old Lady Thornbury was aghast at her own forgetfulness.

"Oh, of course, I remember The Book. I should have thought of it before. I must be getting senile. It was here when I was a child. I remember my father sending it away during the war for safe keeping. It is of national historical importance, so they say, and quite lovely as I recall although very moth eaten and musty. All down the ages, members of the family have written and made comments in it, right back to the Norman Conquest. That's when my family came here you know dear, in 1066."

"Yeah, mine too!" thought Laura wryly, but she said nothing, not yet ready to divulge her discovery.

On her way home, as she passed through the garden and park to the small cottage where she had lived all her life, the voices of her forebears seemed to follow. Their shadows eddied about her room and perched on the end of her bed while she thought about the mysterious book. Why had the Thornburys made those entries? What made human beings so keen to leave an indelible mark on a future they would not know?

Late September 2005

Laura's boots clumped across the piazza where people relaxed upon benches around the perimeter. Students pulled furtively on cigarettes, and fusty looking professors, engrossed in their newspapers, munched sandwiches and drank tea from thermos flasks. The place was vast, built of brick and stone, the words **British Library** emblazoned everywhere, just in case you should forget where you were. At the entrance, the security guard rummaged through her rucksack, presumably looking for a bomb but when satisfied she presented no immediate risk to national security, he directed her toward the reception.

"Leave your bag in a locker and make sure you take only a pencil and paper into the reading room."

The receptionist was clearly bored with repeating the same instruction throughout the day and did not so much as glance at Laura. She was probably in her fifties, her hair dyed an unlikely shade of red and her earrings jangled irritatingly as she explained when questioned, that it would take approximately thirty minutes for the manuscript to be brought from the archive. Laura smiled and nodded and asked the way to the coffee shop. She hadn't eaten since breakfast and was famished; a cappuccino and a salad roll would tide her over until teatime.

Her body fizzed with anticipation as she waited, certain that the history of Thornhold Manor was now her own, As she sipped her coffee and gazed up at an enormous wall of ancient books towering above the dining room, she wondered if her own family book was among them. A glance at her watch told her the thirty minutes were almost up and, collecting her notebook and pencil, Laura made her way to the elevators.

Speaking in whispers, a librarian offered Laura a pair of white cotton gloves before placing the heavy book on a cushion. The woman blinked earnestly as she indicated where Laura could find her should she be required; then she tiptoed away. Laura wondered if the woman ever had the impulse to raise her voice or stamp her feet; or perhaps she was so accustomed to the monastic silence that it was ingrained and followed her into her private life.

The book waited quietly on its cushion. It was larger than she had expected, and the faded red velvet cover and tarnished metal work revealed no hint of the secrets within. The metal lock that would once have kept it closed was broken; Laura reached out to open it and drew in a sharp breath.

The pages were so bright they could have been painted yesterday. Although the vellum was yellowed and dotted with age spots, and the edges seemed to have been scorched at some time, the illuminations gleamed brightly. The monkish hand, written in what she presumed was Latin script stood out blackly from the page.

Each historiated letter was embellished with tiny red dots and must represent hours of devoted work. Laura turned the pages slowly, examining each perfect decoration and noted with puzzlement, several glaring errors. But the book had become more than just another book of gospel; over the centuries the Thornburys had made their mark, transforming it into a personal history.

Laura's ancestors seemed to whisper like leaves in the wind. She looked up to see if the people studying nearby could also hear it but, intent on their own books, they were oblivious to all else.

The Thornburys clustered about the table, pointing out items on the pages, their voices overlapping, growing louder. They were like solid beings, pressing against her, she could smell their strange perfume, feel their breath on her cheek. Their thoughts merged with hers until she was unsure where they ended, and she began. Perhaps it was all one and the same.

Laura paused to examine an illustration of a small church and village, decorated with hundreds of dots and swirls. Then, turning another page, she came upon a blemish, the palm print and several fingertips of the infant still clearly discernible.

Who was the child who made it? She wondered. *Why was it there?* It was not carefully done but rather suggested an accident of some kind. She wondered if he'd got into trouble with his elders for it. The page was creased, as though it had been left open at that particular place for a long time or had been weighted down. She ran her fingertip over the mark, jerking her hand away as pain shot through her body. As if she had been stung, she kept both hands clasped at her breast, reluctant to touch it, suspicious of its potency.

"Go on," urged a child's voice at her elbow. "It can't hurt you. It was Richard when he had the pestilence."

Laura searched for the source of the voice. No one else in the room had moved. The voice had been loud, clear as day. She glanced warily at the librarian expecting her to raise a finger and tell her to hush.

Wishing she could read Latin, Laura turned another page and the words seemed to dance, as if in promise of some indeterminate reward. As she neared the end of the book, the application of gold leaf and the blue lapis lazuli increased, and the margins became richer and more spiritual in execution. The last few pages, however, were plain with no decoration at all, but there were lines of script, which was clearly written by unskilled hands.

Some entries were in Latin or French, and some in what appeared to be an old-fashioned form of English. Luckily, someone at a later date had added rough translations in pencil beneath the original script. Laura read each inscription, starting at the top and when she neared the bottom of the page she almost cried out in exultation. For there was Melissa Thornbury's handwriting, recording the death of her son, Jamie.

He'd been killed at Balaclava! Oh, poor, poor Lily to lose him to war. And poor Melissa too. It took some time before it began to dawn on Laura that the Jamie in question was her own great, great, great, great grandfather, and by the time she had realised it, her finger had come to rest upon another entry.

The writing was faded to a light brown and was barely distinguishable. She leaned forward and spelled out; J-o-a-n-n-a T-h-o-r-n-b-u-r-y.

Joanna Thornbury! She knew that name. She had seen it many times in the graveyard at home, she was the one who had lost all those babies and had lived to be a hundred and two. With her heart beating rapidly and feeling as if she had encountered an old friend, Laura traced a finger along the lines of old handwriting.

Immediately, the room was suffused with the smell of sun-warmed lavender, and she heard the crunch of gravel, evoking the unmistakable memory of the knot garden at Thornhold. Slowly and painstakingly, Laura read out the words.

"To Joanna Thornbury, this seventeenth day of March 1686, was born an heir to Thornhold Manor named Joseph James, and his twin, Margaret May."

Margaret May Thornbury. After all those dead babies Joanna had not one baby survive, but two. Twins, Joseph and Margaret! Margaret wasn't buried at Thornhold though, probably because she had married and moved away to raise her own family.

Delighted at solving so many questions, Laura ceased to mind the shadows pressing around her; a silken bodice rubbed her elbow, and a tawny-haired fellow in velvet breeches smiled at her from across the table.

She scanned up the page, keeping her finger on the text all the while and Joanna and her companion drifted away. Almost as soon as they'd gone, Laura became aware of a grinning boy in a monk's habit. He was thin, and his dank and slightly herby aroma filled her nostrils. He indicated with a grubby nail that she should read on. She turned back to the page.

"It is good to be here. Here man more purely lives, less oft doth fall, more promptly rises, walks with stricter need, more safely rests, dies happier, is freed earlier from cleansing fires, and gains withal a brighter crown."

The words made no sense to Laura, but she made a note of them in her book to research later. Suddenly feeling desperately tired, she buried her face in her hands and then leaned back in her chair scooping her hair into a knot behind her head. She closed her eyes and at once seemed to be at Thornhold, or rather at Thornhold as it had been before she knew it, as it was when her ancestors were there.

Her ears rang, and bright lights pierced the darkness in her mind as she experienced their miseries and joys, shared their pain as if it were her own.

A fair-haired girl walked heedlessly into a flooding river, and a stone tower crumbled as flames leapt in the night's sky. She heard a horse scream amid the clash of battle, and a broken-hearted woman weeping in the dark. At the bedside of her child, the woman prayed, the stench of sickness in the air. It was a time of decay, a time of death.

And then, she saw an old woman cursing, a bony finger raised in warning, as wolves encircled Thornhold bringing peril and division. The mists swirled, and fighting to clear her head, Laura passed into a clearing where a half-built wooden church nestled at the edge of a wood. She saw a priest and a child looking out to sea where long ships brought terror and war. A sharp-bladed axe somersaulted through the air, and a red-haired woman slumped in the sand.

***

When Laura opened her eyes, the whispering librarian was urging her to take a glass of water while a cluster of academics hovered nearby. They sat her up, assisted her to the coffee shop and sat her at a chrome table, with a cup of Americano. Comforted by the modern music jangling reassuringly from the speakers, Laura was glad of the din and the chattering of the diners, but she hardly dared raise her head to look at her other companions.

Grouped around her table, they watched her intently. Joanna Thornbury and the man with the tawny hair each held a struggling two-year-old on their knee. Behind them, an old woman grasped the arm of a girl with thick braids and fierce eyes. A bowman with a leaping stag emblazoned upon his chest guarded a girl with sloe dark eyes. They pressed so close that Laura could scarcely breathe. She tried to stand but, forestalling her, the boy priest pushed past a fair-haired child and a bandaged Hussar, and pushed his face close to Laura's. His tainted breath wafted in her face, his voice ringing clear.

"We want you to write it," he said. "The story of Thornhold. We want you to write it down, as we tell you, before the memories fade."

The End

If you have enjoyed this please consider leaving a review or rating on Amazon.

Author Biography

A lifelong history enthusiast and avid reader, Judith holds a BA in English/Creative writing and an MA in Medieval Studies. She lives on the coast of West Wales where she writes both fiction and non-fiction. She is best known for her novels set in the Medieval and Tudor period, focussing on the perspective of historical women but recently she has been writing from the perspective of Henry VIII himself.

Judith is also a founder member of a re-enactment group called The Fyne Companye of Cambria which is when she began to experiment with sewing historical garments. She now makes clothes and accessories both for the group and others. She is not a professionally trained sewer but through trial, error and determination has learned how to make authentic looking, if not strictly historically accurate clothing. She is currently working on a non-fiction book about Tudor clothing which will be published by Pen and Sword.

Her novels in chronological order include:

A Song of Sixpence: the Story of Elizabeth of York

The Beaufort Chronicle: the Life of Lady Margaret Beaufort three book series comprising of:

The Beaufort Bride

The Beaufort Woman

The King's Mother

A Matter of Conscience: Henry VIII, The Aragon Years (Book One of The Henrician Chronicle)

A Matter of Faith: Henry VIII, The Days of the Phoenix (Book Two of The Henrician chronicle)

A Matter of Time: Henry VIII, The Dying of the Light (Book Three of The Henrician Chronicle)

The Kiss of the Concubine: A Story of Anne Boleyn

The Winchester Goose: At The Court of Henry VIII

Intractable Heart: The Story of Katheryn Parr

Sisters of Arden: On The Pilgrimage of Grace

The Heretic Wind: The Life of Mary Tudor, Queen of England

Peaceweaver

The Forest Dwellers

The Song of Heledd

The Book of Thornhold

Webpage: www.judithmarnopp.com
Books: author.to/juditharnoppbooks
Blog: www.juditharnoppnovelist.blogspot.co.uk/
You can also find Judith on most social media platforms.